P9-CJR-540

LAT.

TOWN BOY

WITHDRAWN

First Second

New York & London

:01

First Second

Copyright © 1980 by Lat

Published by First Second
First Second is an imprint of Roaring Brook Press, a division of
Holtzbrinck Publishing Holdings Limited Partnership
175 Fifth Avenue, New York, NY 10010

All rights reserved.

Photograph of Ipoh class of 1963 courtesy of Hj. Anuar Zaini

Distributed in Canada by H. B. Fenn and Company Ltd.
Distributed in the United Kingdom by Macmillan Children's
Books, a division of Pan Macmillan.

Design by Mark Siegel

Library of Congress Cataloging-in-Publication Data

Lat.
   Town boy / Lat. -- 1st American ed.
      p. cm.
   Originally published: Kuala Lumpur : Berita Pub., 1980.
   ISBN-13: 978-1-59643-331-1
   ISBN-10: 1-59643-331-0
   1. Graphic novels. I. Title.
   PN6790.M353L39 2007
   741.5'9595--dc22
                          2006102857

First Second books are available for special
promotions and premiums.
For details, contact: Director of Special Markets,
Holtzbrinck Publishers.

First American Edition October 2007

Printed in China

10 9 8 7 6 5 4 3 2 1

Ipoh's class of 1963. Lat is fourth from the right in the back row.

The editor wishes to thank Férid and Christiane Kaddour, without whose
precious help and exquisite French editions of Lat's work under the *Thé-Troc*
imprint, these new releases of Lat's work may not have been possible.

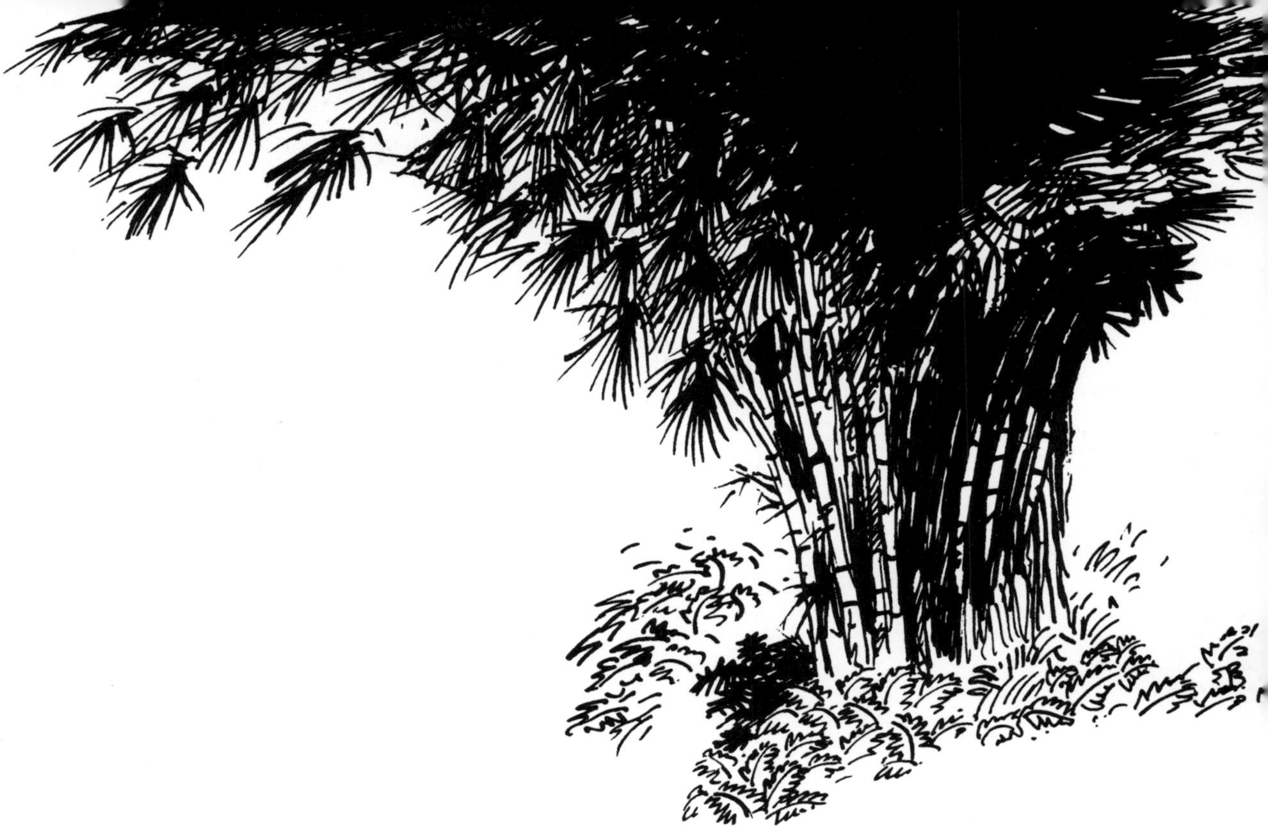

To all my friends

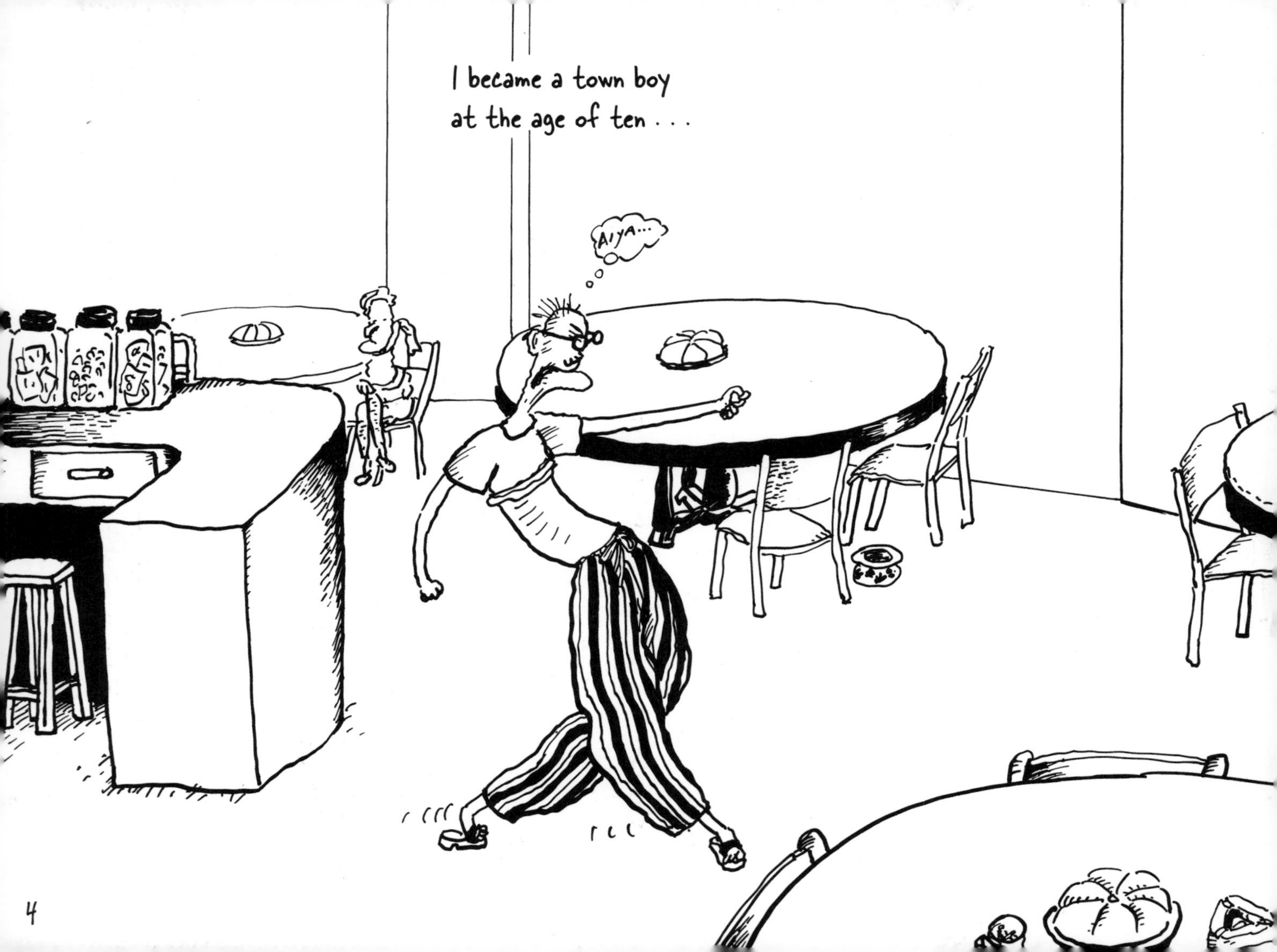
I became a town boy
at the age of ten . . .
AIYA...

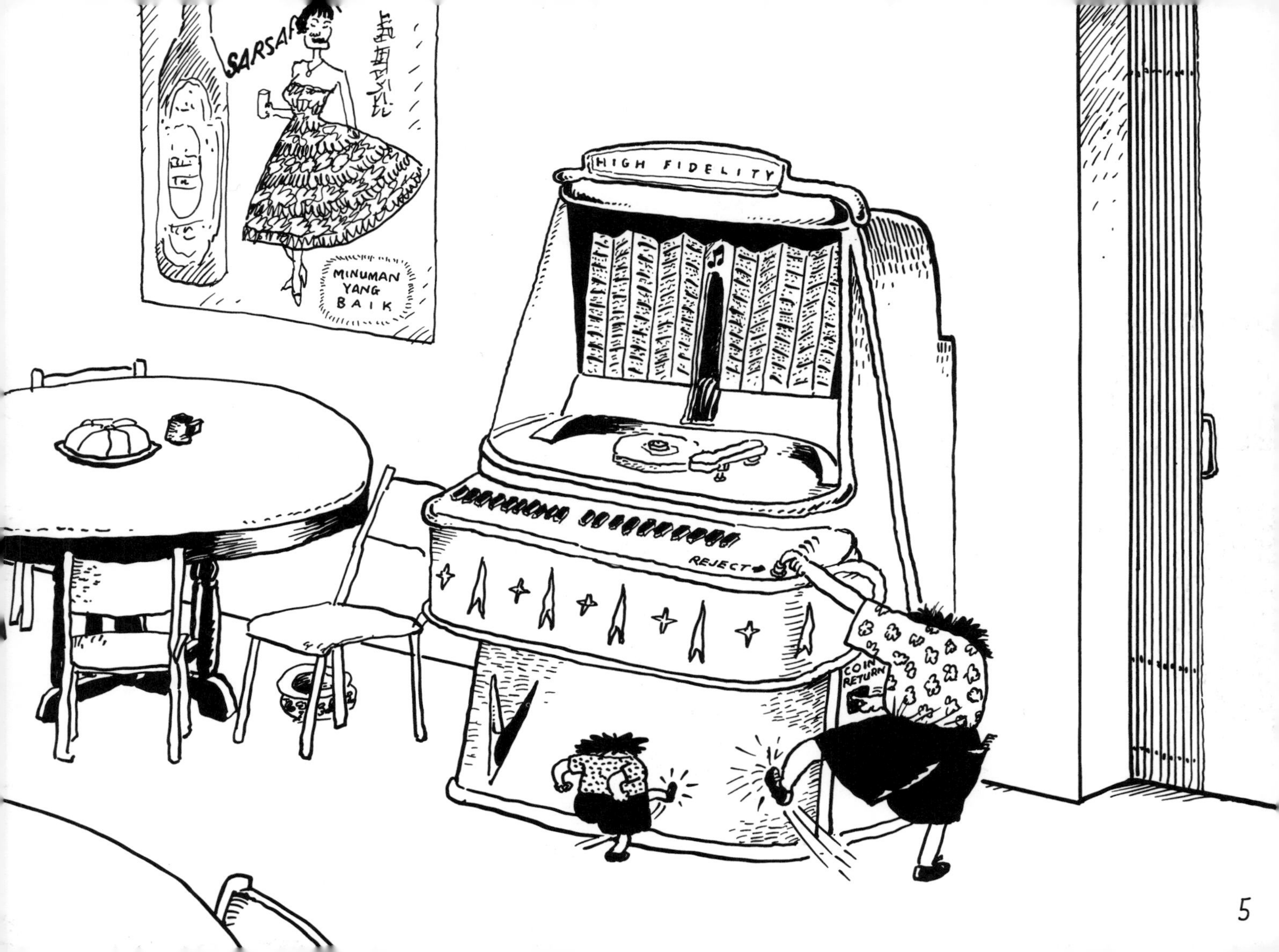
SARSAF
MINUMAN YANG BAIK
HIGH FIDELITY
REJECT
COIN RETURN

I was born in the kampung, of course. But at the age of ten I went to Ipoh to pursue my studies and stayed in the school hostel.

The hostel didn't hold many memories for, as it turned out, I only spent a short while there. Less than a year.

The picture on the right shows a typical scene at the hostel on every Tuesday afternoon. When the dhobi man, Mr. Ng, came for his fee the entire hostel suddenly turned quiet and no one was in sight . . .

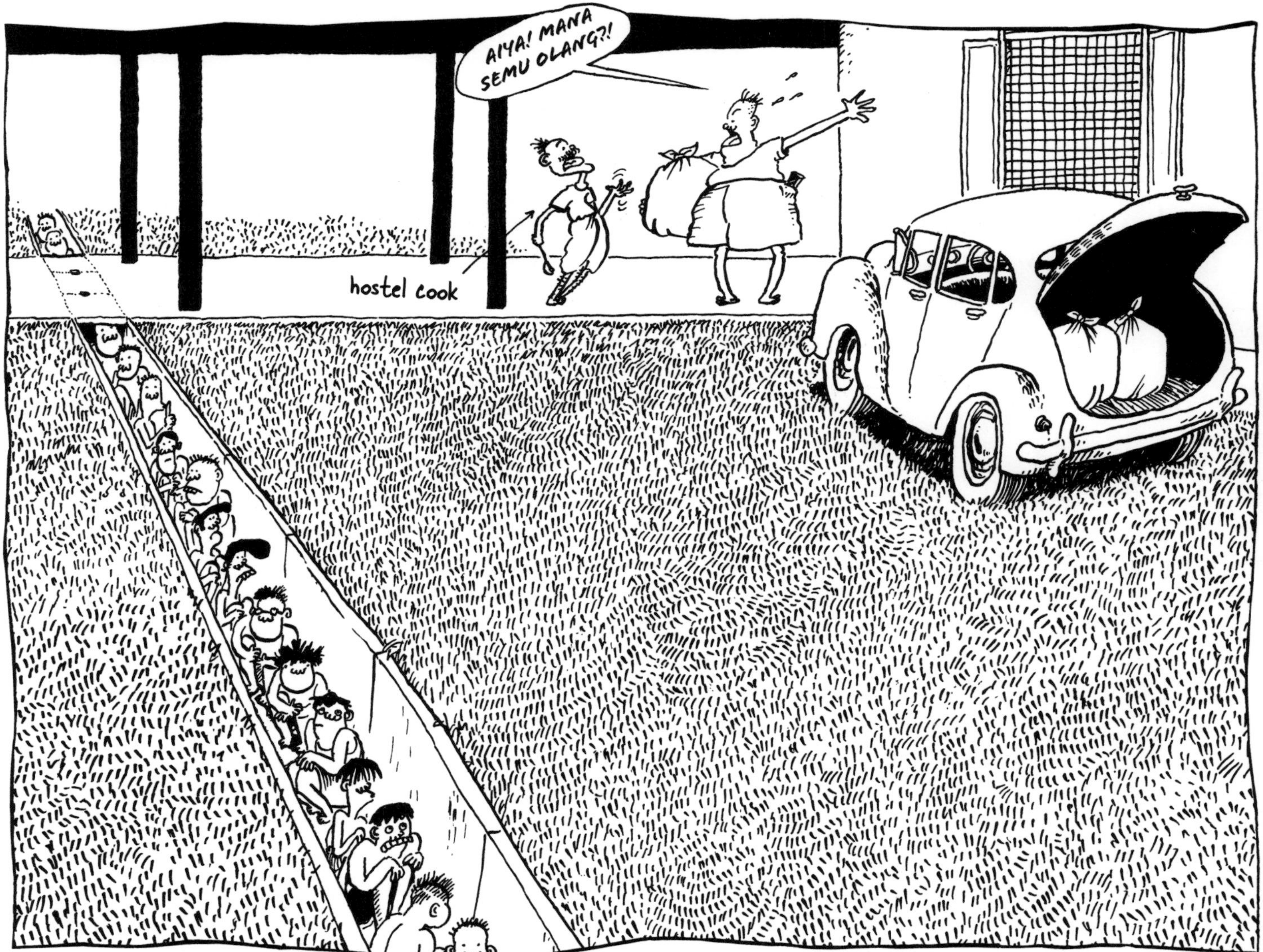
AIYA! MANA SEMU OLANG?!
hostel cook

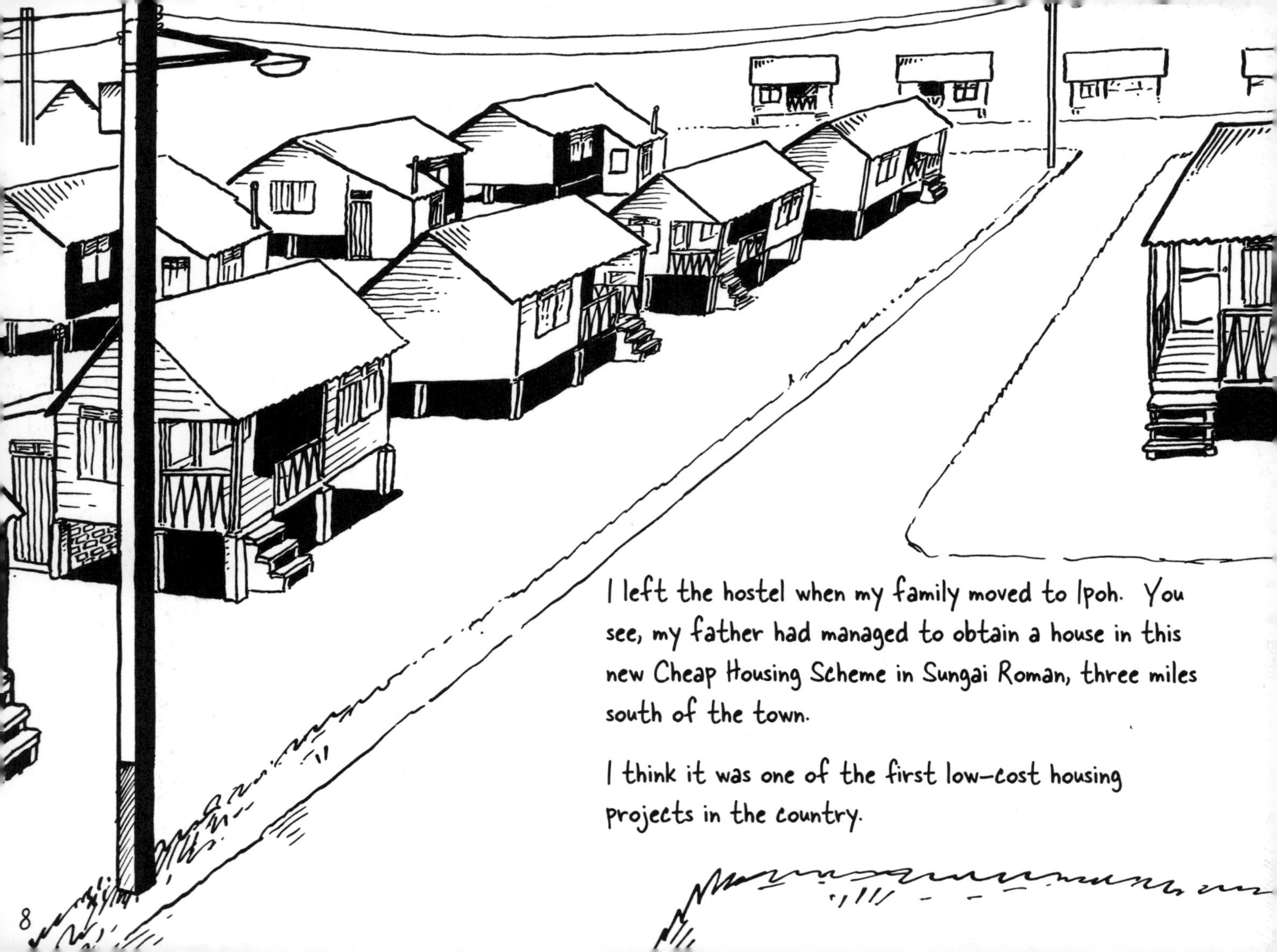
I left the hostel when my family moved to Ipoh. You see, my father had managed to obtain a house in this new Cheap Housing Scheme in Sungai Roman, three miles south of the town.
I think it was one of the first low-cost housing projects in the country.

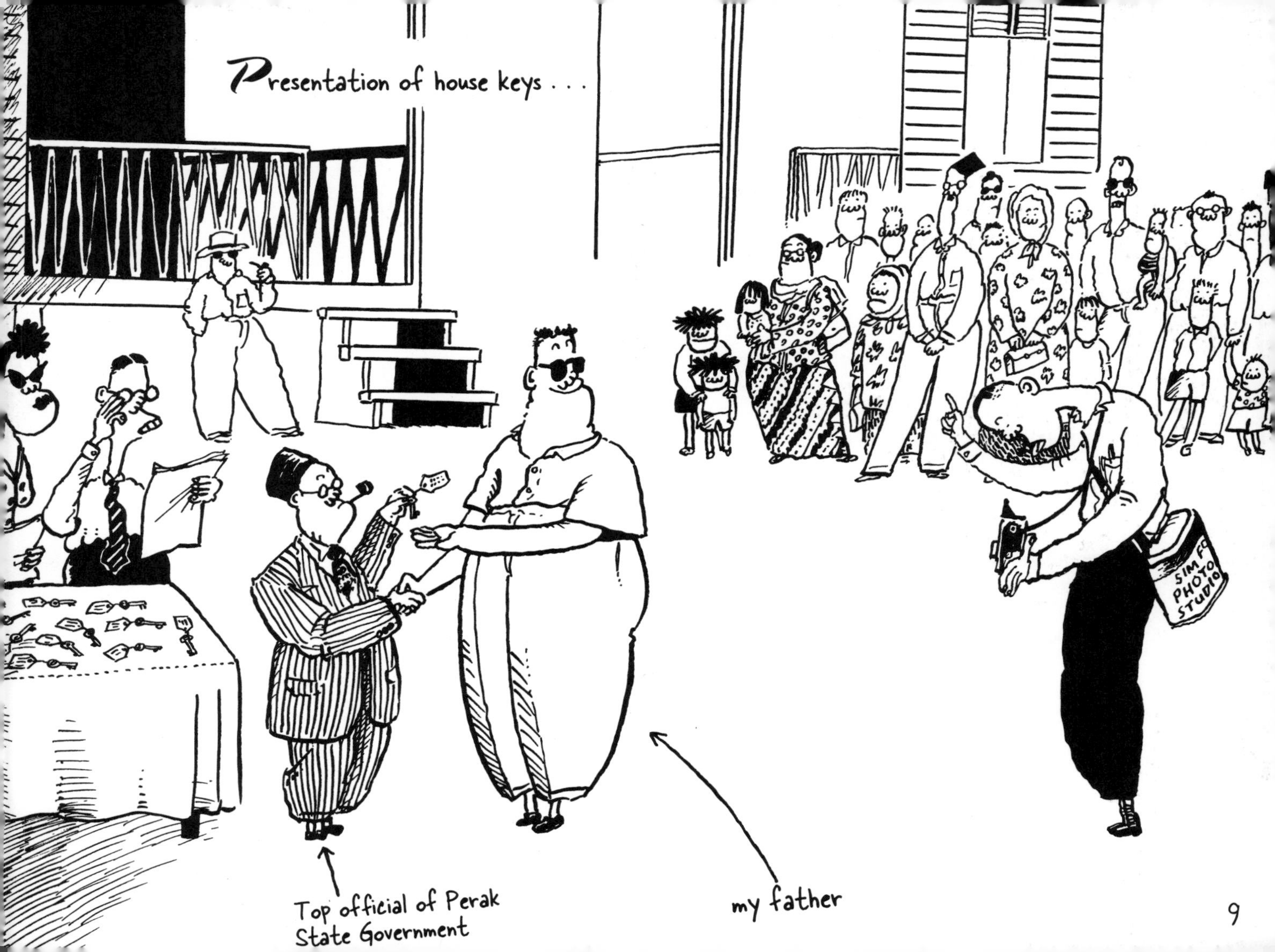
Presentation of house keys . . .
SIM F
PHOTO
STUDIO
Top official of Perak State Government
my father

After receiving the keys, off we went to look for our new home—its address indicated on a tag that came with the keys.

How eager we were to look at our house. So was every other resident, of course.
It was a happy day.

And so . . . there we were—my family and I . . .
beginning a new life in this new place.

We had become town people . . .

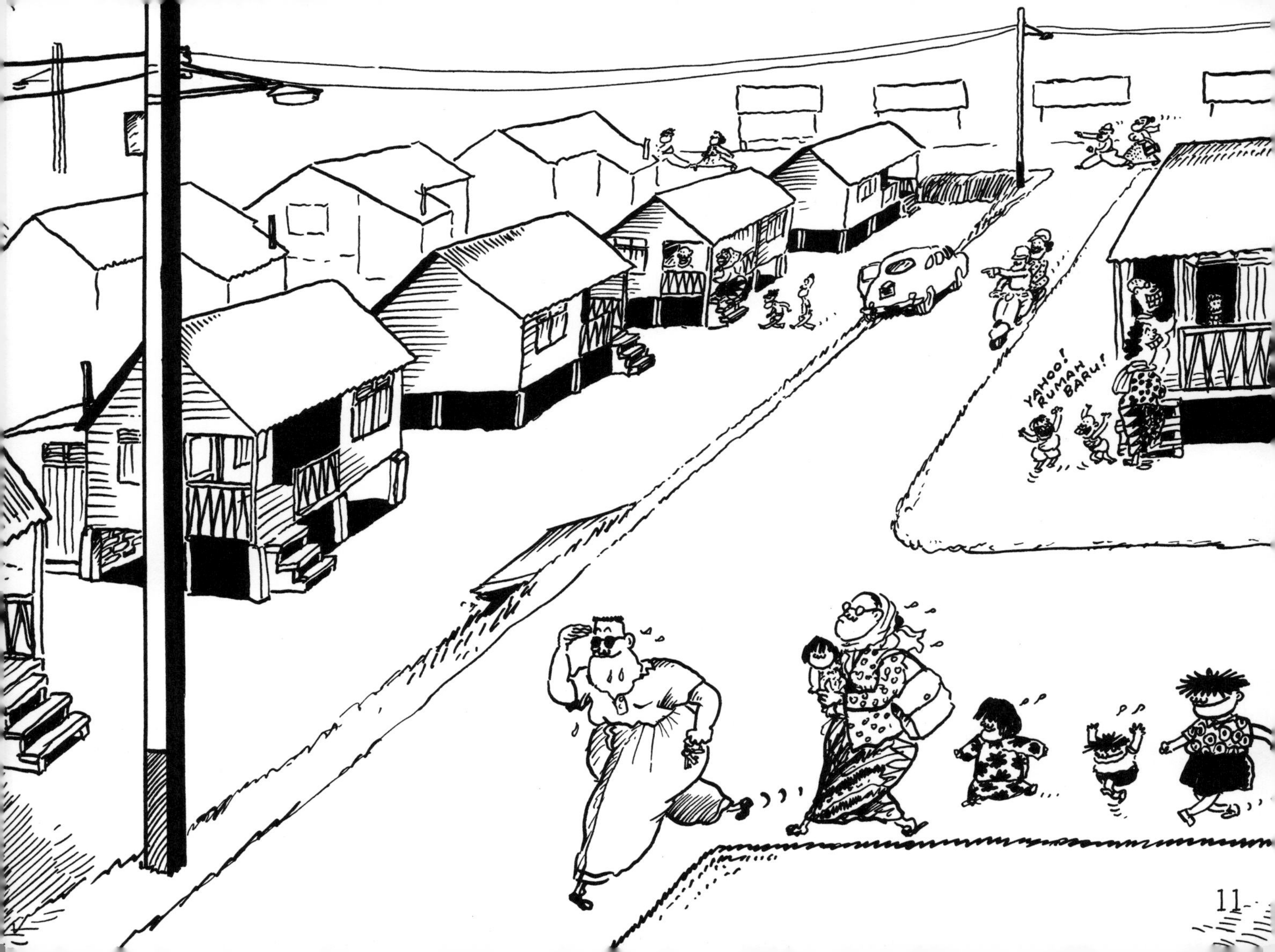
YAHOO! RUMAH BARU!

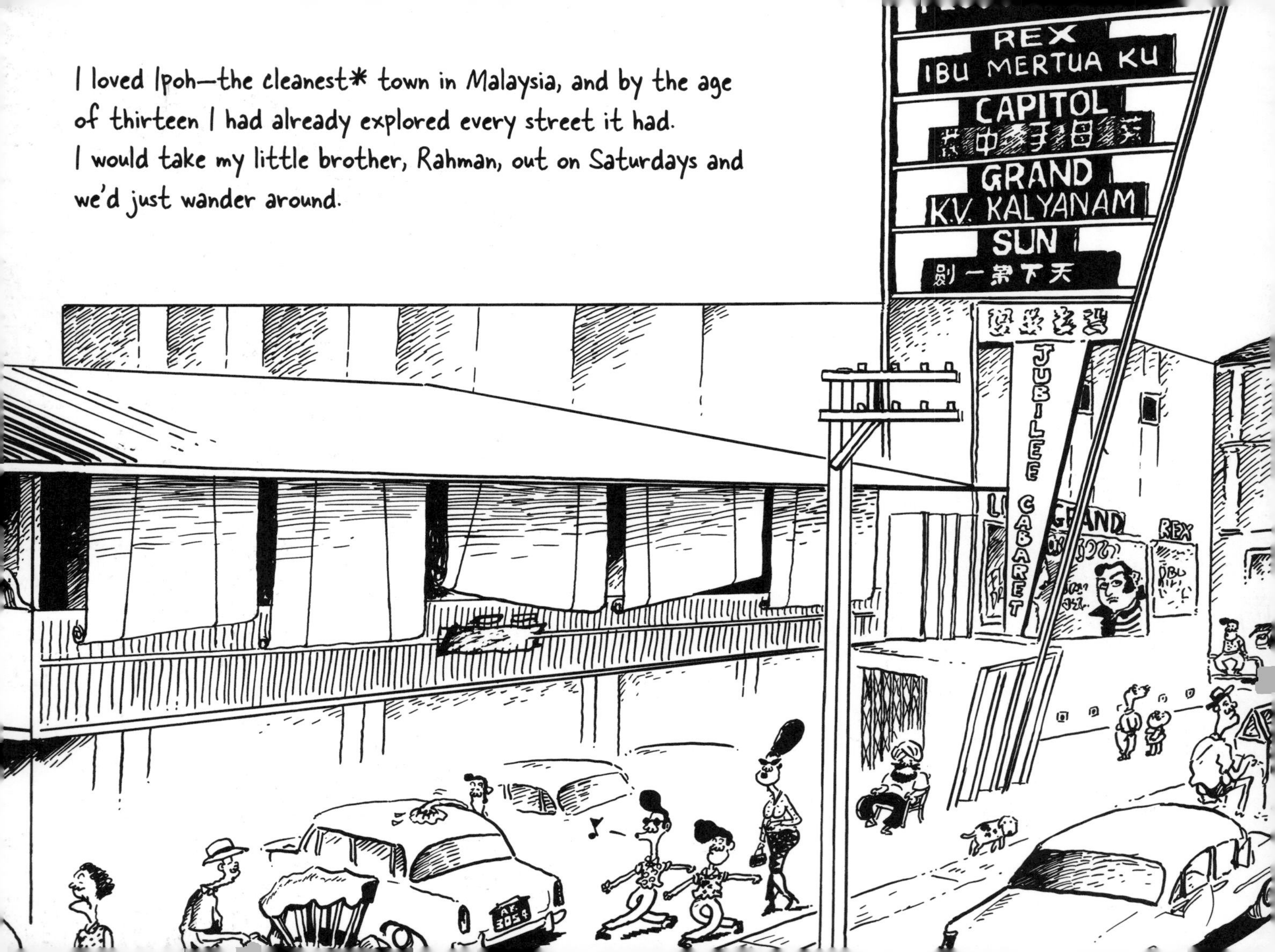
I loved Ipoh—the cleanest* town in Malaysia, and by the age of thirteen I had already explored every street it had.
I would take my little brother, Rahman, out on Saturdays and we'd just wander around.
REX
IBU MERTUA KU
CAPITOL
GRAND
K.V. KALYANAM
SUN
JUBILEE CABARET
GRAND
REX

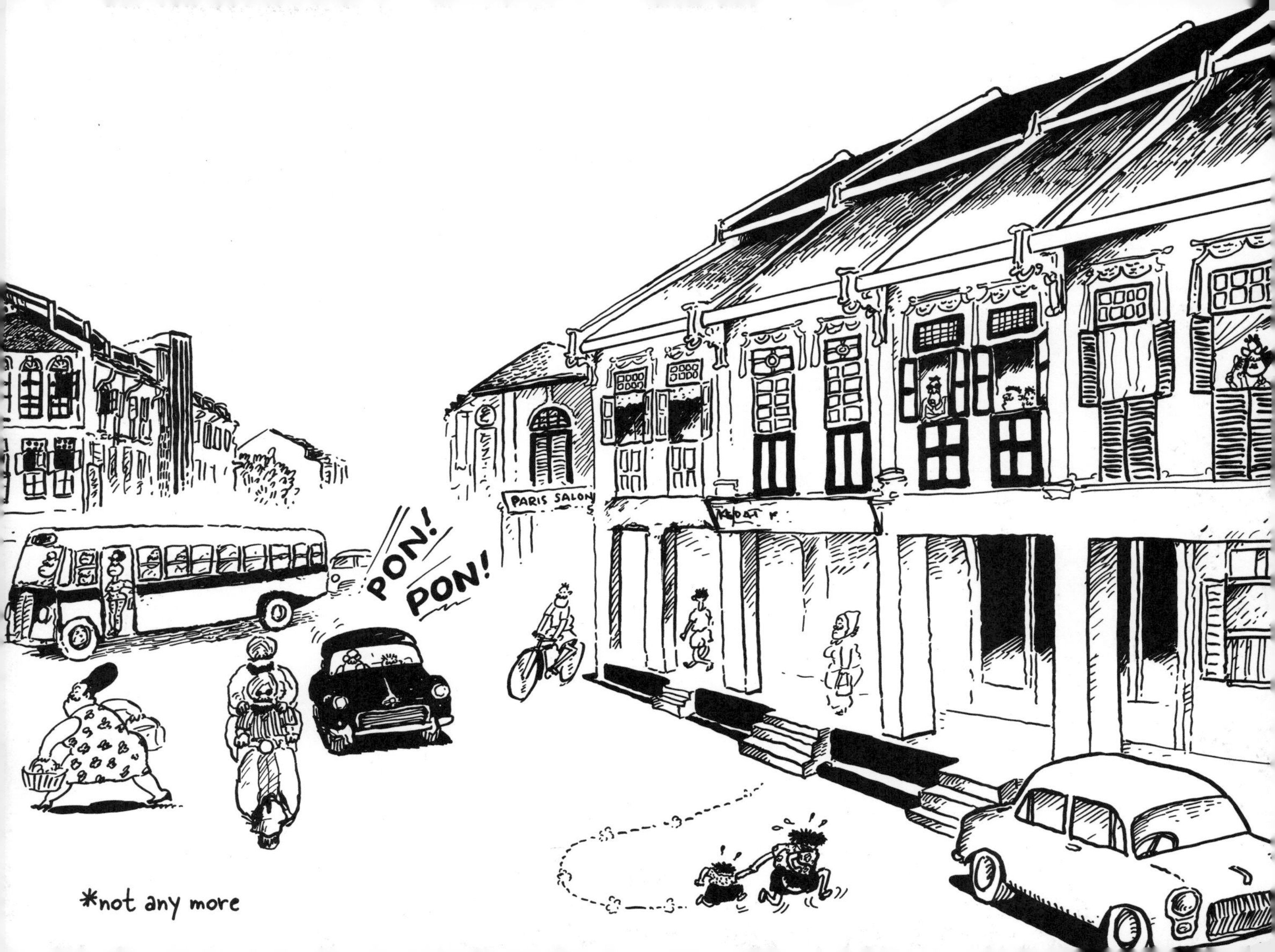
PARIS SALON
PON!
PON!

*not any more

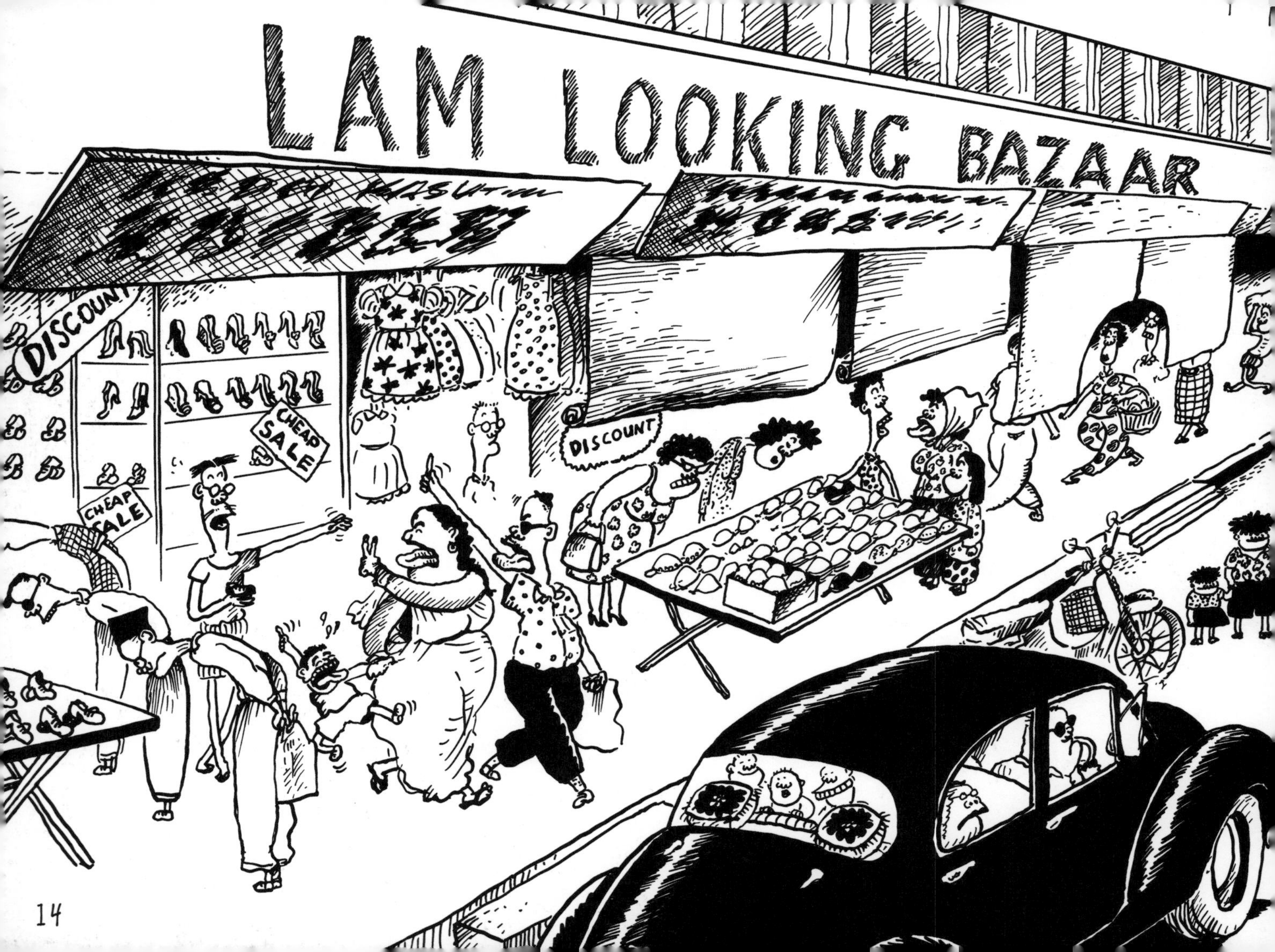
LAM LOOKING BAZAAR
DISCOUNT
CHEAP SALE
CHEAP SALE
DISCOUNT

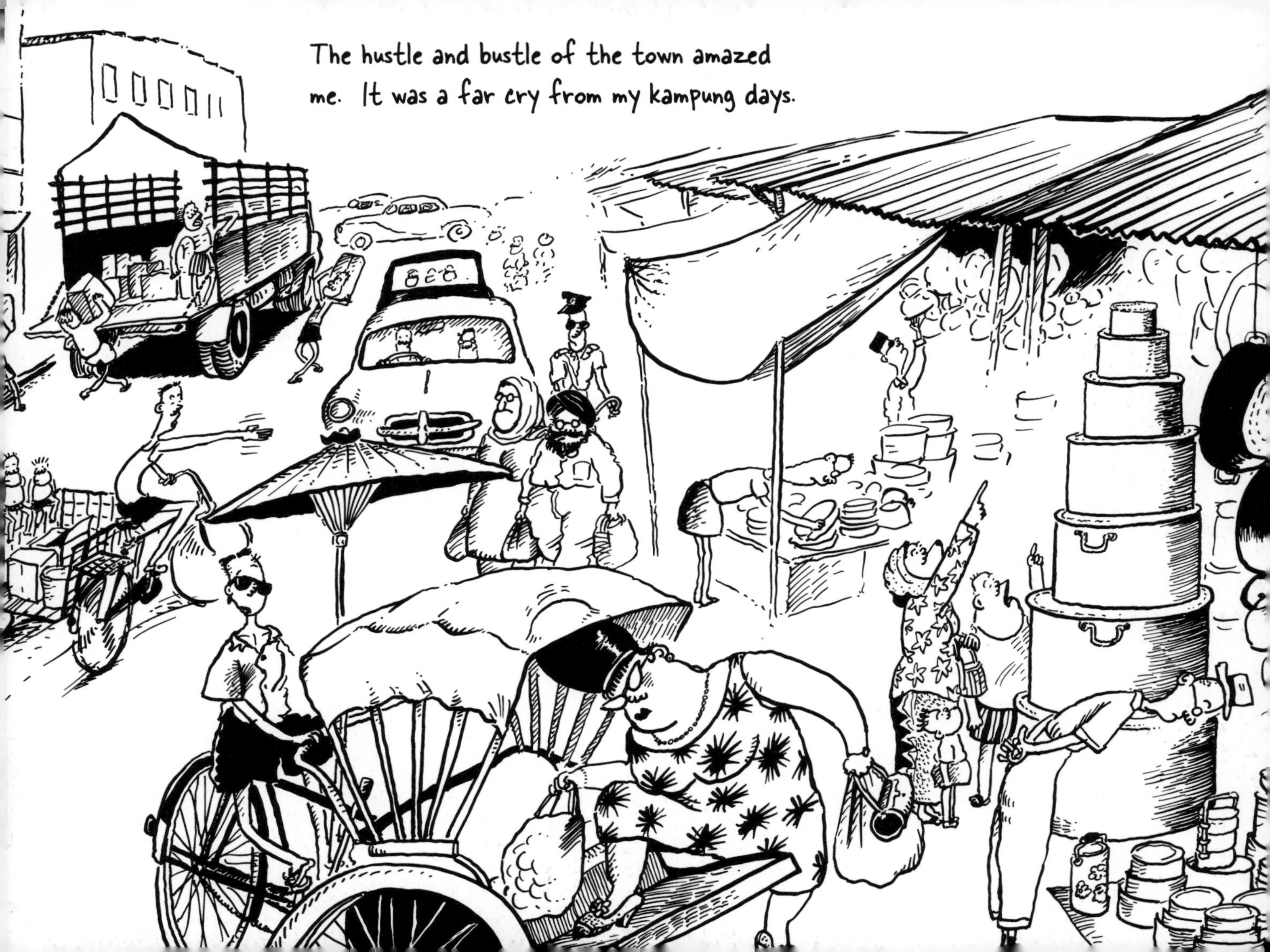
The hustle and bustle of the town amazed me. It was a far cry from my kampung days.

At the age of thirteen

I was a quiet boy, come to think of it. Having no close friends, I cycled alone to school. But this didn't mean that I was not in the mainstream of things.

My hobby was drawing (watercolor) and music (radio). My favorite color was pink and my favorite subjects in school were geography and arts and crafts.

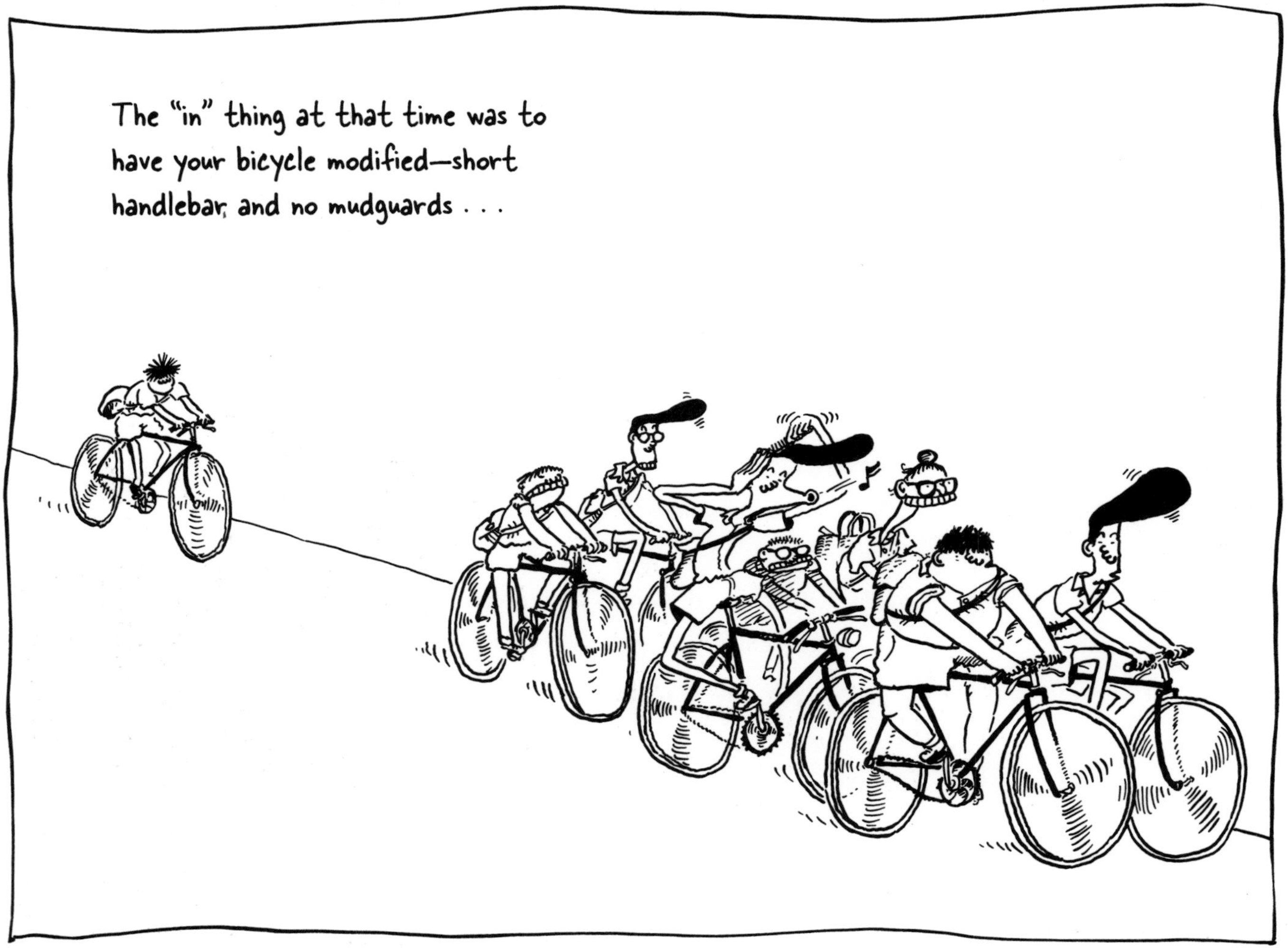
The "in" thing at that time was to have your bicycle modified—short handlebar, and no mudguards . . .

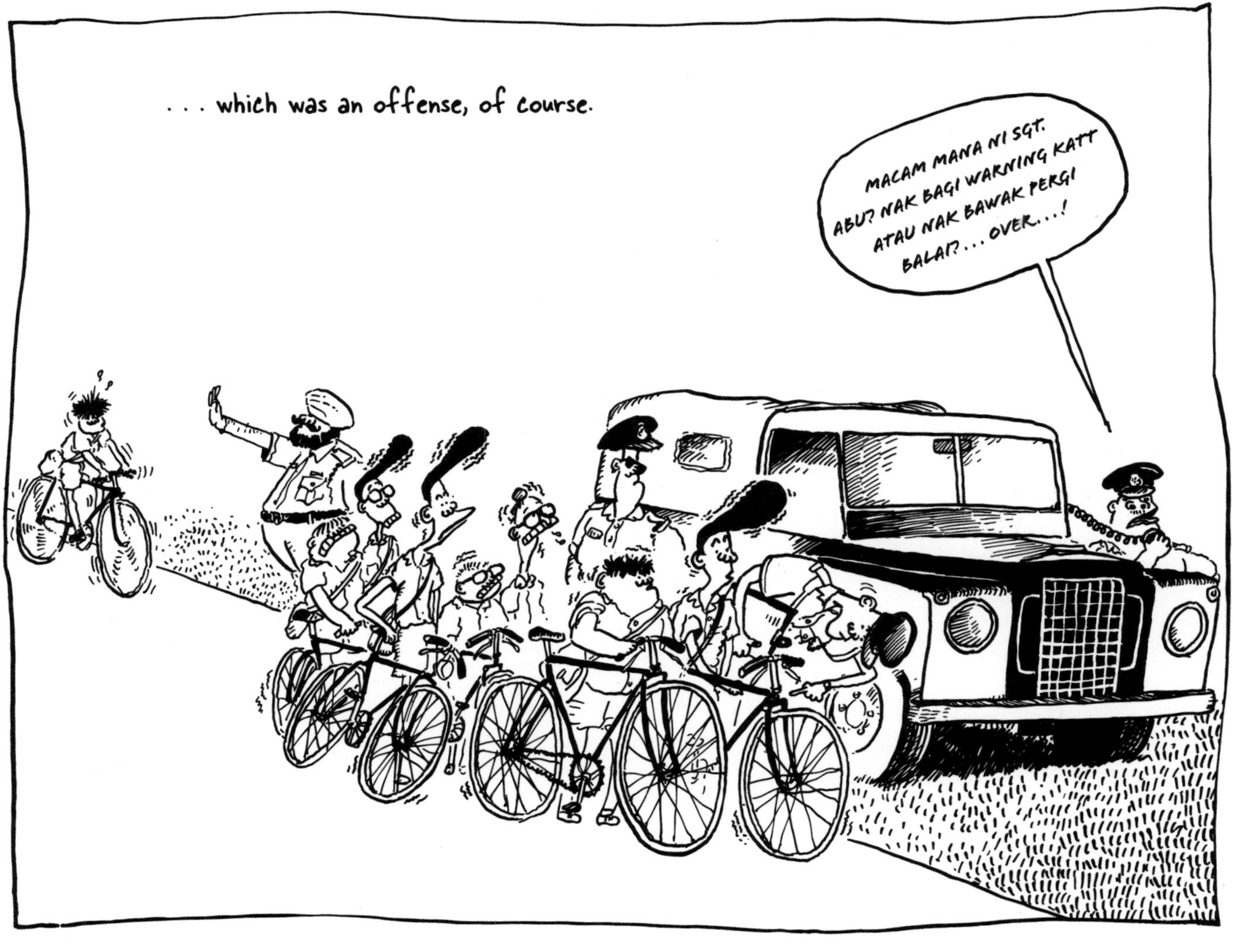
. . . which was an offense, of course.
MACAM MANA NI SGT. ABU? NAK BAGI WARNING KATT ATAU NAK BAWAK PERGI BALAI? . . . OVER . . . !

Anyway . . . it was on this one particular day that something came about.

It was recess time. Suddenly, I heard my name being called out loud.

It came from a . . . well . . . rather typical Chinese fellow you'd see anywhere.

I didn't know him.

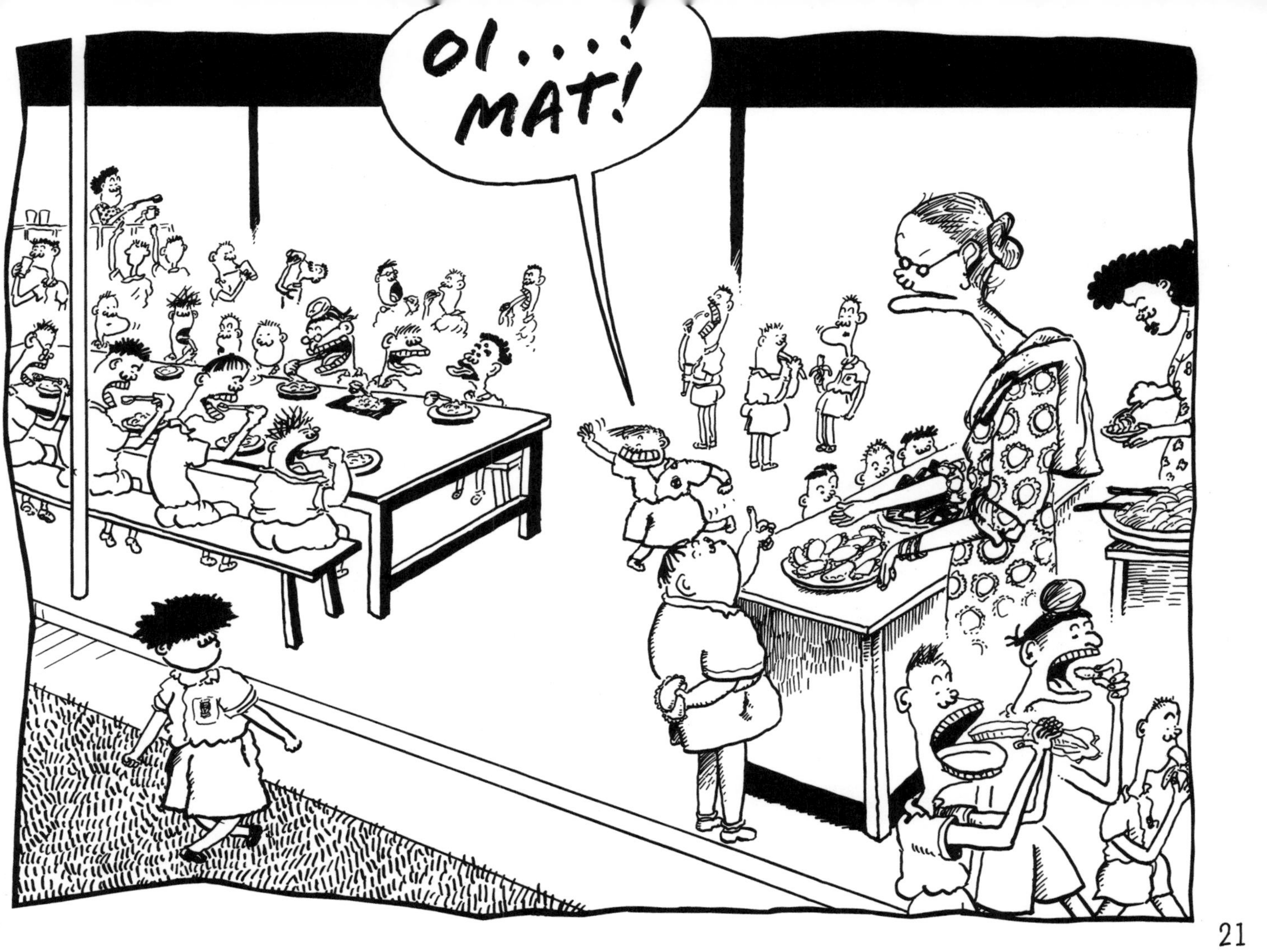
OI....!
MAT!

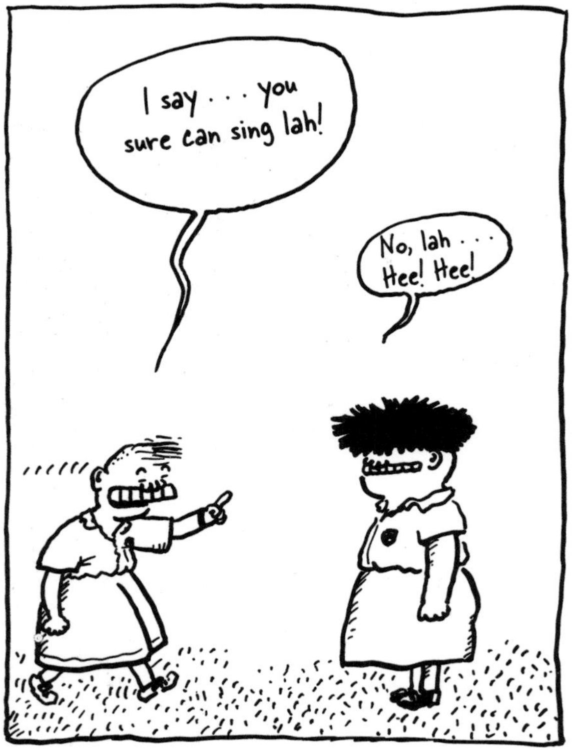
I say . . . you sure can sing lah!
No, lah . . . Hee! Hee!

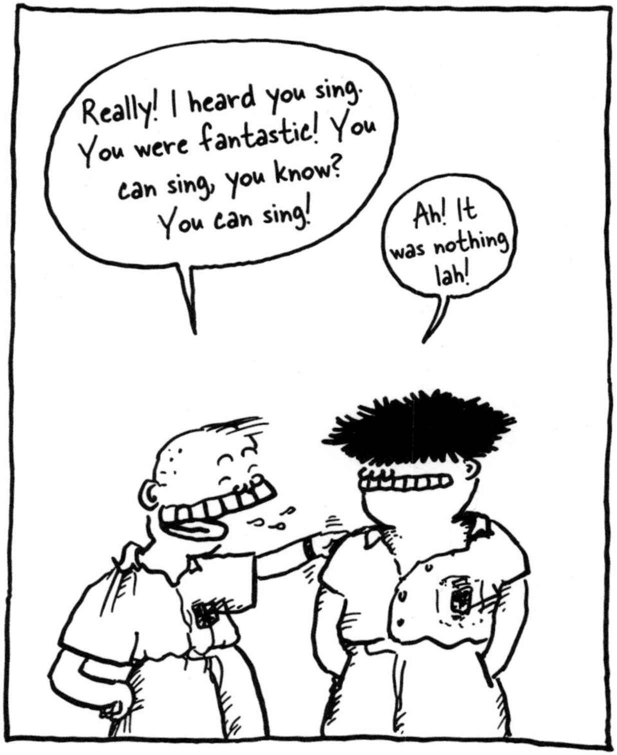
Really! I heard you sing. You were fantastic! You can sing, you know? You can sing!
Ah! It was nothing lah!

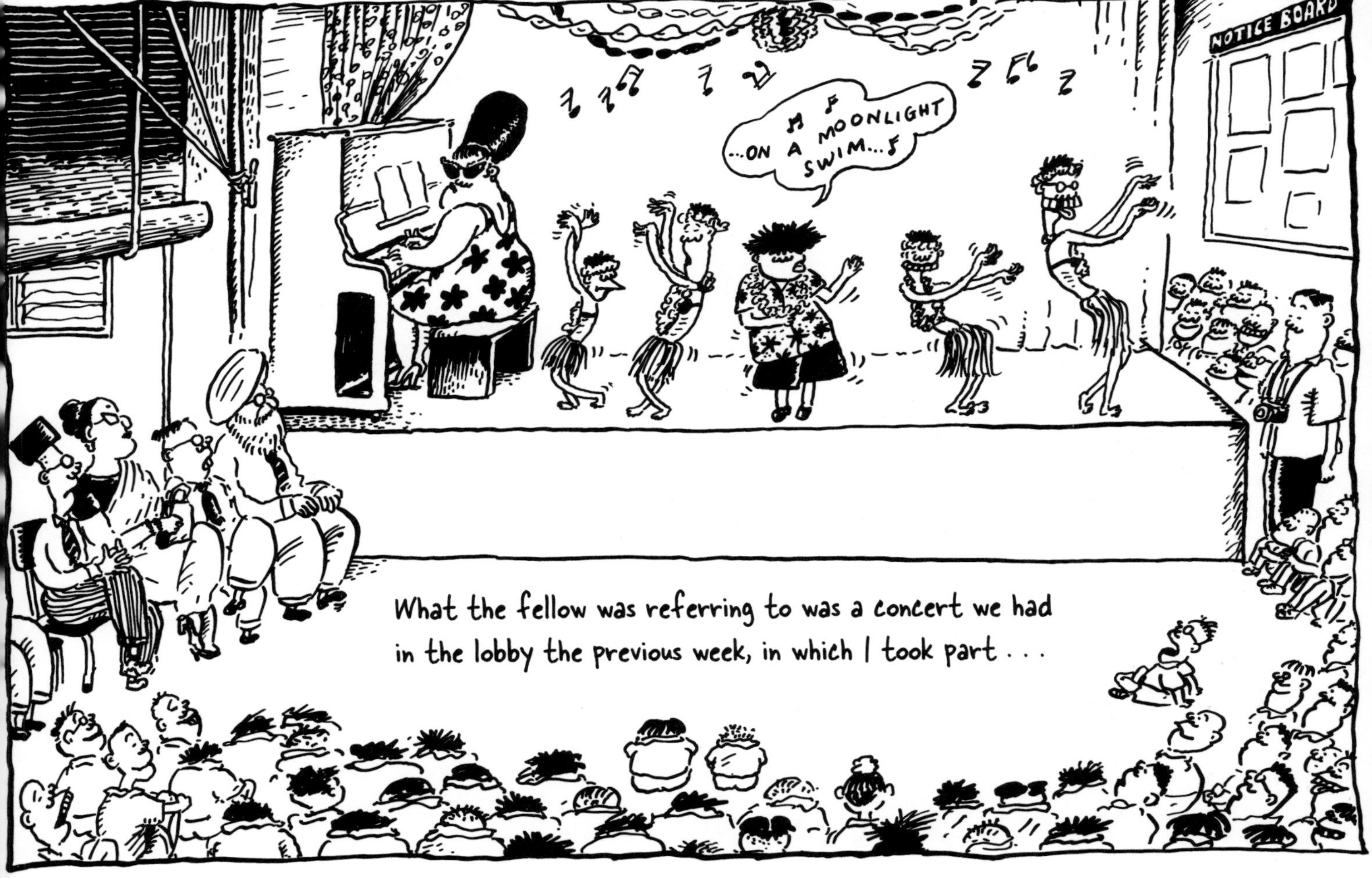
NOTICE BOARD
...ON A MOONLIGHT SWIM...

What the fellow was referring to was a concert we had in the lobby the previous week, in which I took part . . .

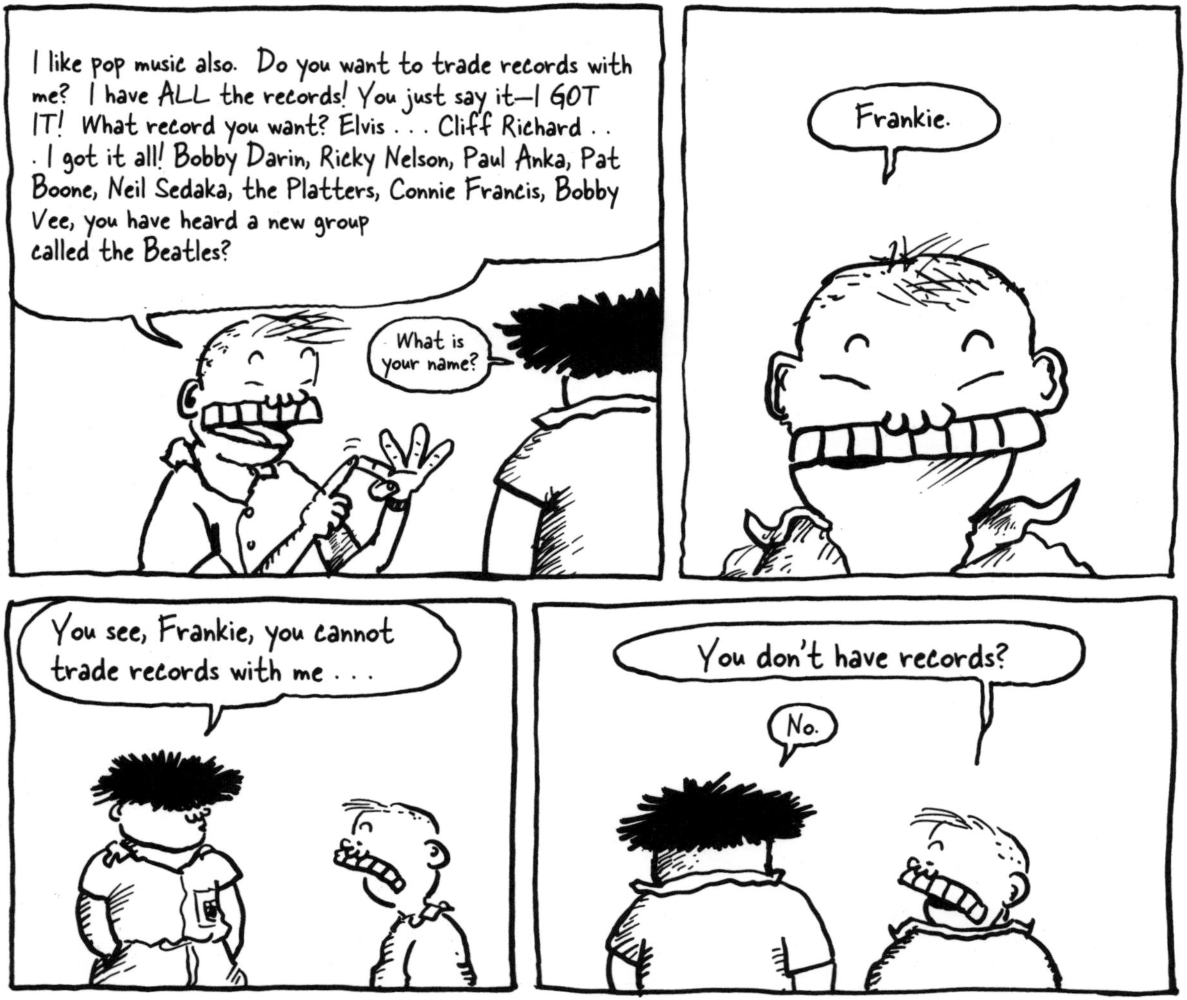
I like pop music also. Do you want to trade records with me? I have ALL the records! You just say it—I GOT IT! What record you want? Elvis . . . Cliff Richard . . . I got it all! Bobby Darin, Ricky Nelson, Paul Anka, Pat Boone, Neil Sedaka, the Platters, Connie Francis, Bobby Vee, you have heard a new group called the Beatles?
What is your name?
Frankie.
You see, Frankie, you cannot trade records with me . . .
You don't have records?
No.

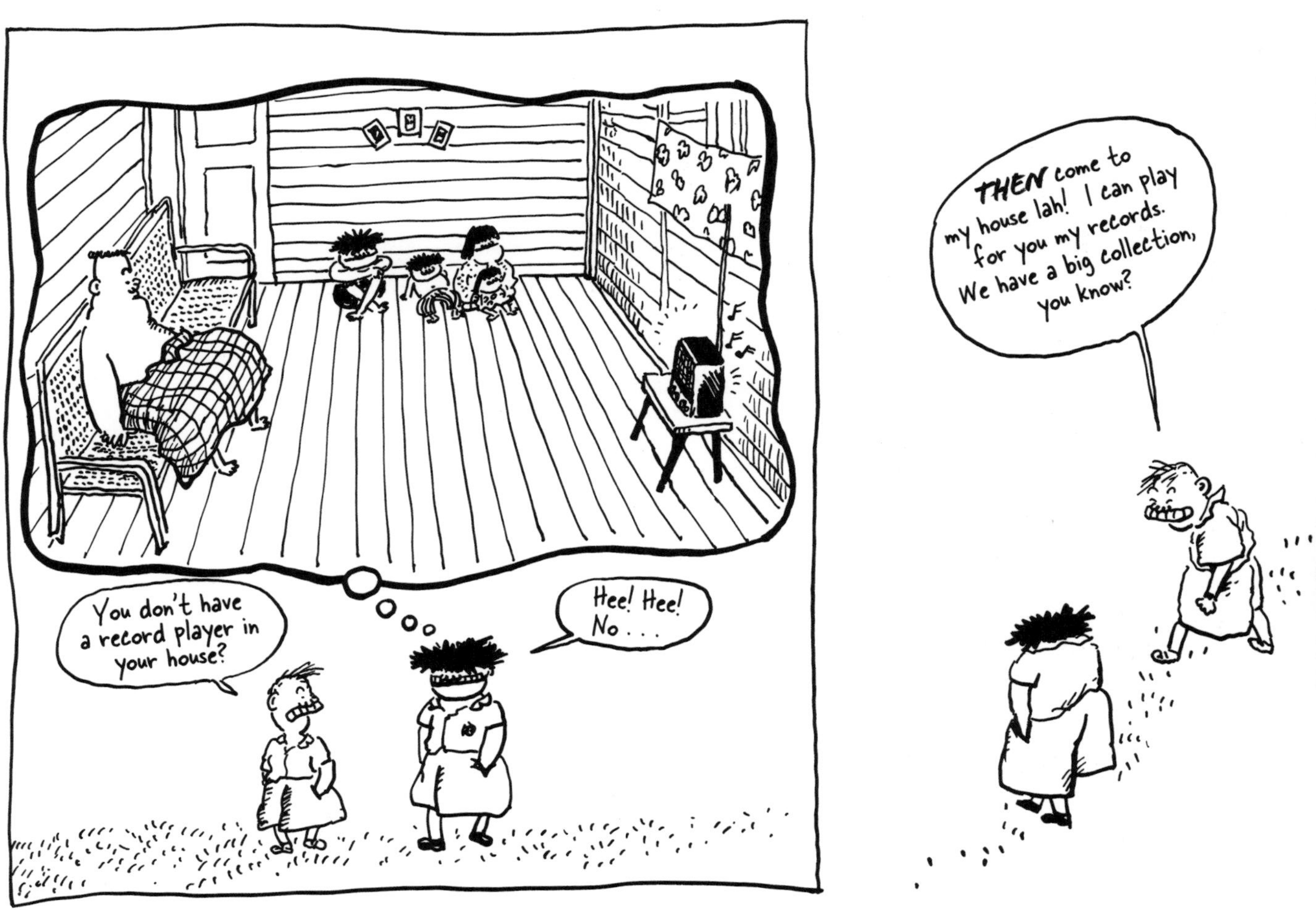
You don't have a record player in your house?
Hee! Hee! No . . .
THEN come to my house lah! I can play for you my records. We have a big collection, you know?

Frankie meant what he said (about the invitation), for he kept asking me to go to his house days later.

I was very interested, naturally, but at the same time I was also shy.

Frankie knew music. At first I thought I knew a lot but it seemed sitting alone by myself beside the radio at home could not make me understand much after all.

From that day onward we'd meet during recess to have a chat that I always looked forward to. Frankie seemed to like it also.

I had a feeling he too had been searching for someone who was interested in music.

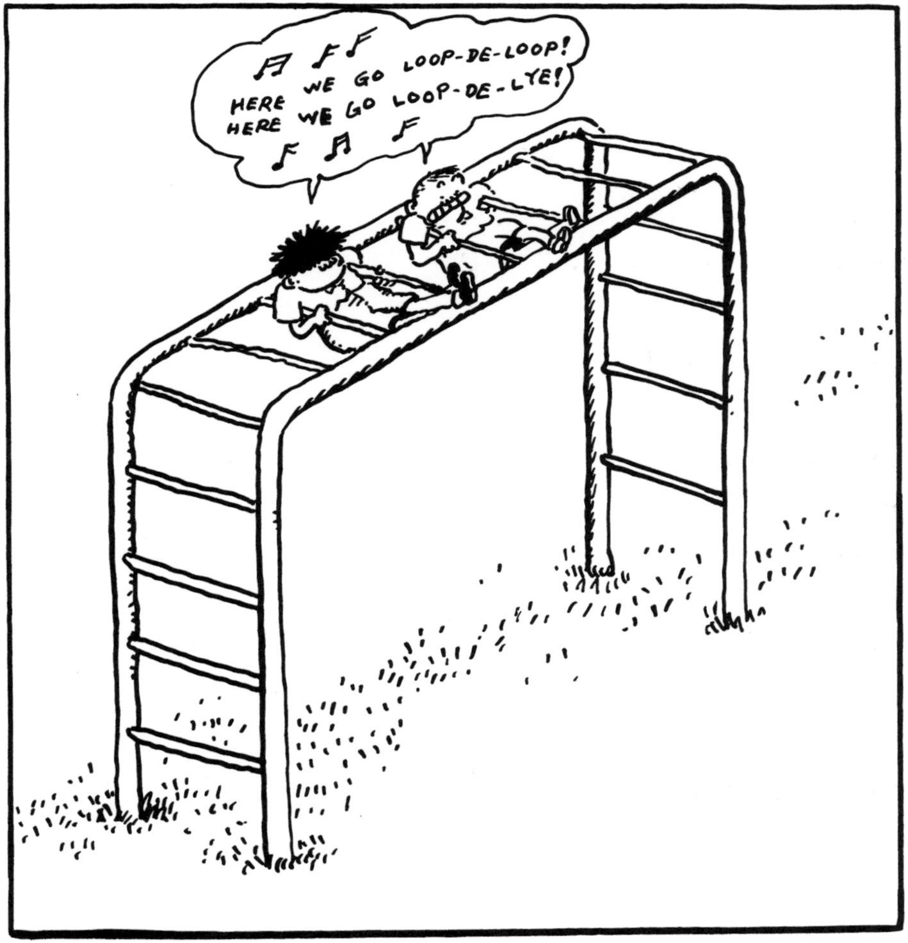
HERE WE GO LOOP-DE-LOOP!
HERE WE GO LOOP-DE-LYE!

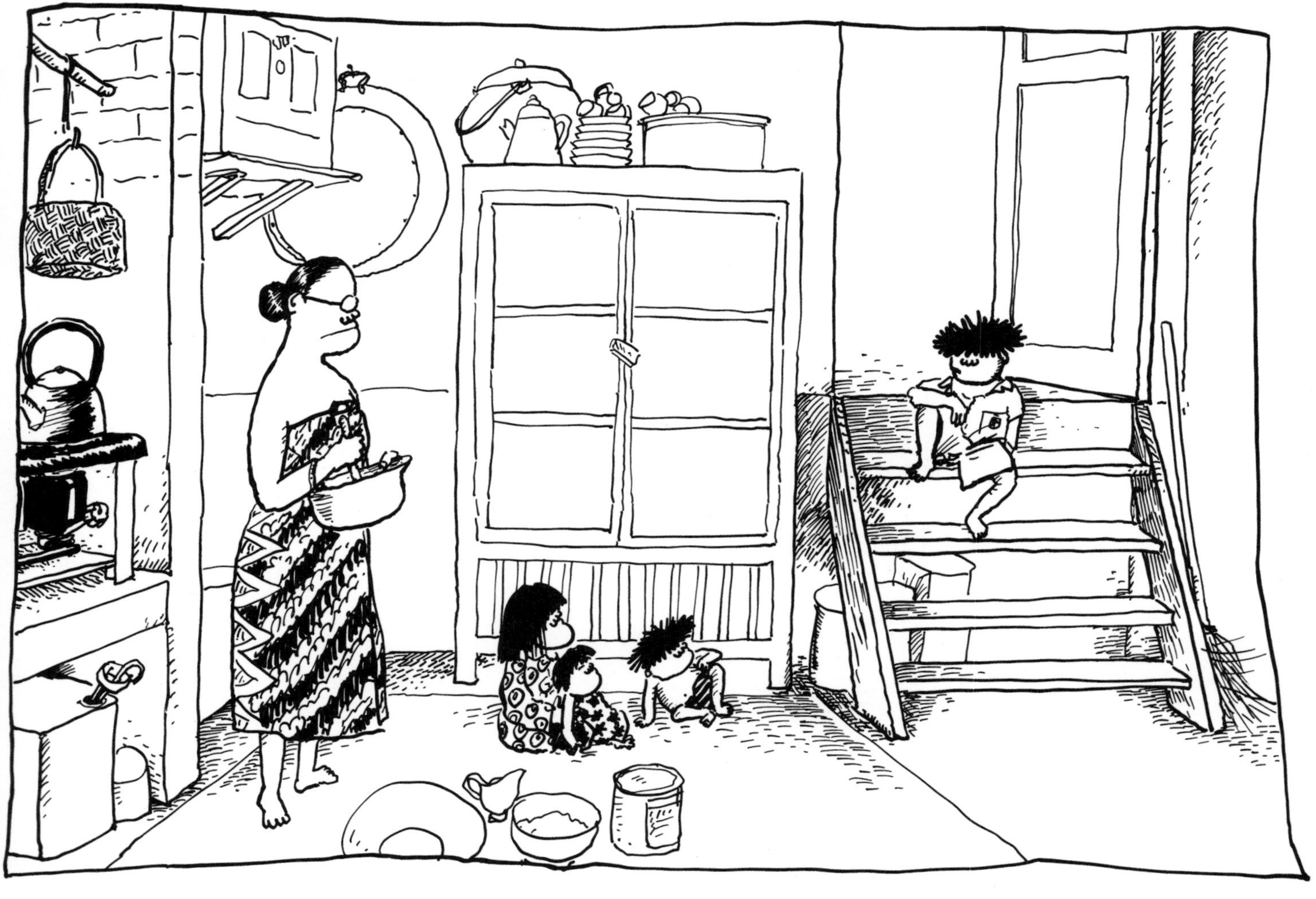

One day I told my mother that I'd be home late the following day because I was going to a friend's place to listen to records.

And just as I had expected, Mum wanted to know more about this friend.

I told her the only details I knew: Frankie lived in a shop house in New Town. His father ran a coffee shop downstairs. Mum said a coffee shop was always busy and that she didn't want me to go and "disturb Frankie's folks."

I said Frankie had already asked his parents about it and he said not to worry.

Mum said it was O.K. if I went just for a while because "we don't know your friend's parents and they don't know you," and if I would come straight back after listening to records.

All right.

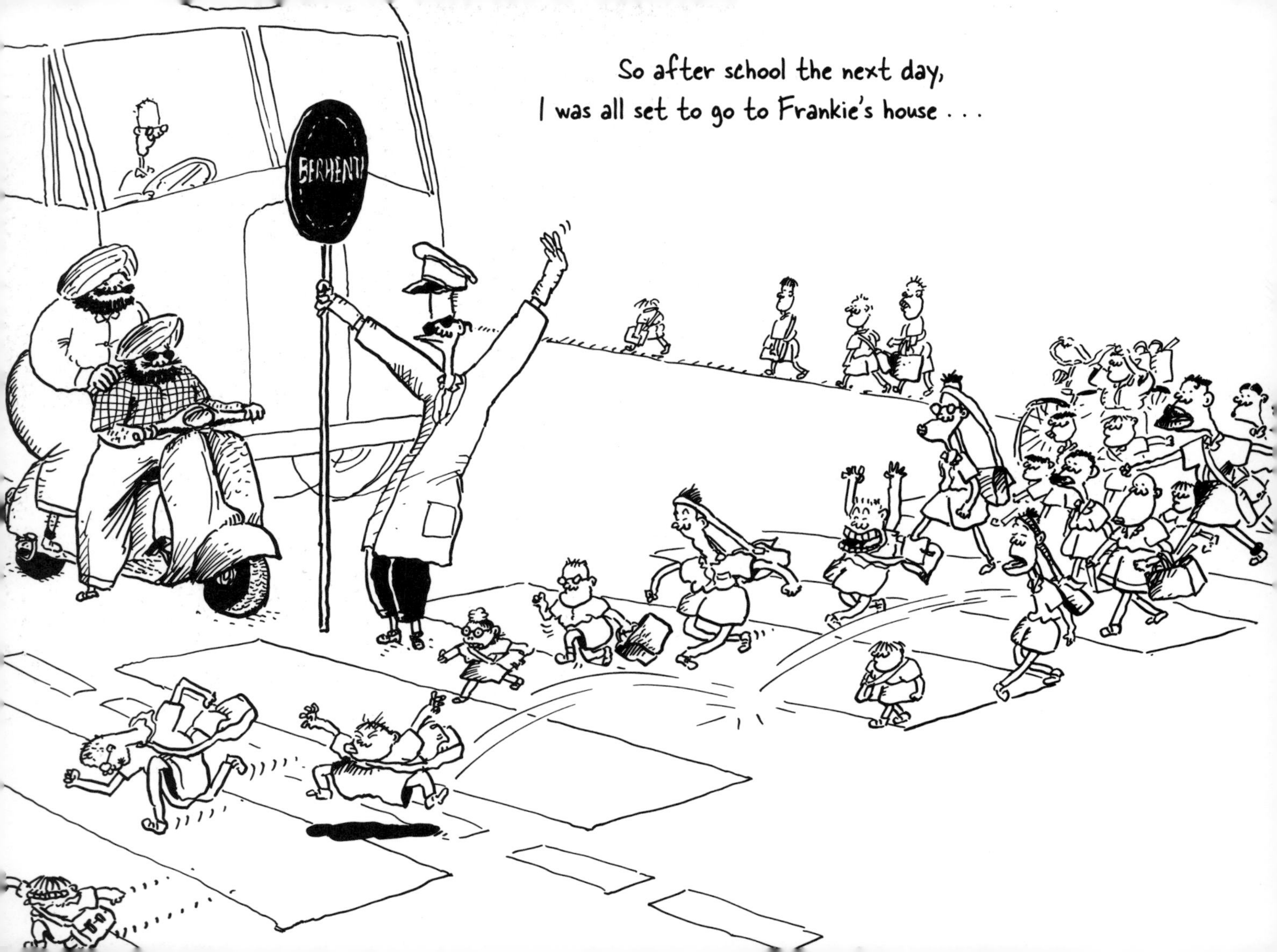
So after school the next day,
I was all set to go to Frankie's house . . .
BERHENTI

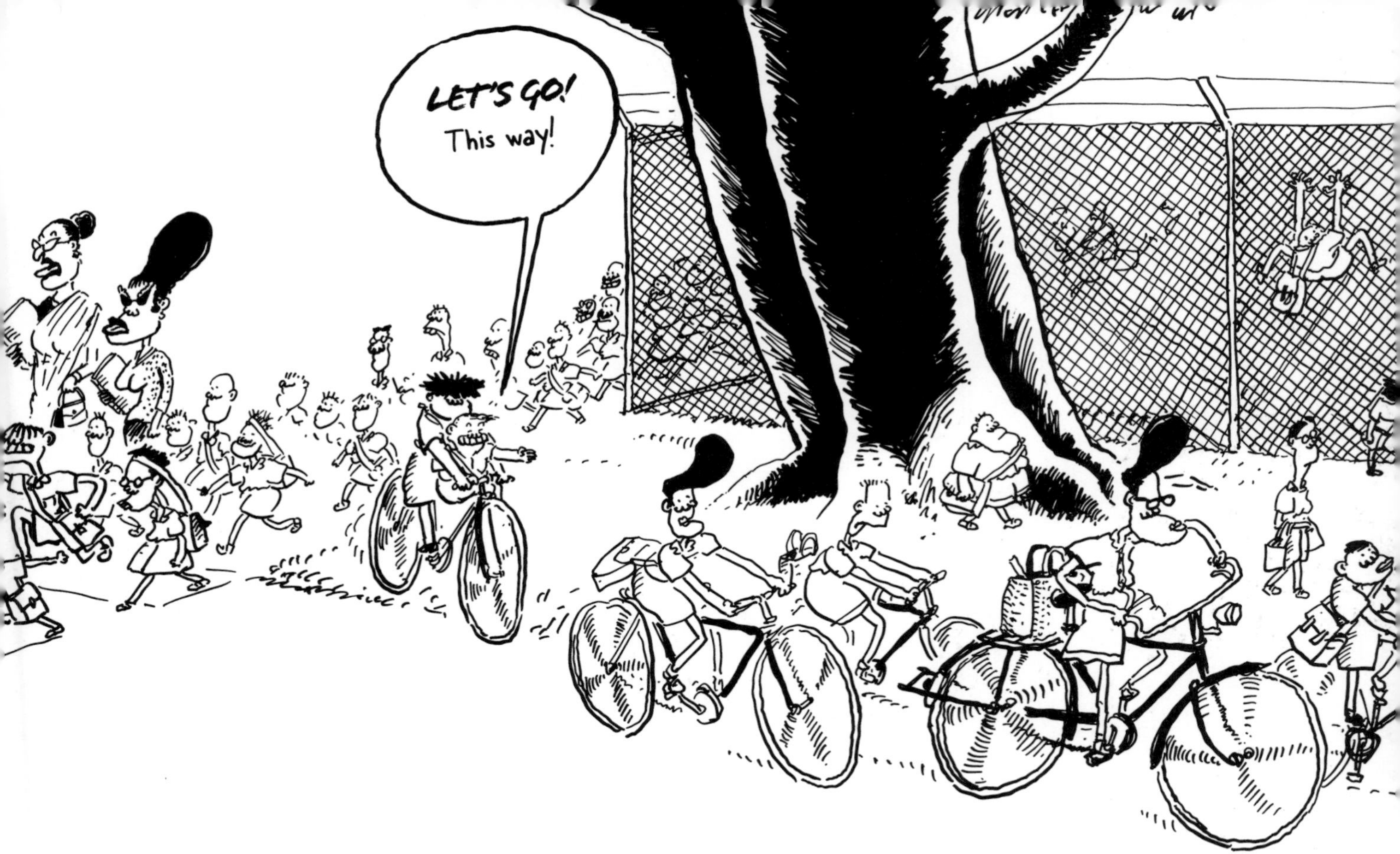
LET'S GO!
This way!

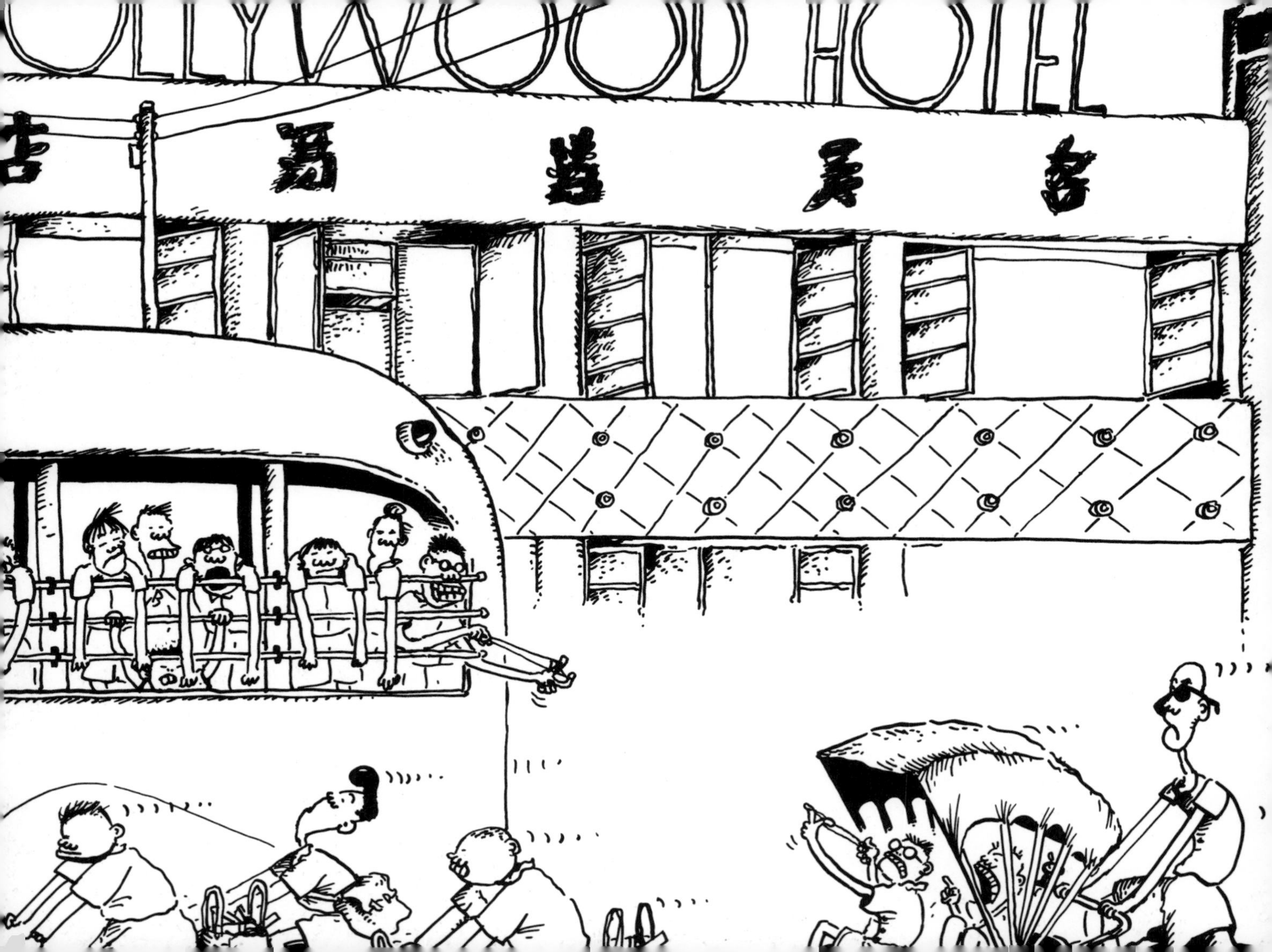
OLLYWOOD HOTEL

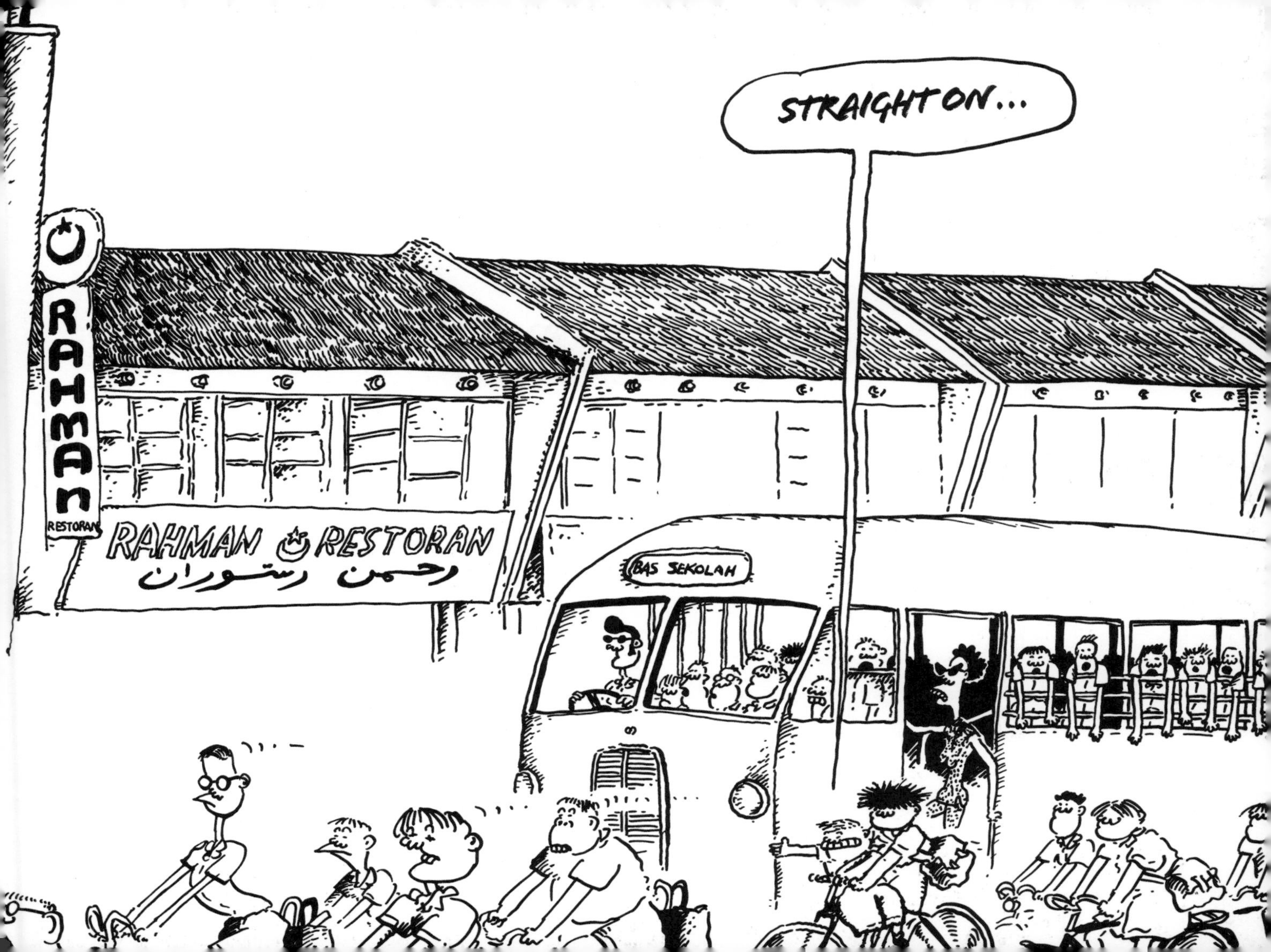

STRAIGHT ON...
RAHMAN
RESTORAN
RAHMAN RESTORAN
رحمن رستوران
BAS SEKOLAH

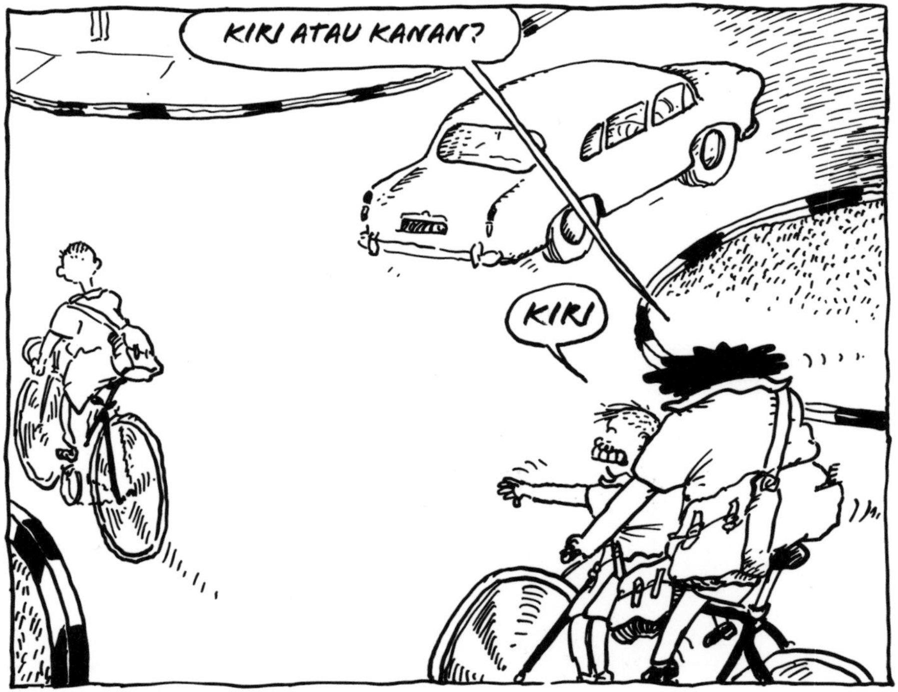
KIRI ATAU KANAN?
KIRI

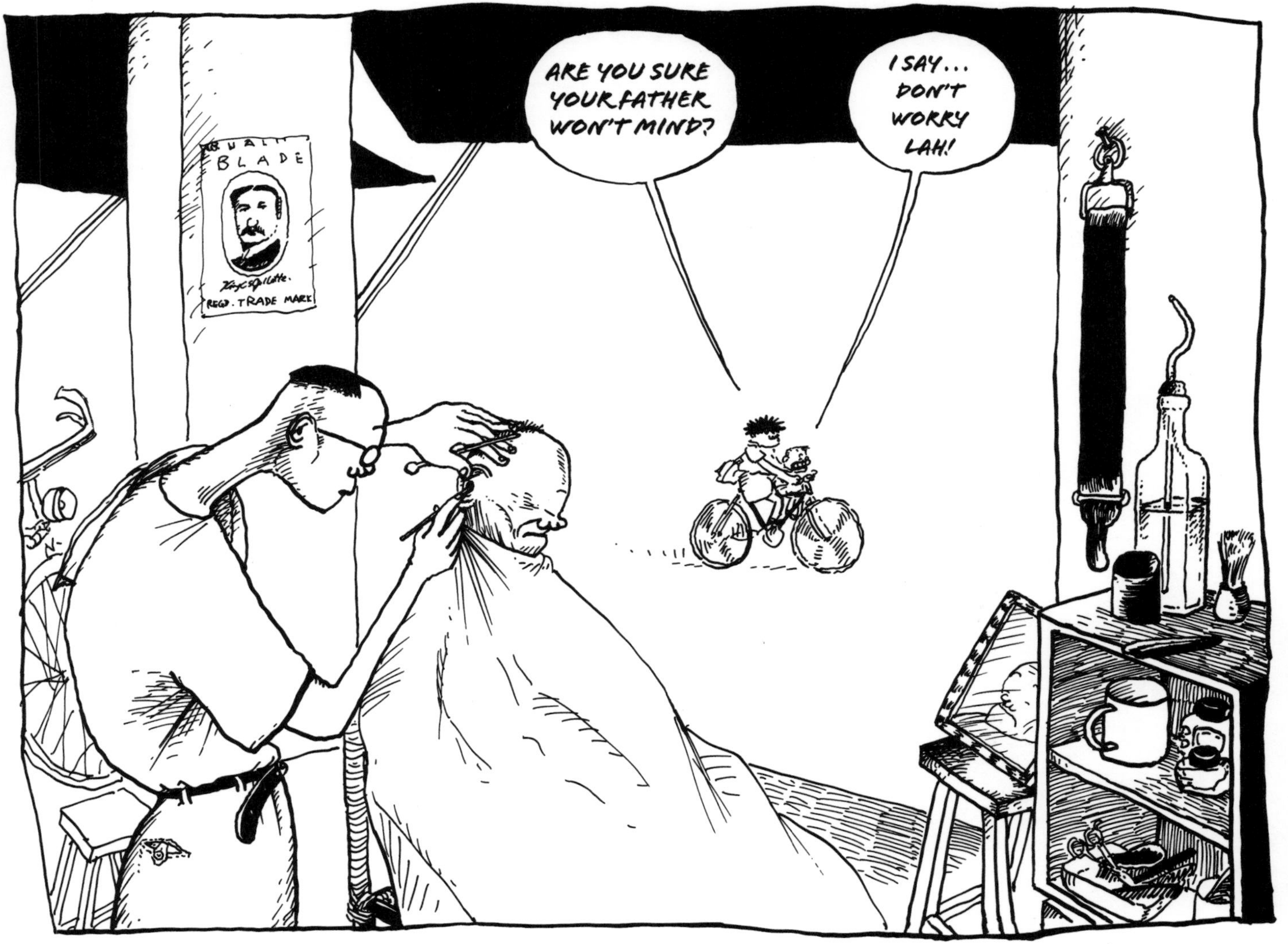
BLADE
REGD. TRADE MARK
ARE YOU SURE YOUR FATHER WON'T MIND?
I SAY... DON'T WORRY LAH!

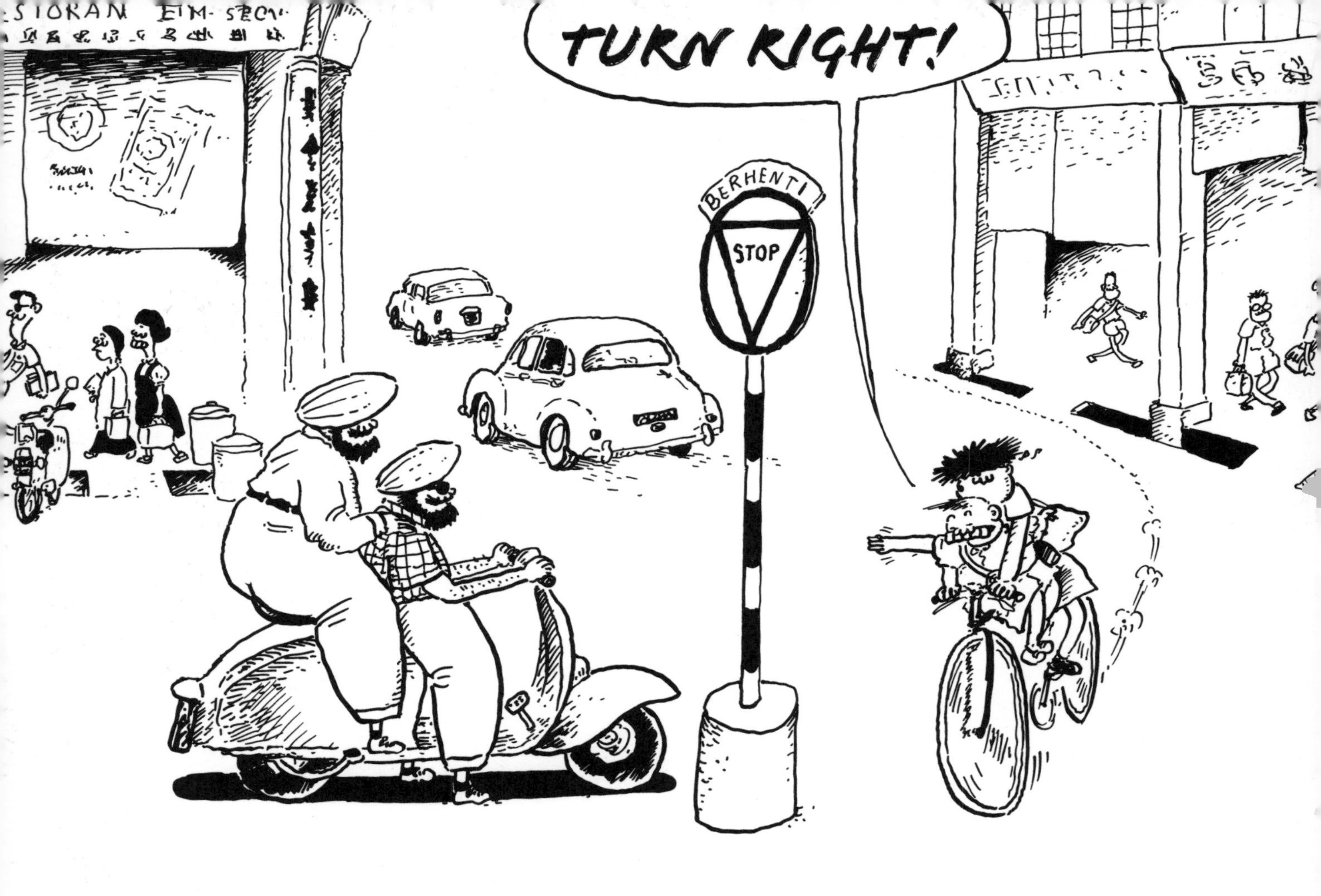
TURN RIGHT!
BERHENTI
STOP

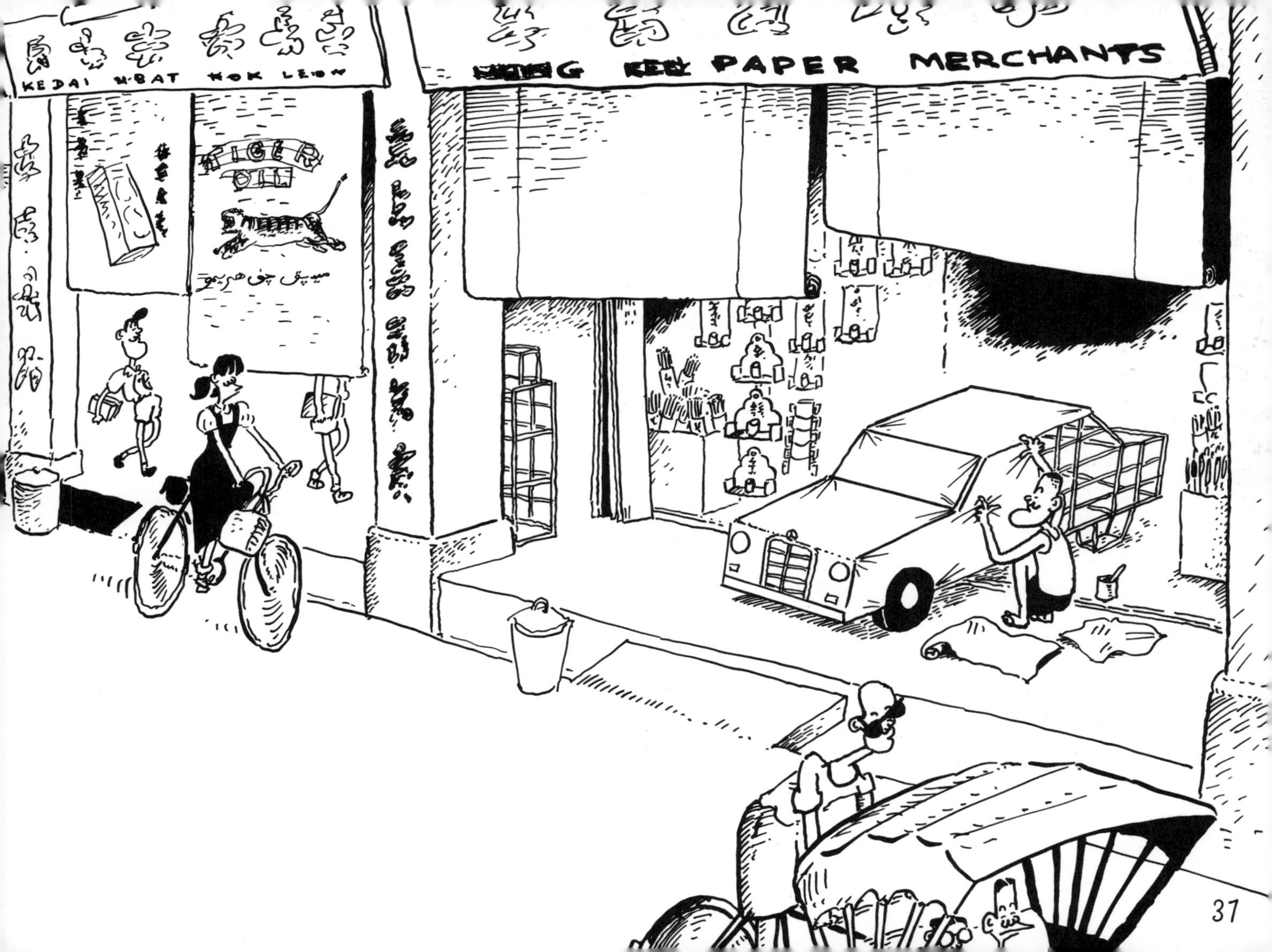
KEDAI UBAT KOK LEON
PAPER MERCHANTS
TIGER OIL

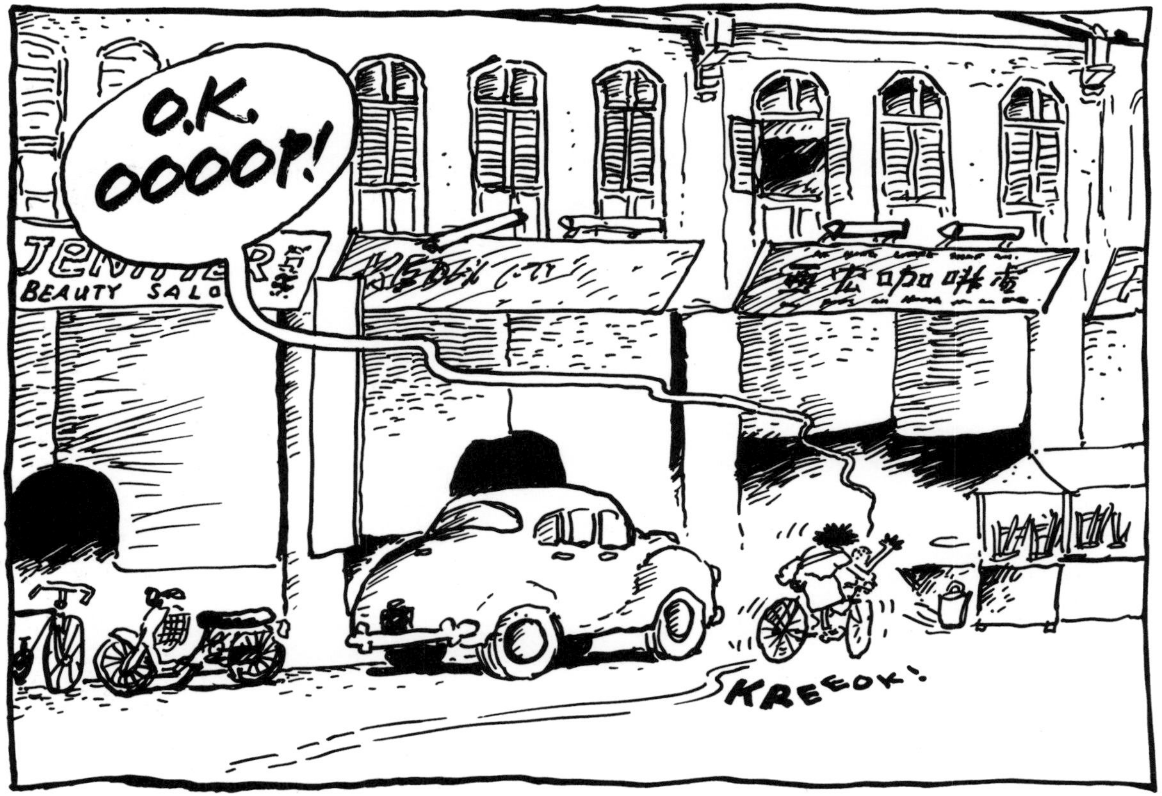
O.K.
OOOOP!
BEAUTY SALO
KREEOK!

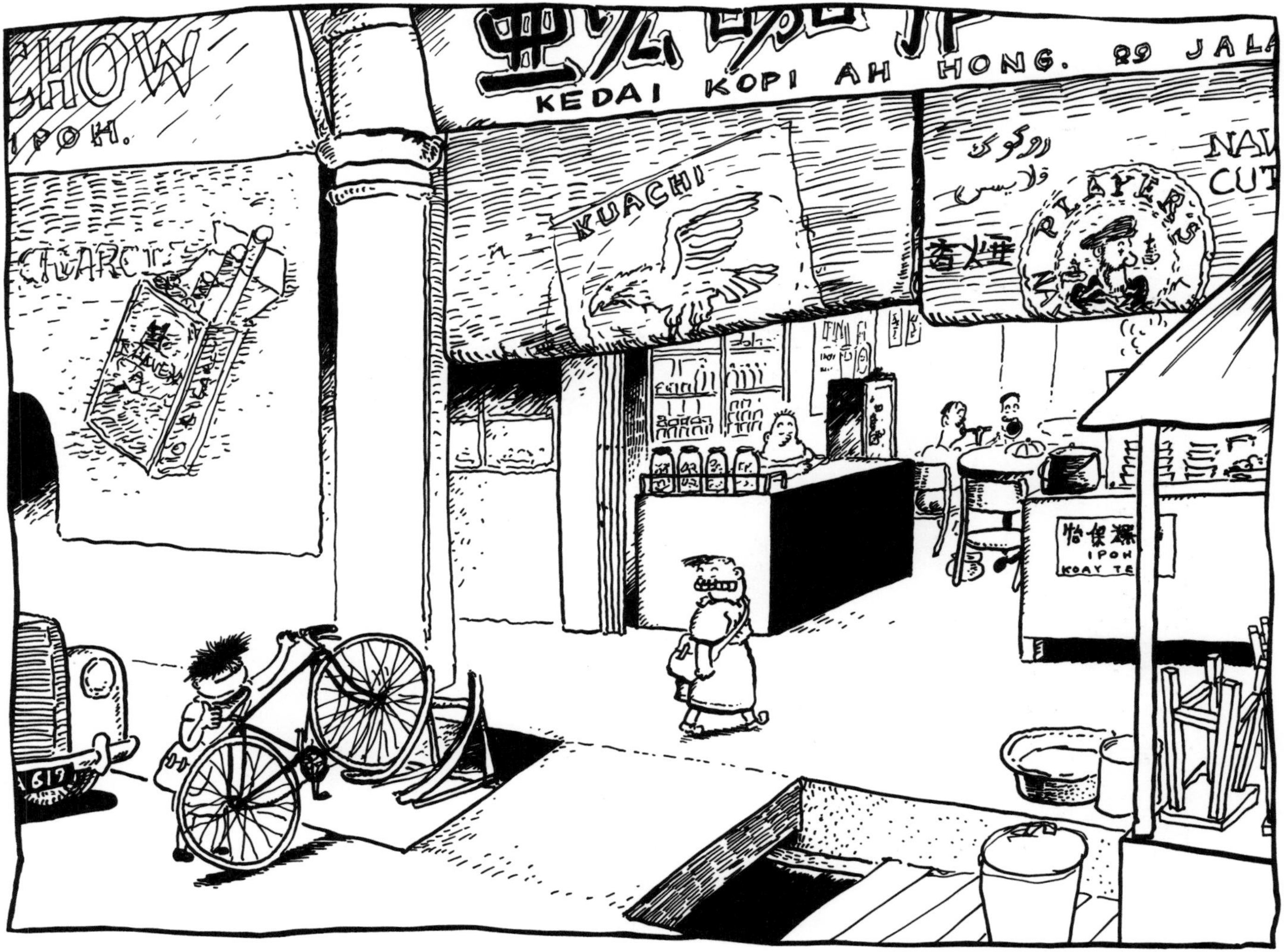
CHOW
IPOH.
KEDAI KOPI AH HONG. 29 JALA
KUACHI
PLAYER'S
NAV
CUT
IPOH
KOAY TE

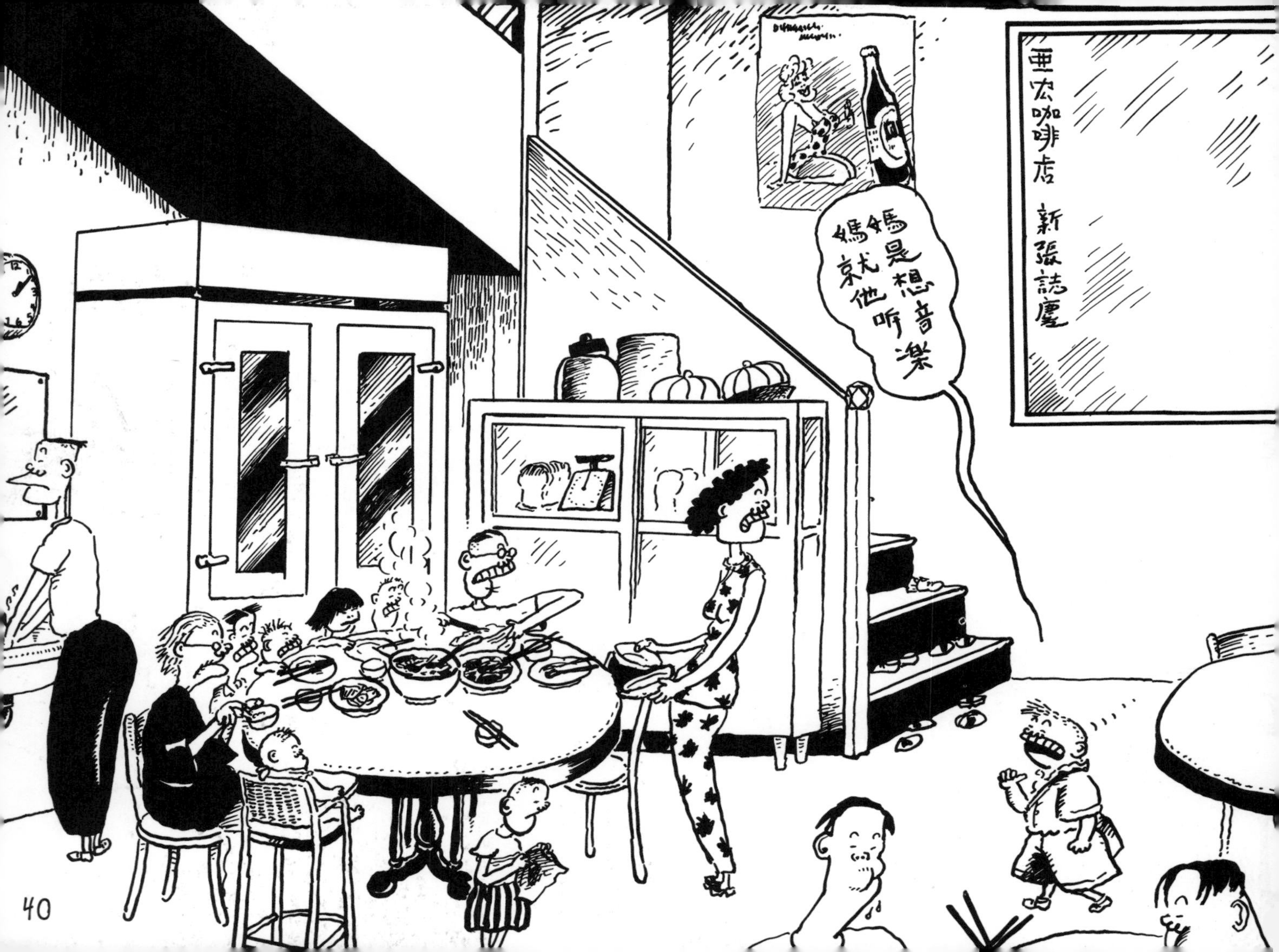
新張誌慶
亜宏咖啡店
媽媽就是想他听音樂

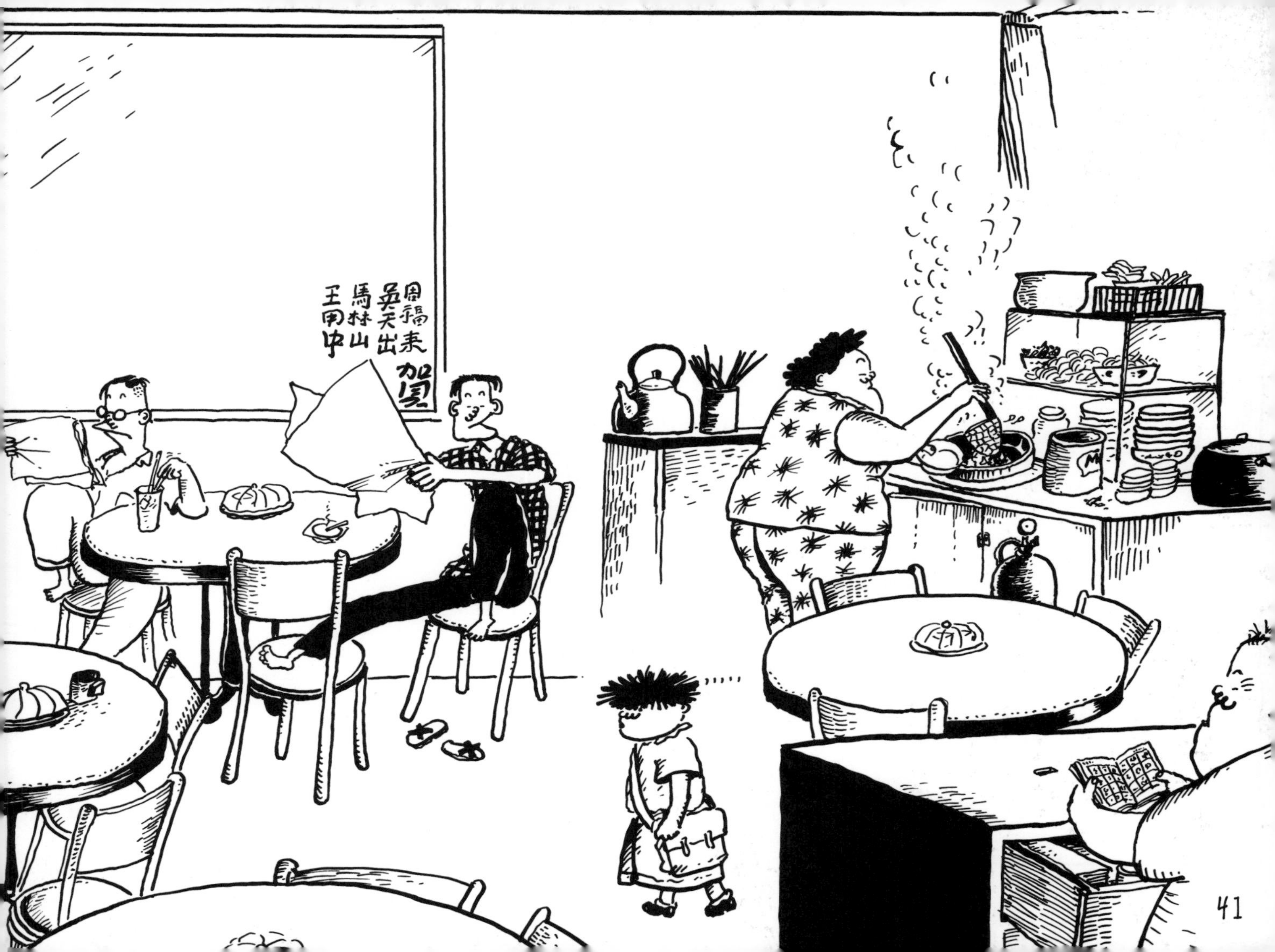

馬林山

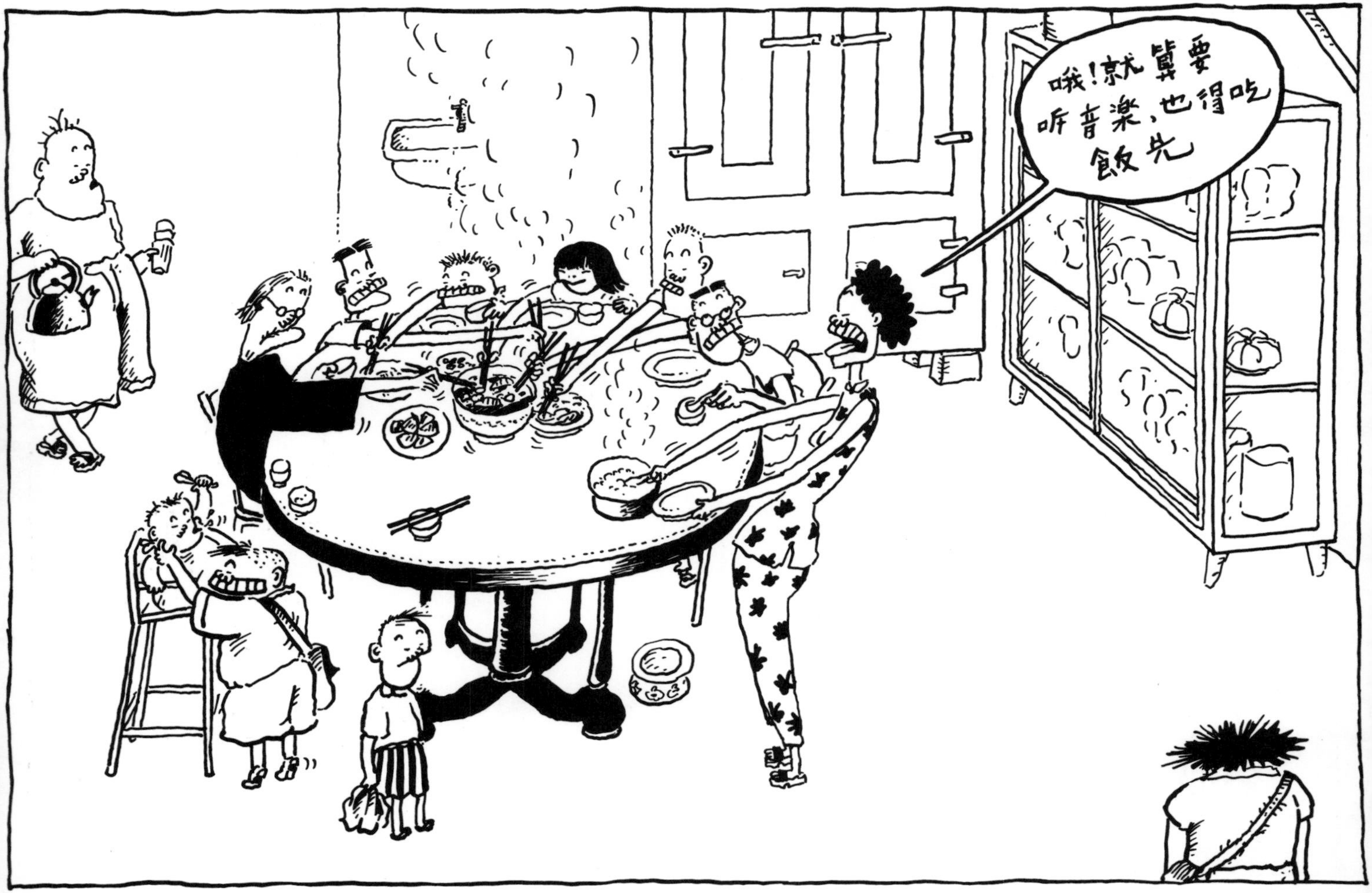
哦!就算要听音樂，也得吃飯先

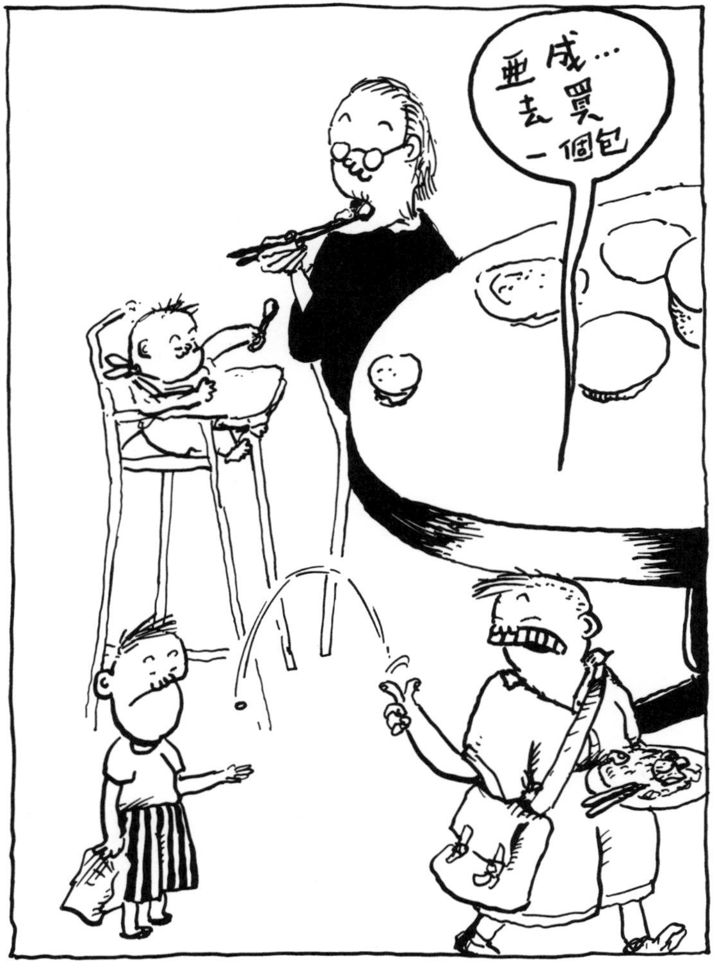

亚成...
去買
一個包

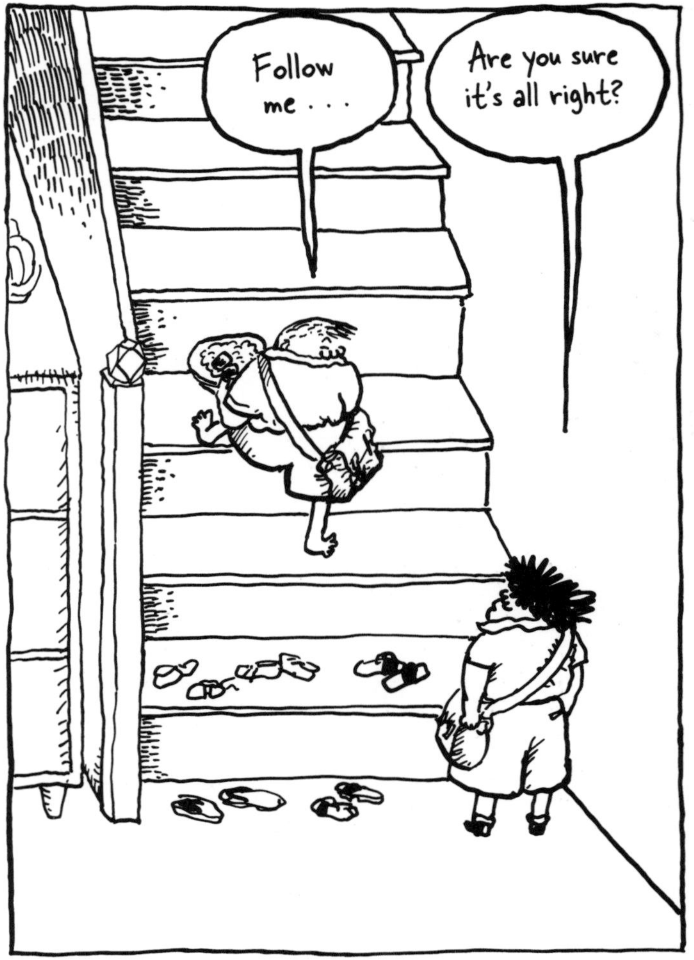

Follow me . . .
Are you sure it's all right?

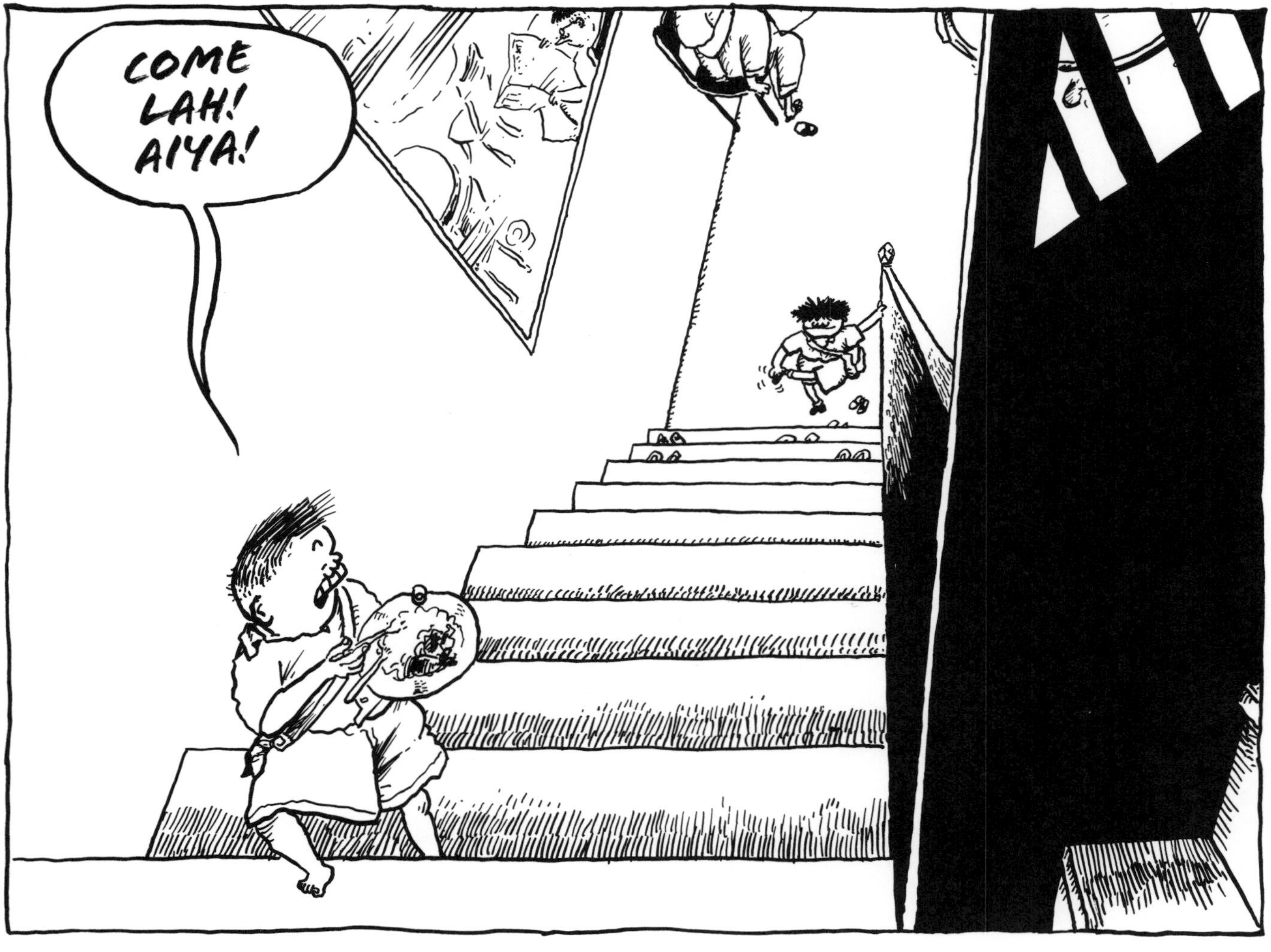
COME LAH! AIYA!

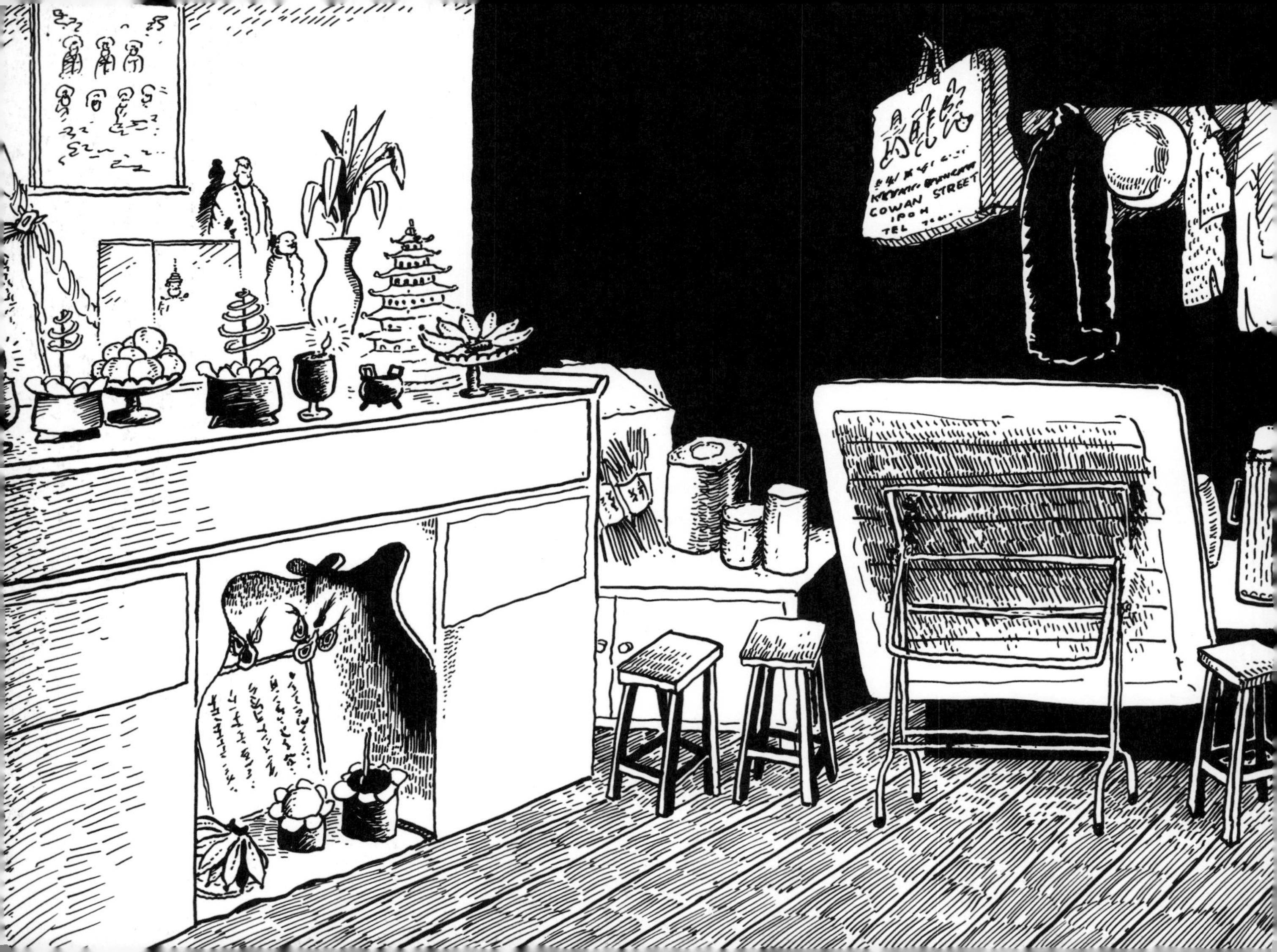
COWAN STREET
IPOH
TEL

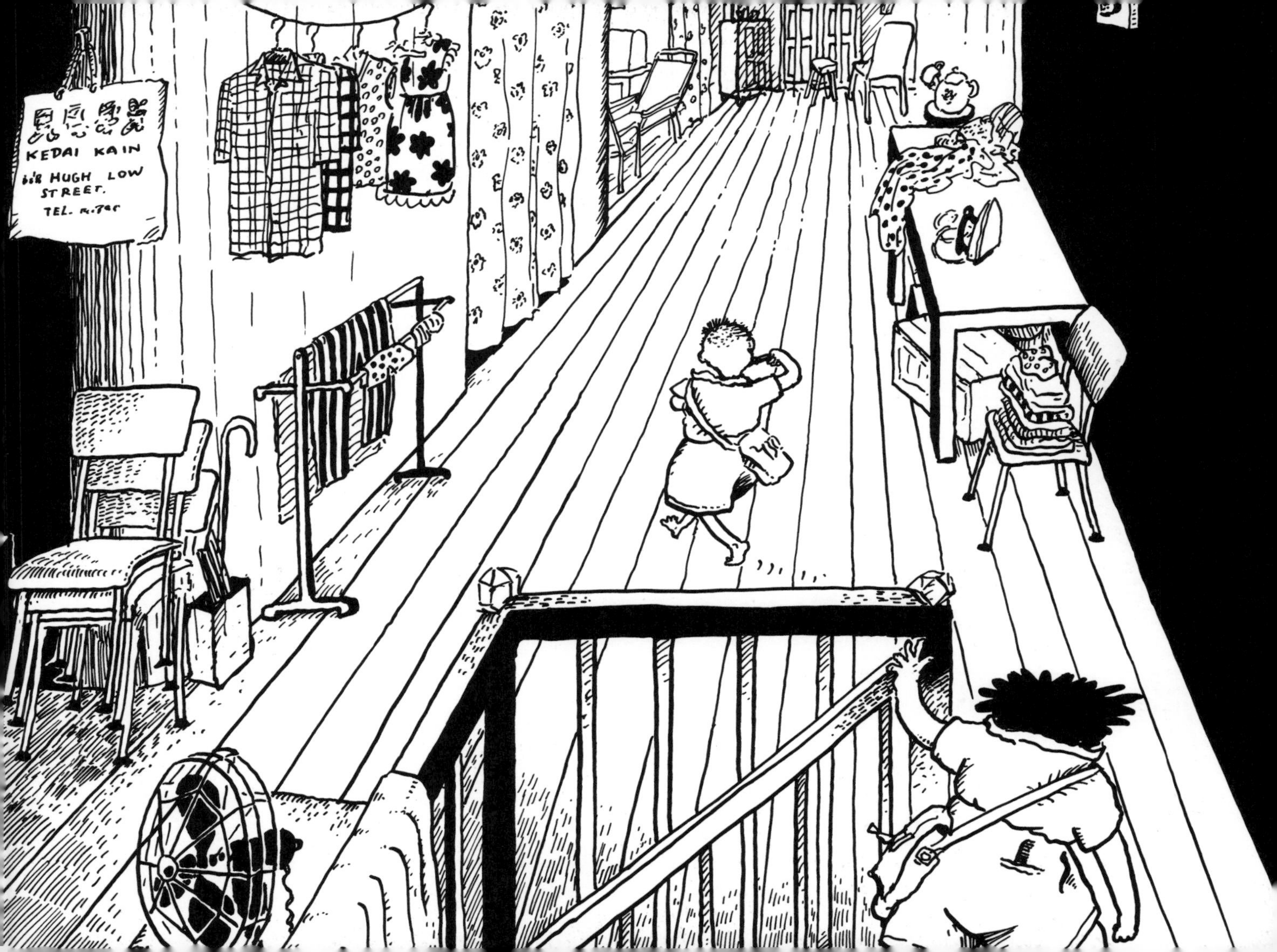
KEDAI KAIN
HUGH LOW
STREET.
TEL.

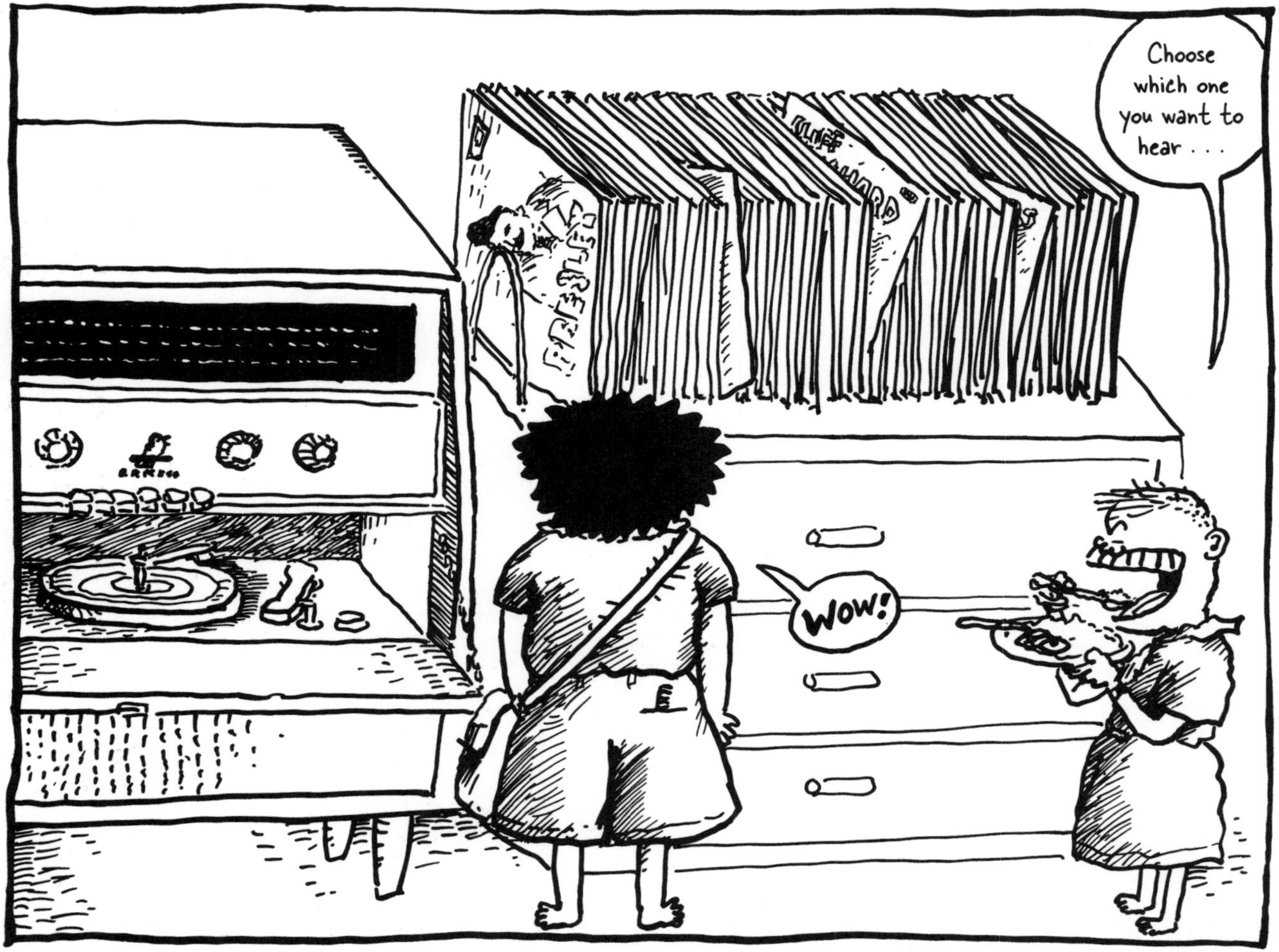
Choose which one you want to hear . . .
WOW!

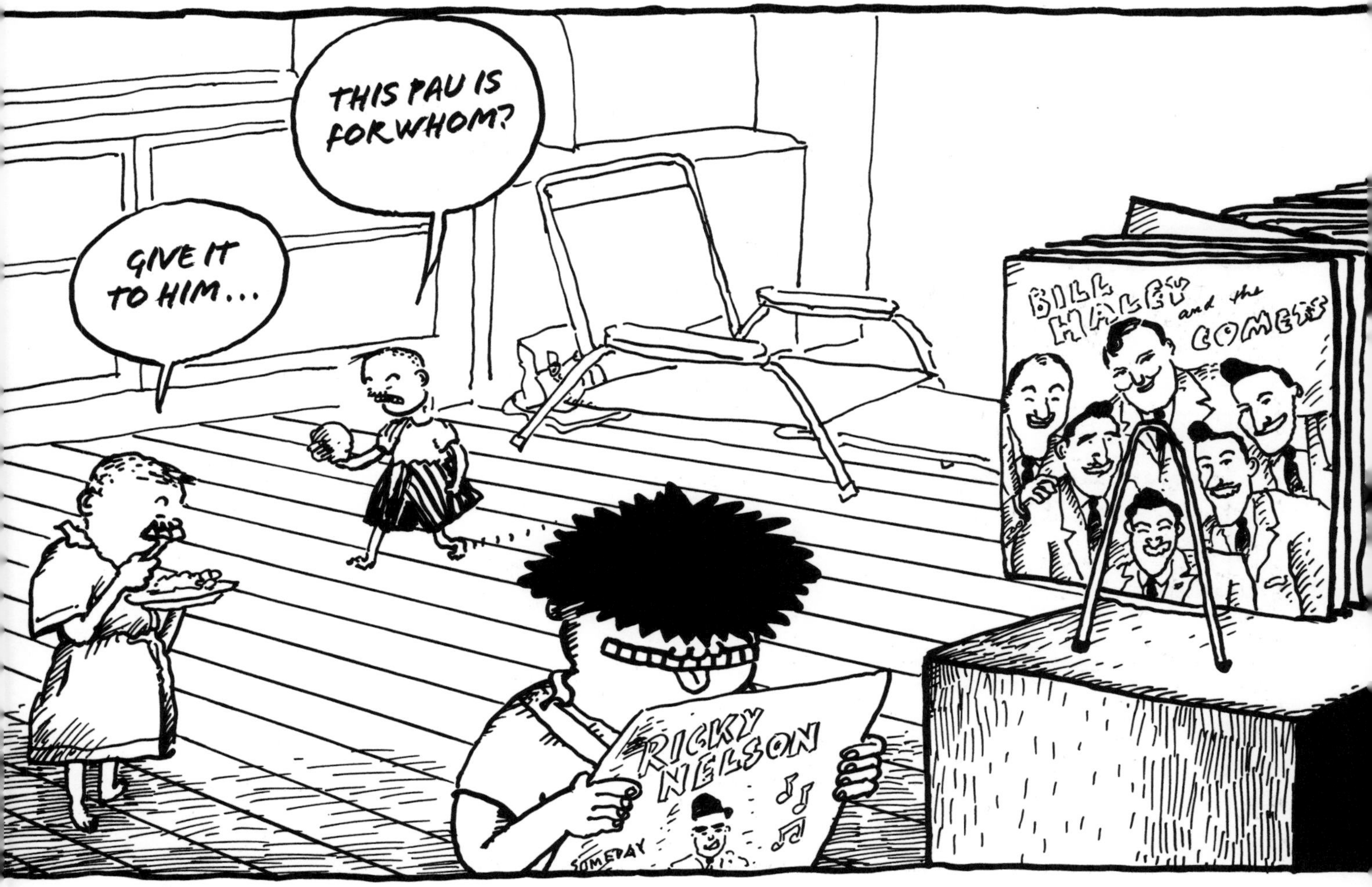
THIS PAU IS FOR WHOM?
GIVE IT TO HIM...
BILL HALEY and the COMETS
RICKY NELSON
SOMEDAY

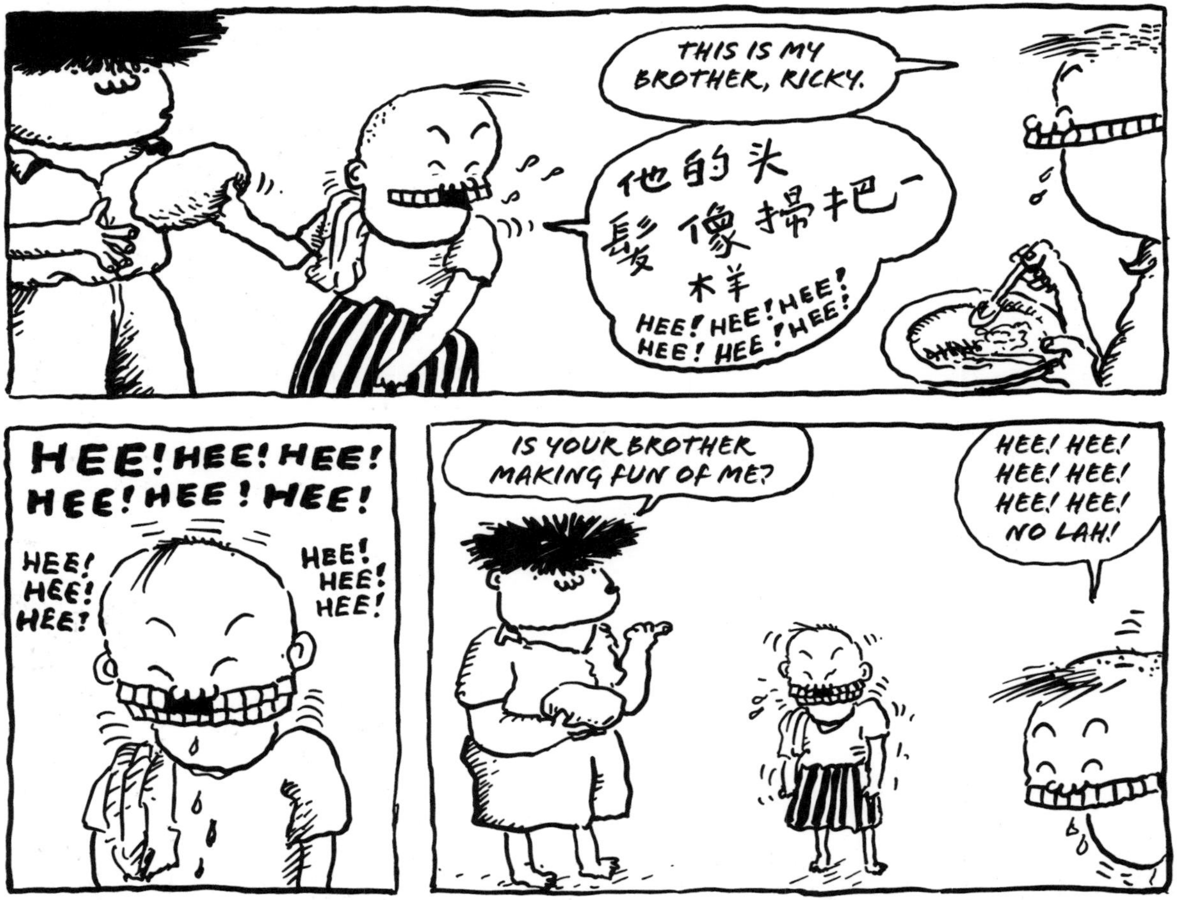
THIS IS MY BROTHER, RICKY.
他的头
髮像掃把一
样
HEE! HEE! HEE! HEE! HEE! HEE!
HEE! HEE! HEE! HEE! HEE! HEE!
HEE! HEE! HEE!
HEE! HEE! HEE!
IS YOUR BROTHER MAKING FUN OF ME?
HEE! HEE! HEE! HEE! HEE! HEE! NO LAH!

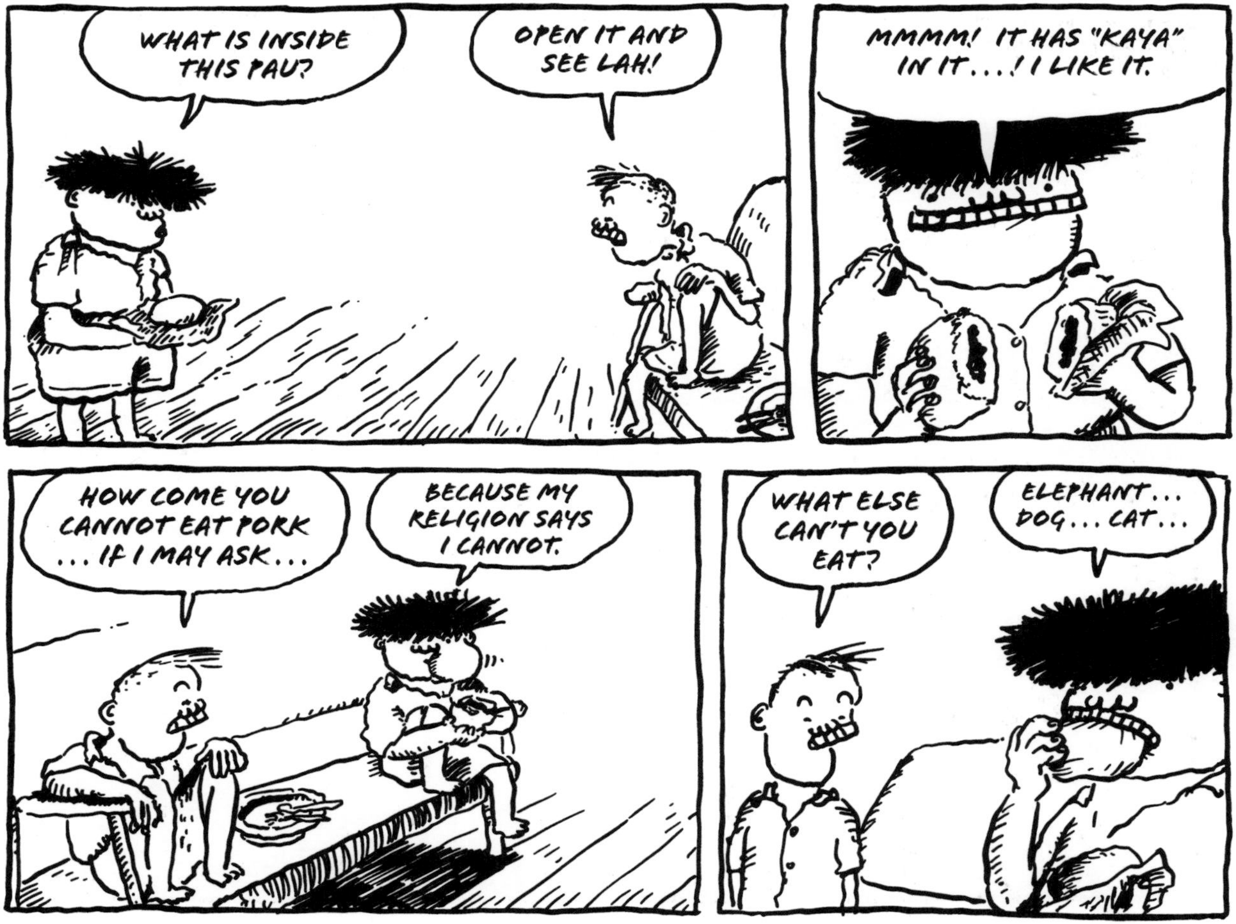
WHAT IS INSIDE THIS PAU?
OPEN IT AND SEE LAH!
MMMM! IT HAS "KAYA" IN IT....! I LIKE IT.
HOW COME YOU CANNOT EAT PORK ... IF I MAY ASK...
BECAUSE MY RELIGION SAYS I CANNOT.
WHAT ELSE CAN'T YOU EAT?
ELEPHANT... DOG... CAT...

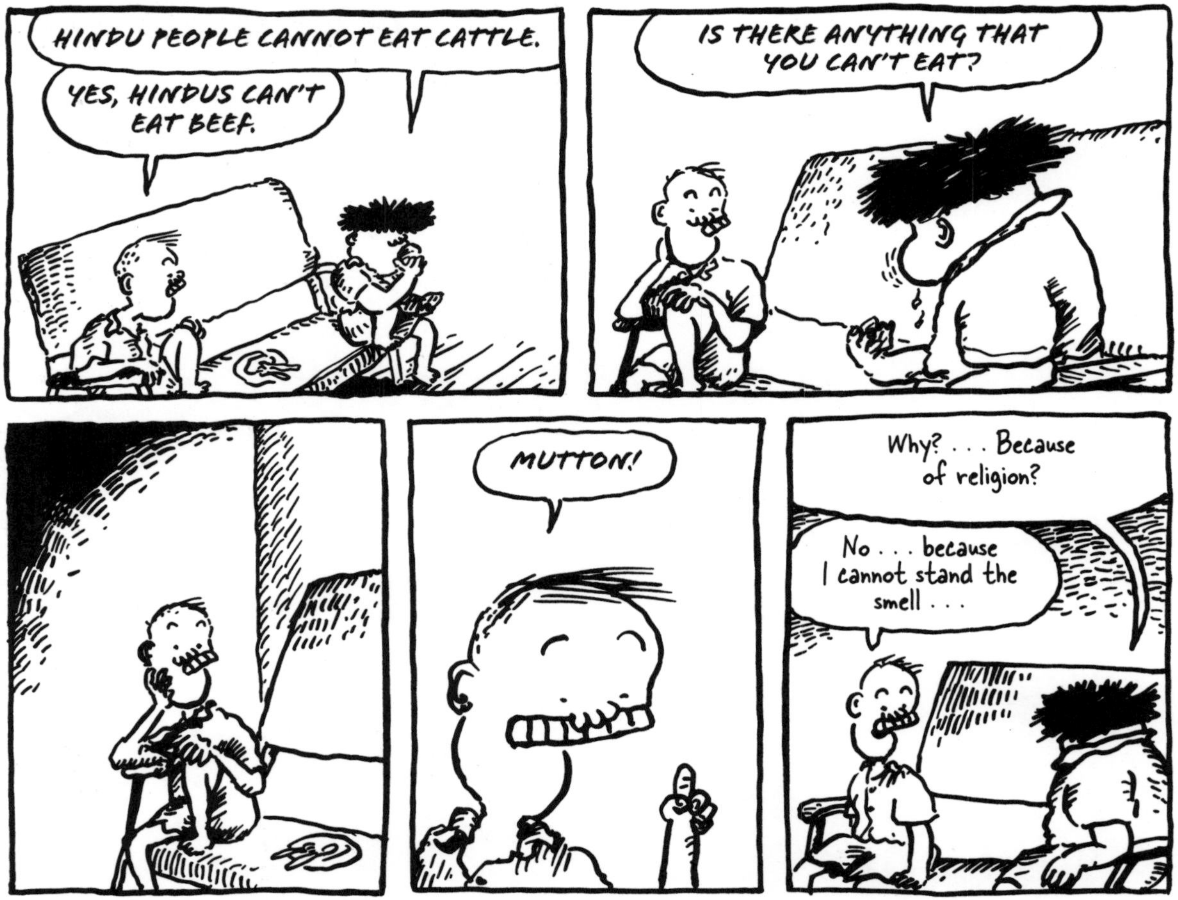
HINDU PEOPLE CANNOT EAT CATTLE.
YES, HINDUS CAN'T EAT BEEF.
IS THERE ANYTHING THAT YOU CAN'T EAT?
MUTTON!
Why? . . . Because of religion?
No . . . because I cannot stand the smell . . .

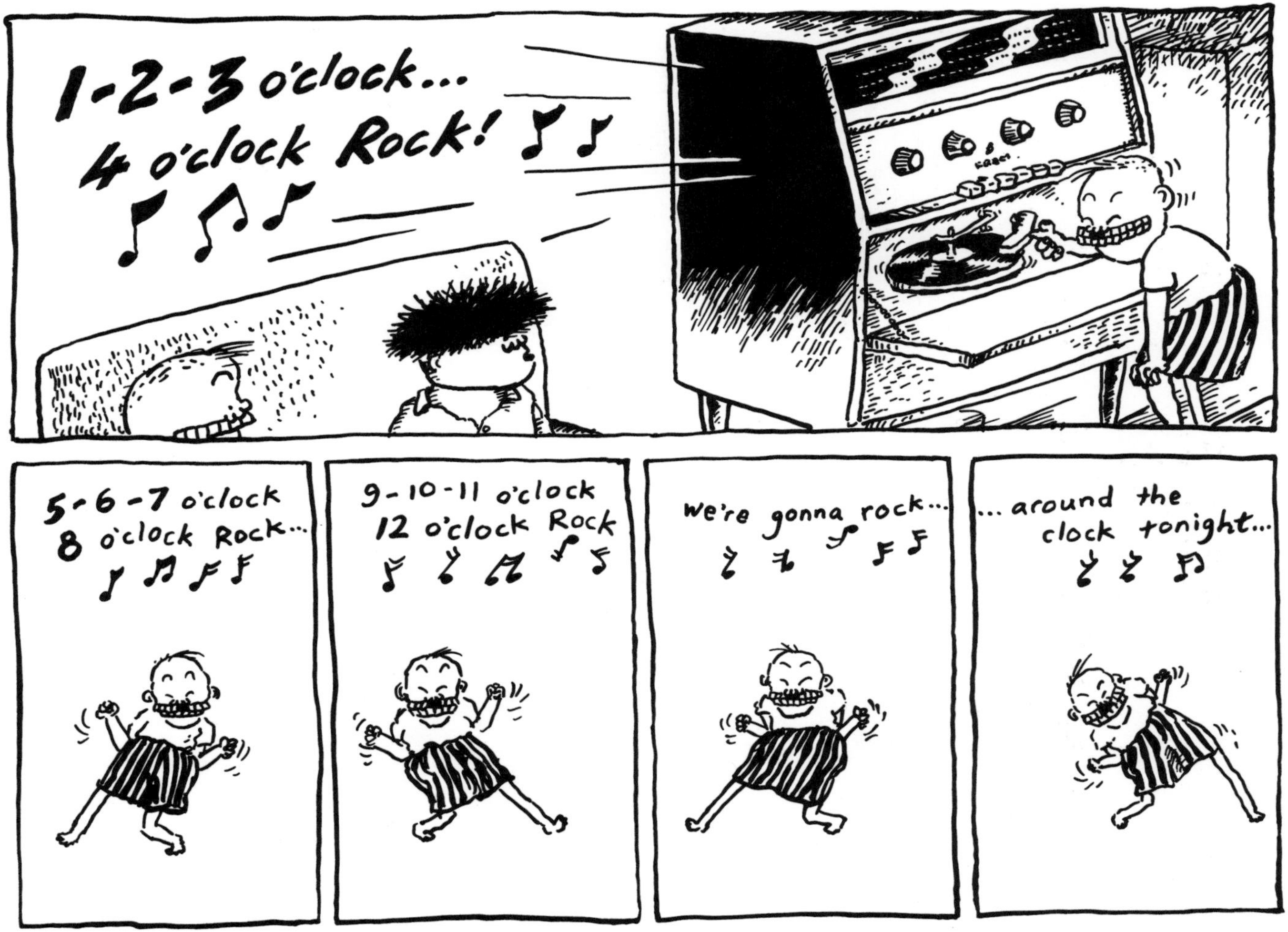

1-2-3 o'clock...
4 o'clock Rock!
5-6-7 o'clock
8 o'clock Rock...
9-10-11 o'clock
12 o'clock Rock
we're gonna rock...
...around the clock tonight...

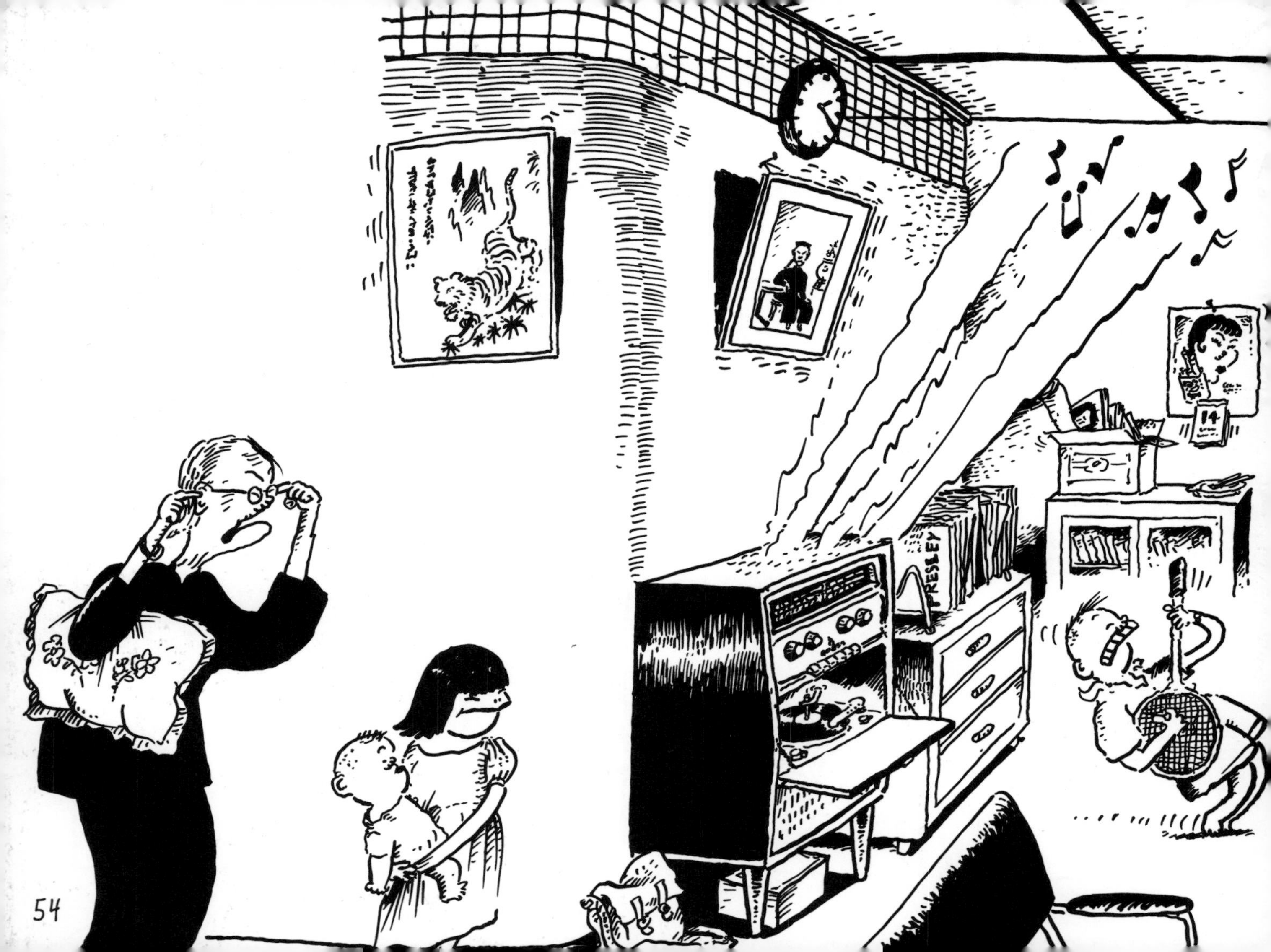
PRESLEY
14

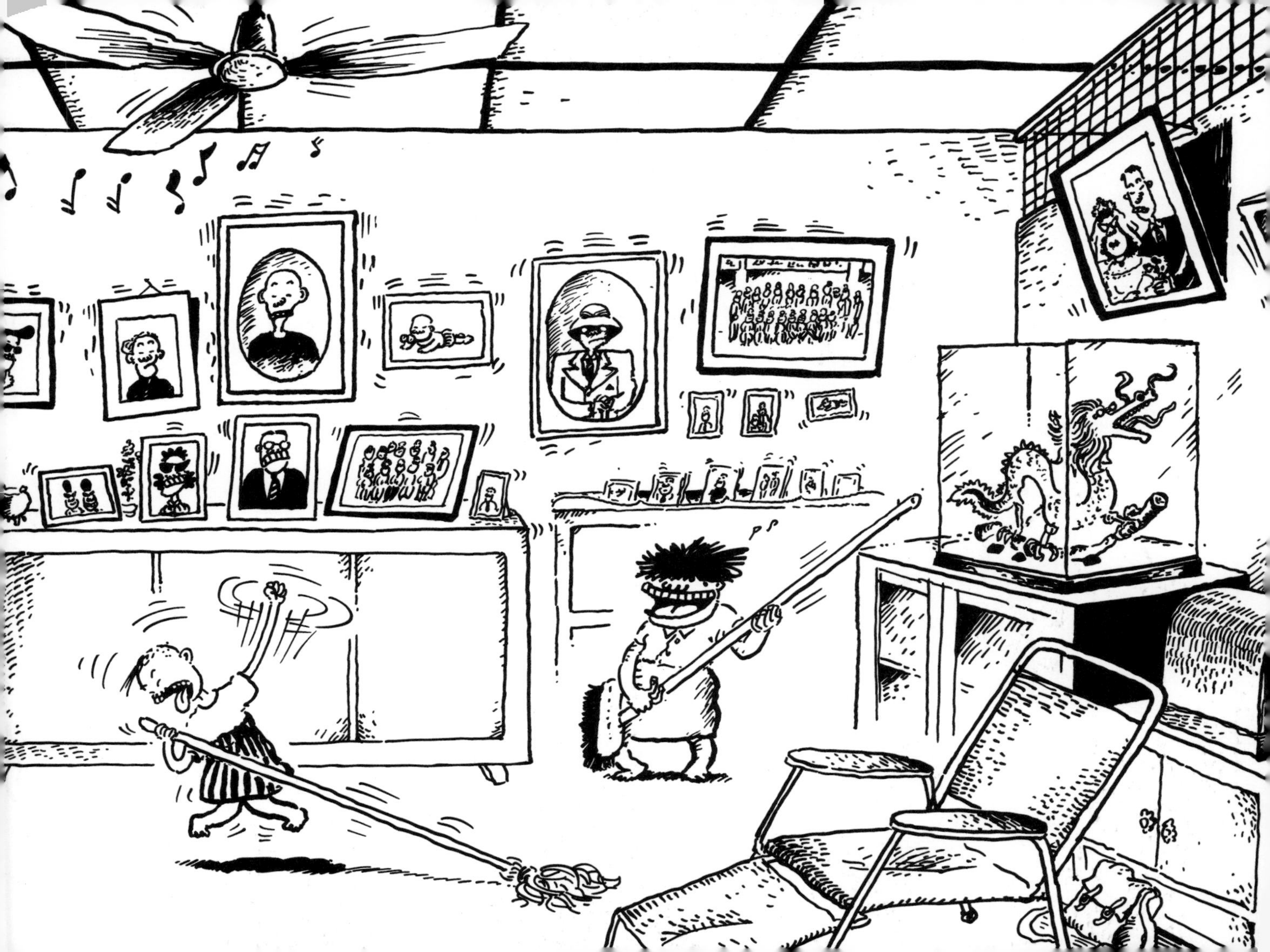

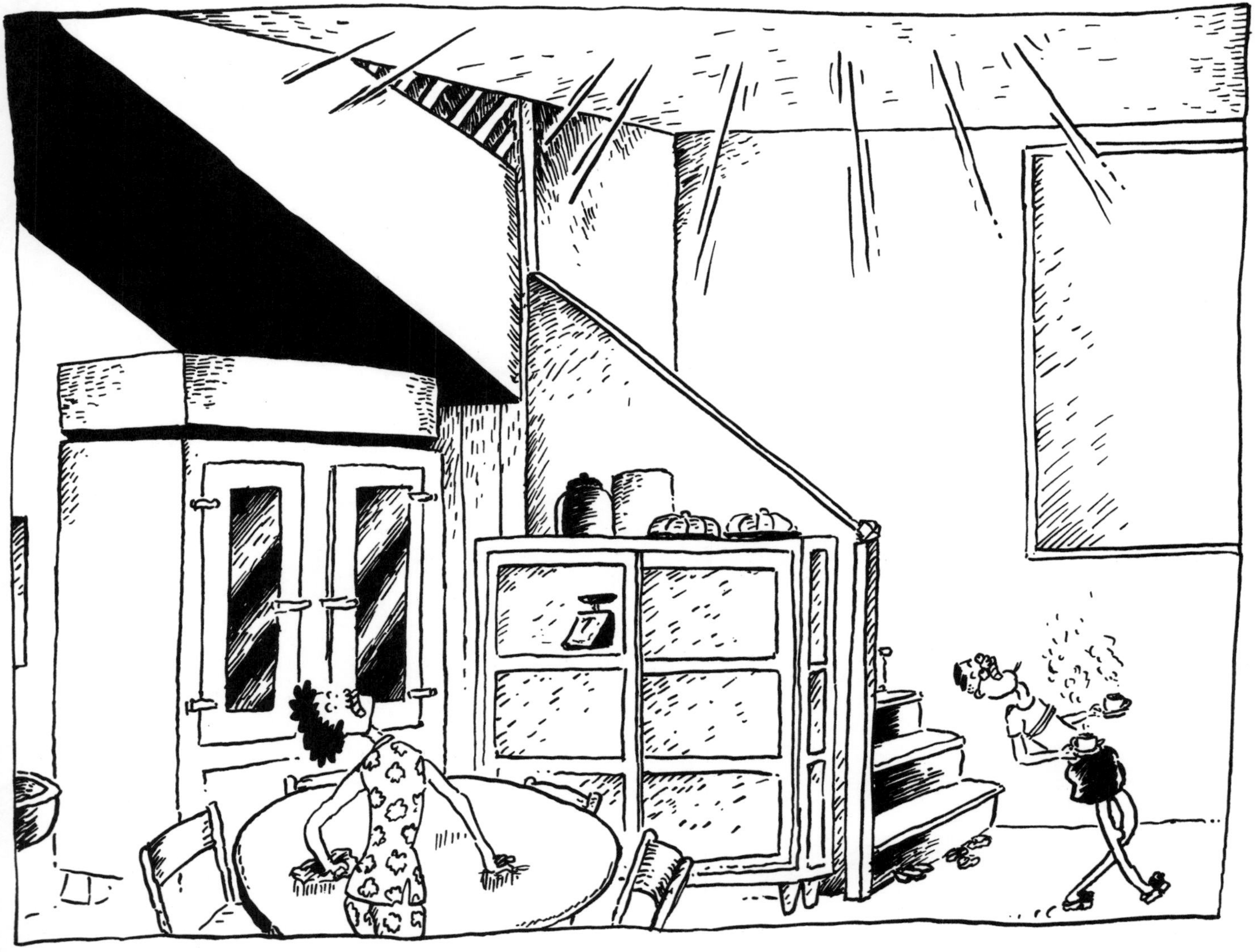

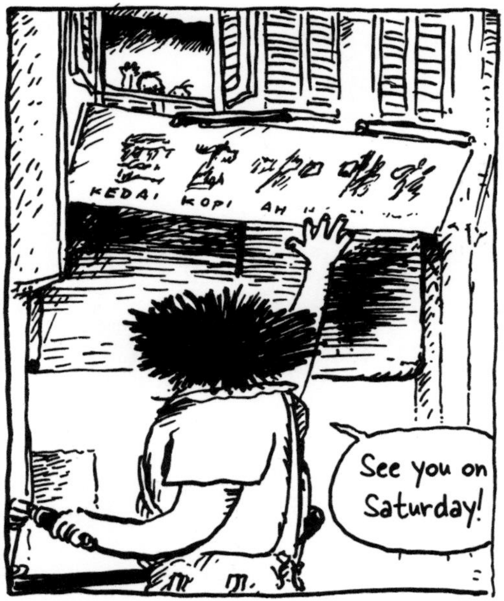
KEDAI KOPI AH
See you on Saturday!

At 3:30 Frankie's dad came up and told him that it was time to do his homework.

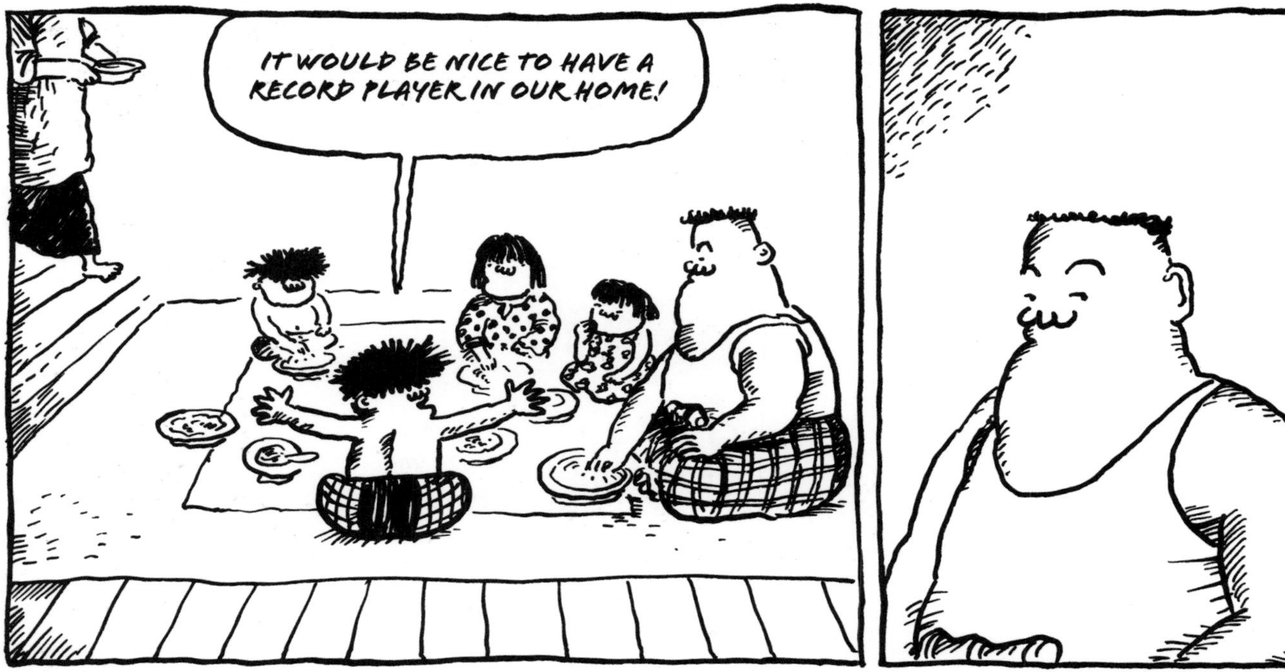
IT WOULD BE NICE TO HAVE A RECORD PLAYER IN OUR HOME!

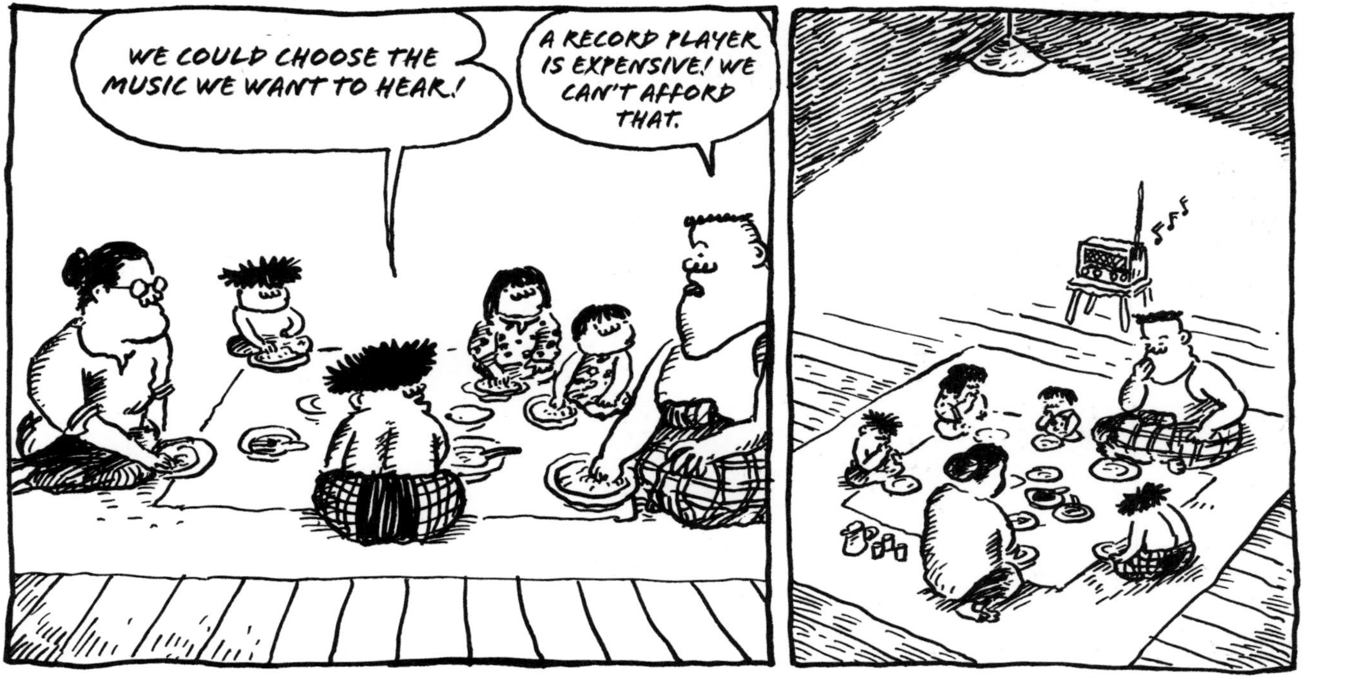
WE COULD CHOOSE THE MUSIC WE WANT TO HEAR!
A RECORD PLAYER IS EXPENSIVE! WE CAN'T AFFORD THAT.

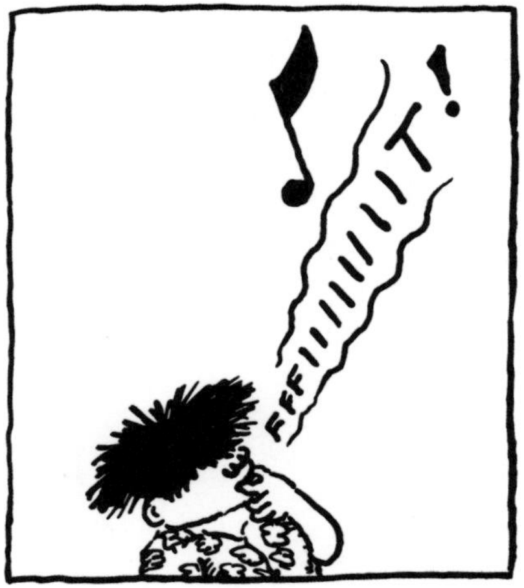
FFFIIIIIIIIT!

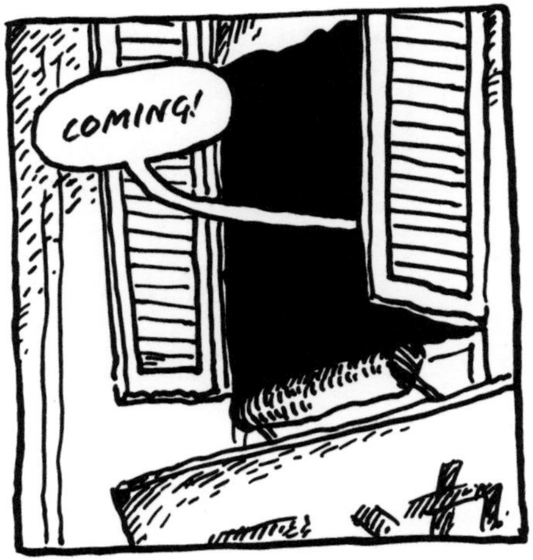
COMING!

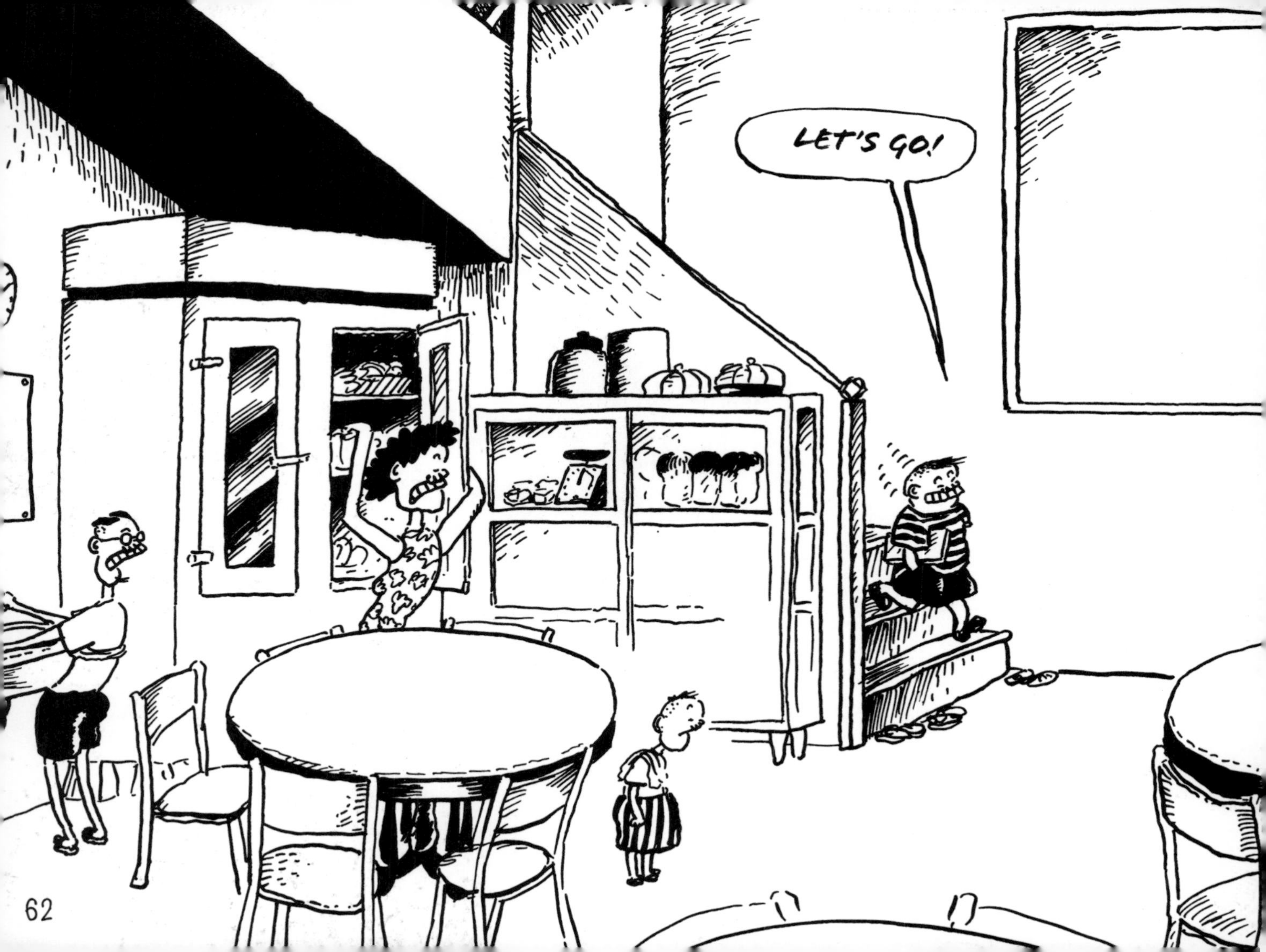
LET'S GO!

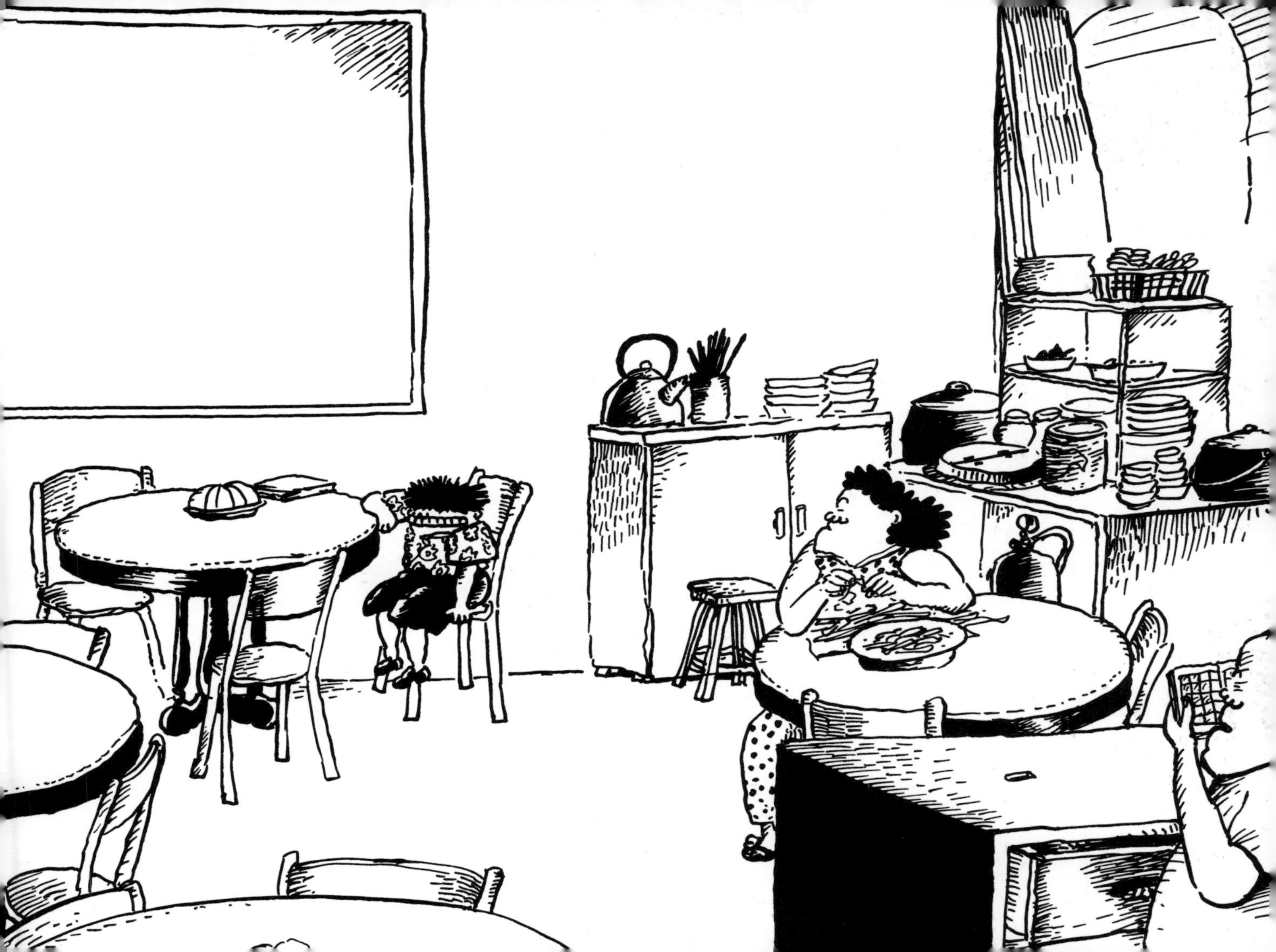

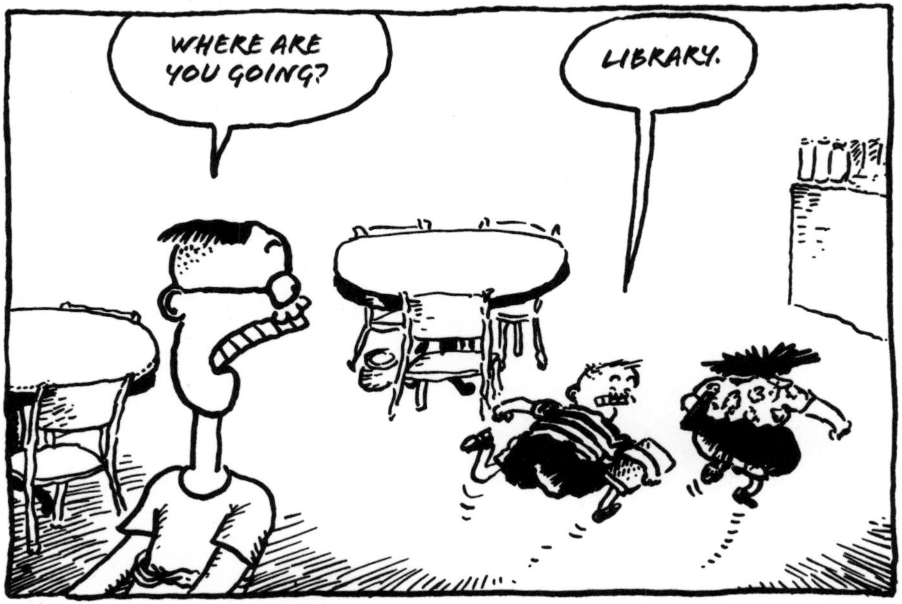
WHERE ARE YOU GOING?
LIBRARY.

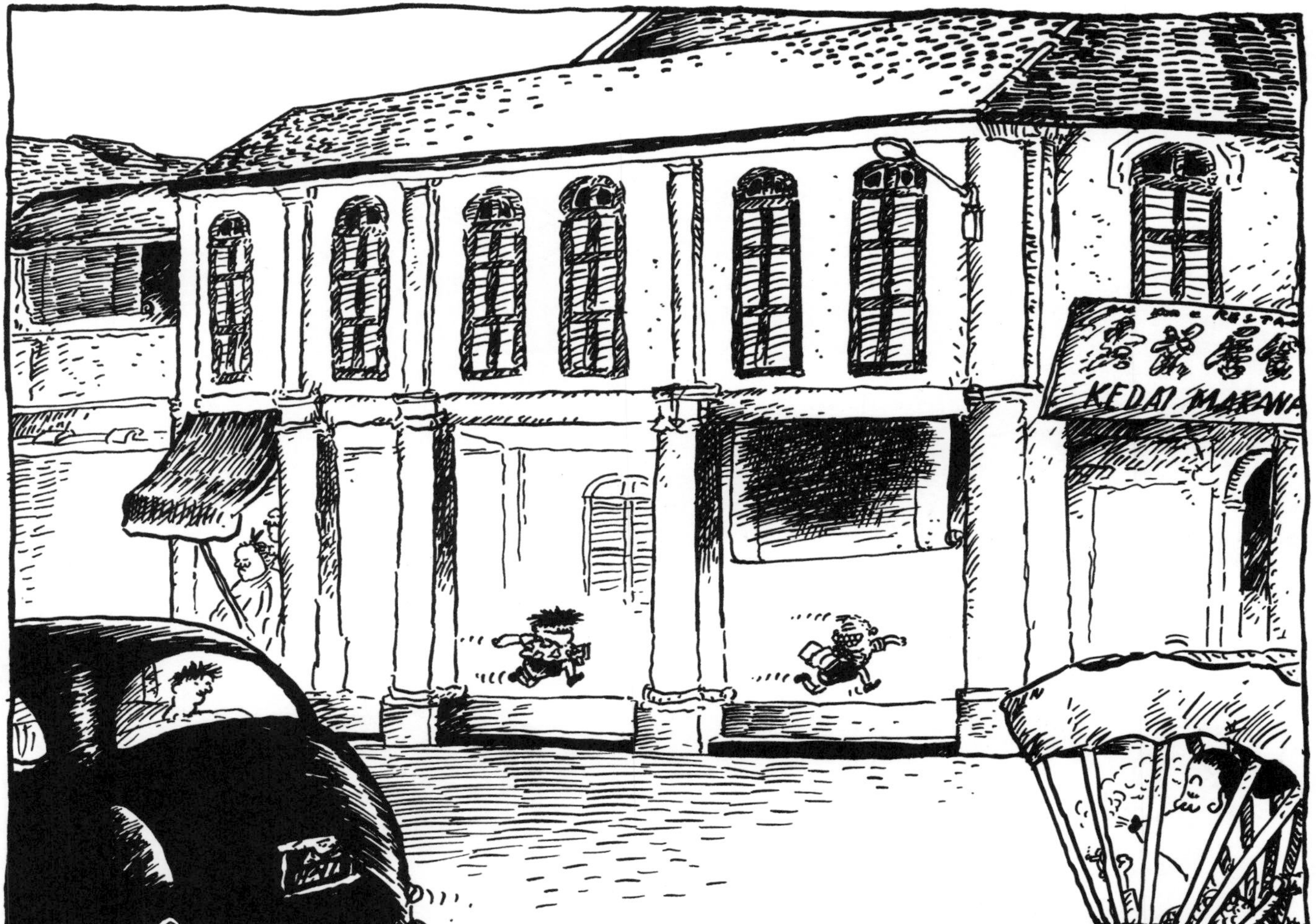
KEDAI

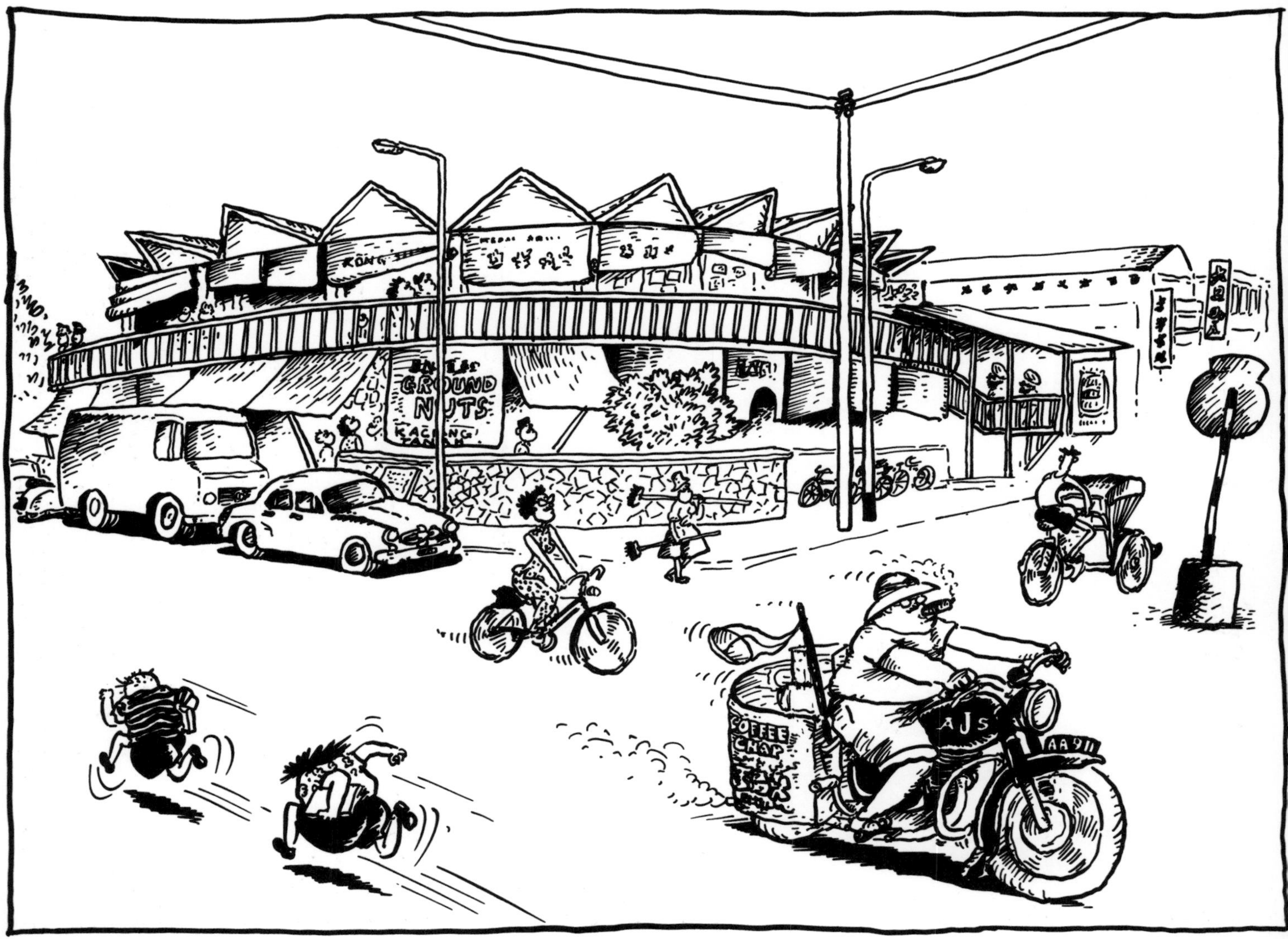
GROUND NUTS
COFFEE CHAP
AJS
AA 911

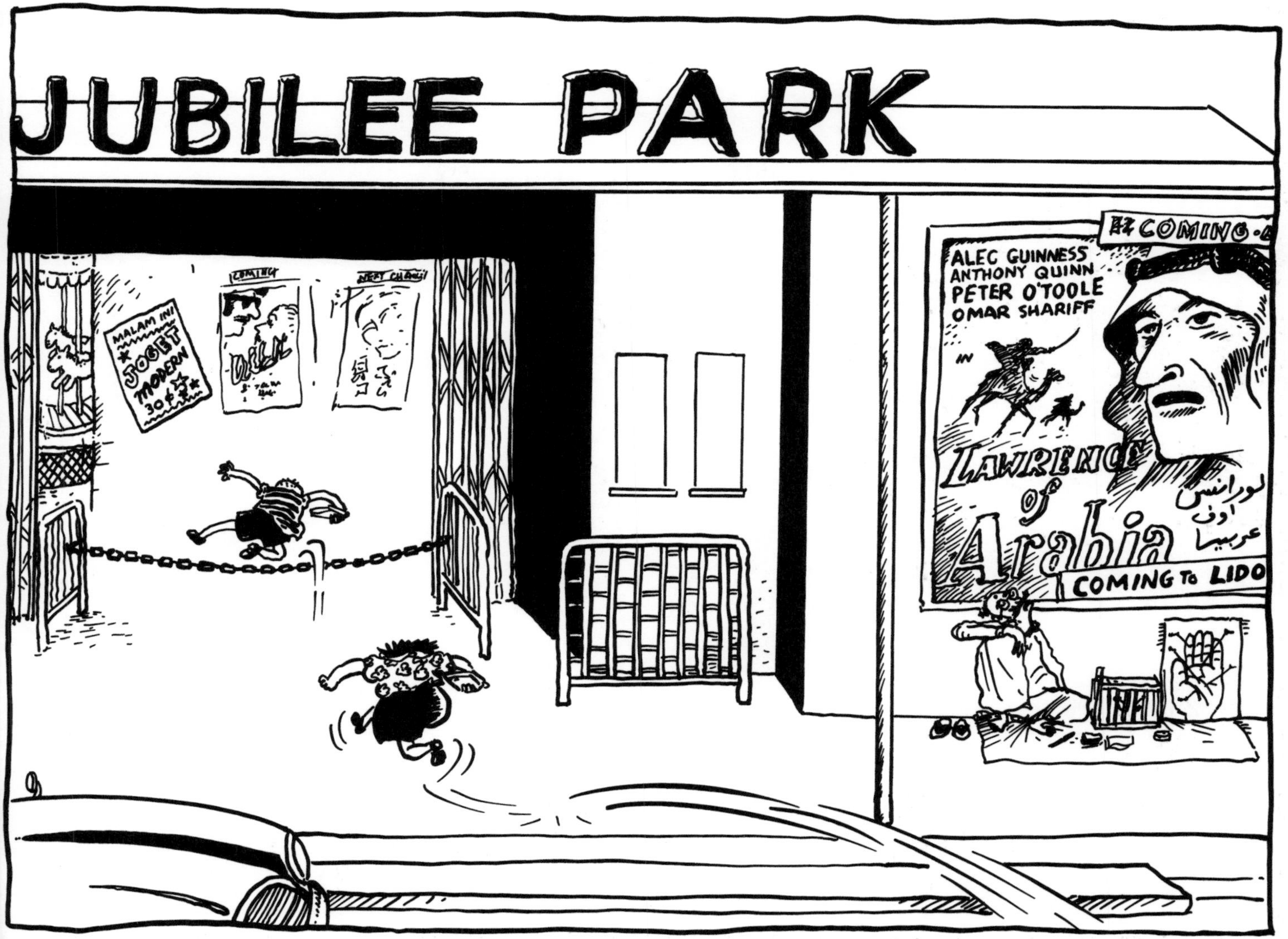

JUBILEE PARK
MALAM INI
JOGET MODERN
30¢
COMING
ALEC GUINNESS
ANTHONY QUINN
PETER O'TOOLE
OMAR SHARIFF
IN
LAWRENCE of Arabia
لورانس
اوف
عربيا
COMING TO LIDO

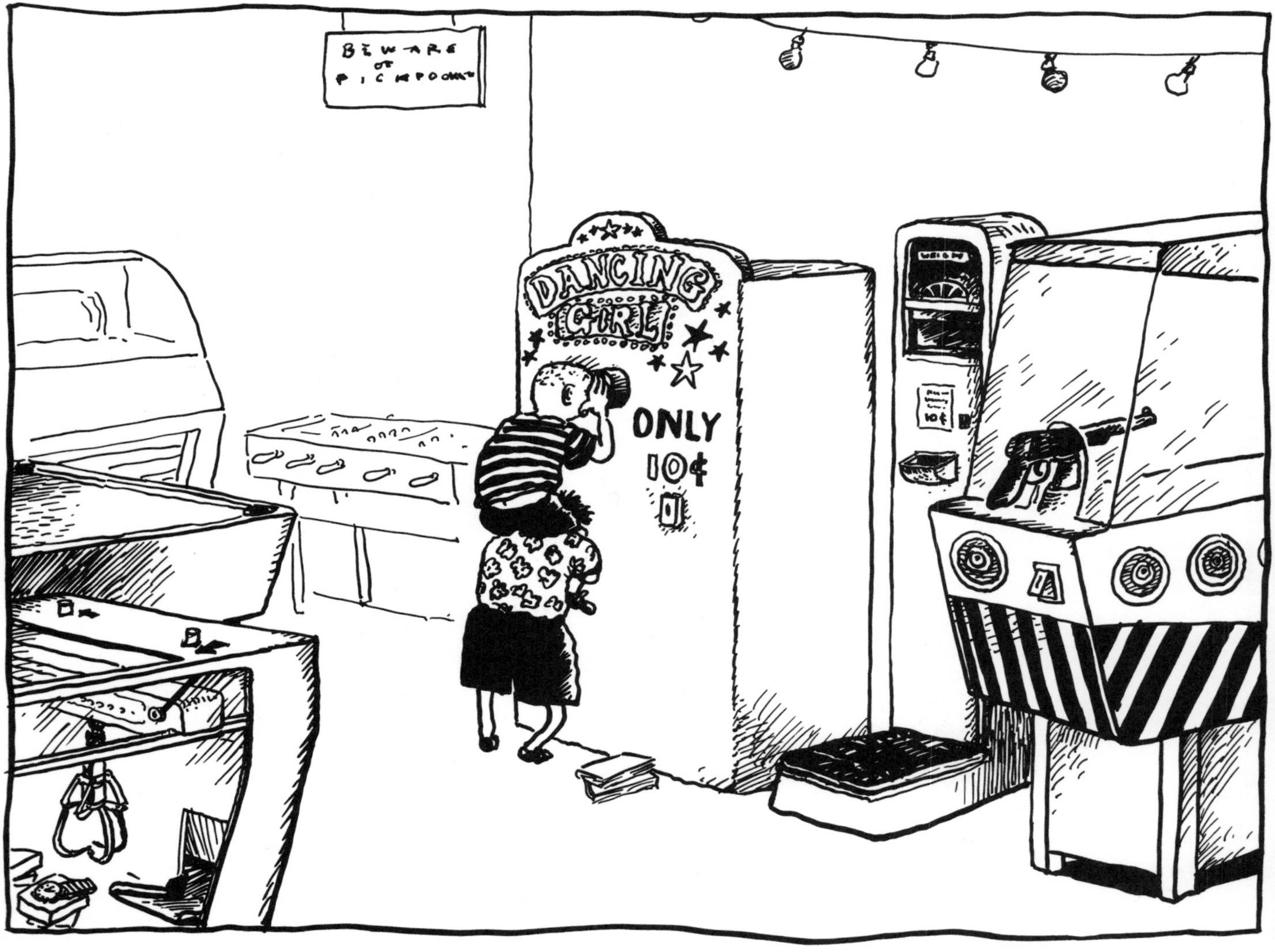
BEWARE OF PICKPOCKETS
DANCING GIRL
ONLY 10¢

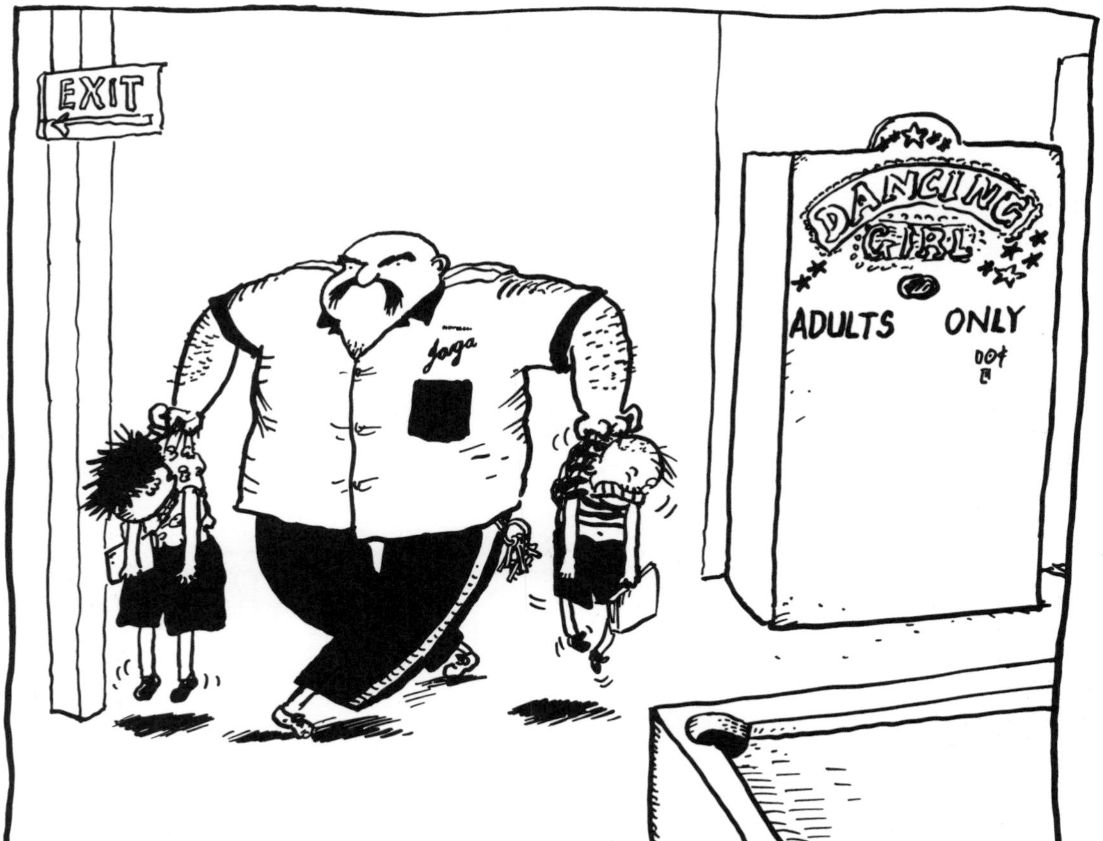
EXIT
Jorga
DANCING GIRL
ADULTS ONLY

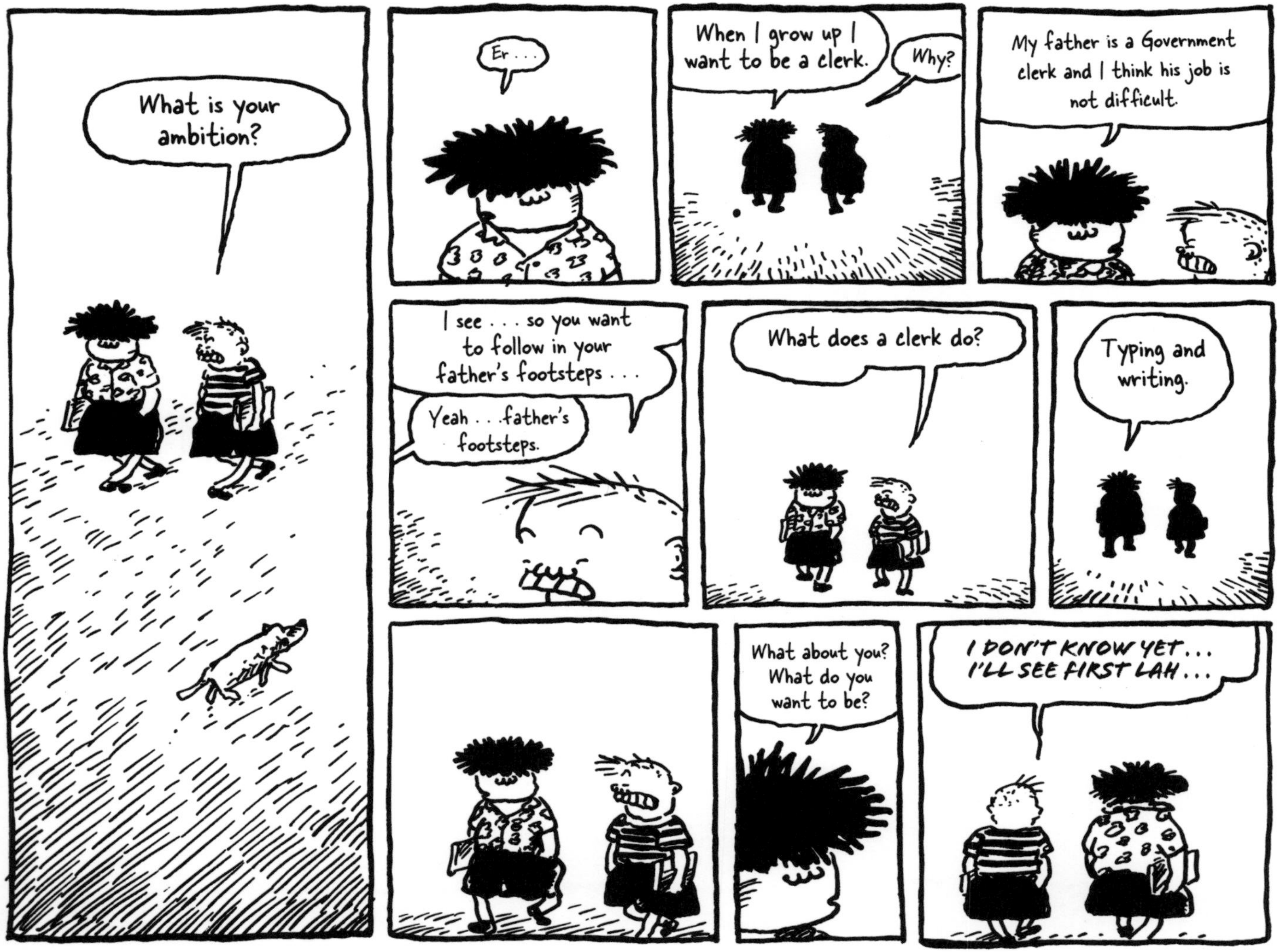

What is your ambition?
Er . . .
When I grow up I want to be a clerk.
Why?
My father is a Government clerk and I think his job is not difficult.
I see . . . so you want to follow in your father's footsteps . . .
Yeah . . . father's footsteps.
What does a clerk do?
Typing and writing.
What about you? What do you want to be?
I DON'T KNOW YET . . . I'LL SEE FIRST LAH . . .

Frankie and I went to the same secondary school—Anderson School, Ipoh.

One of the new things that I experienced in the secondary school was the cross-country race which began at the Coronation Park (now Taman D.R. Seenivasagam).

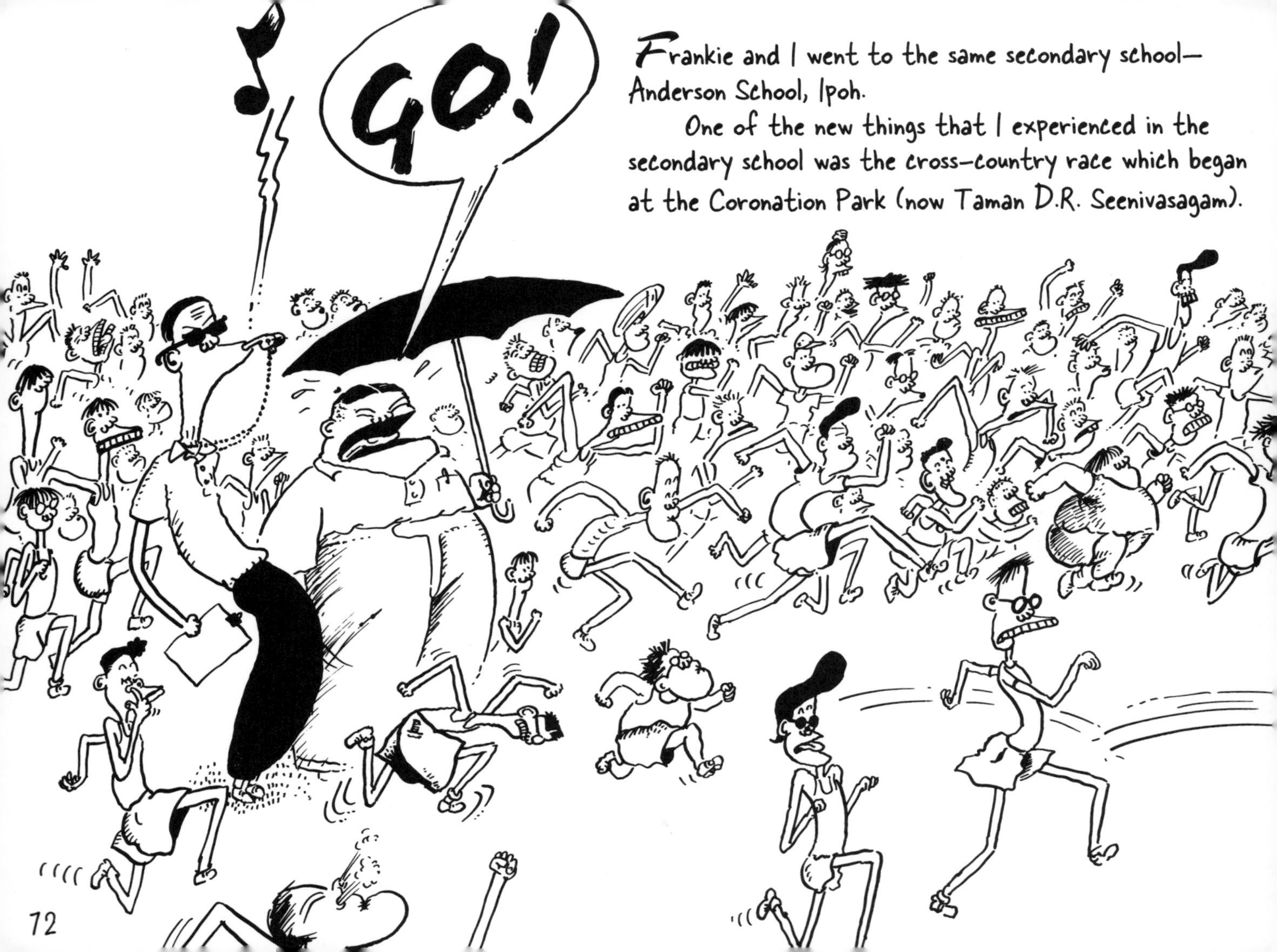
GO!

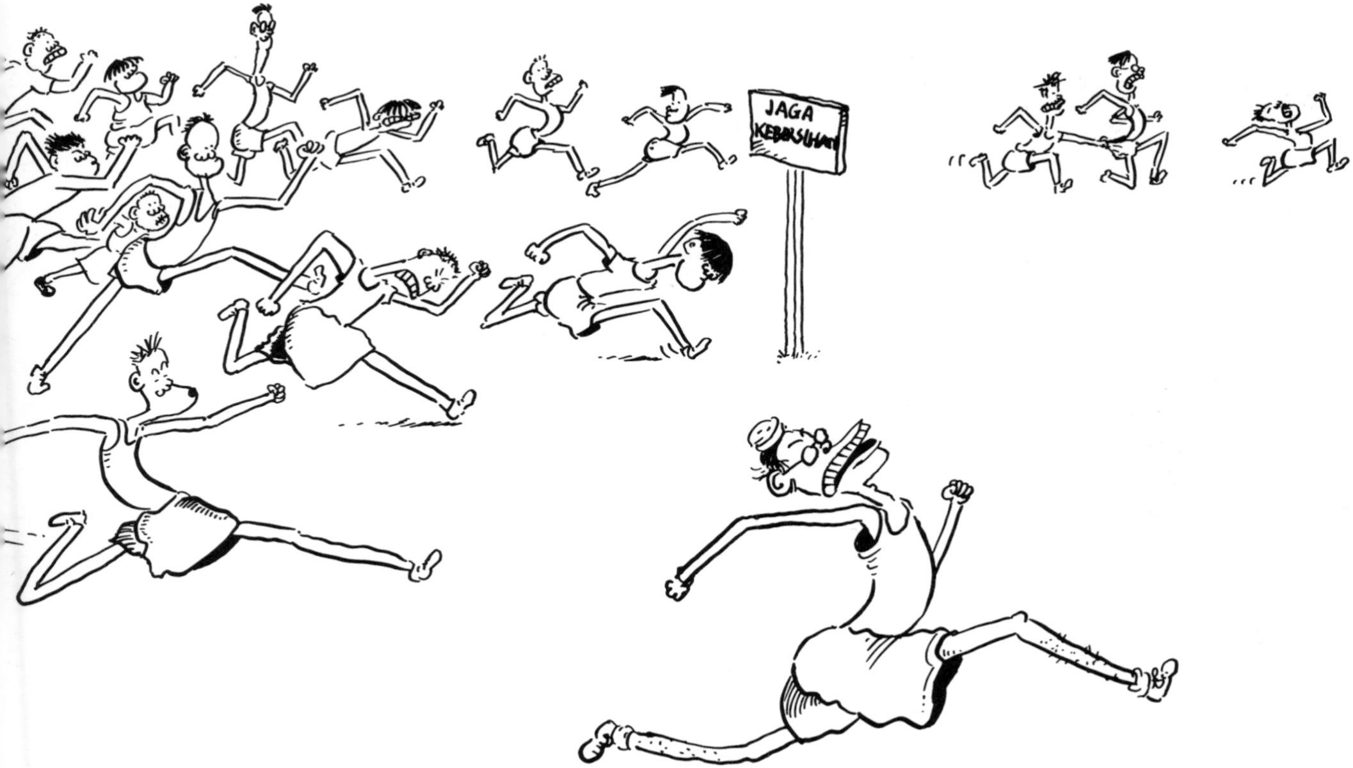
JAGA
KEBERSIHAN

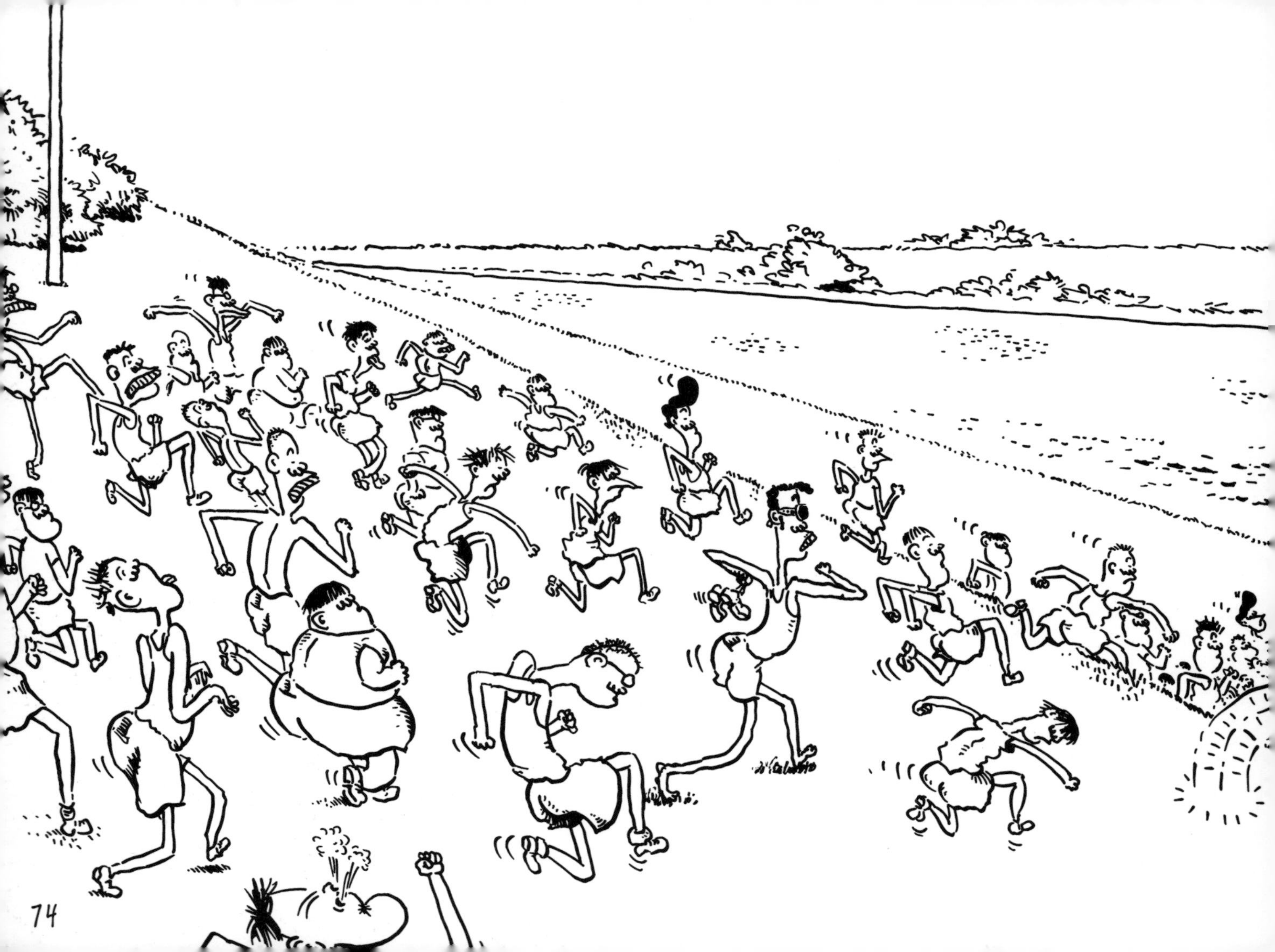

Running the six-mile track was O.K. with me but the dreadful part was crossing the Kinta River.

They wouldn't let you use the bridge!

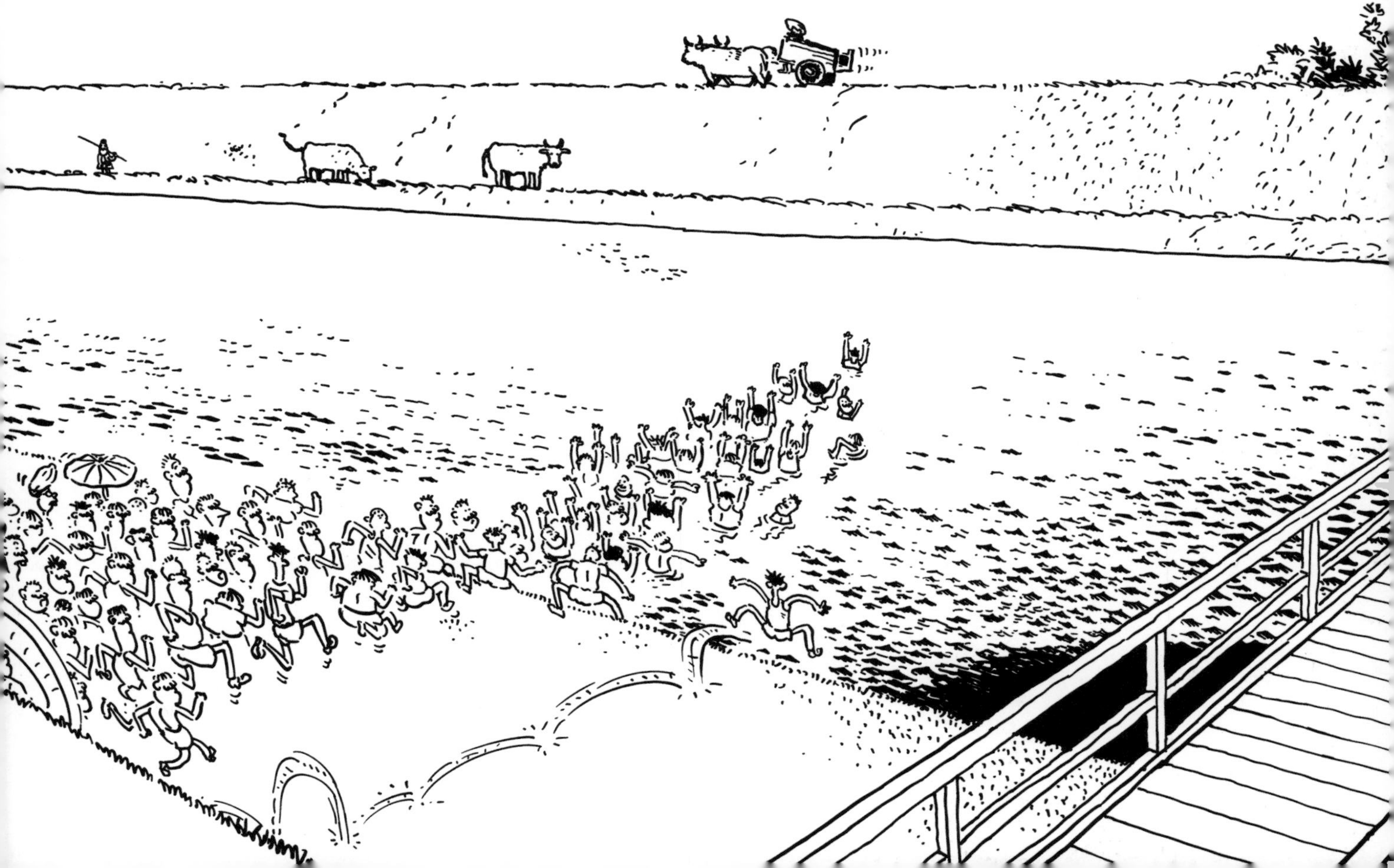

One day we broke the rule . . .

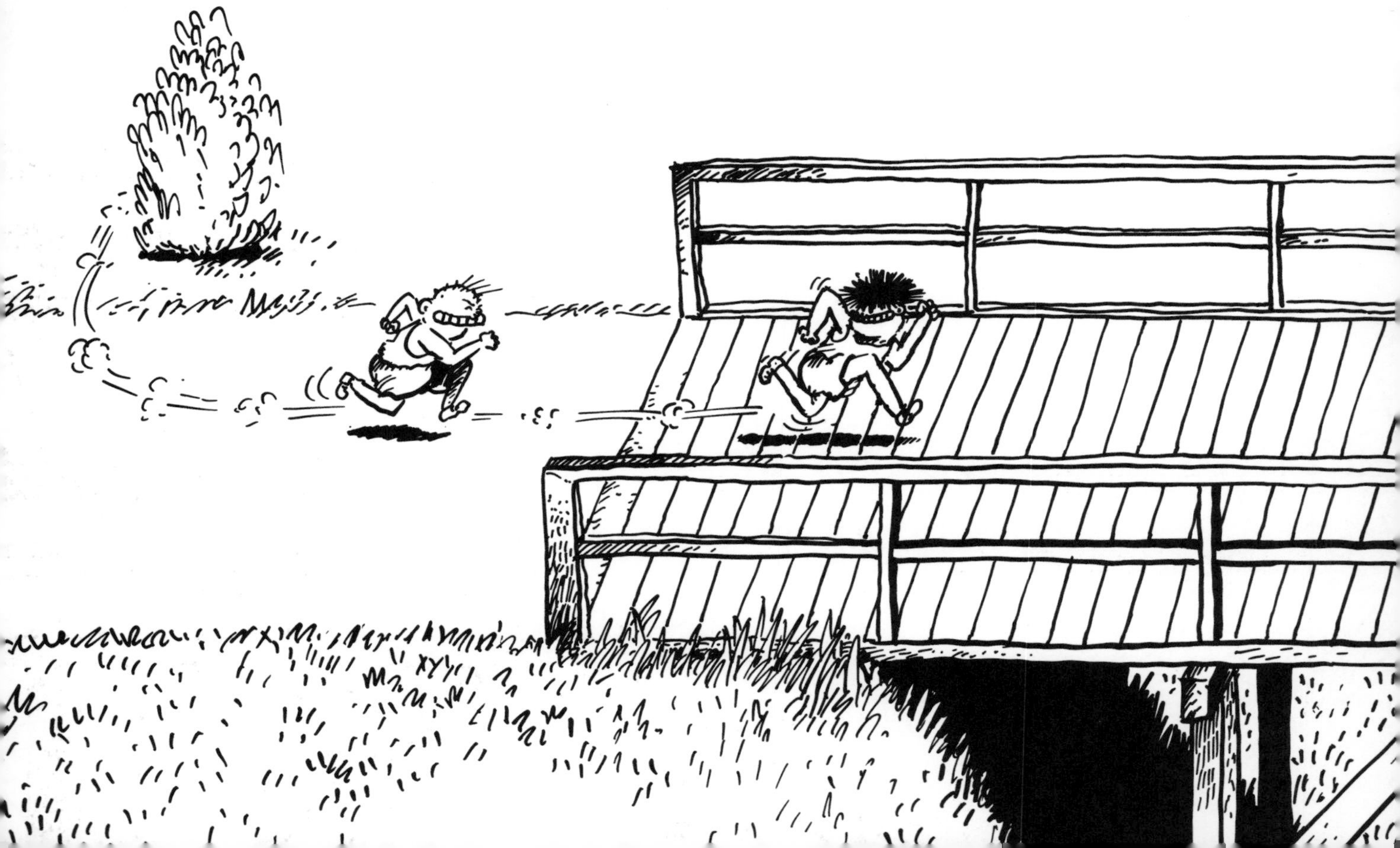

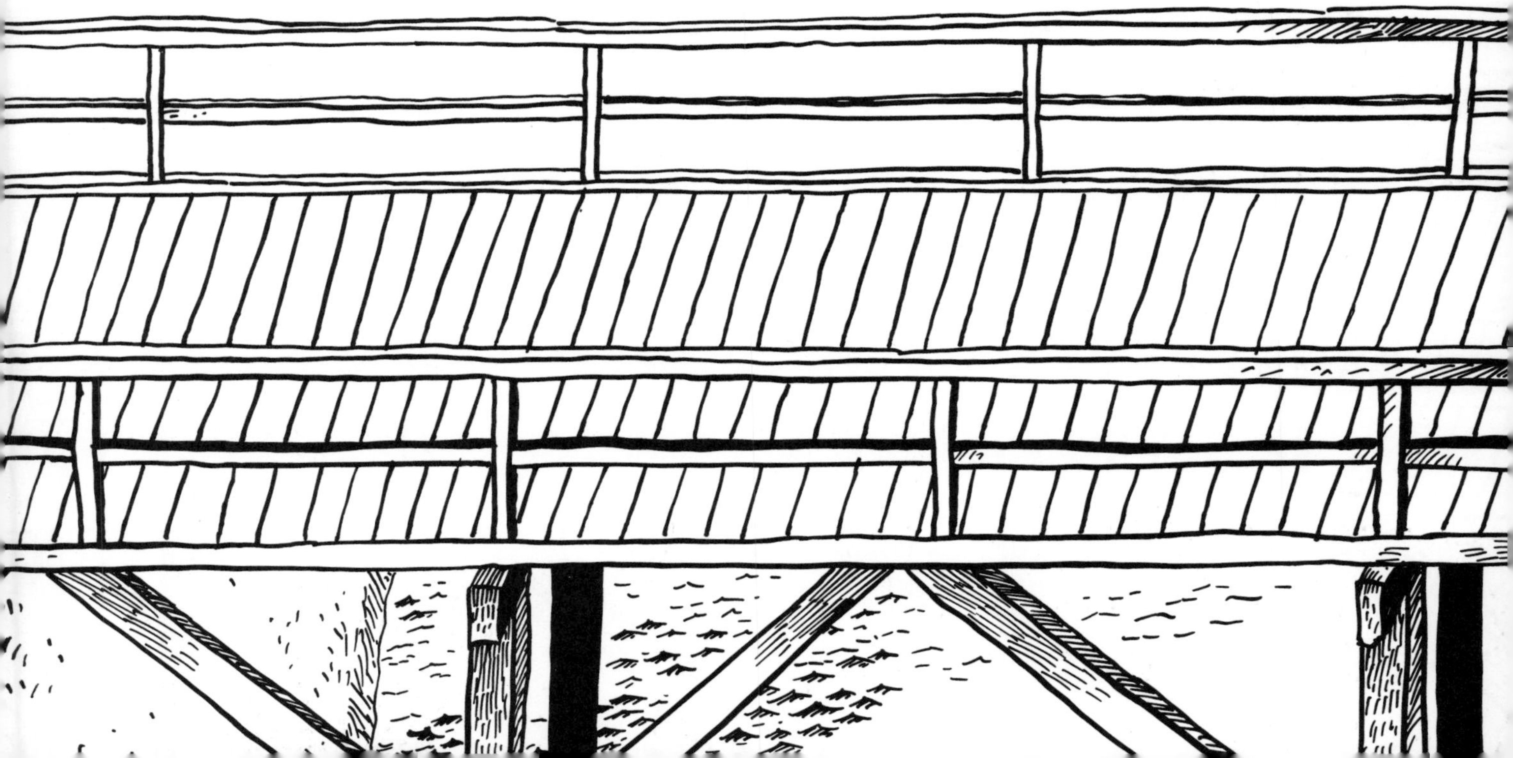

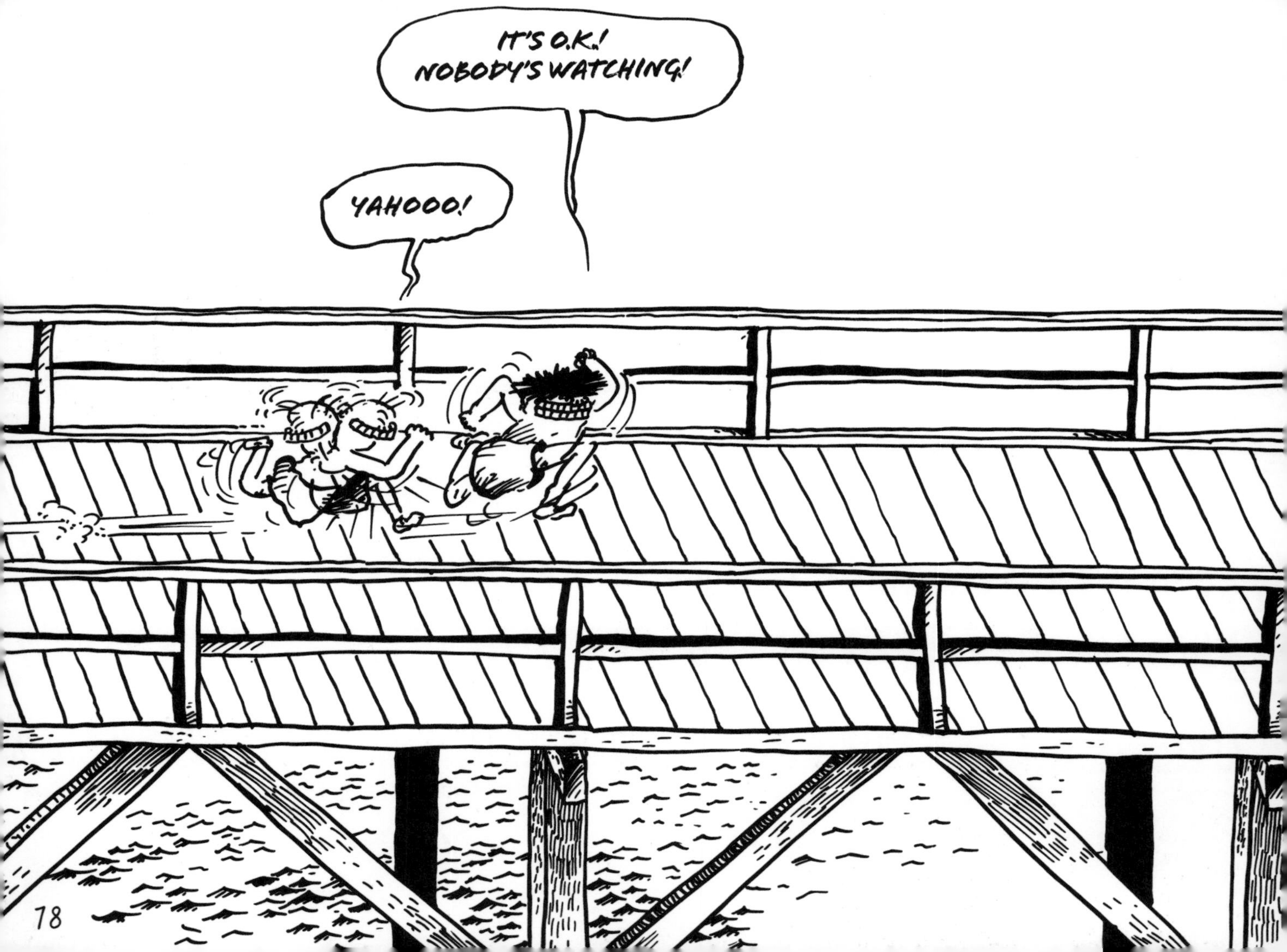
IT'S O.K.! NOBODY'S WATCHING!
YAHOOOO!

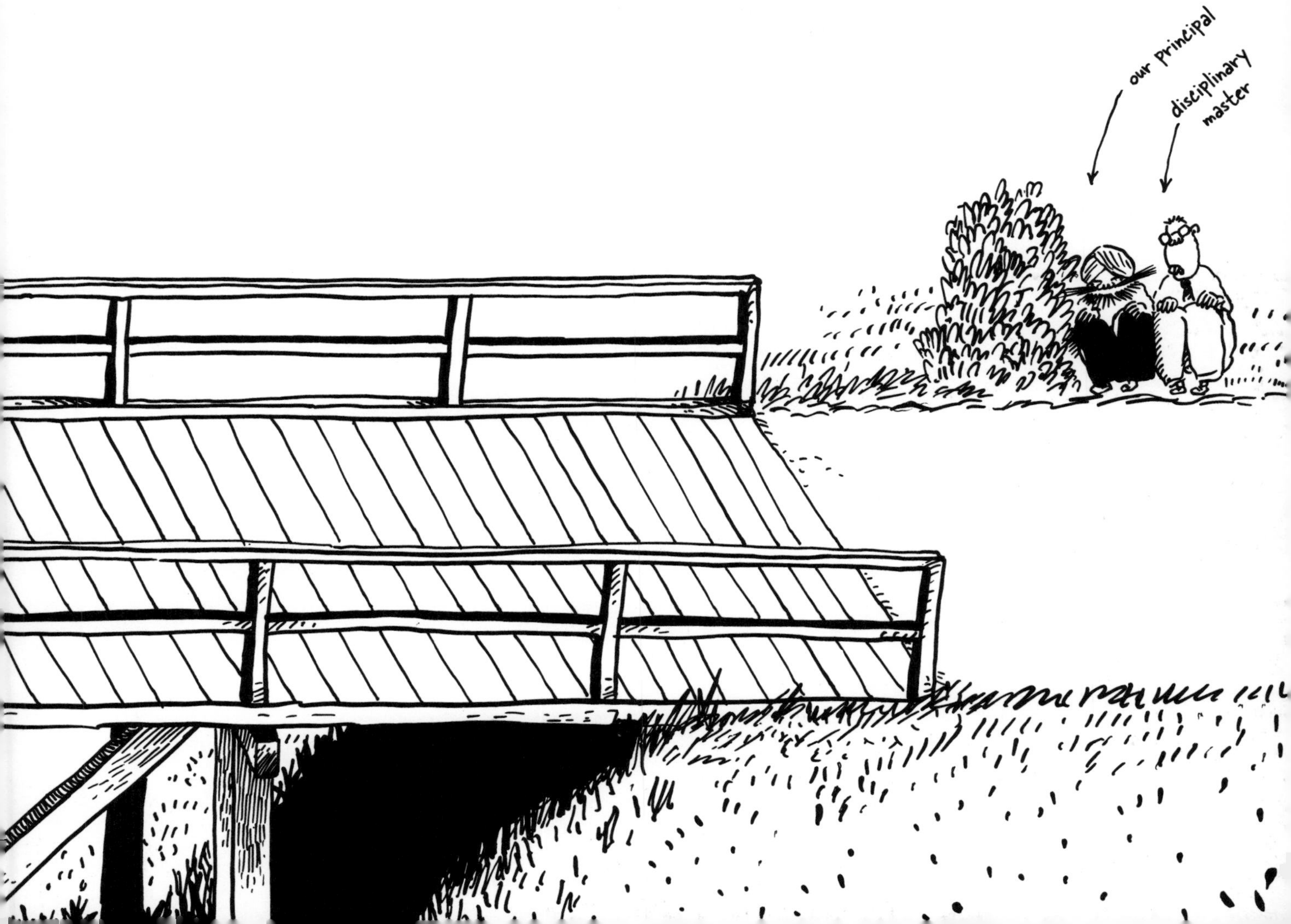
our principal
disciplinary master

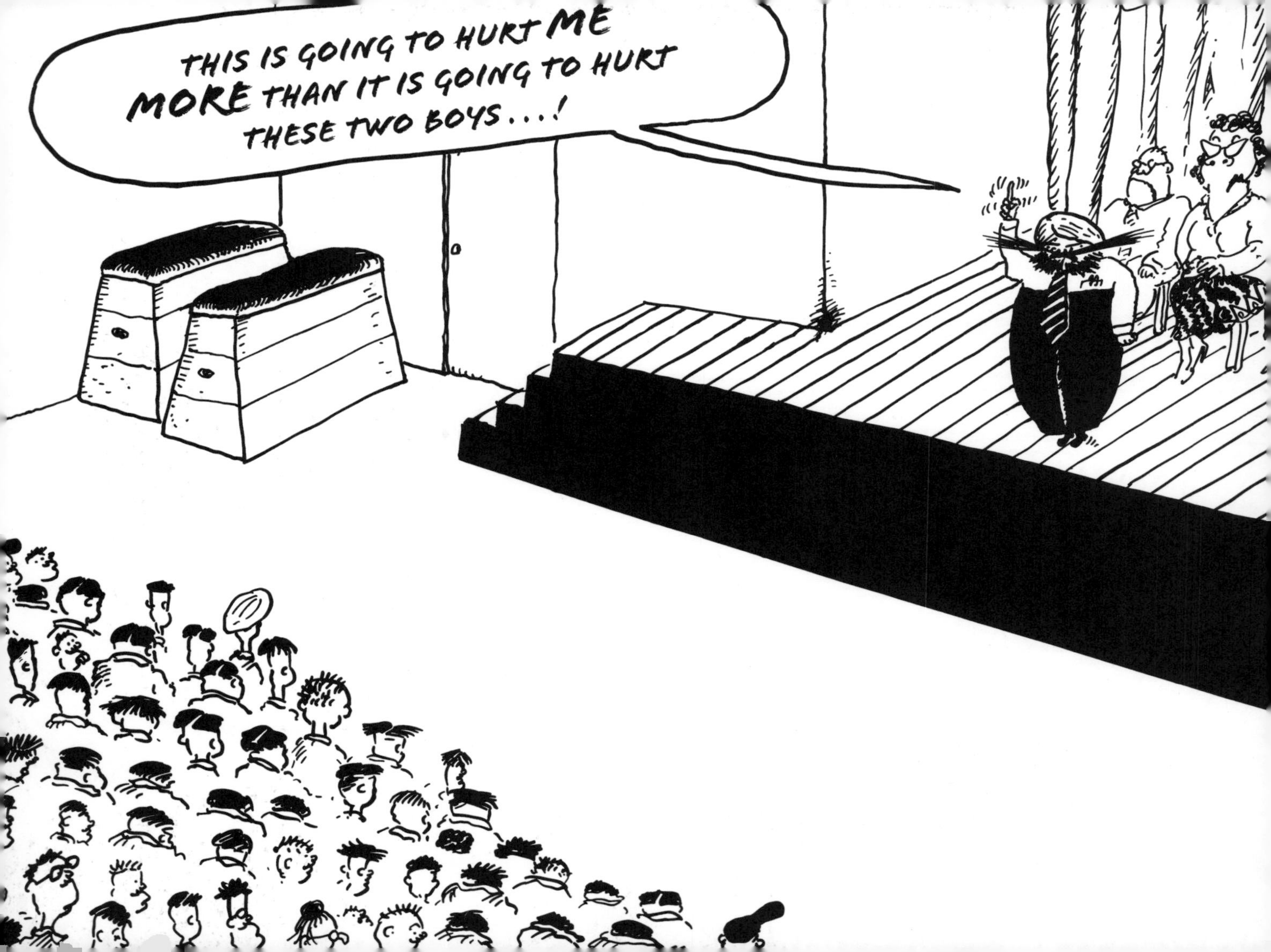
THIS IS GOING TO HURT ME MORE THAN IT IS GOING TO HURT THESE TWO BOYS....!

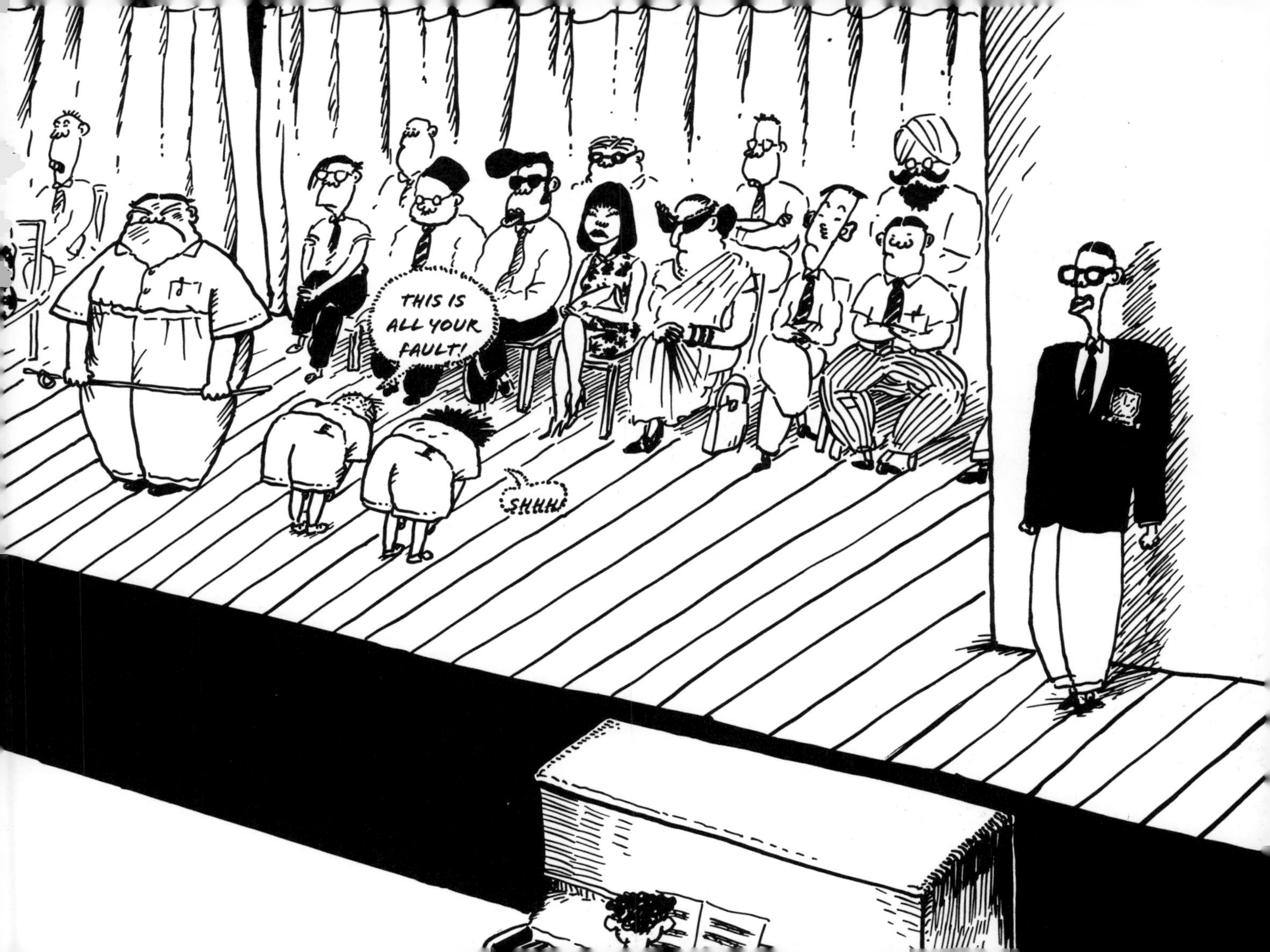
THIS IS ALL YOUR FAULT!
SHHH

1968

was a momentous year . . .

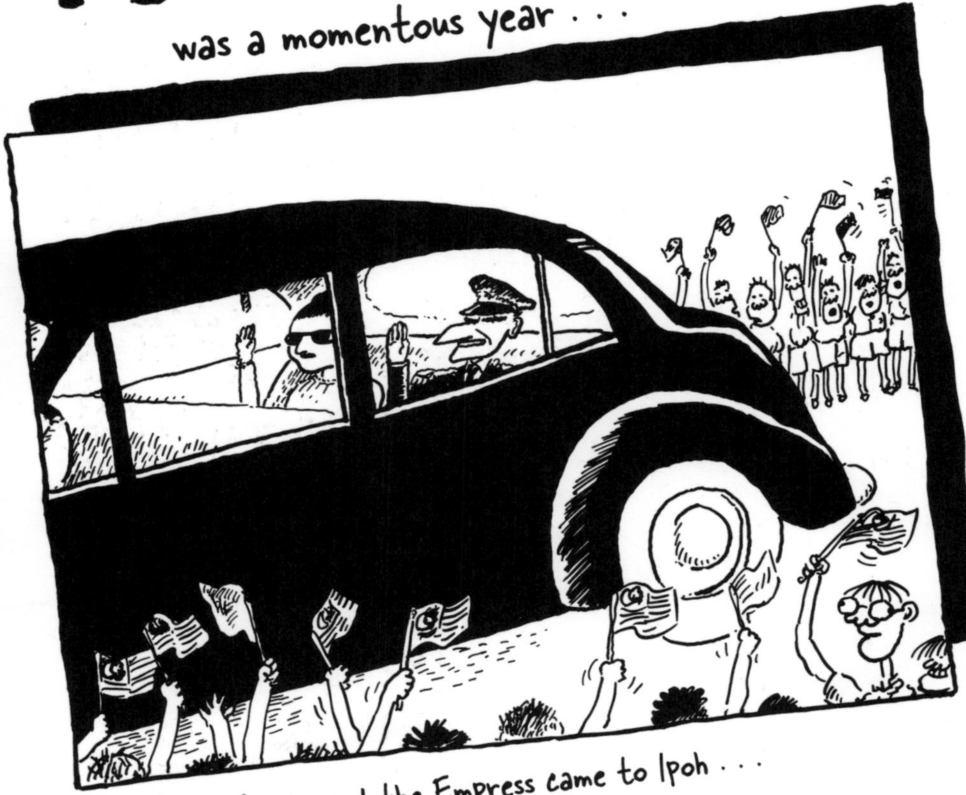

The Shah of Iran and the Empress came to Ipoh . . .

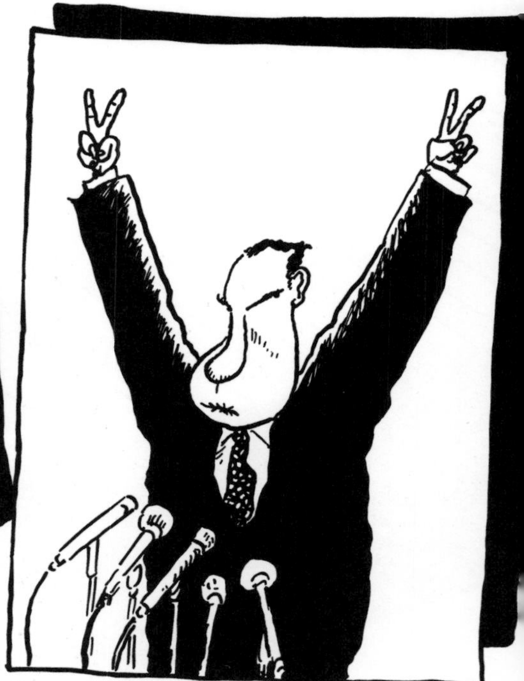

Richard Nixon was elected President of the United States . . .

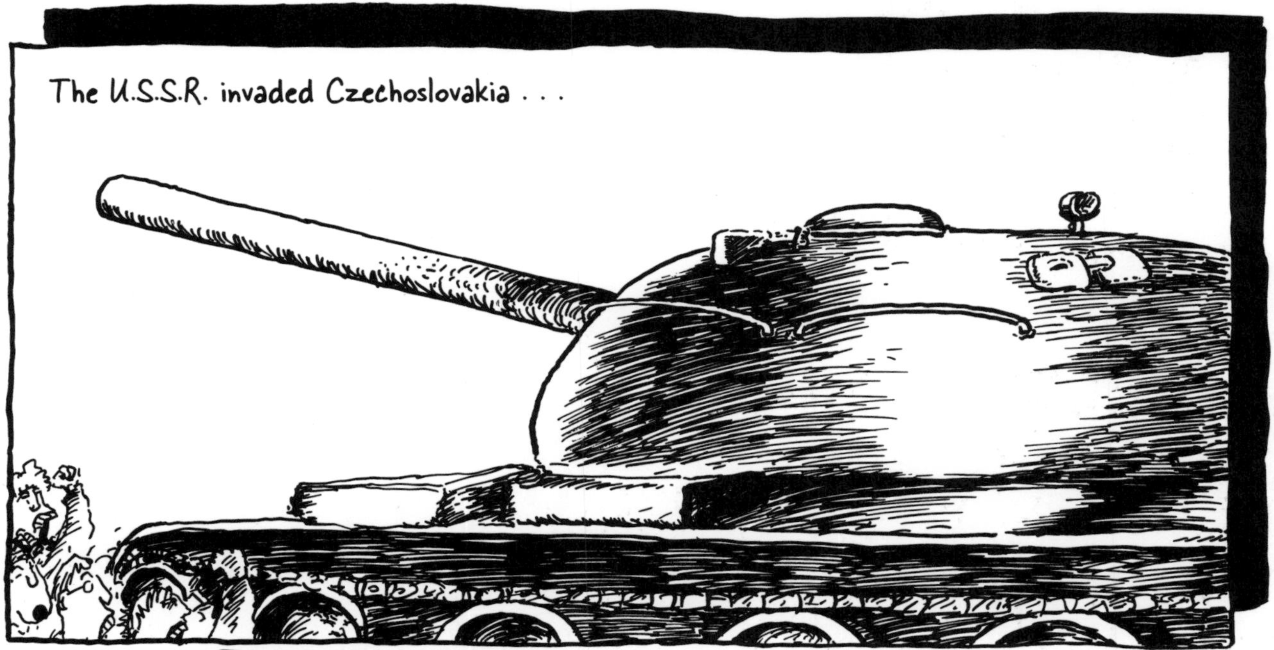
The U.S.S.R. invaded Czechoslovakia . . .

The Philippine Government staked a claim on Sabah . . .

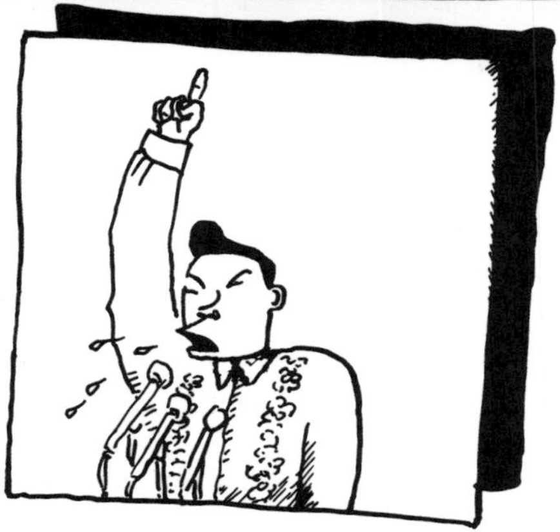

I was seventeen.

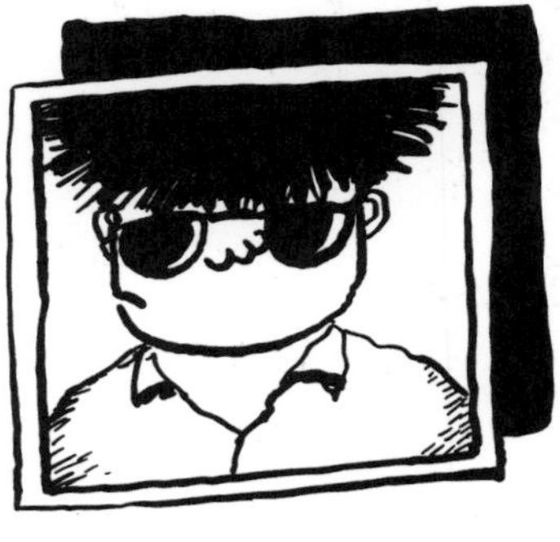

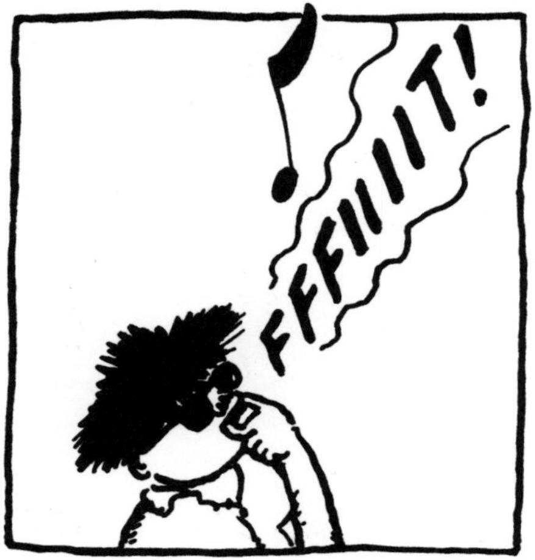
FFWIIT!

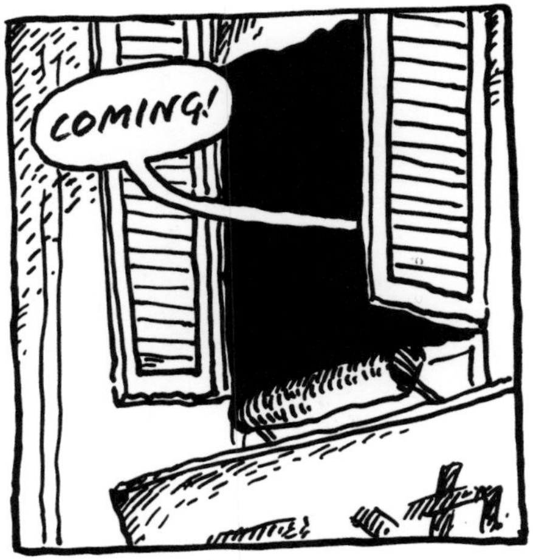
COMING!

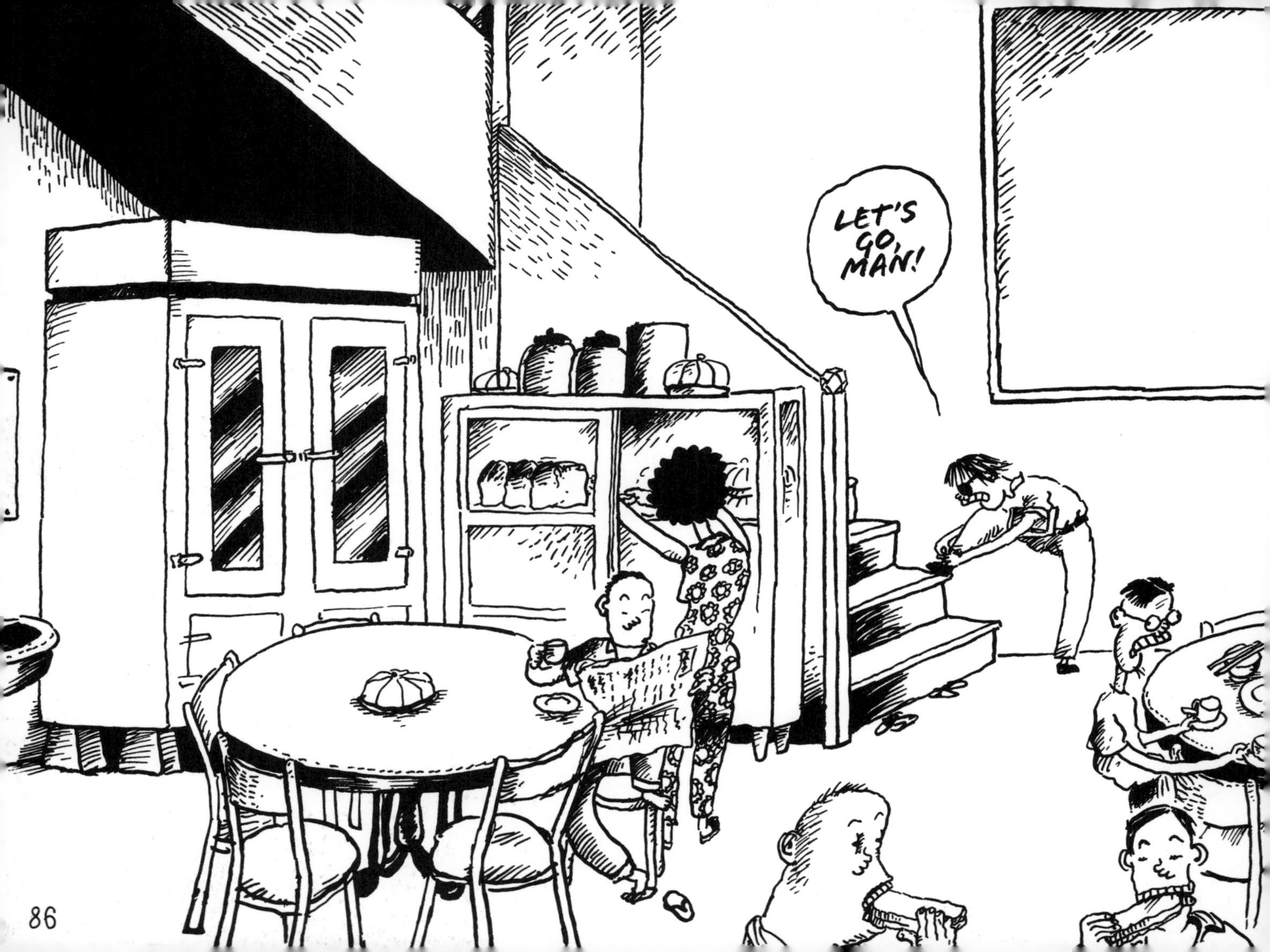
LET'S GO, MAN!

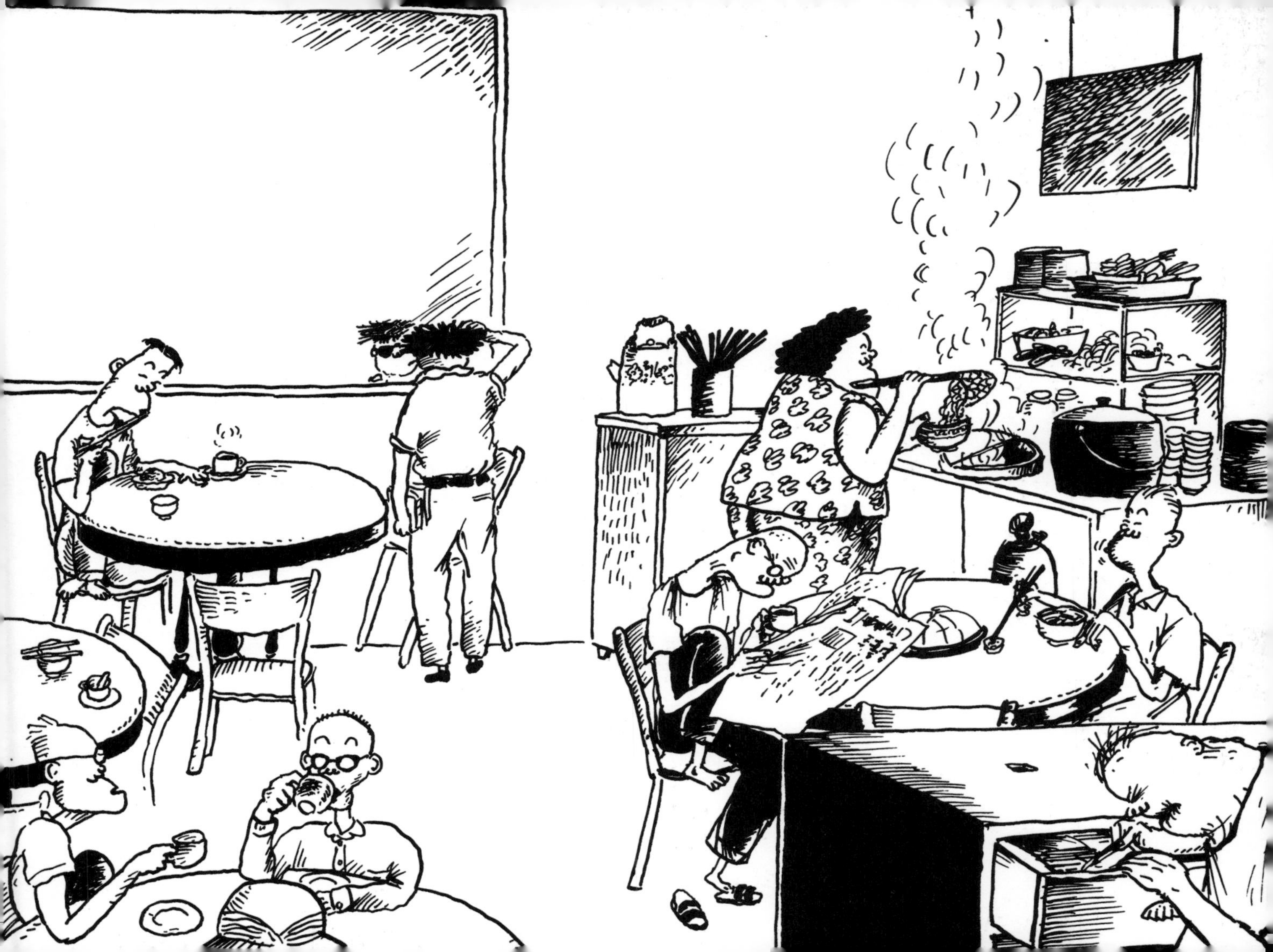

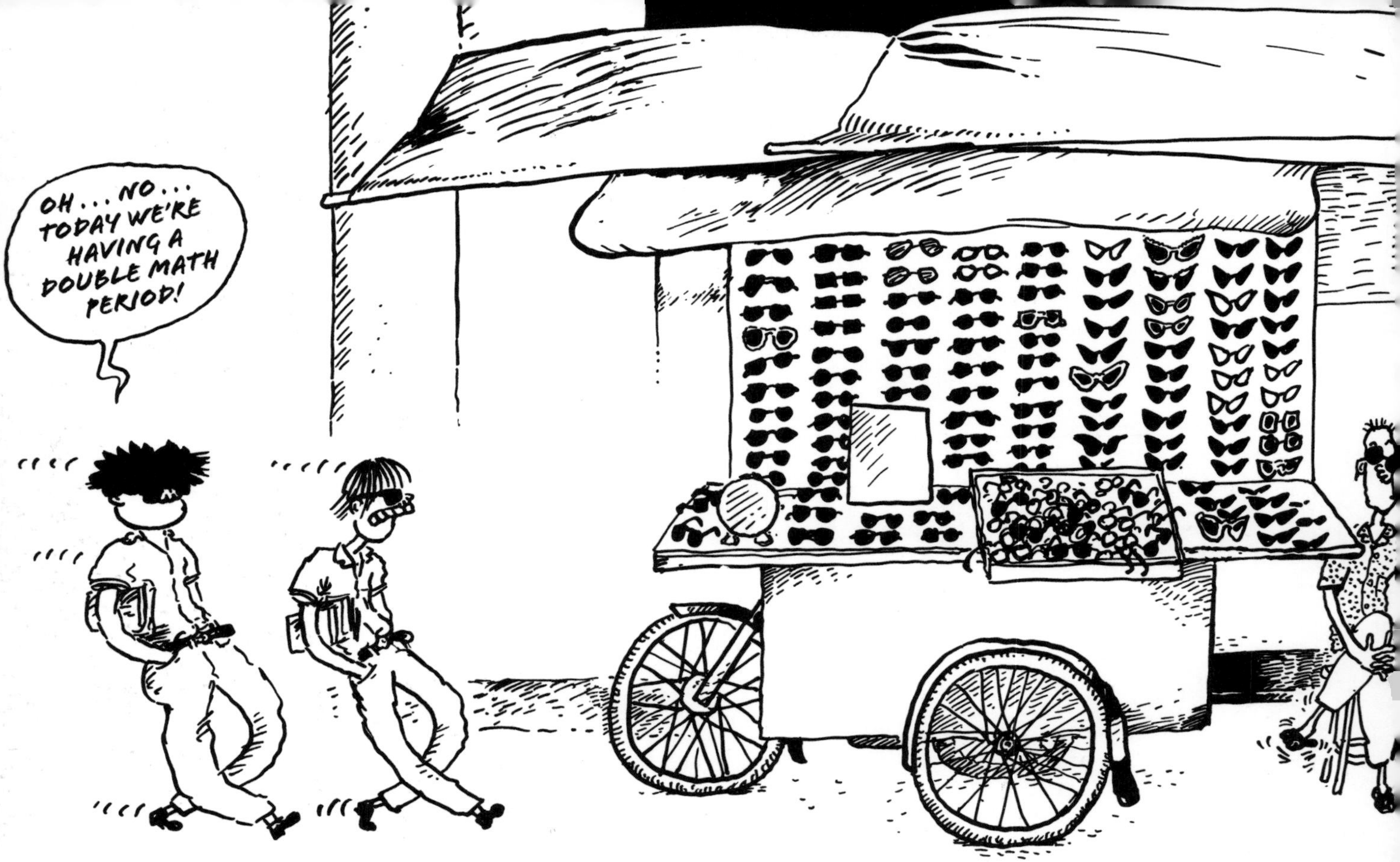
OH... NO... TODAY WE'RE HAVING A DOUBLE MATH PERIOD!

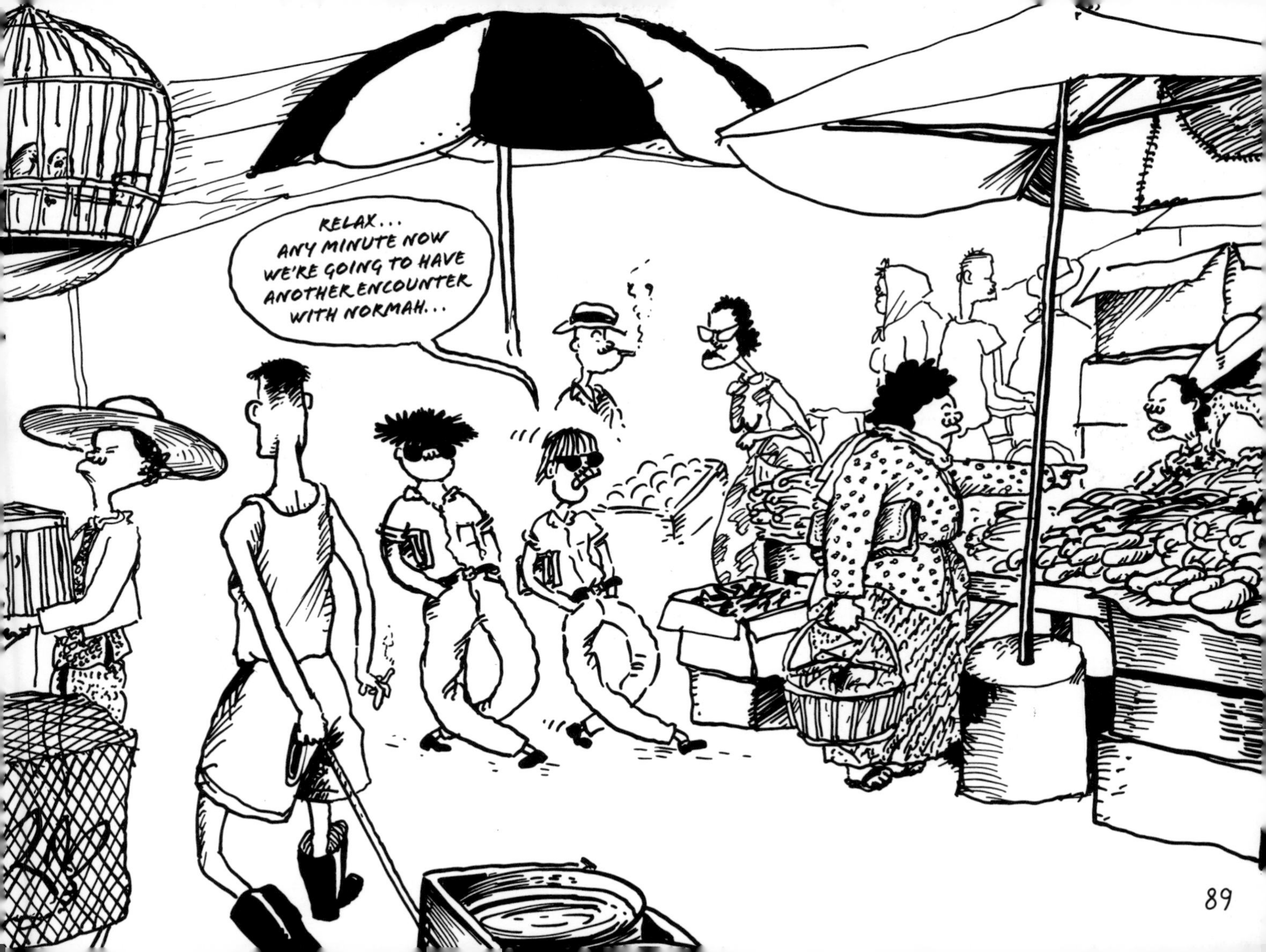
RELAX... ANY MINUTE NOW WE'RE GOING TO HAVE ANOTHER ENCOUNTER WITH NORMAH...

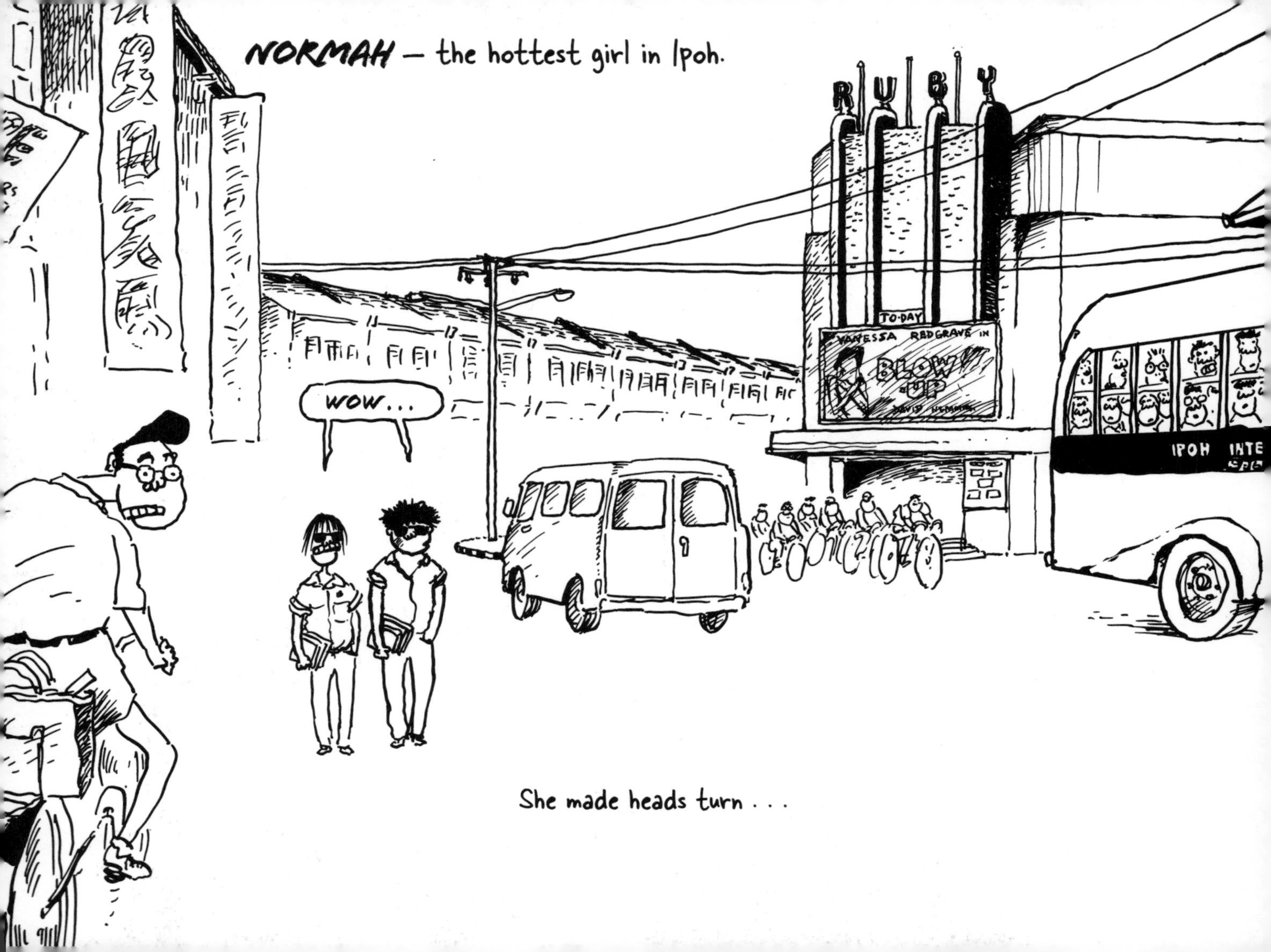
NORMAH — the hottest girl in Ipoh.
RUBY
TO-DAY
VANESSA REDGRAVE IN
BLOW-UP
WOW...
IPOH INTE
She made heads turn . . .

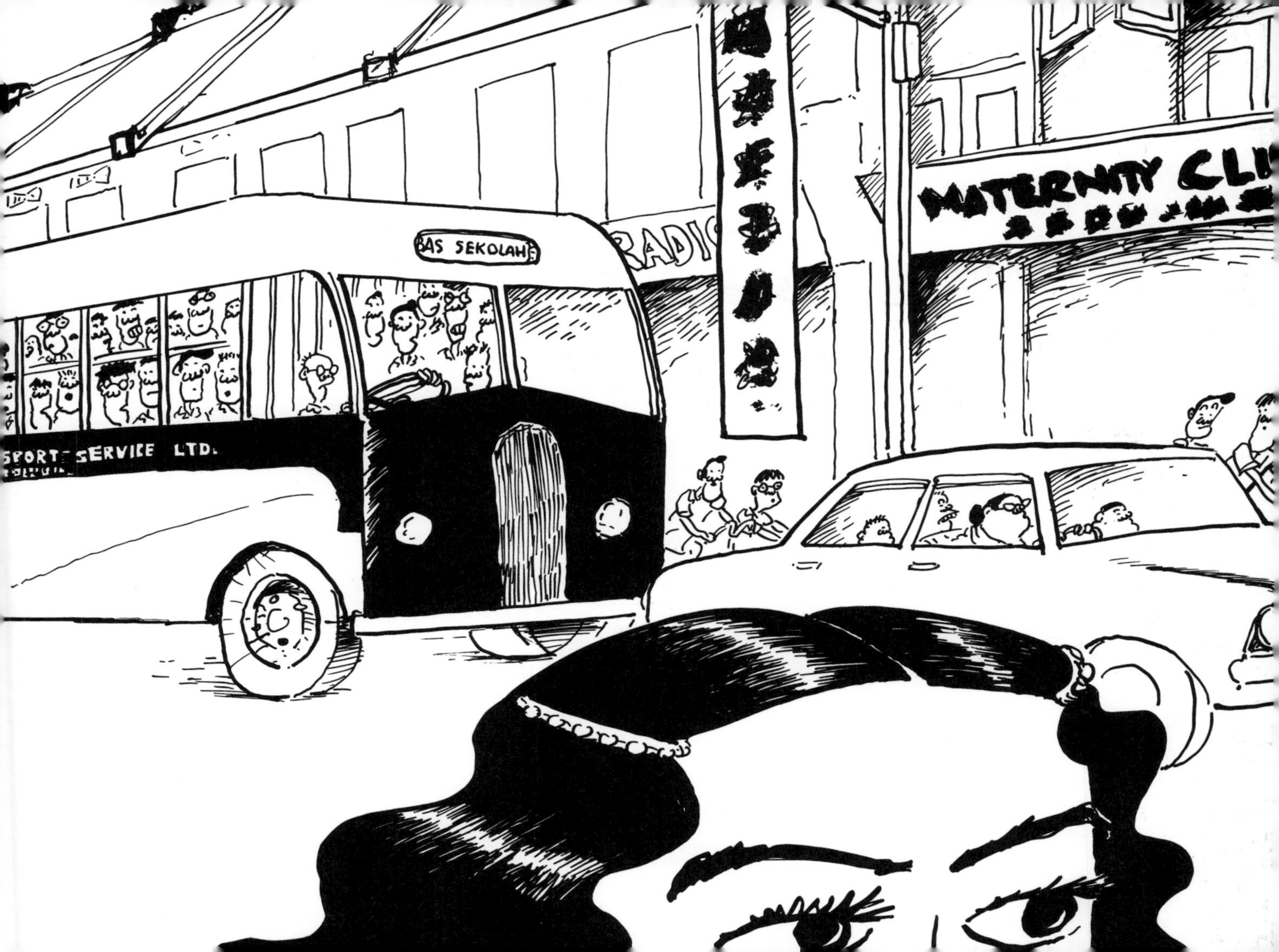
BAS SEKOLAH
RADIO
MATERNITY CLI
SPORT SERVICE LTD.

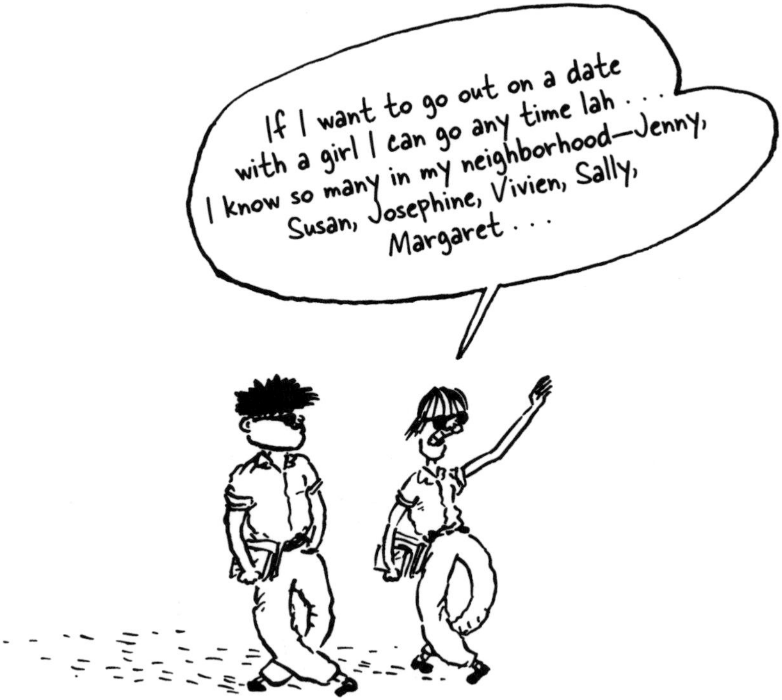
If I want to go out on a date with a girl I can go any time lah . . . I know so many in my neighborhood—Jenny, Susan, Josephine, Vivien, Sally, Margaret . . .

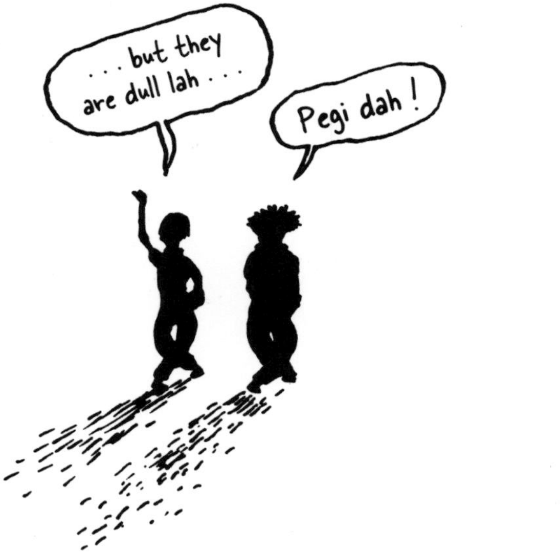
. . . but they are dull lah . . .
Pegi dah !

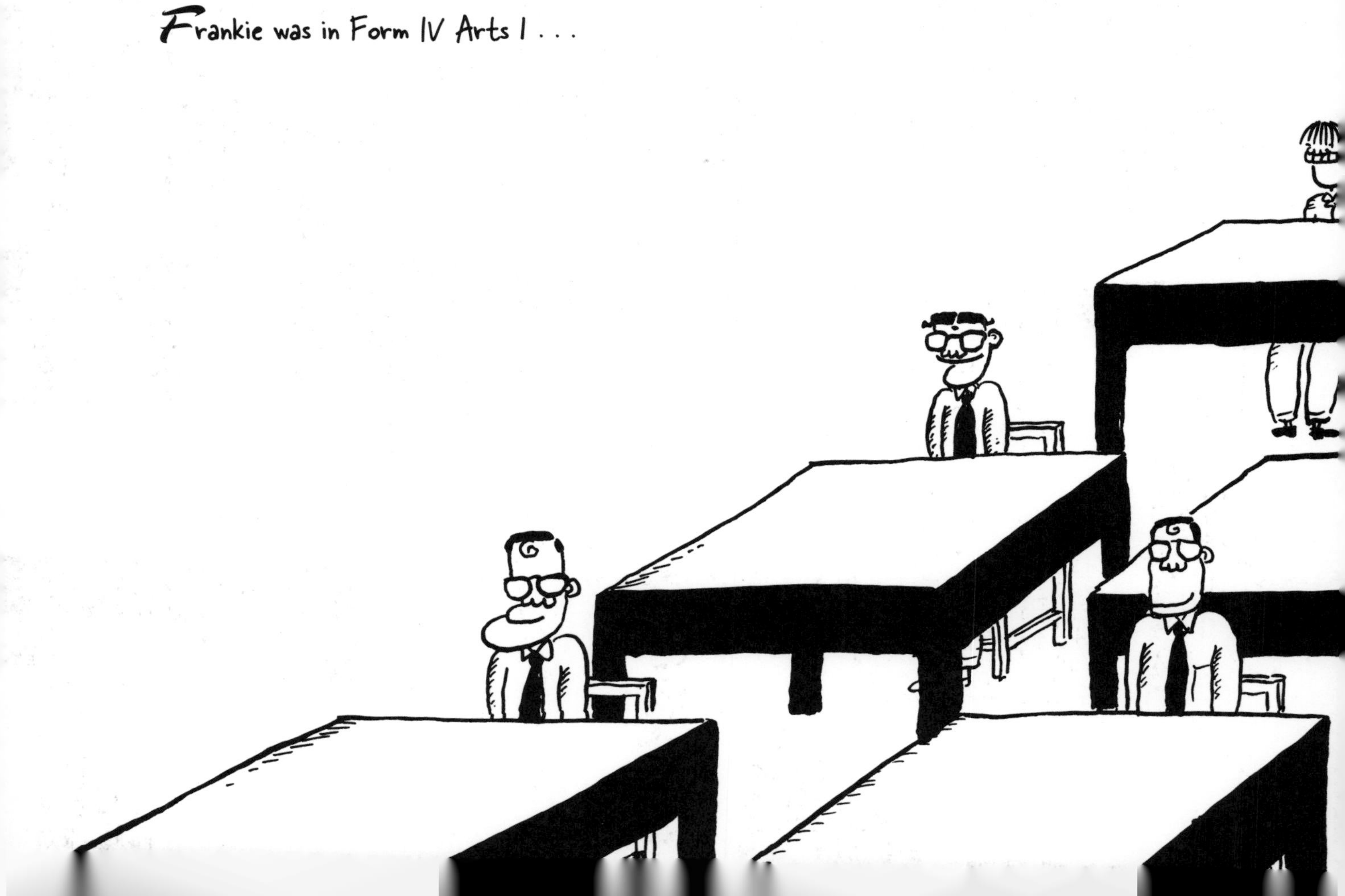
Frankie was in Form IV Arts I . . .

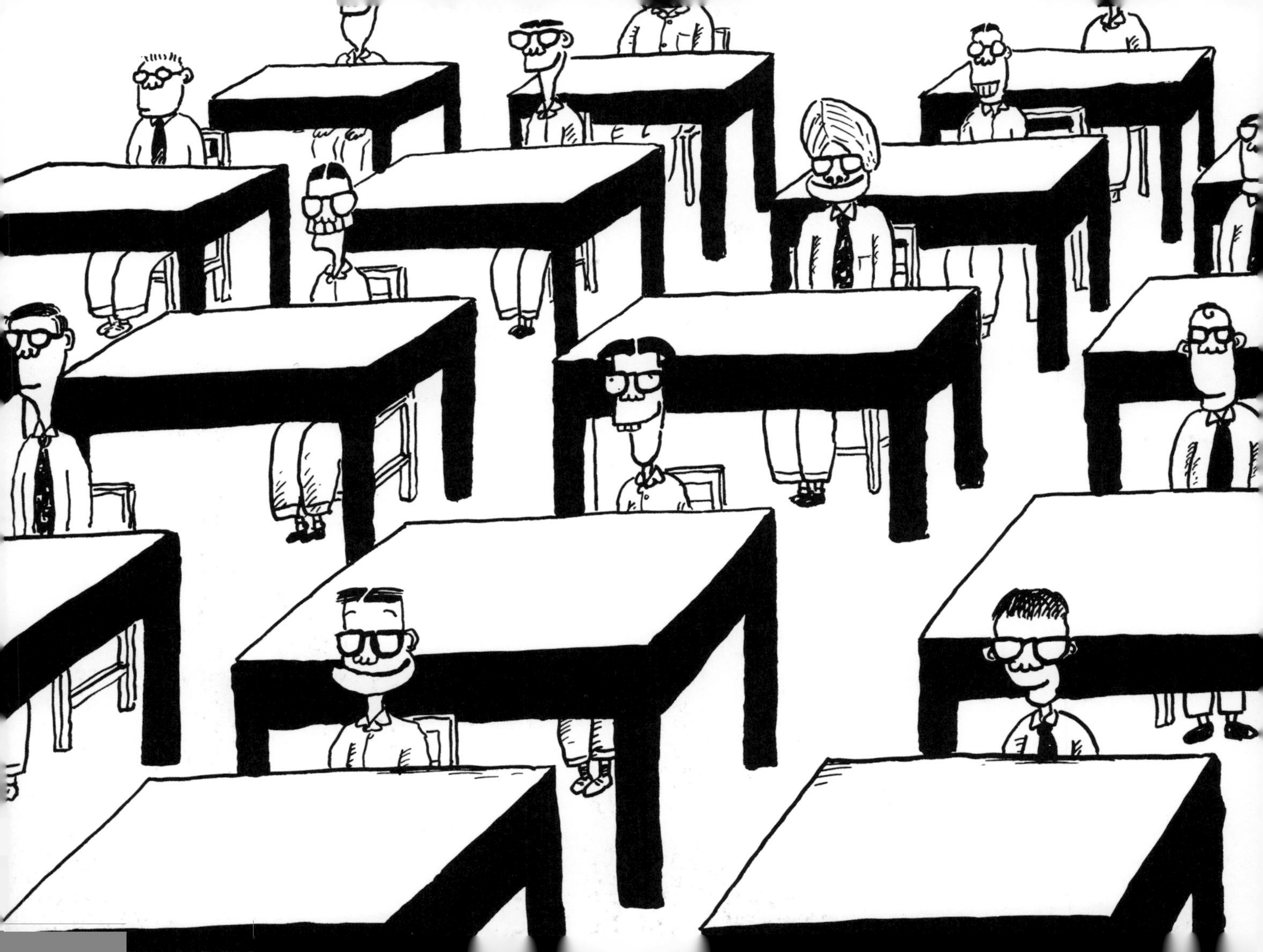

I was in Form IV Arts 3 . . .

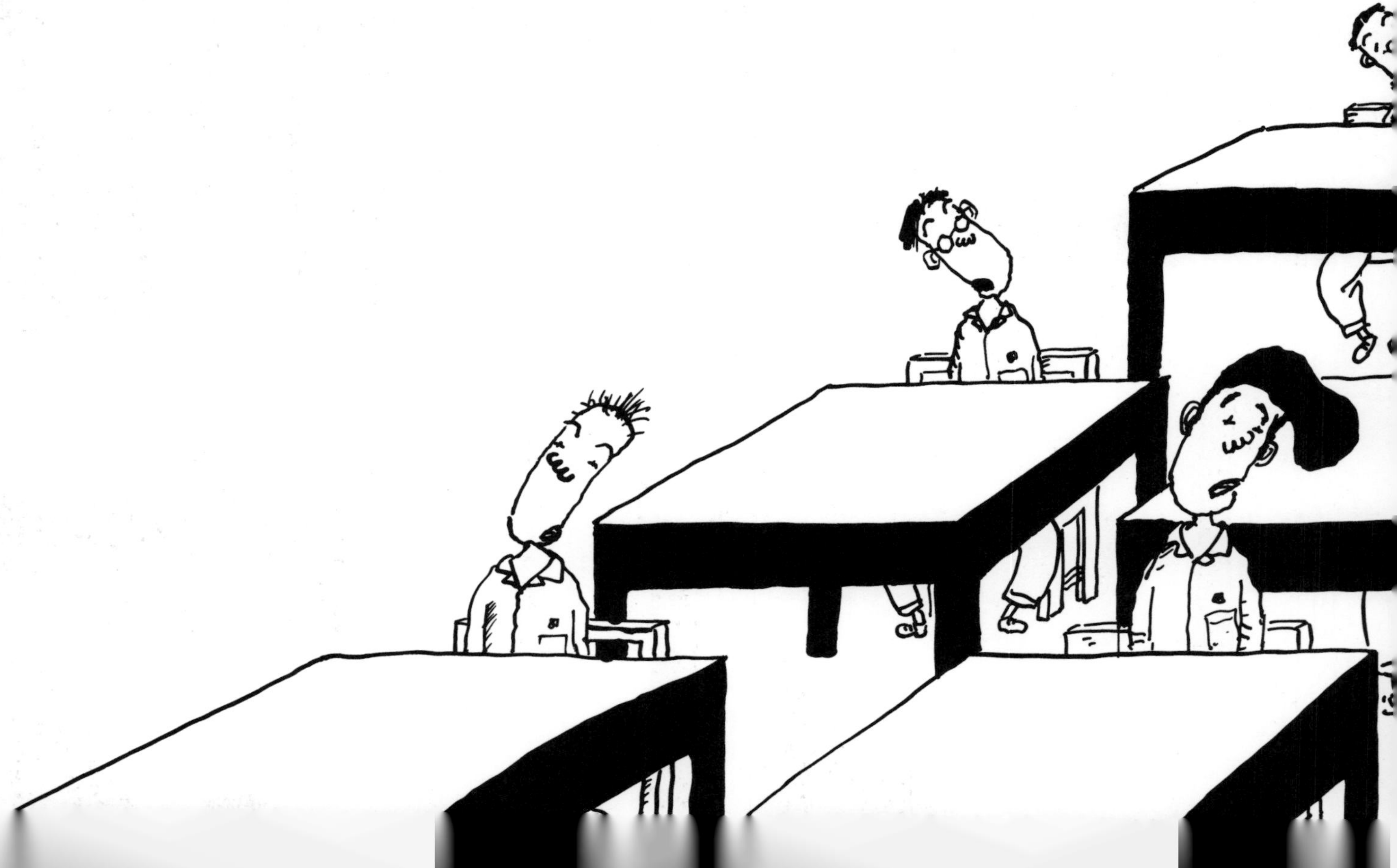

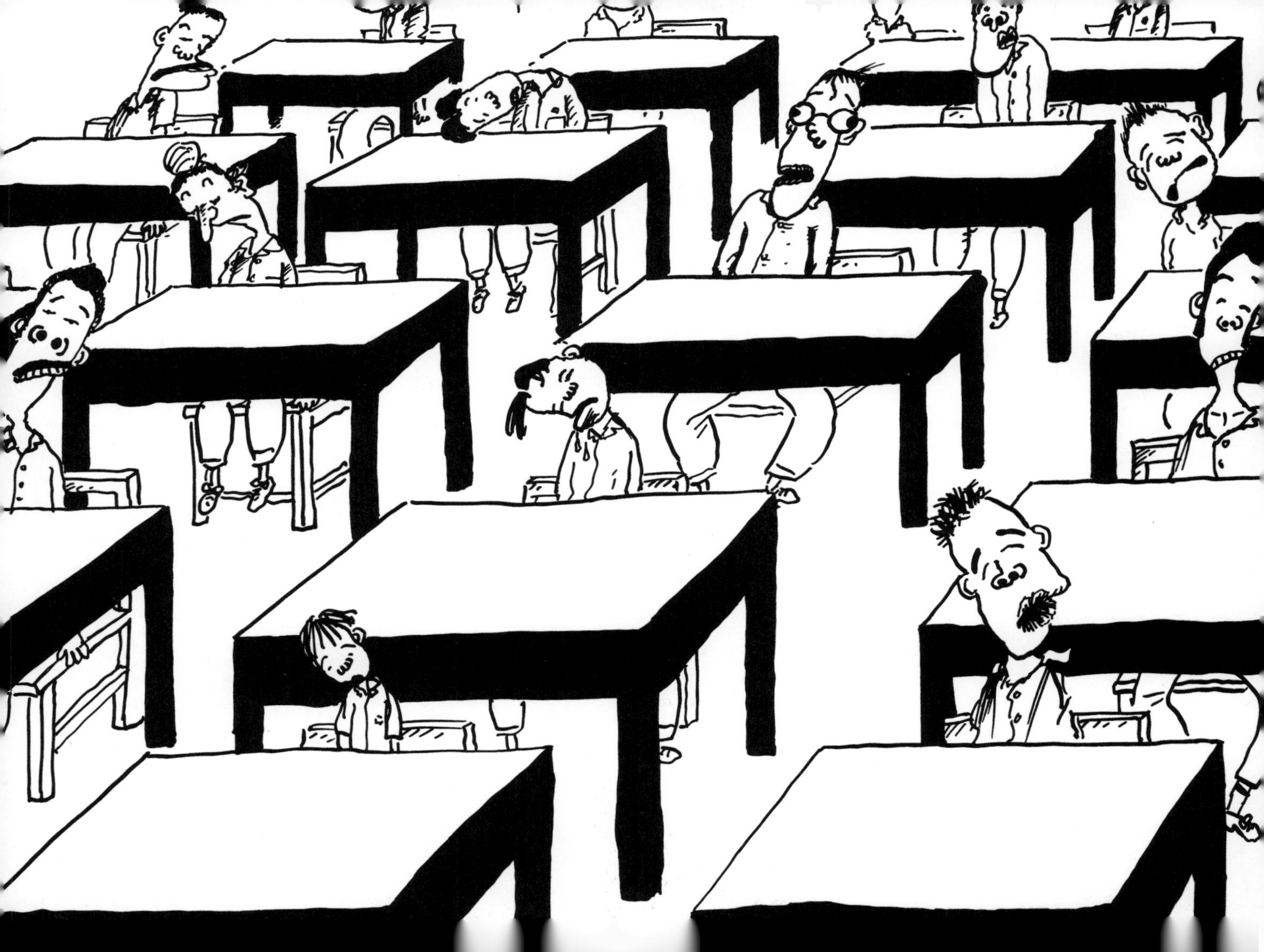

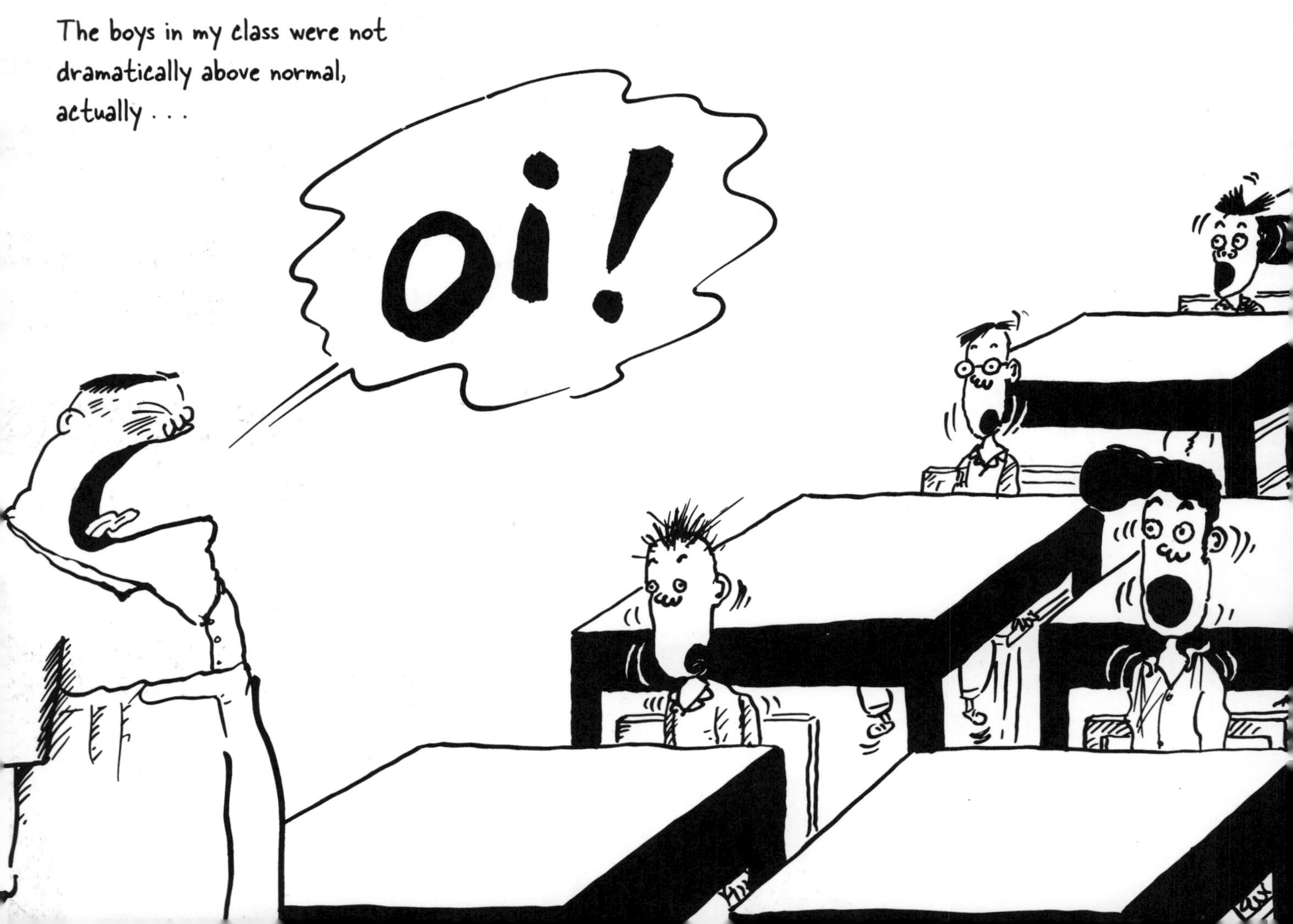
The boys in my class were not dramatically above normal, actually . . .
Oi!

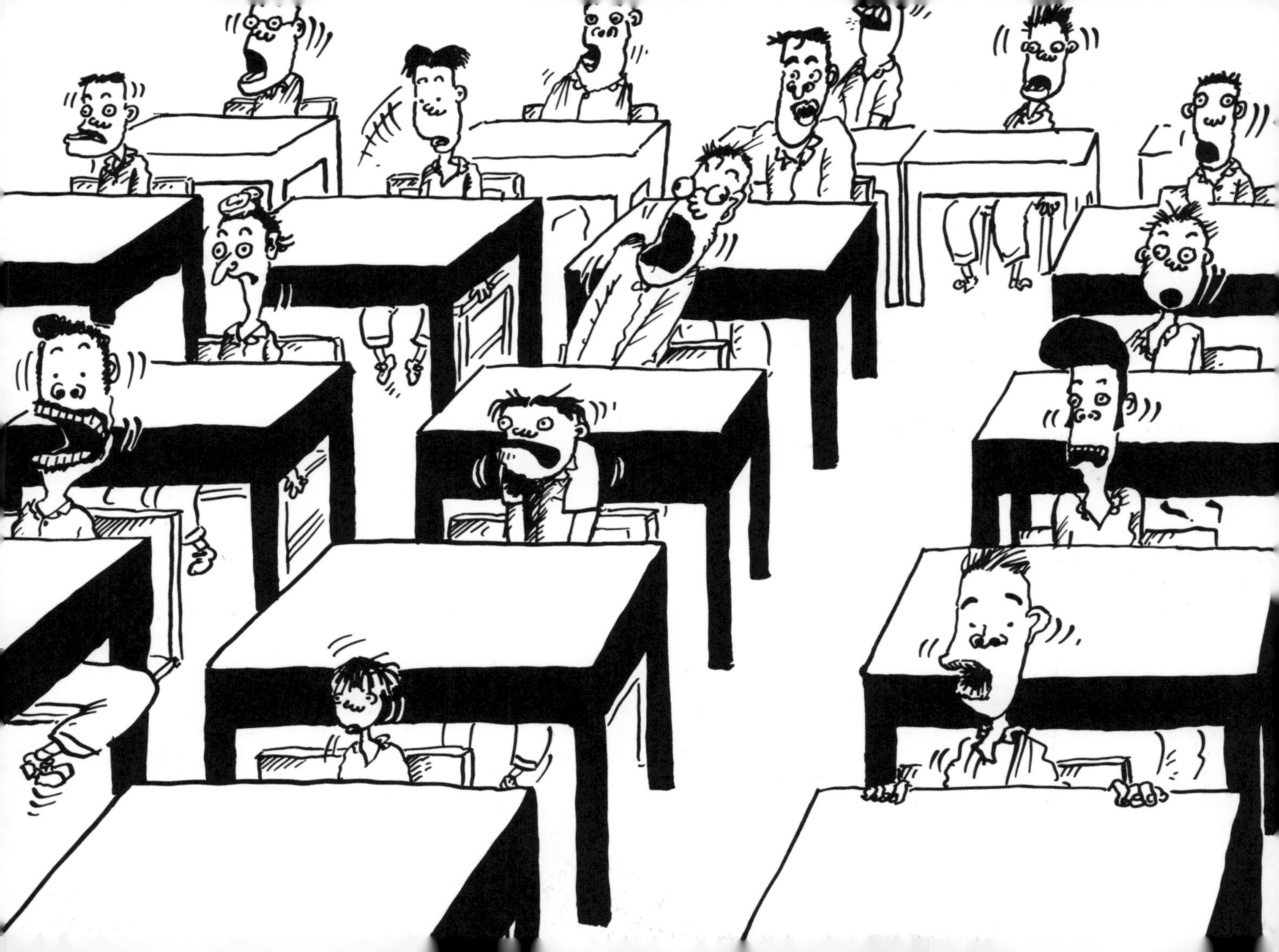

I sat in the back row and the boys in the back row were close friends of mine . . . They were:

THE T.R. TRIO

Din, Hamdan, and Neoh came from Tanjung Rambutan, seven miles away. They were always together.

Mat Sham

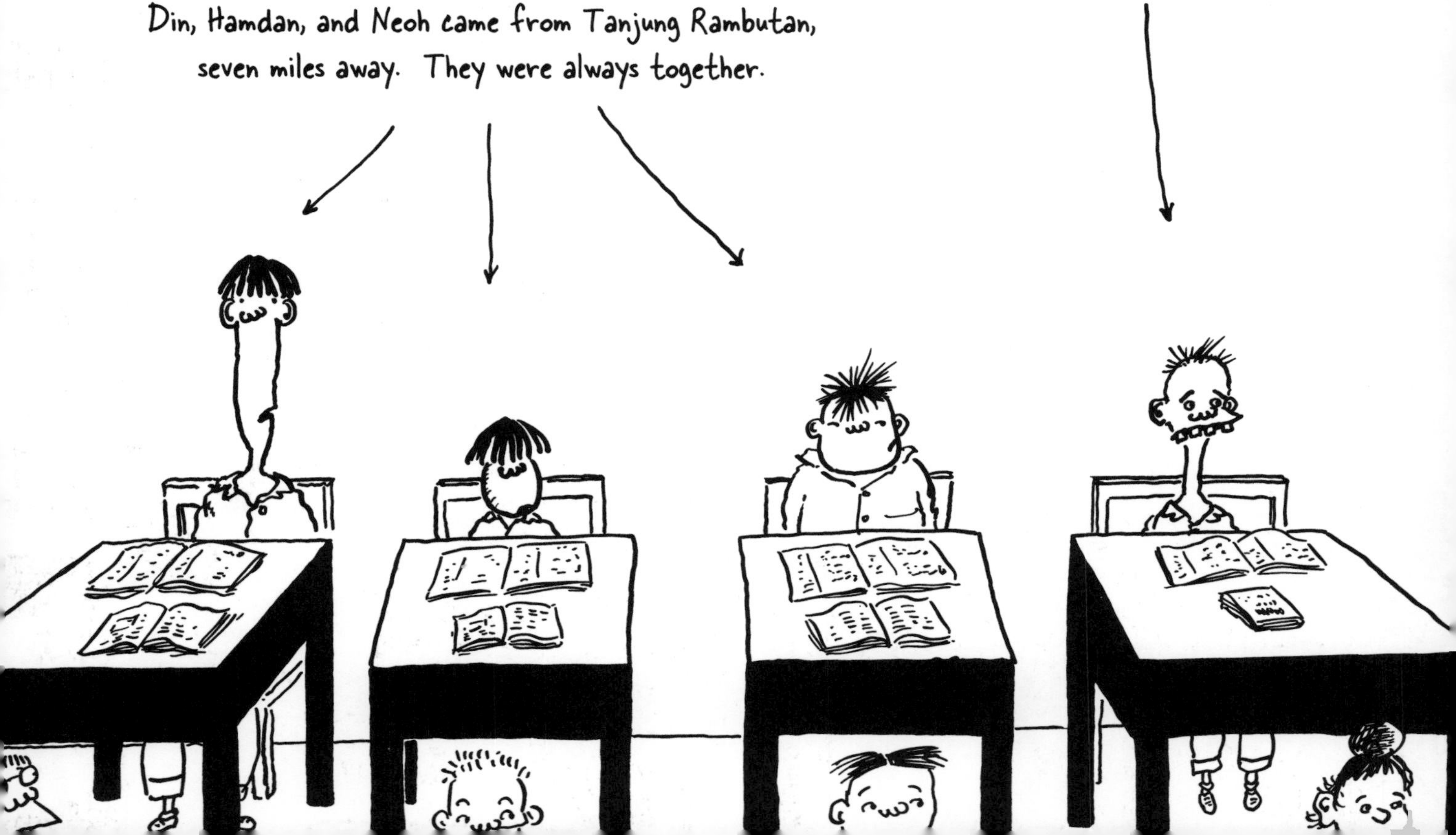

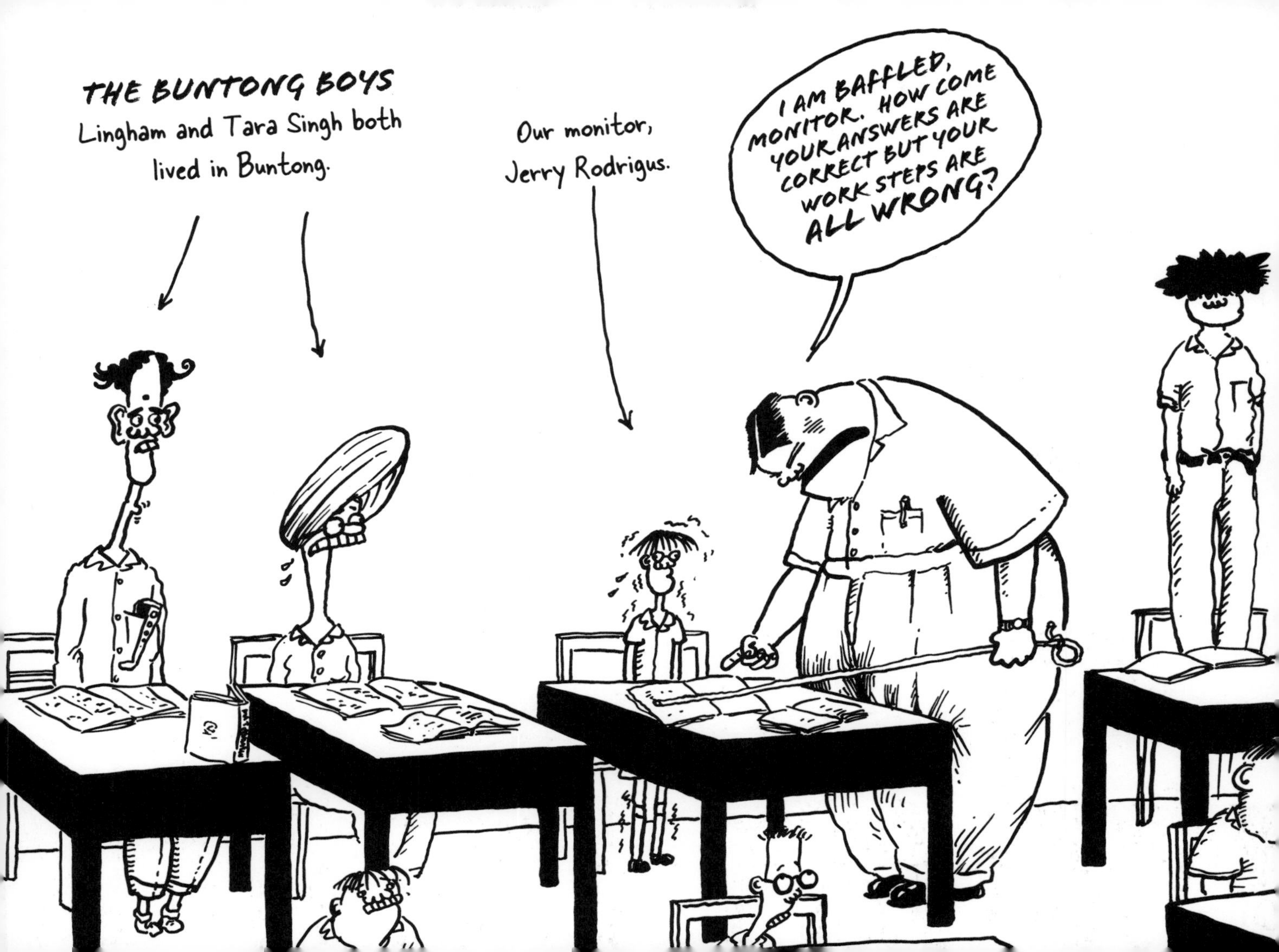
THE BUNTONG BOYS
Lingham and Tara Singh both lived in Buntong.
Our monitor, Jerry Rodrigus.
I AM BAFFLED, MONITOR. HOW COME YOUR ANSWERS ARE CORRECT BUT YOUR WORK STEPS ARE ALL WRONG?

Sometimes Frankie and I and the boys
would go downtown to check out the cinemas.

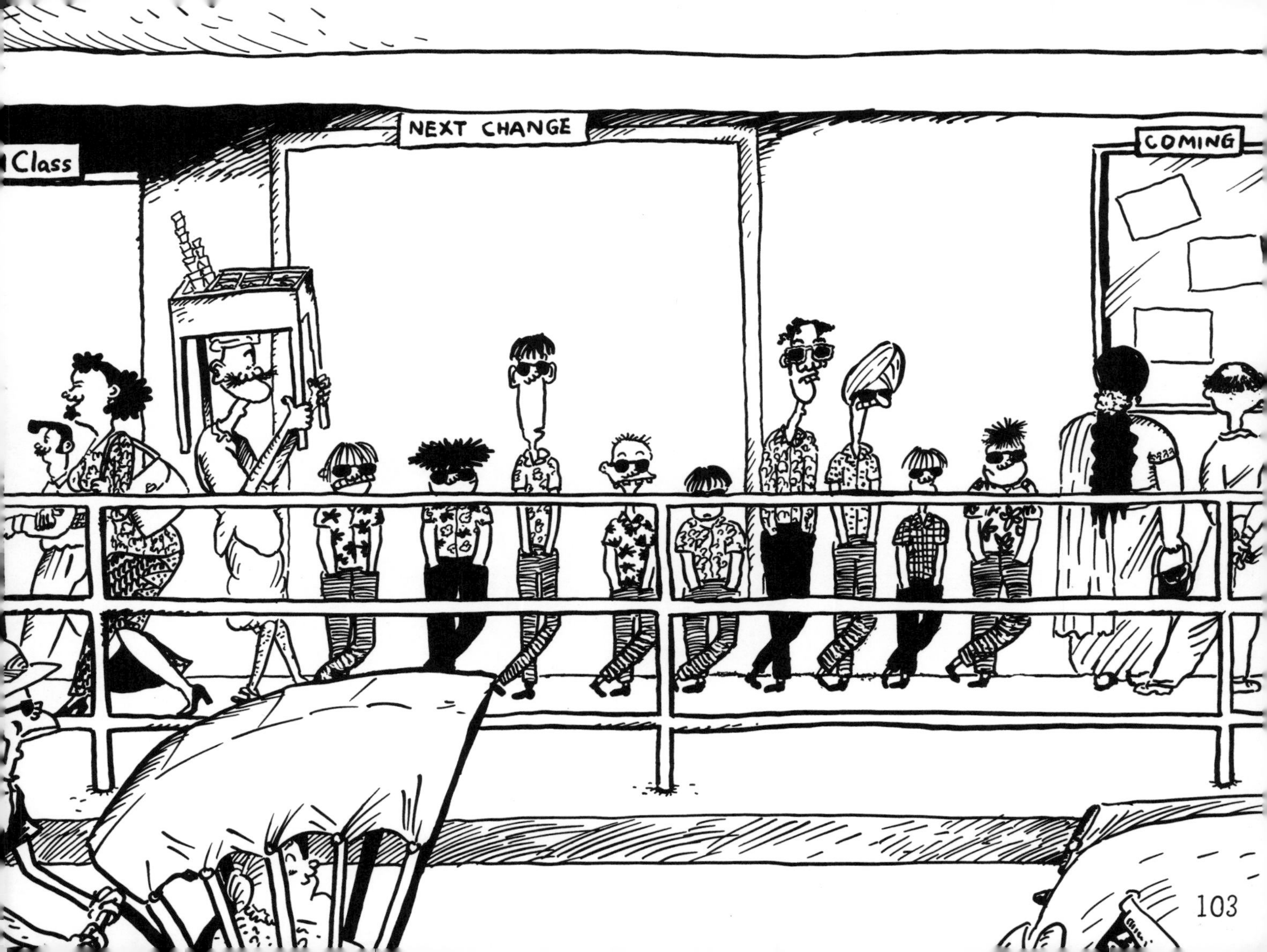

Class
NEXT CHANGE
COMING

Sometimes we'd go to the Jalan Yang Kalthom bus station.

What we probably wanted was attention . . .

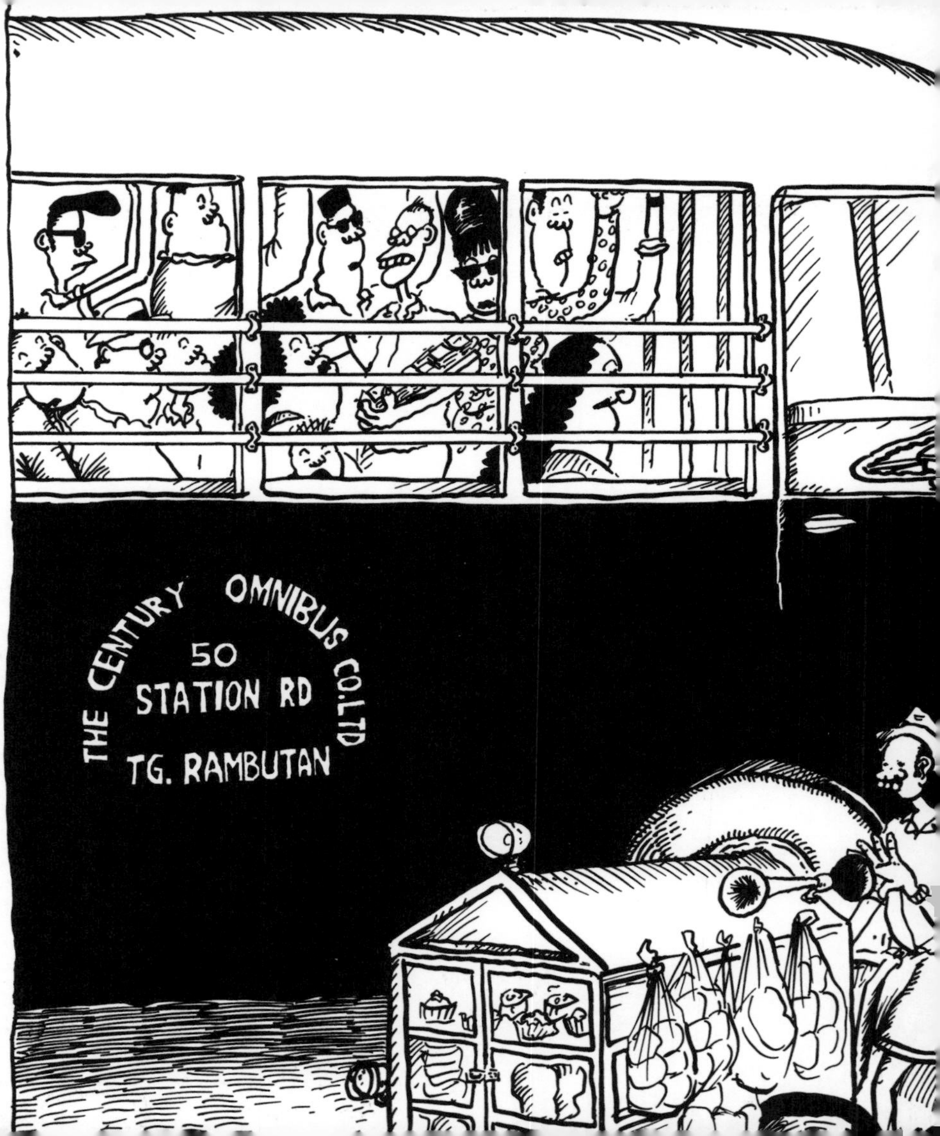
THE CENTURY OMNIBUS CO. LTD
50
STATION RD
TG. RAMBUTAN

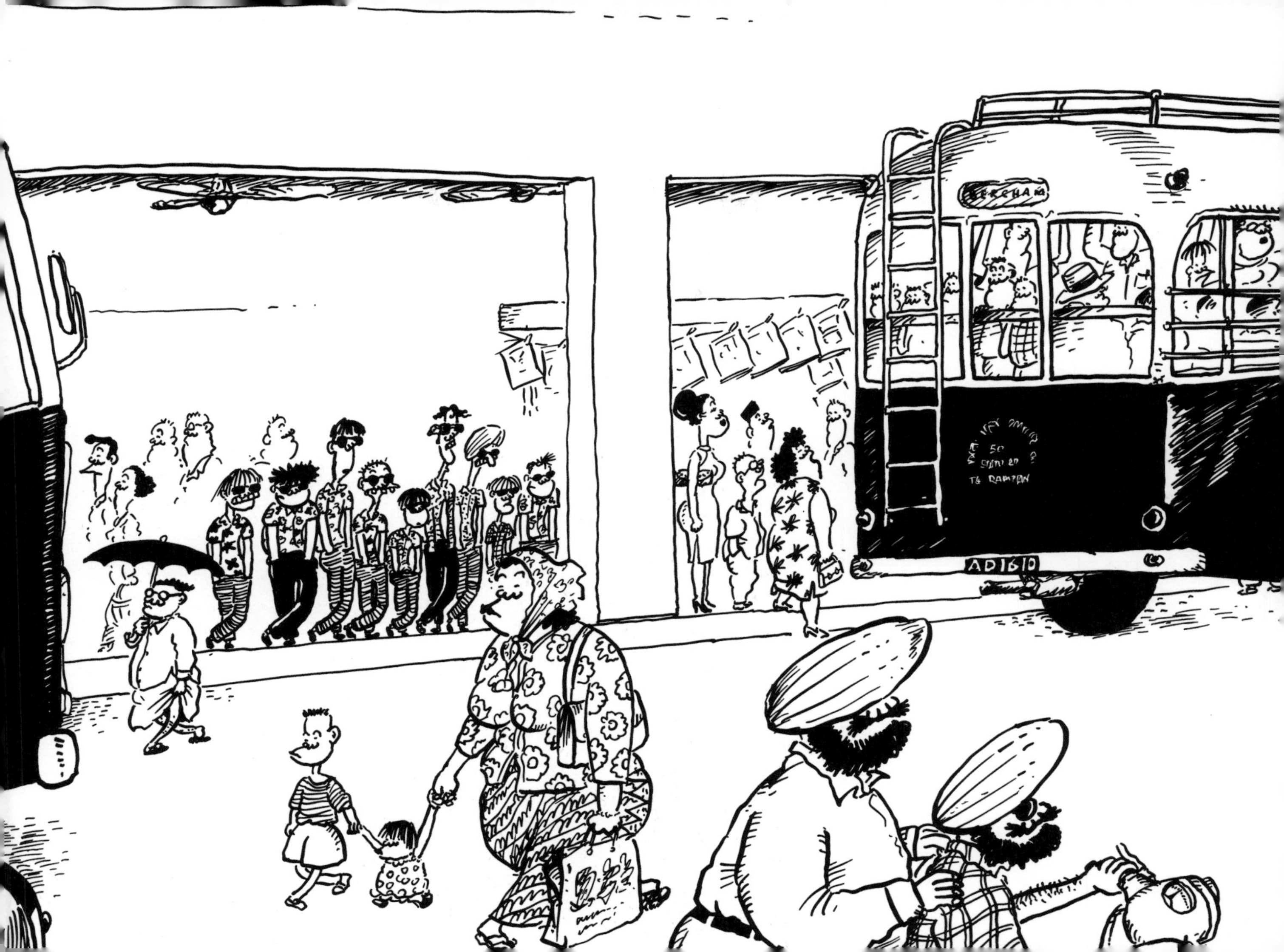
AD1610

My favorite subject in school was art.

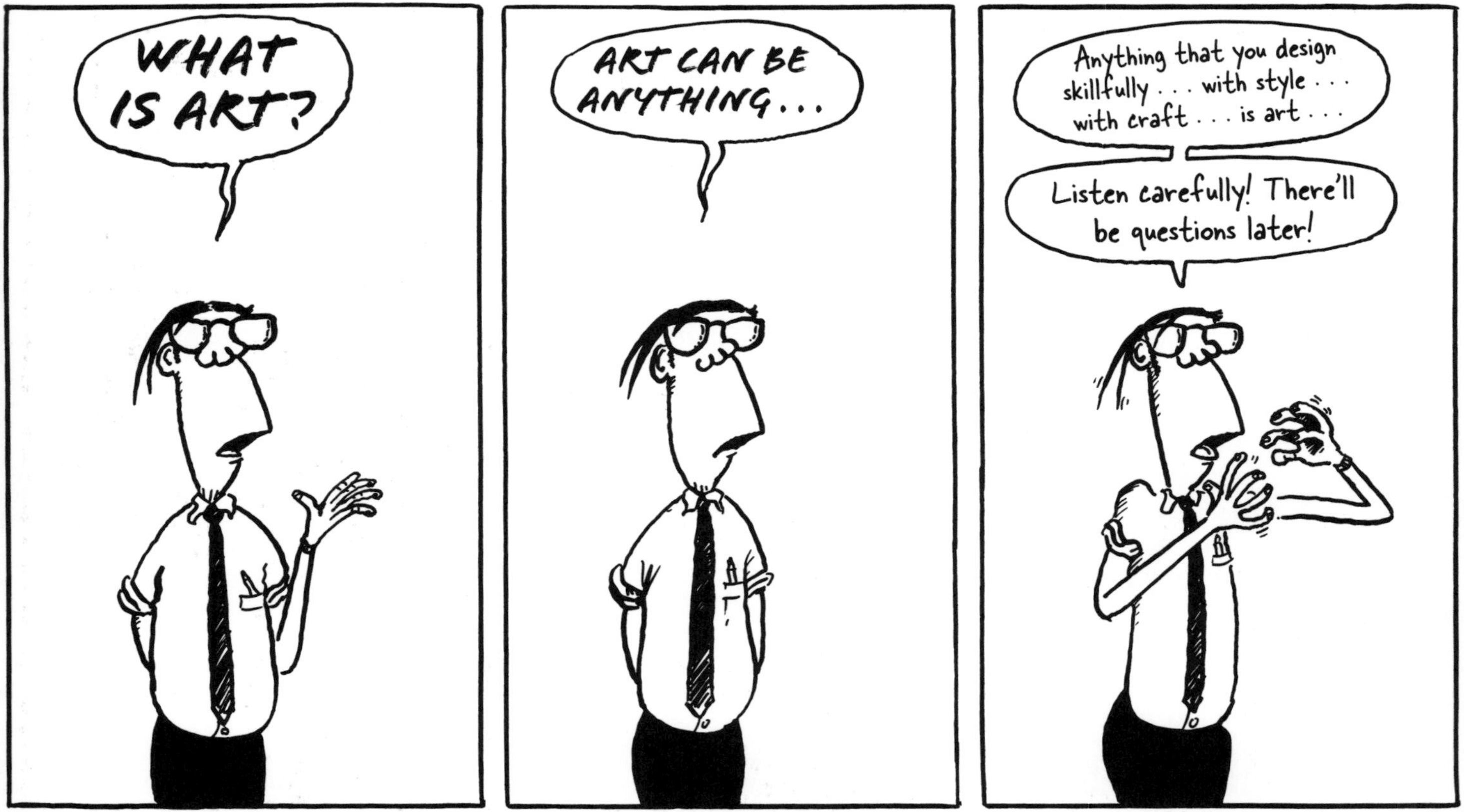
WHAT IS ART?
ART CAN BE ANYTHING...
Anything that you design skillfully . . . with style . . . with craft . . . is art . . .
Listen carefully! There'll be questions later!

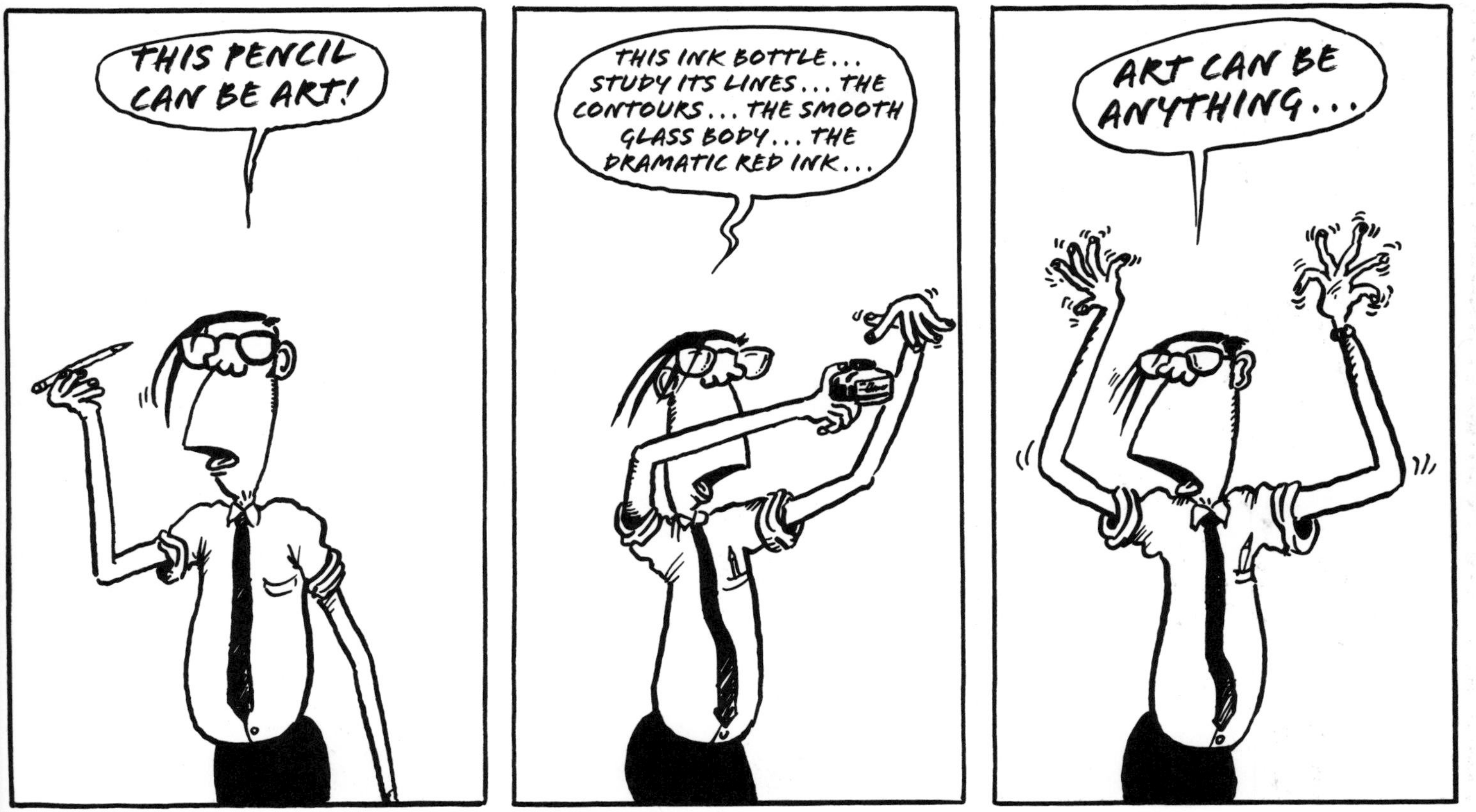
THIS PENCIL CAN BE ART!
THIS INK BOTTLE... STUDY ITS LINES... THE CONTOURS... THE SMOOTH GLASS BODY... THE DRAMATIC RED INK...
ART CAN BE ANYTHING...

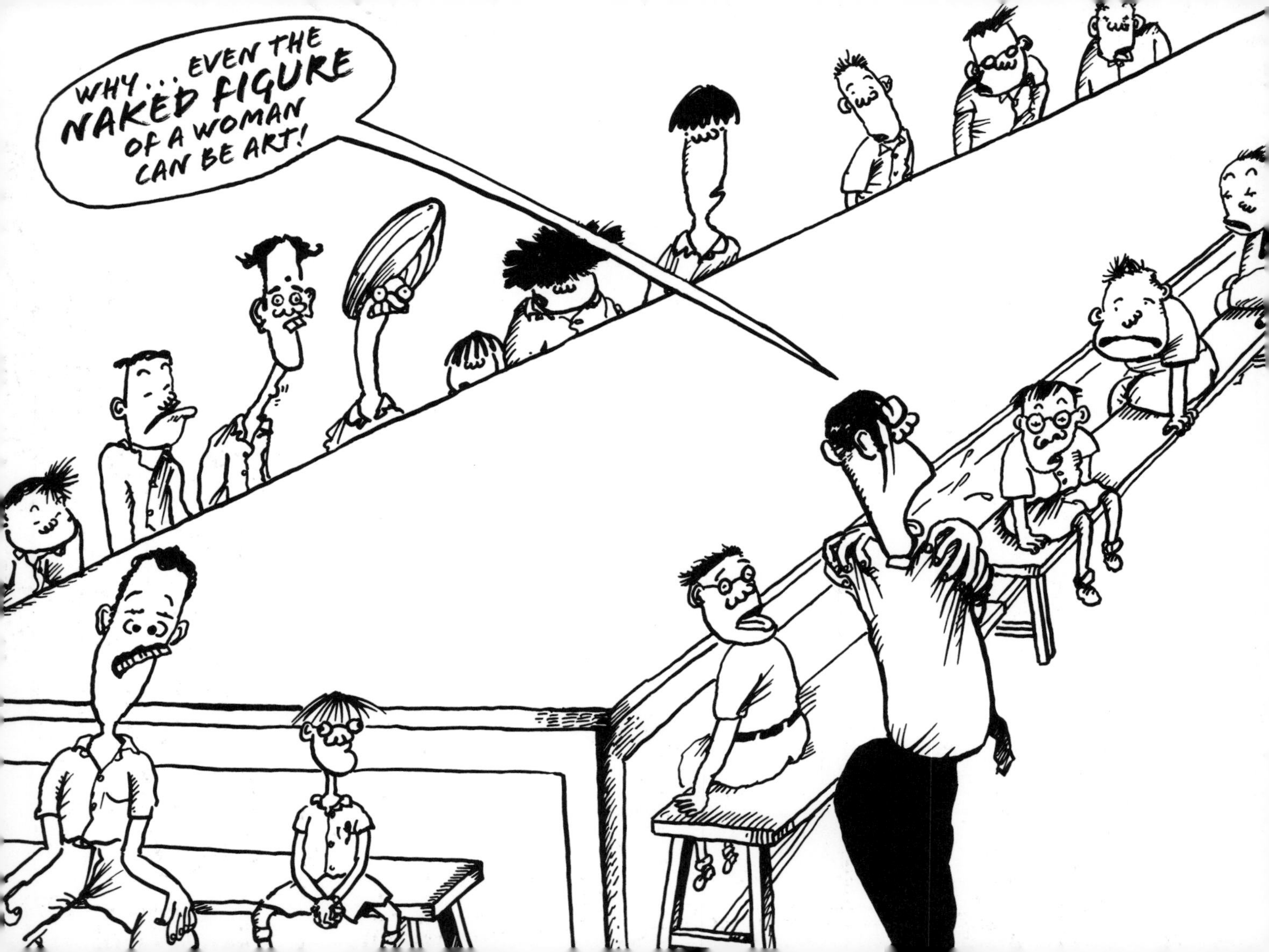
WHY... EVEN THE NAKED FIGURE OF A WOMAN CAN BE ART!

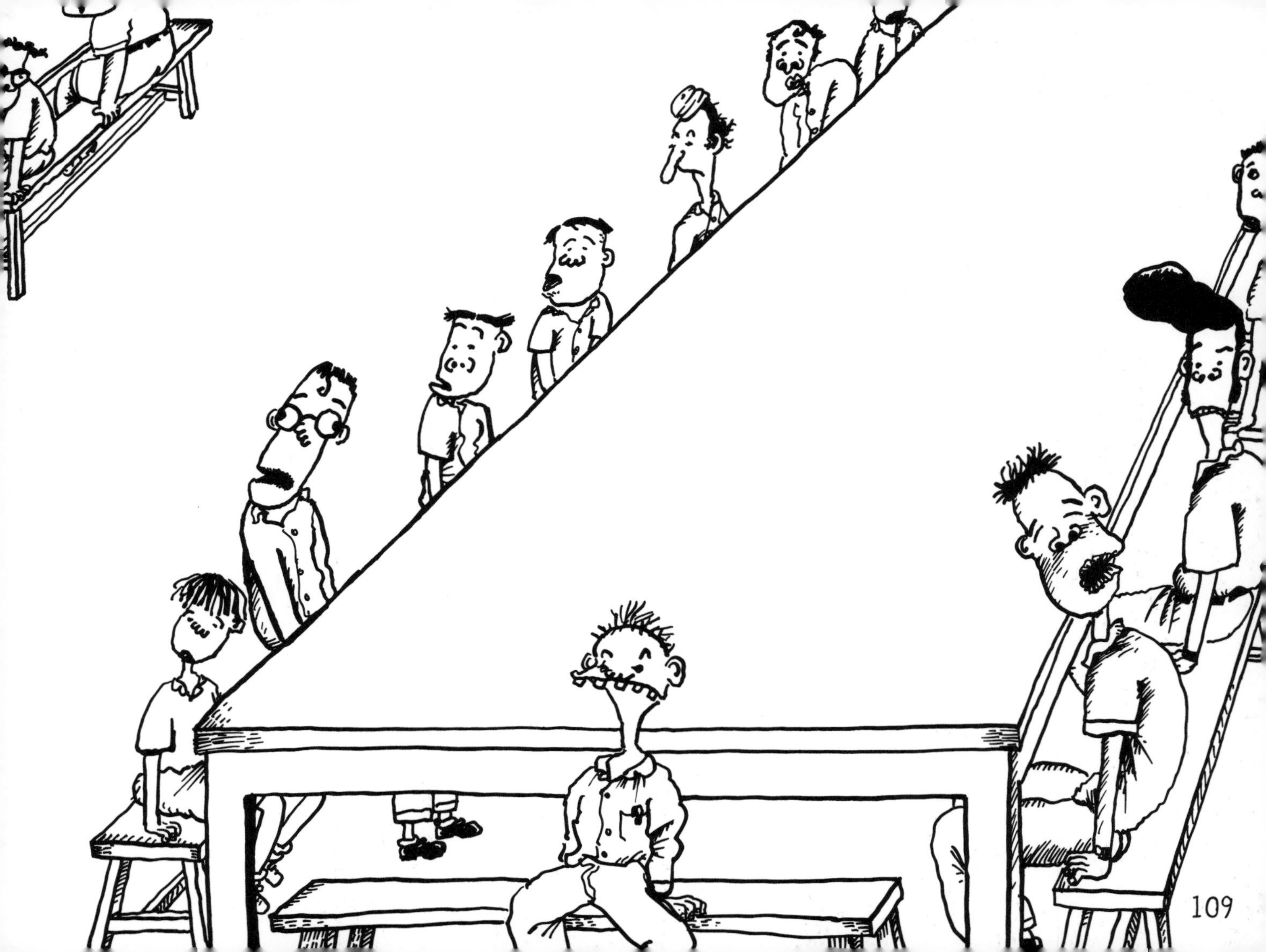

In art schools in Western countries they have figure-drawing classes . . .
. . . where nude models pose for students . . .

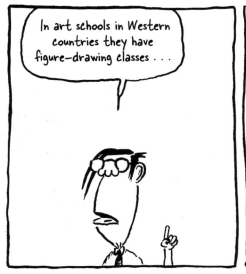

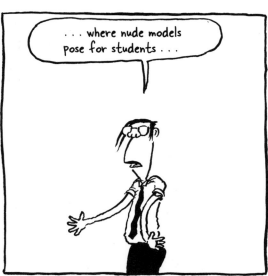

Anyway . . . I haven't seen the work of any of you boys before . . .
So for the next 1½ hours I am going to leave you with your drawing paper, your colors, and your imagination.
You can draw ANYTHING . . .
BUT! . . .
. . . make sure it is Art.

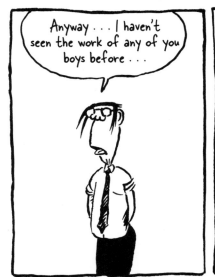

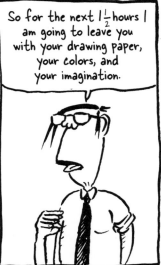

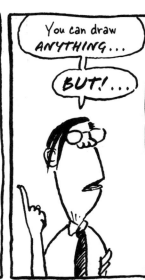

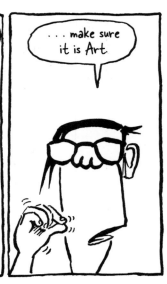

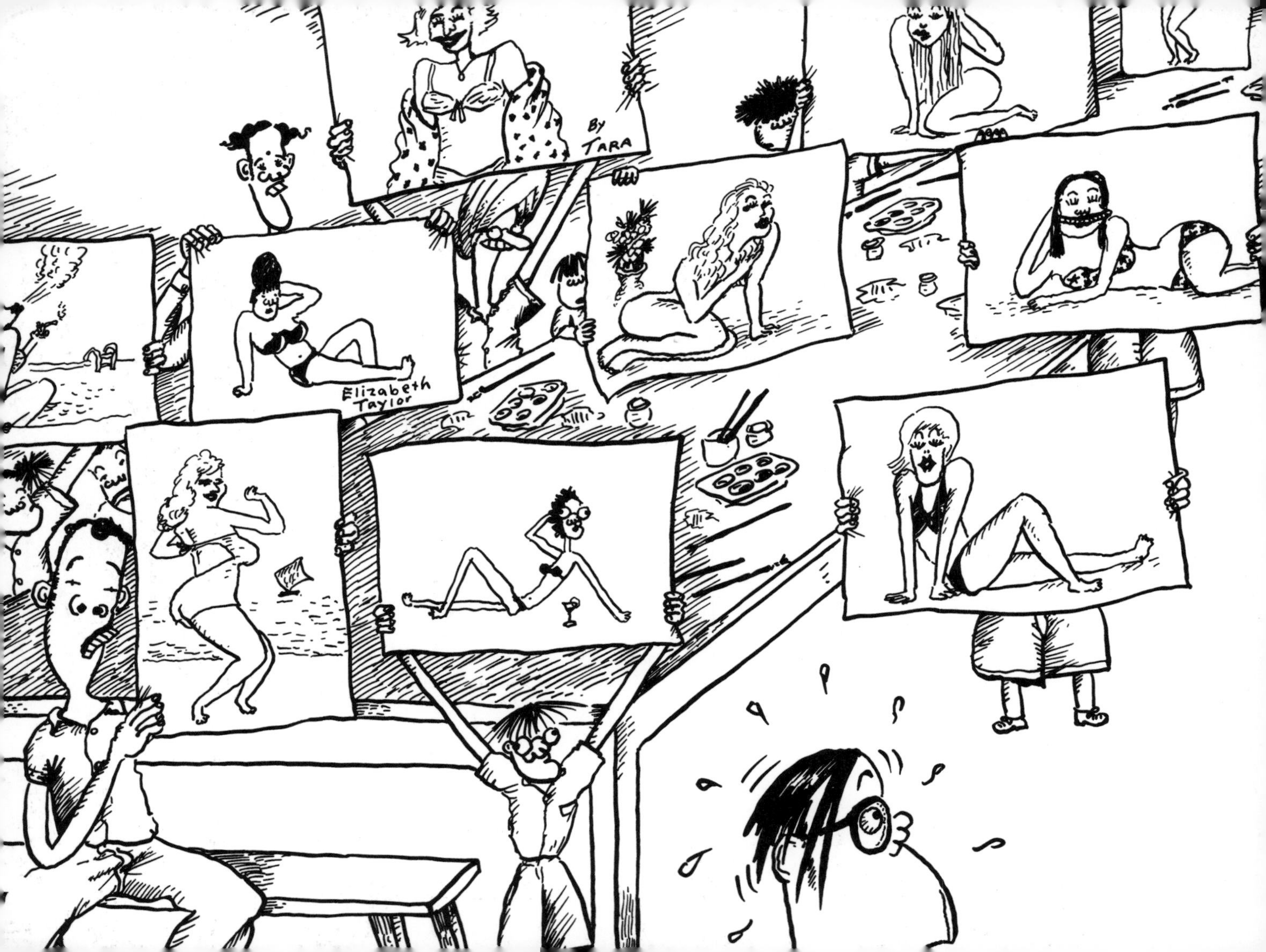

By TARA
Elizabeth Taylor

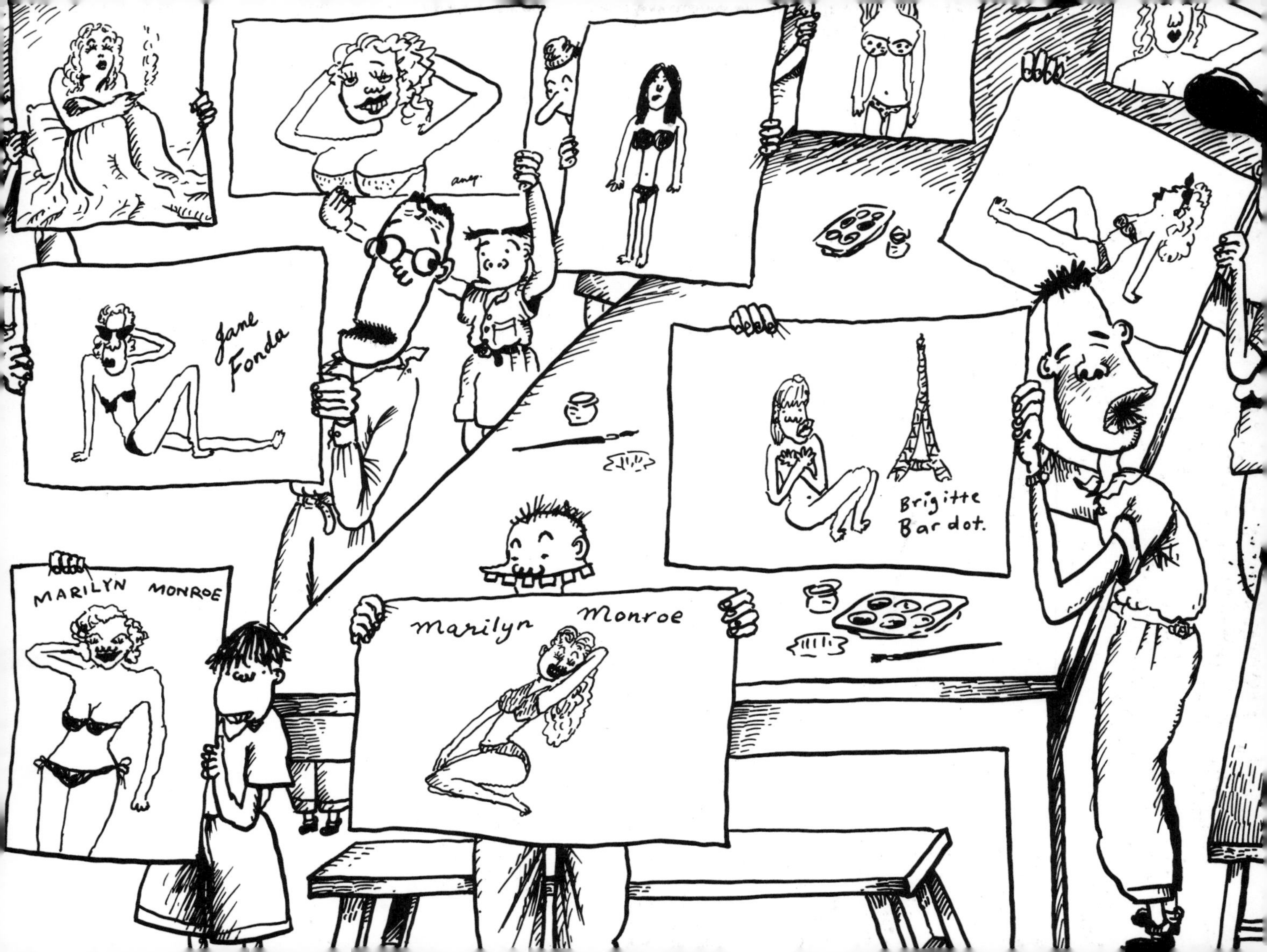
Jane Fonda
Brigitte Bardot.
MARILYN MONROE
Marilyn Monroe

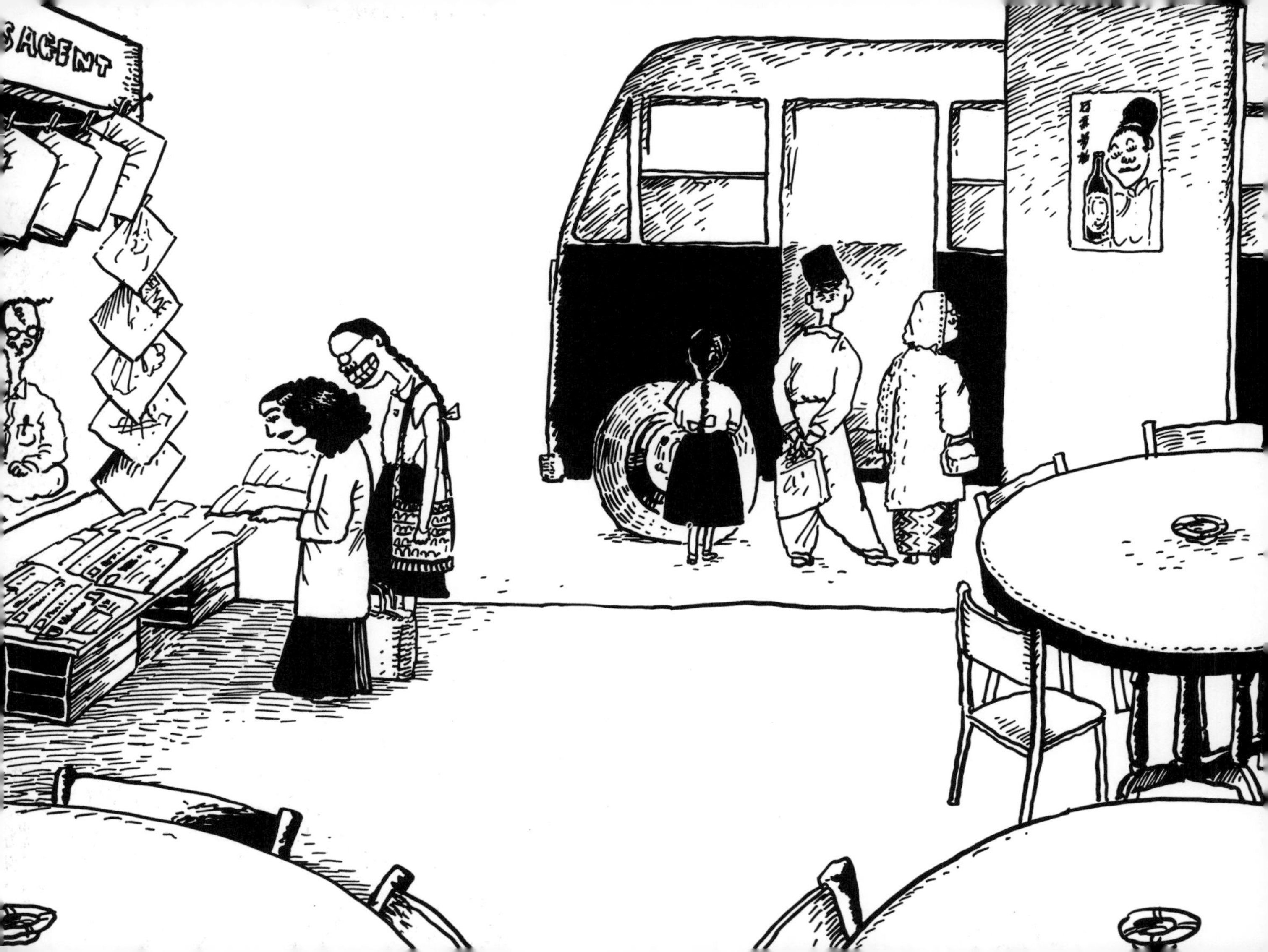
SAGENT

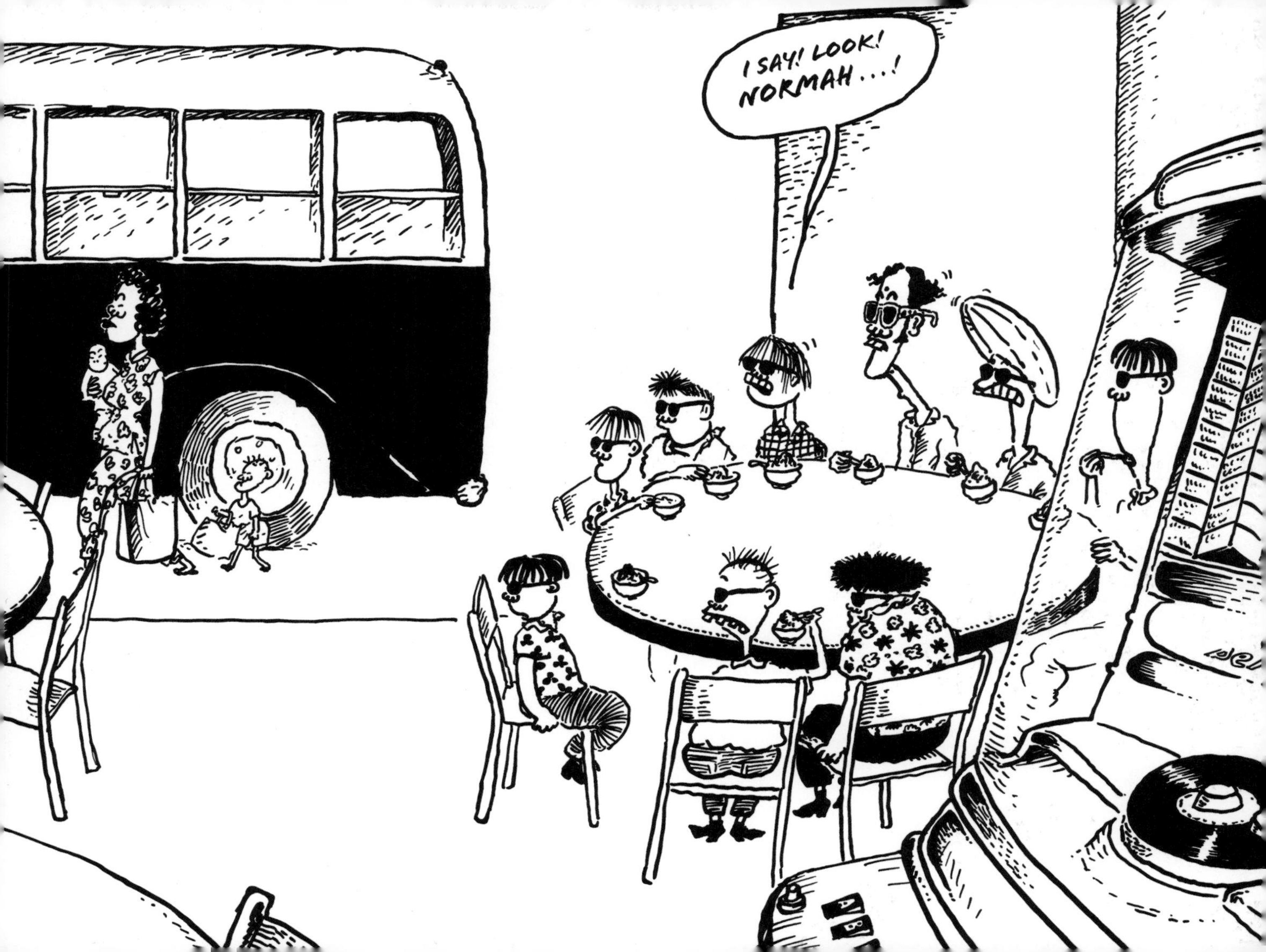
I SAY! LOOK! NORMAH...!

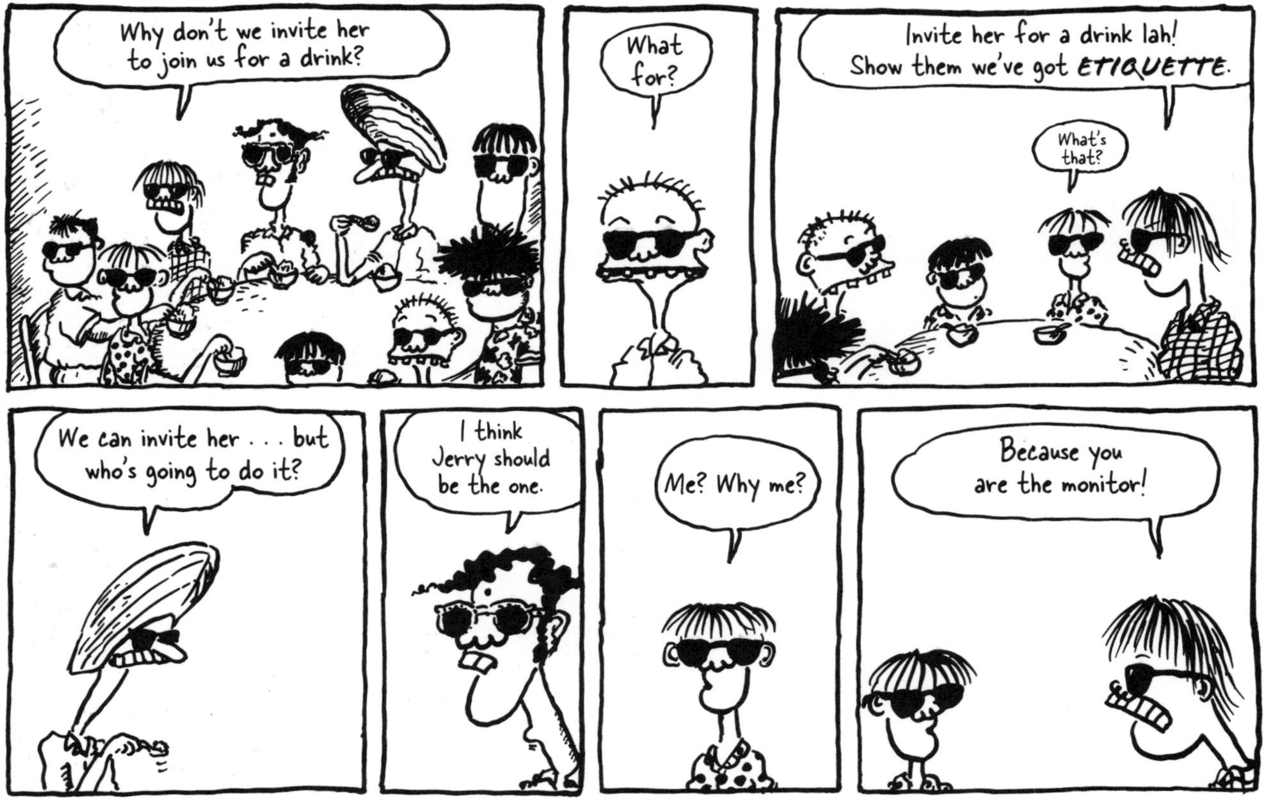
Why don't we invite her to join us for a drink?
What for?
Invite her for a drink lah! Show them we've got ETIQUETTE.
What's that?
We can invite her . . . but who's going to do it?
I think Jerry should be the one.
Me? Why me?
Because you are the monitor!

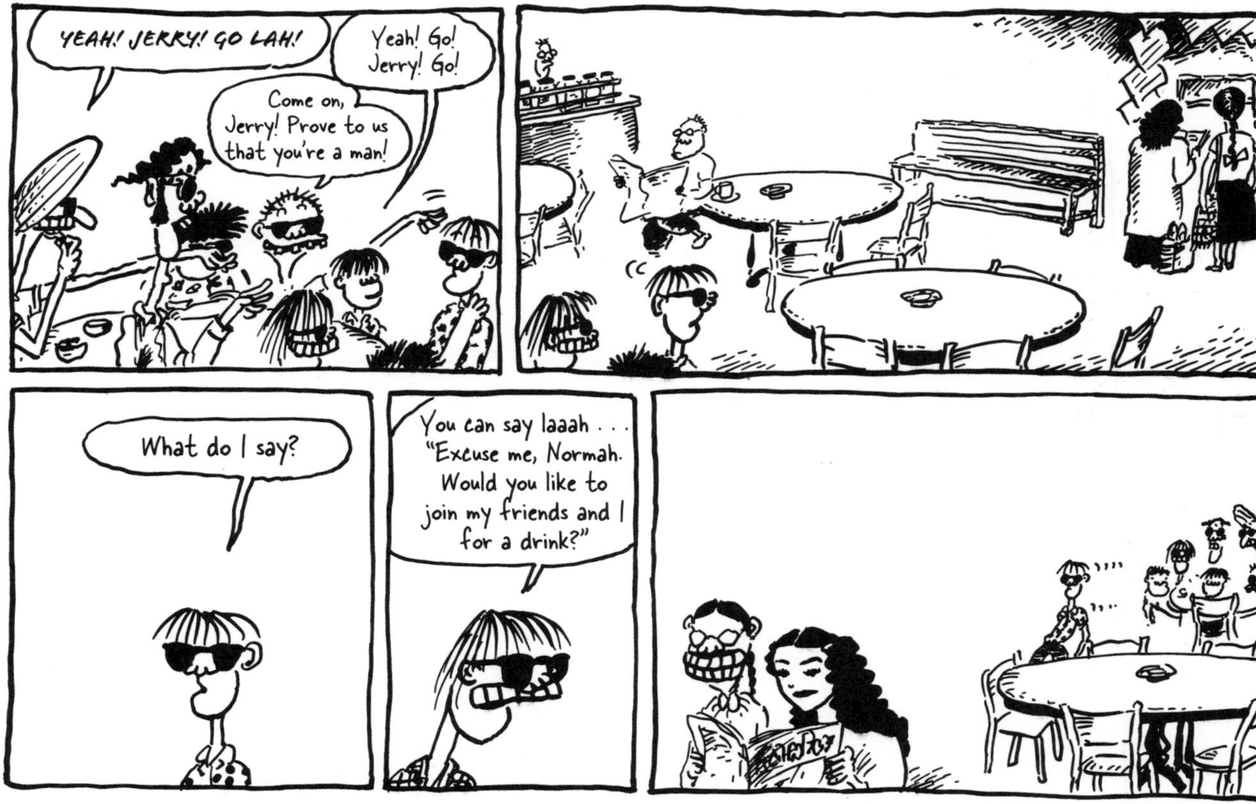
YEAH! JERRY! GO LAH!
Come on, Jerry! Prove to us that you're a man!
Yeah! Go! Jerry! Go!
What do I say?
You can say laaah . . . "Excuse me, Normah. Would you like to join my friends and I for a drink?"

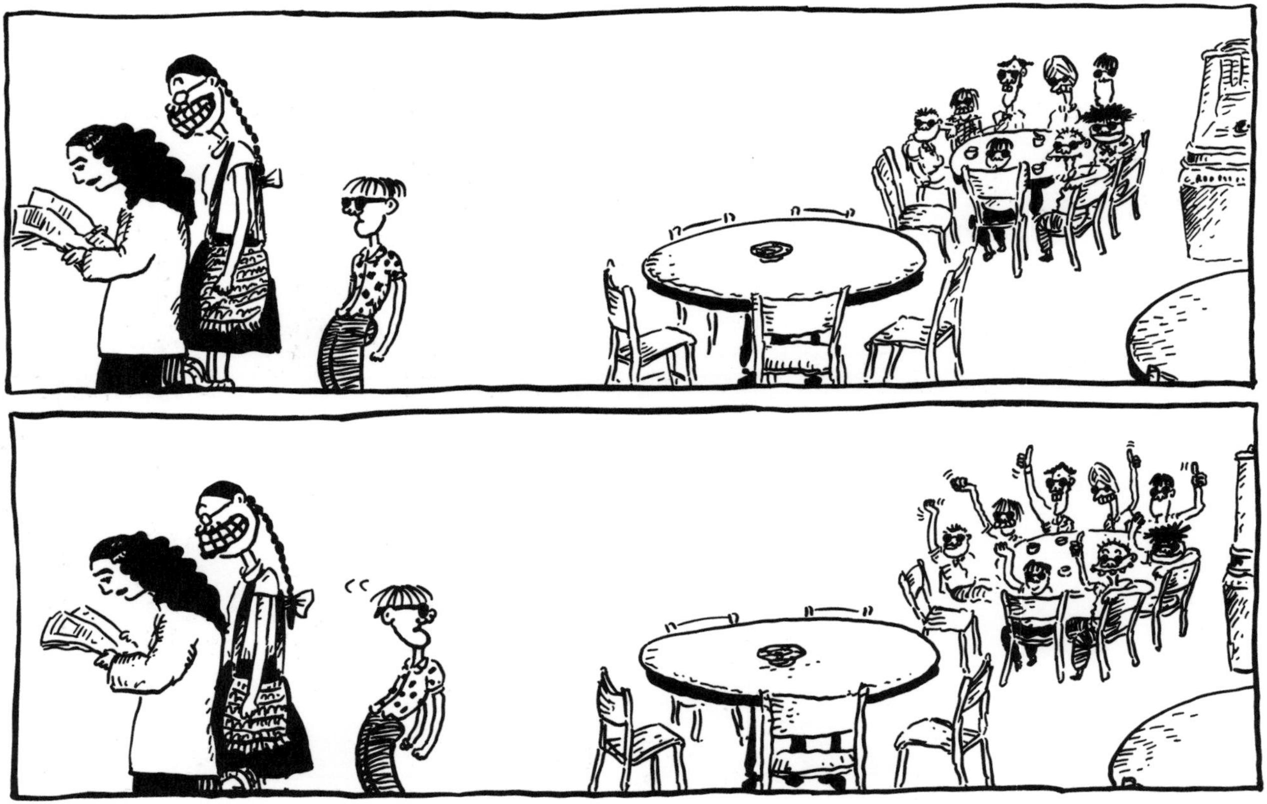

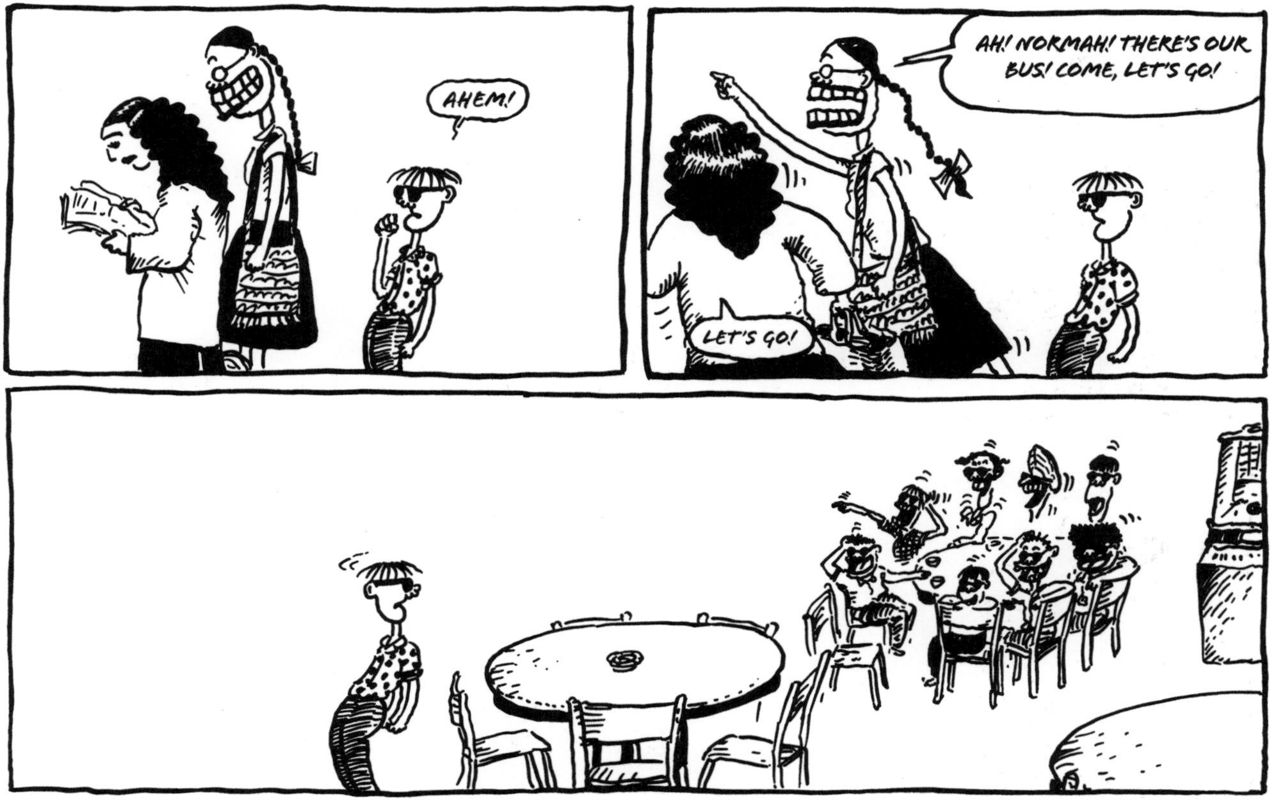
AHEM!
AH! NORMAH! THERE'S OUR BUS! COME, LET'S GO!
LET'S GO!

Extramural activities.

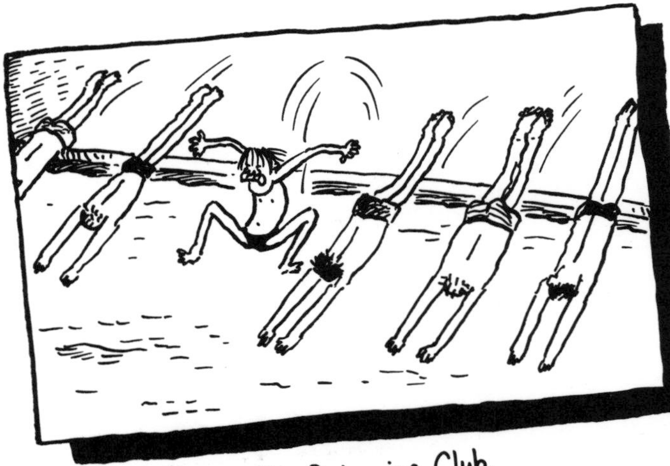

Frankie joined the Swimming Club.

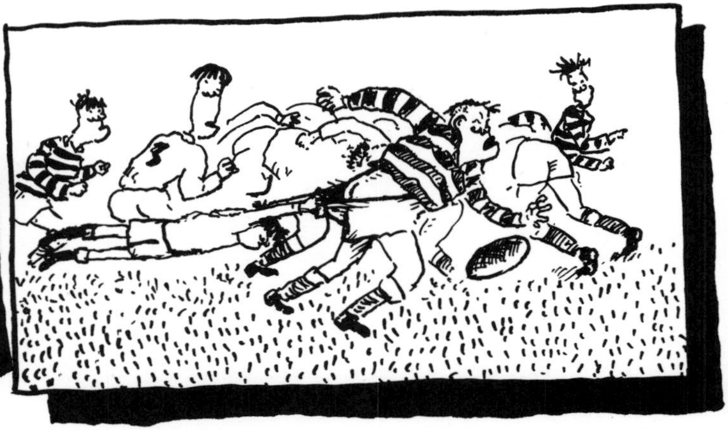

The T. R. Trio was on the school rugby team.

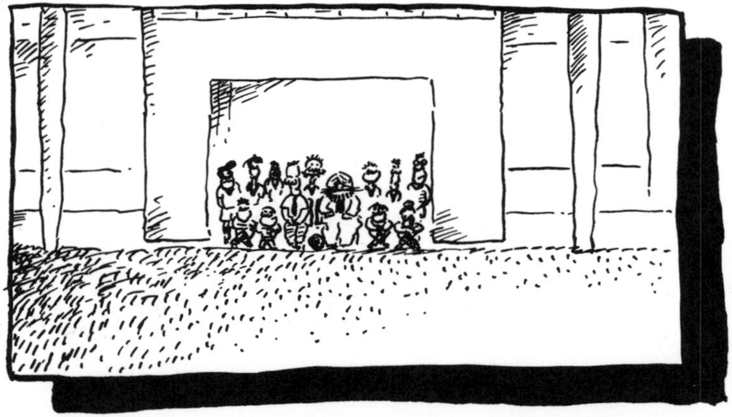

Mat Sham was in the School's 2nd eleven.

Our monitor was the secretary of the Butterfly-Catching Society.

Tara Singh was an active member of the Literary and Debating Society.

YES!

OUR SCHOOL SHOULD BE COEDUCATIONAL.

Lingham and I joined the school cadet band. He played the cymbals and I was a flutist.

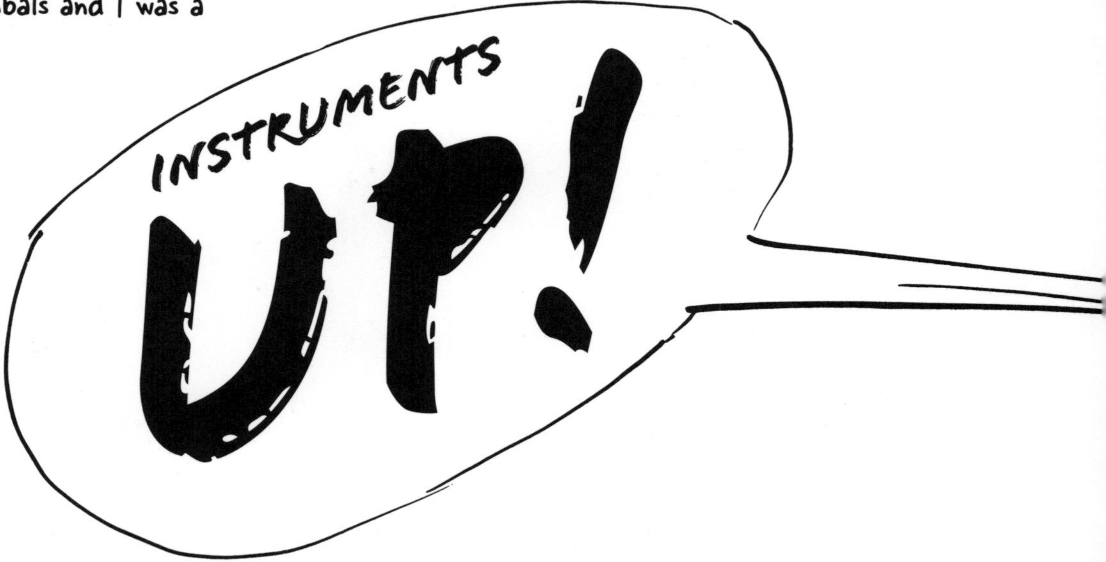
INSTRUMENTS UP!

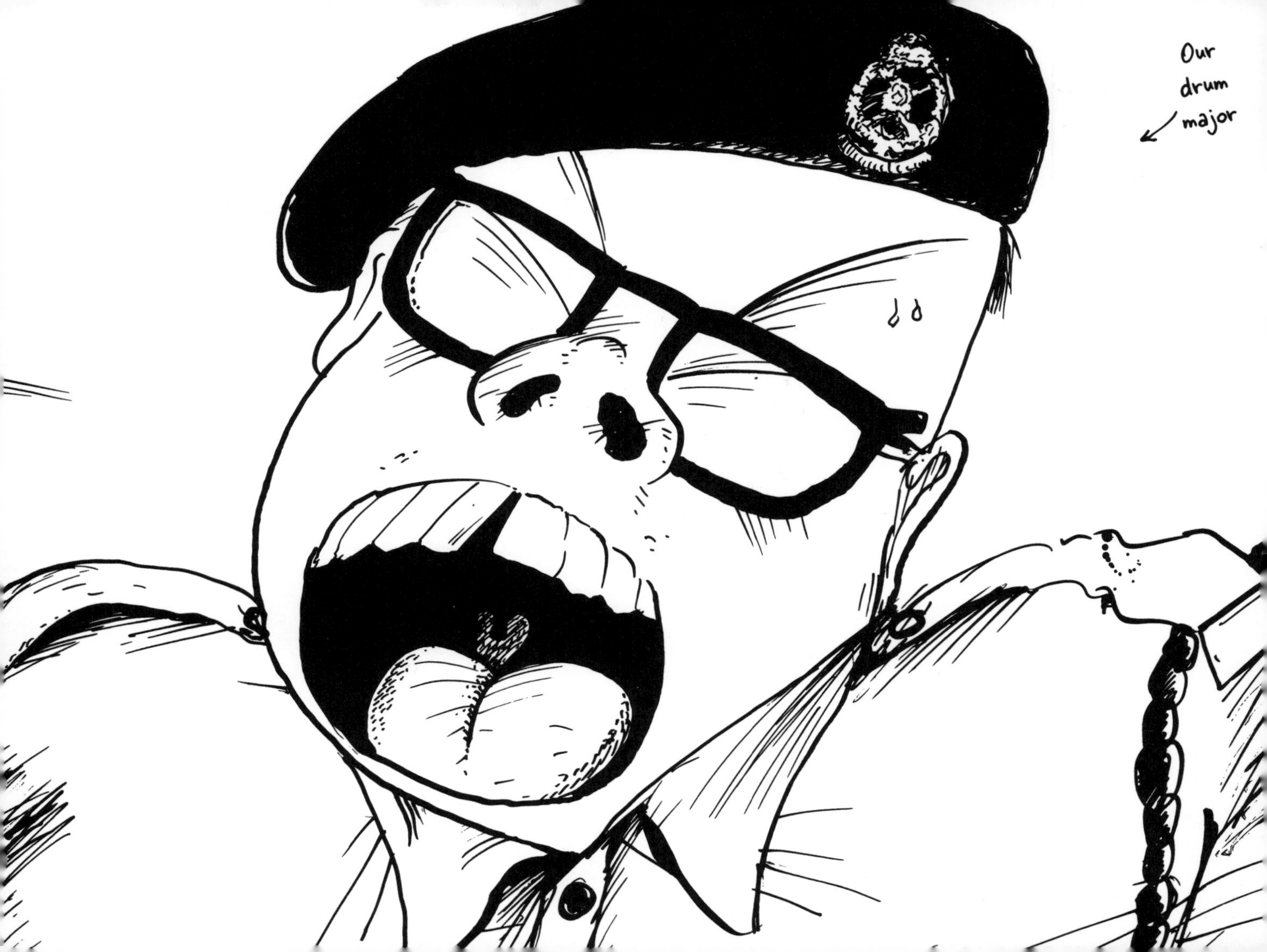
Our
drum
major

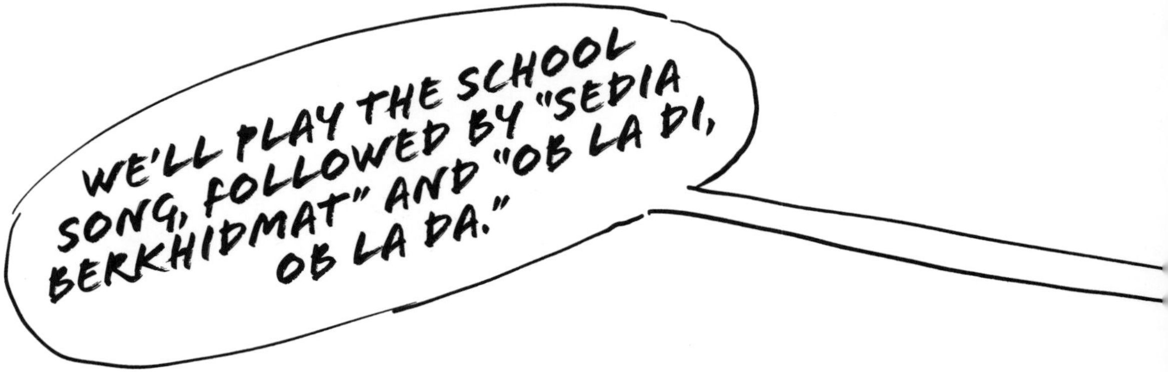
WE'LL PLAY THE SCHOOL SONG, FOLLOWED BY "SEDIA BERKHIDMAT" AND "OB LA DI, OB LA DA."

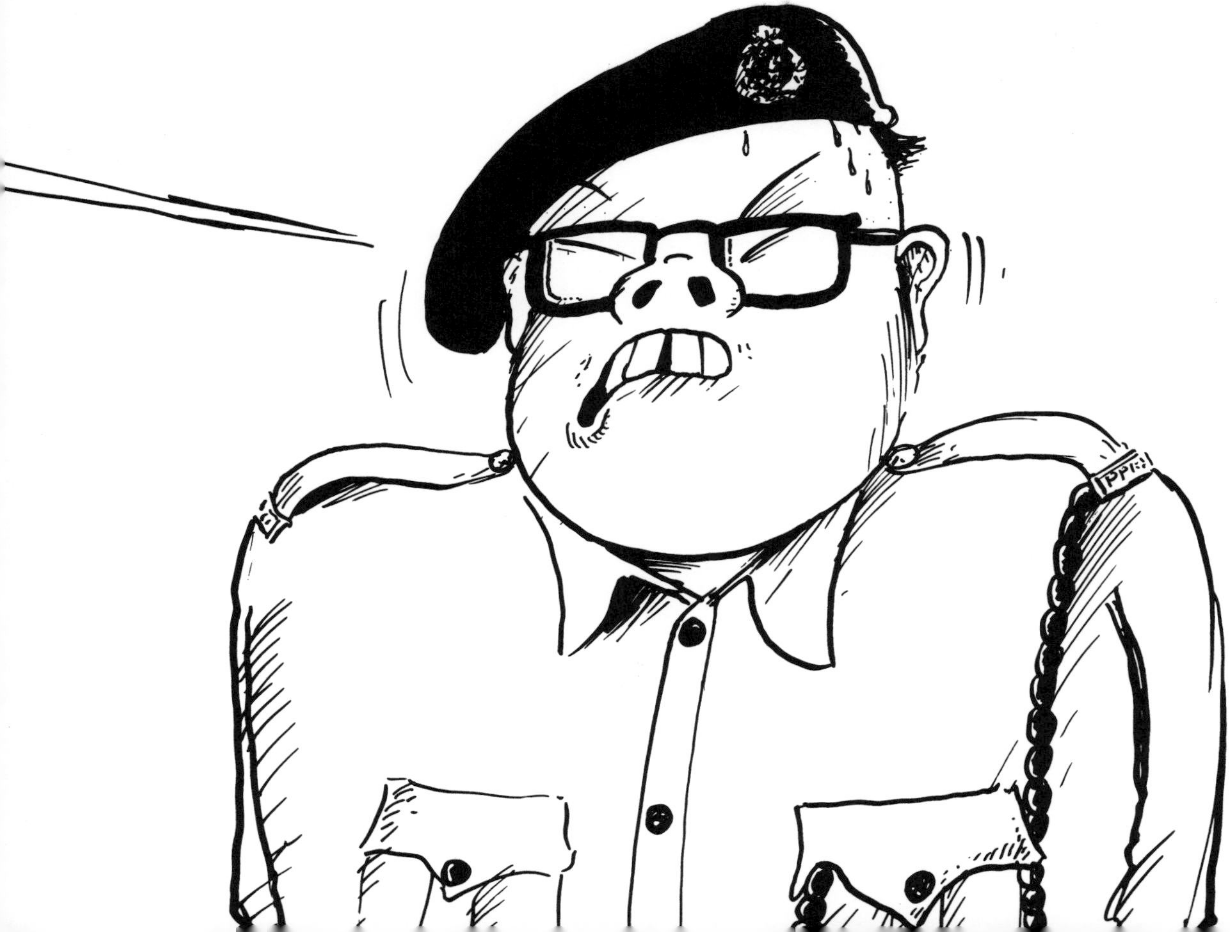

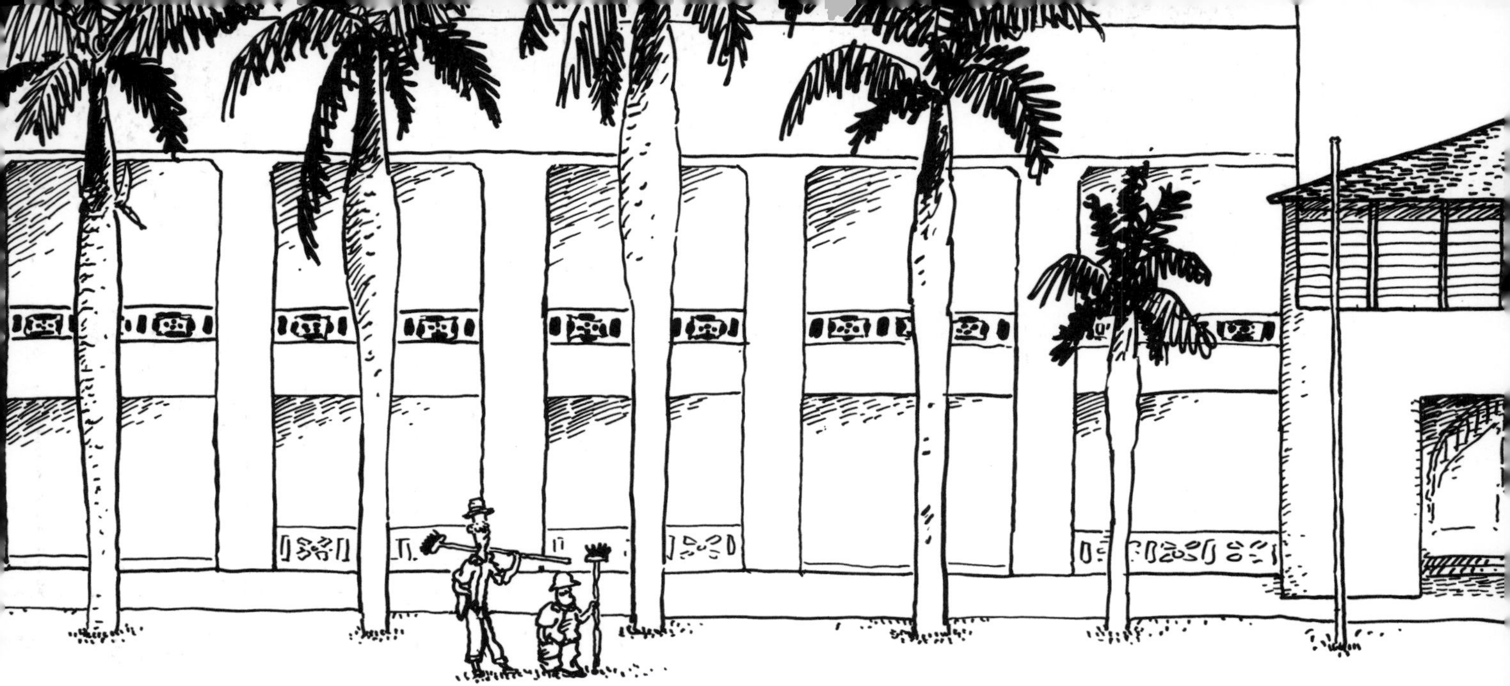

It was not a very big band, actually . . .

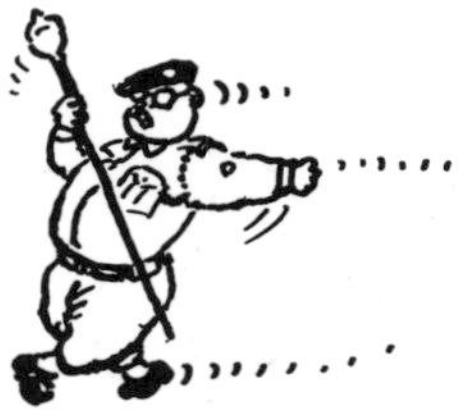

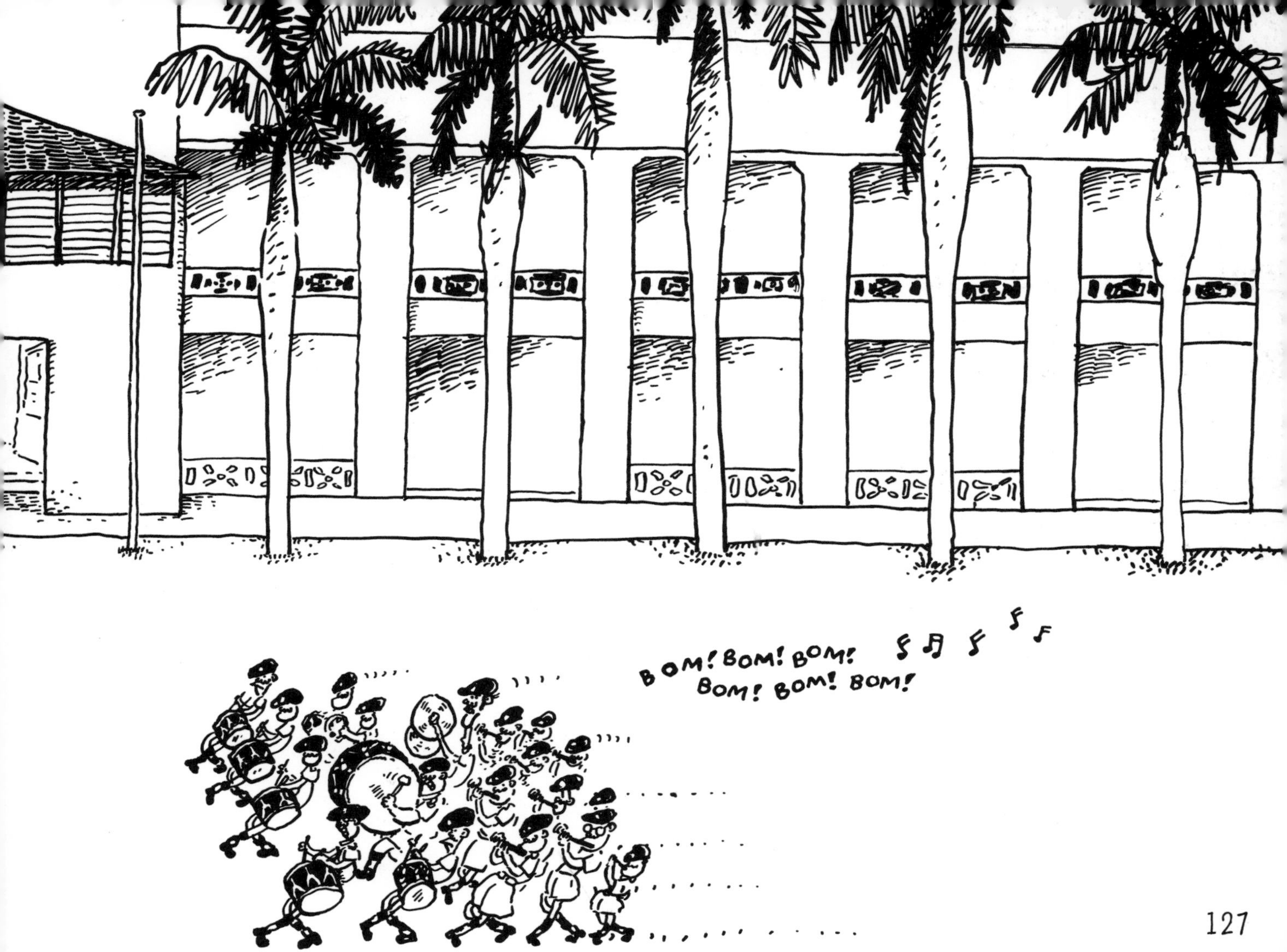
BOM! BOM! BOM!
BOM! BOM! BOM!

It consisted of eleven flutists, six drummers, one bass drummer, one cymbalist, and one tambourine player.

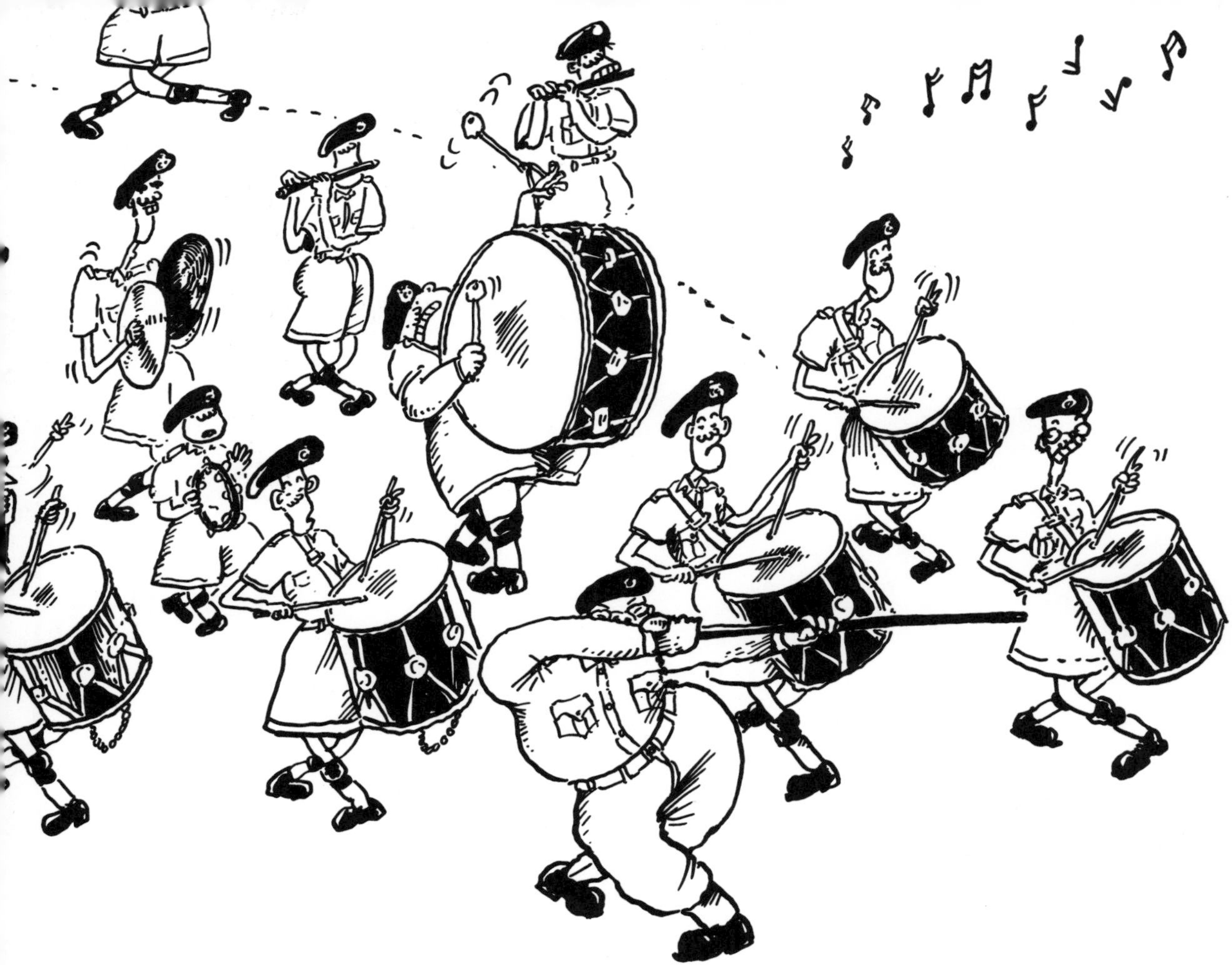

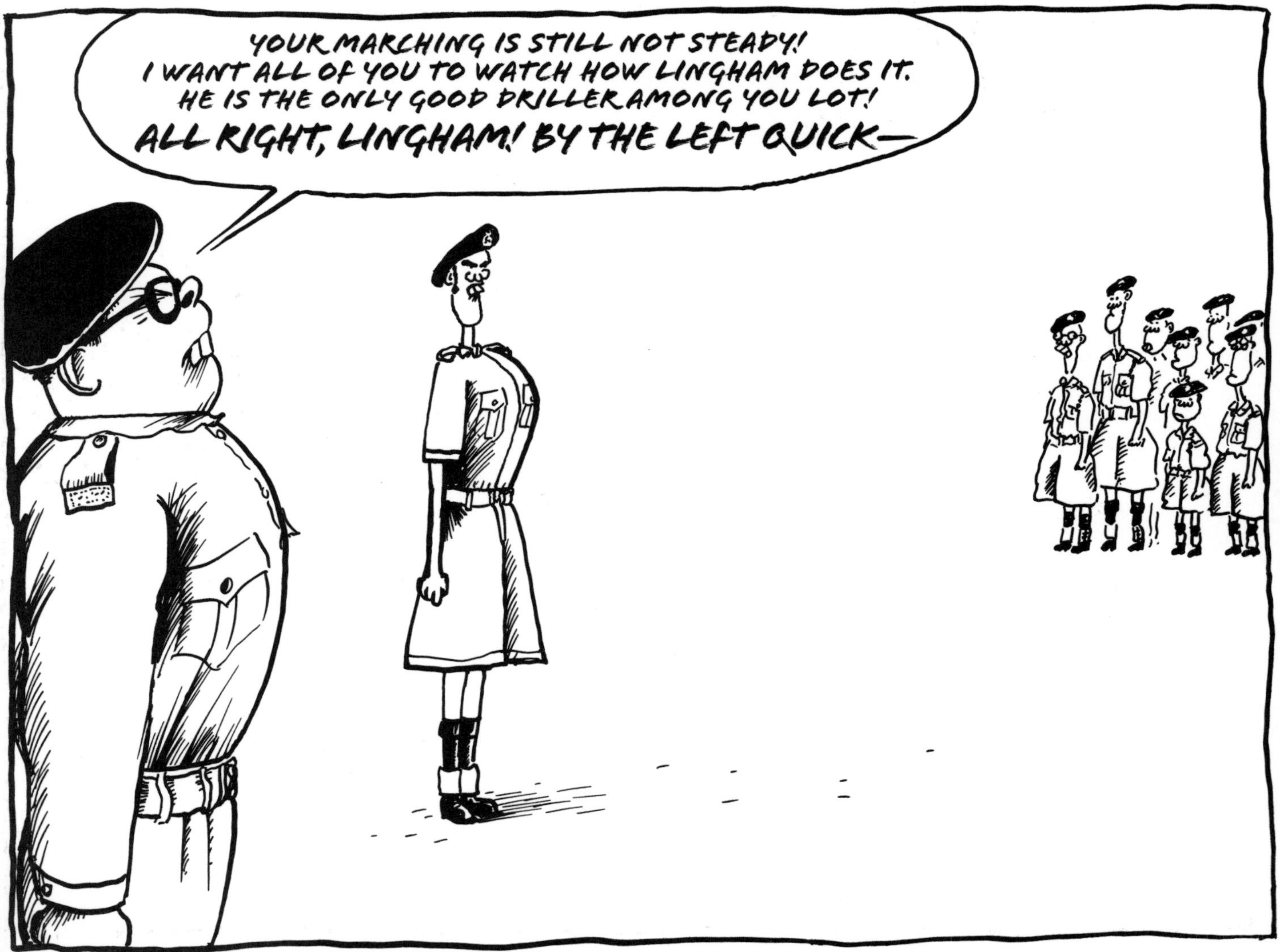
YOUR MARCHING IS STILL NOT STEADY! I WANT ALL OF YOU TO WATCH HOW LINGHAM DOES IT. HE IS THE ONLY GOOD DRILLER AMONG YOU LOT! ALL RIGHT, LINGHAM! BY THE LEFT QUICK—

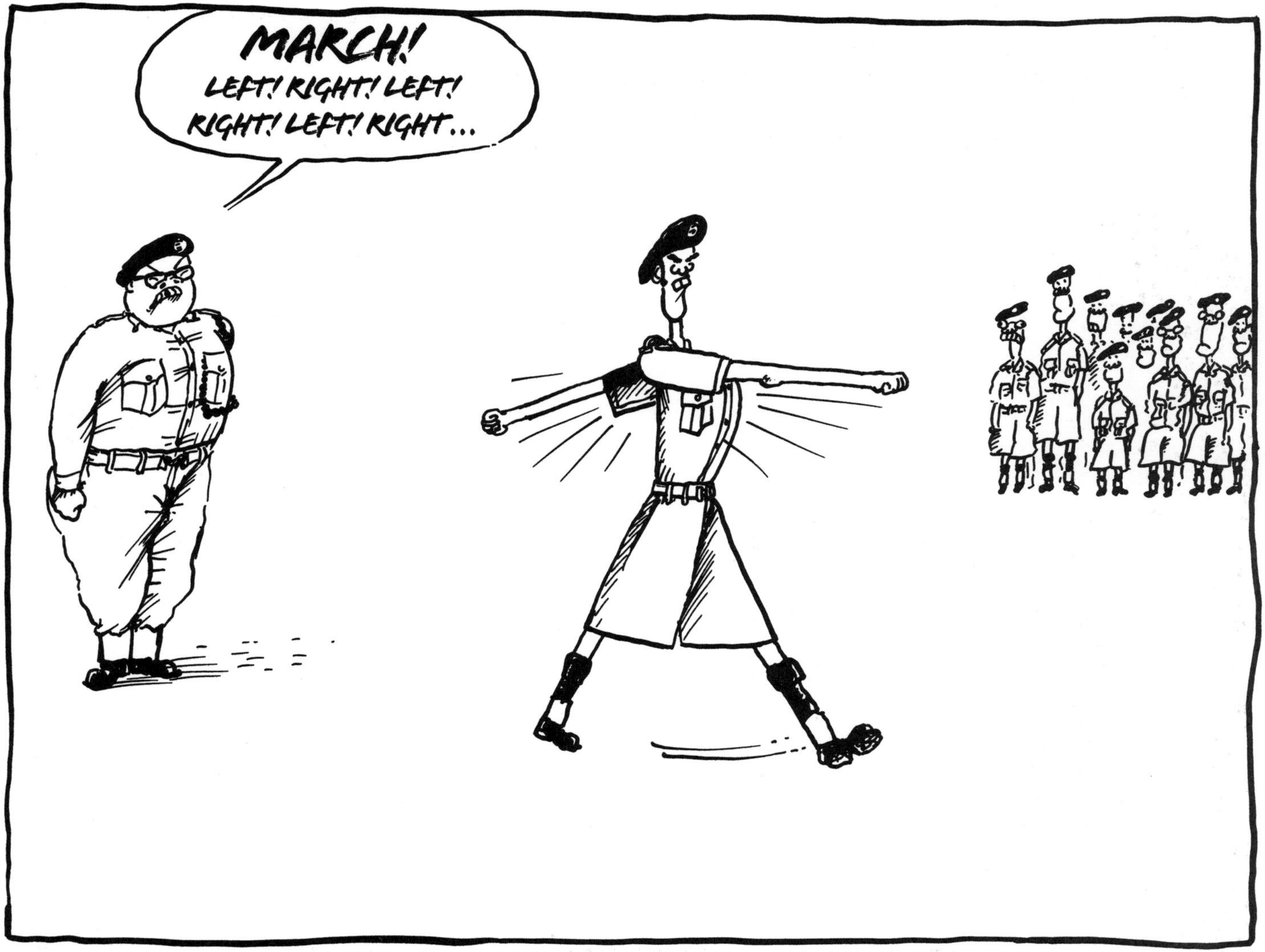
MARCH!
LEFT! RIGHT! LEFT!
RIGHT! LEFT! RIGHT...

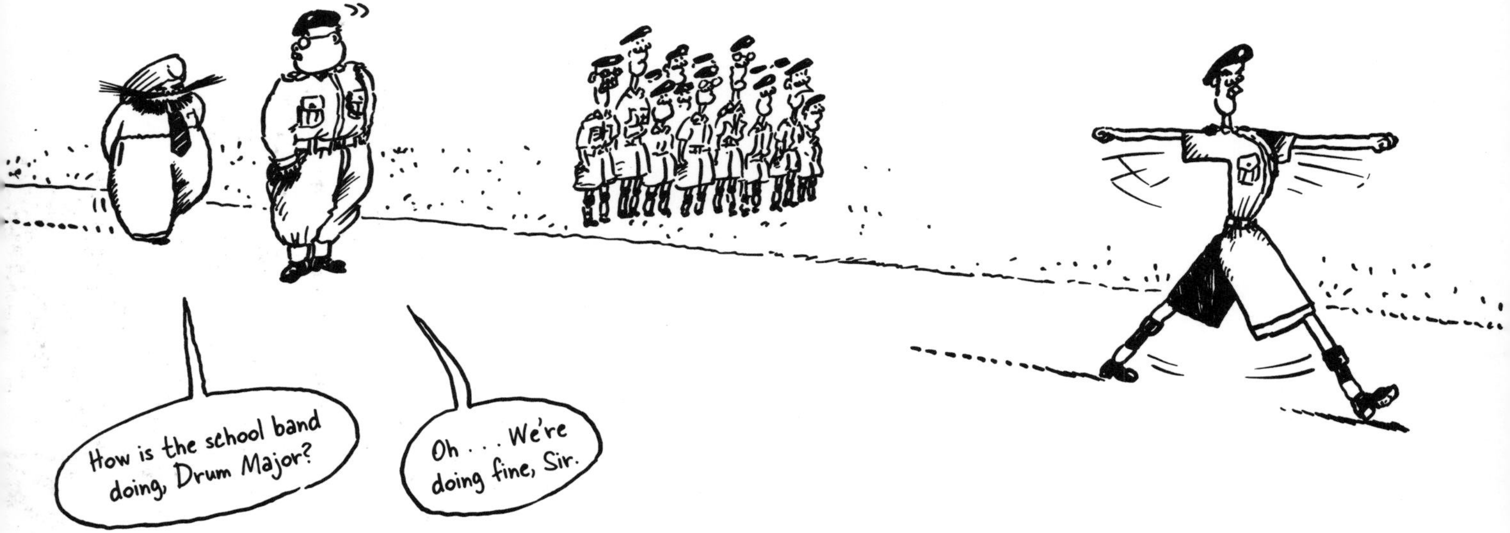
How is the school band doing, Drum Major?
Oh . . . We're doing fine, Sir.

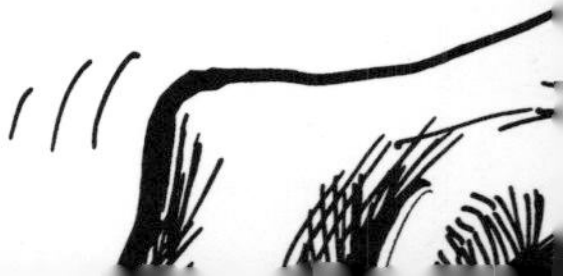

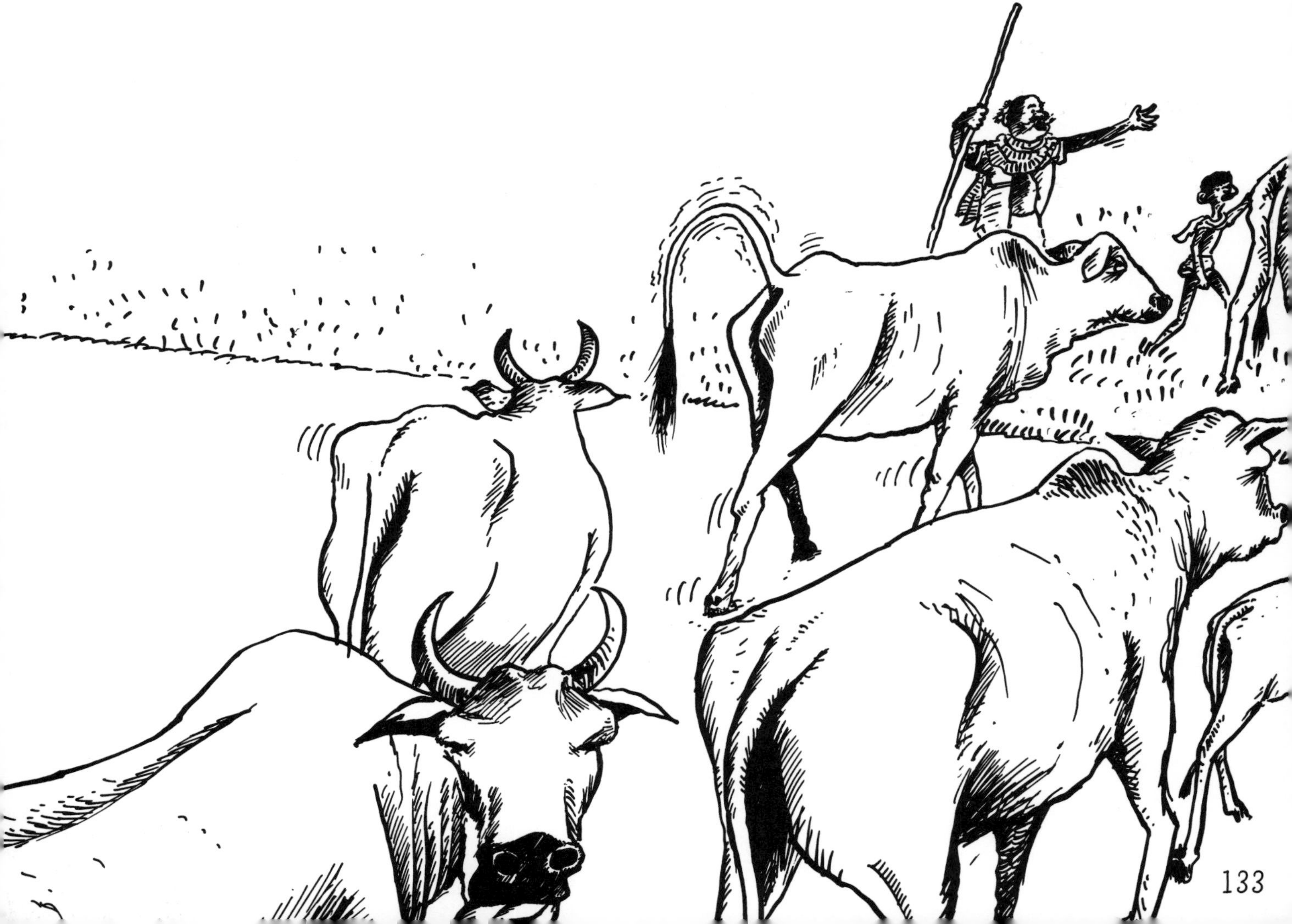

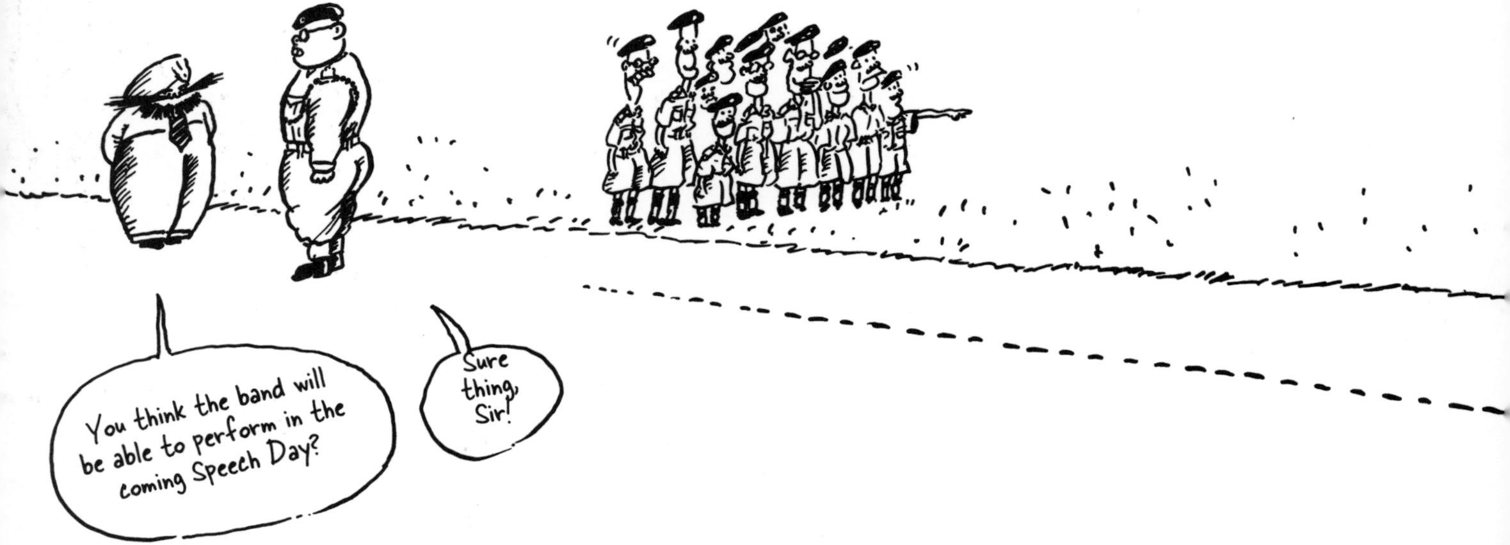
You think the band will be able to perform in the coming Speech Day?
Sure thing, Sir!

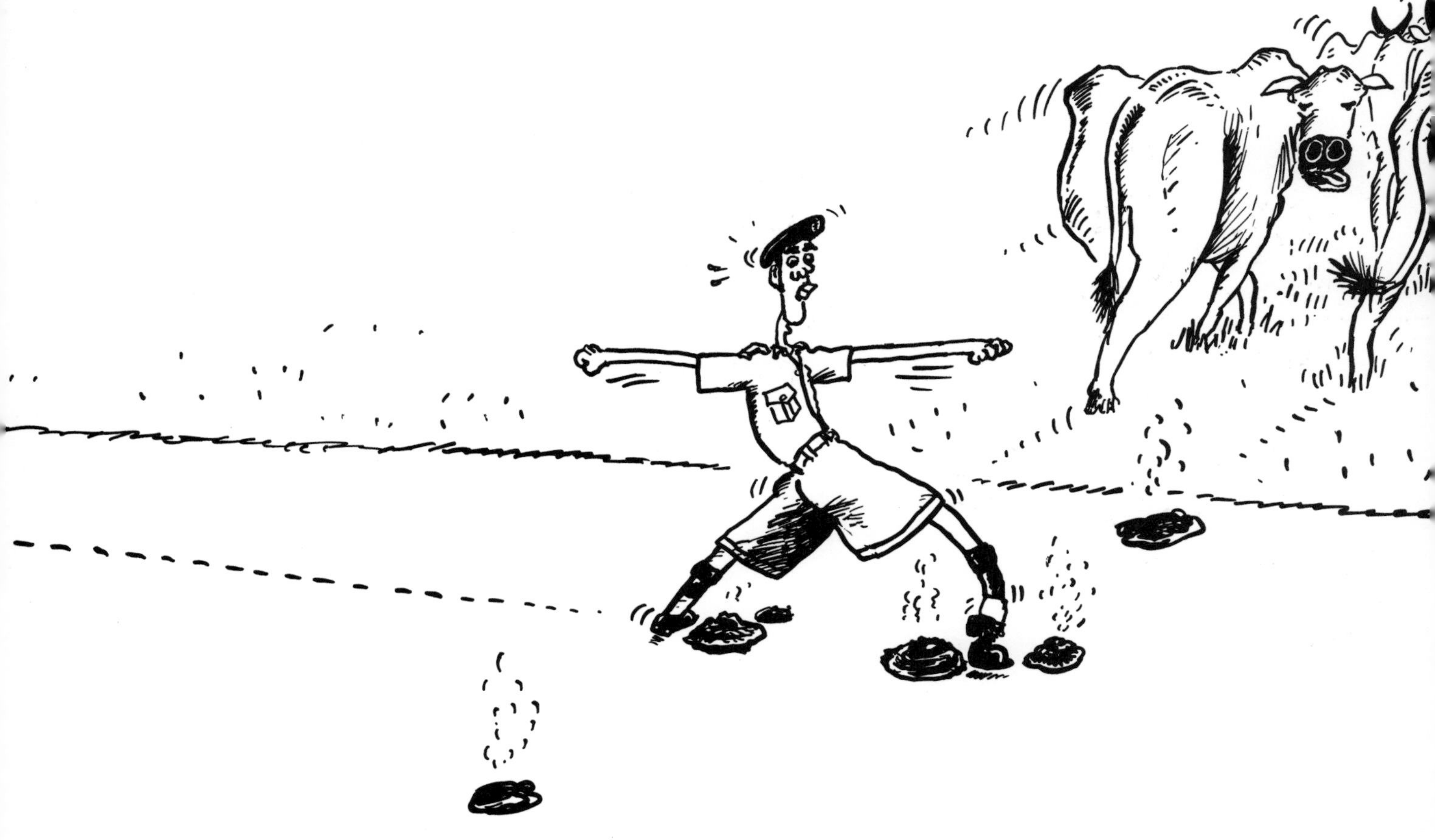

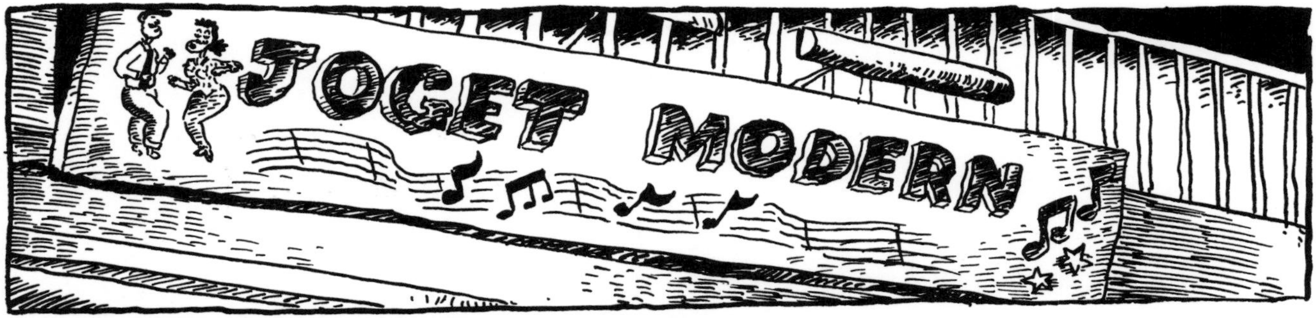
JOGET MODERN

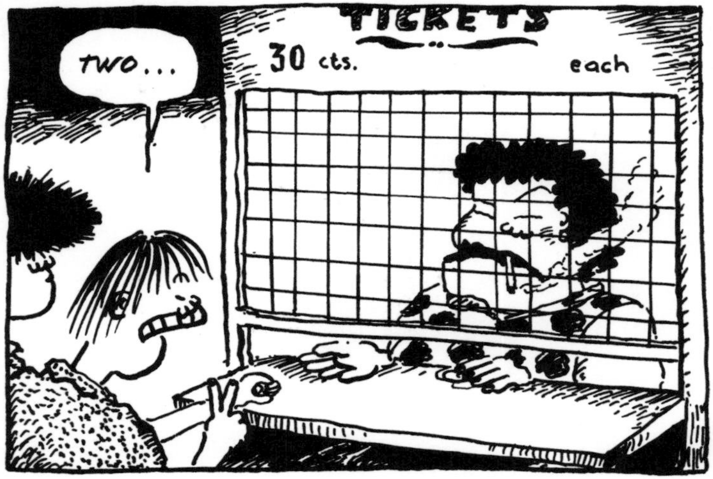
TICKETS
30 cts. each
TWO...

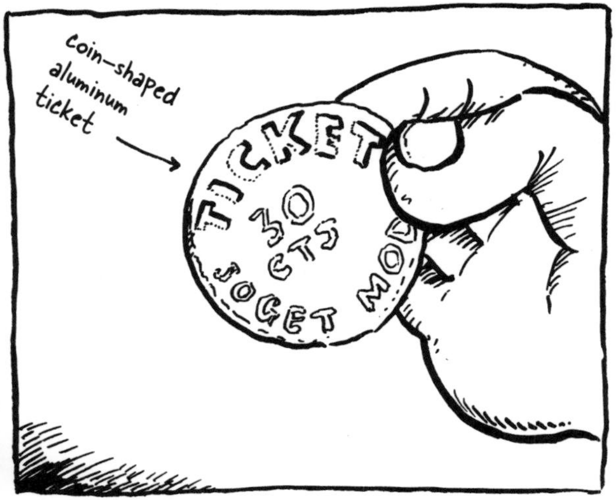
coin-shaped aluminum ticket
TICKET 30 CTS JOGET MOD

ROUND 26...
OFF-BEAT CHA-CHA!
O.K., EVERYBODY...

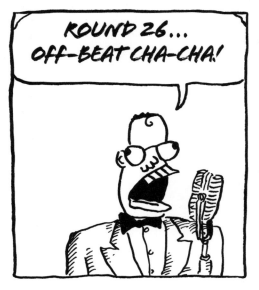

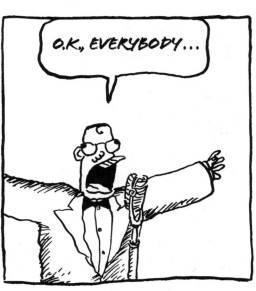

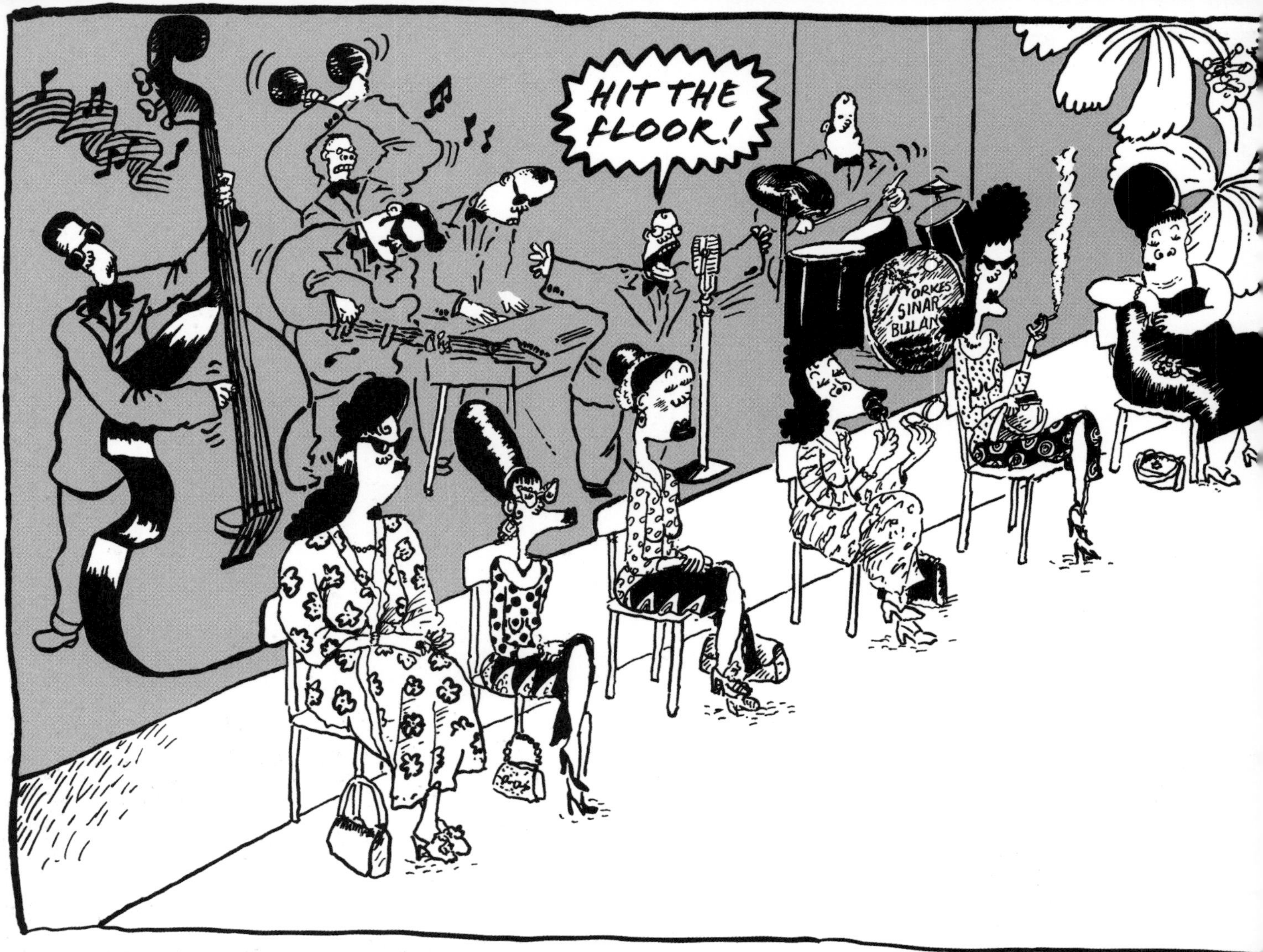
HIT THE FLOOR!
ORKES SINAR BULAN

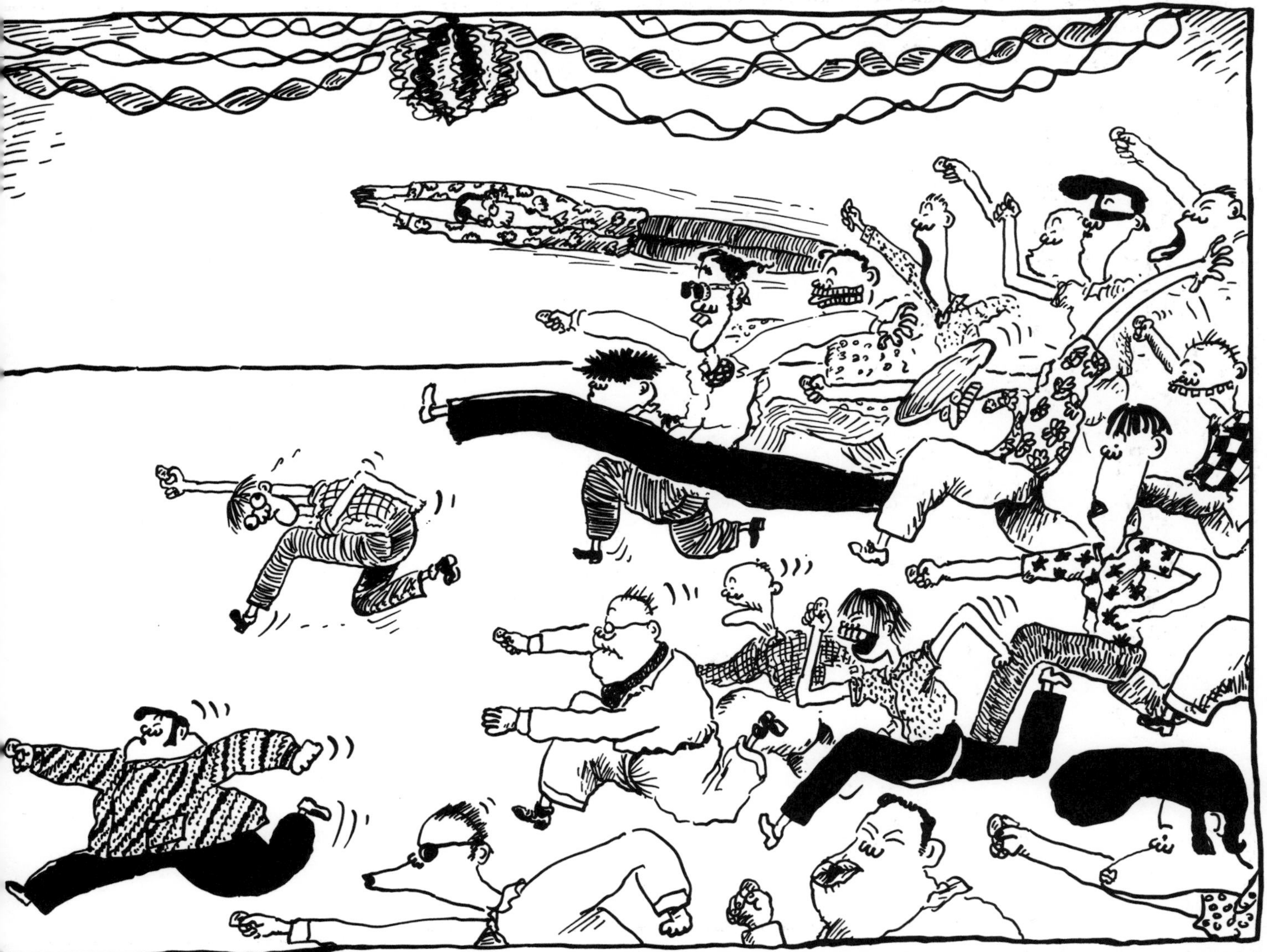

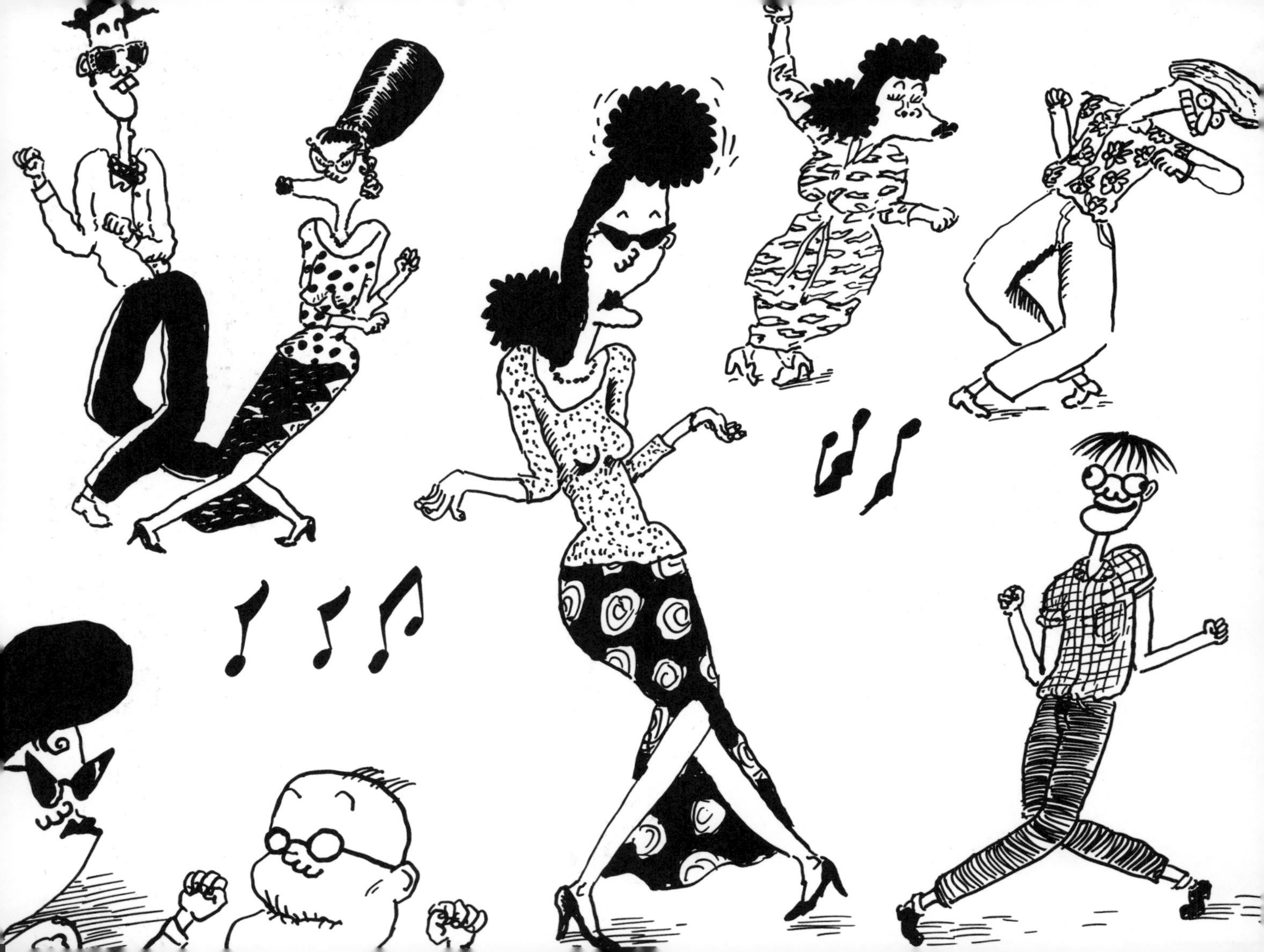

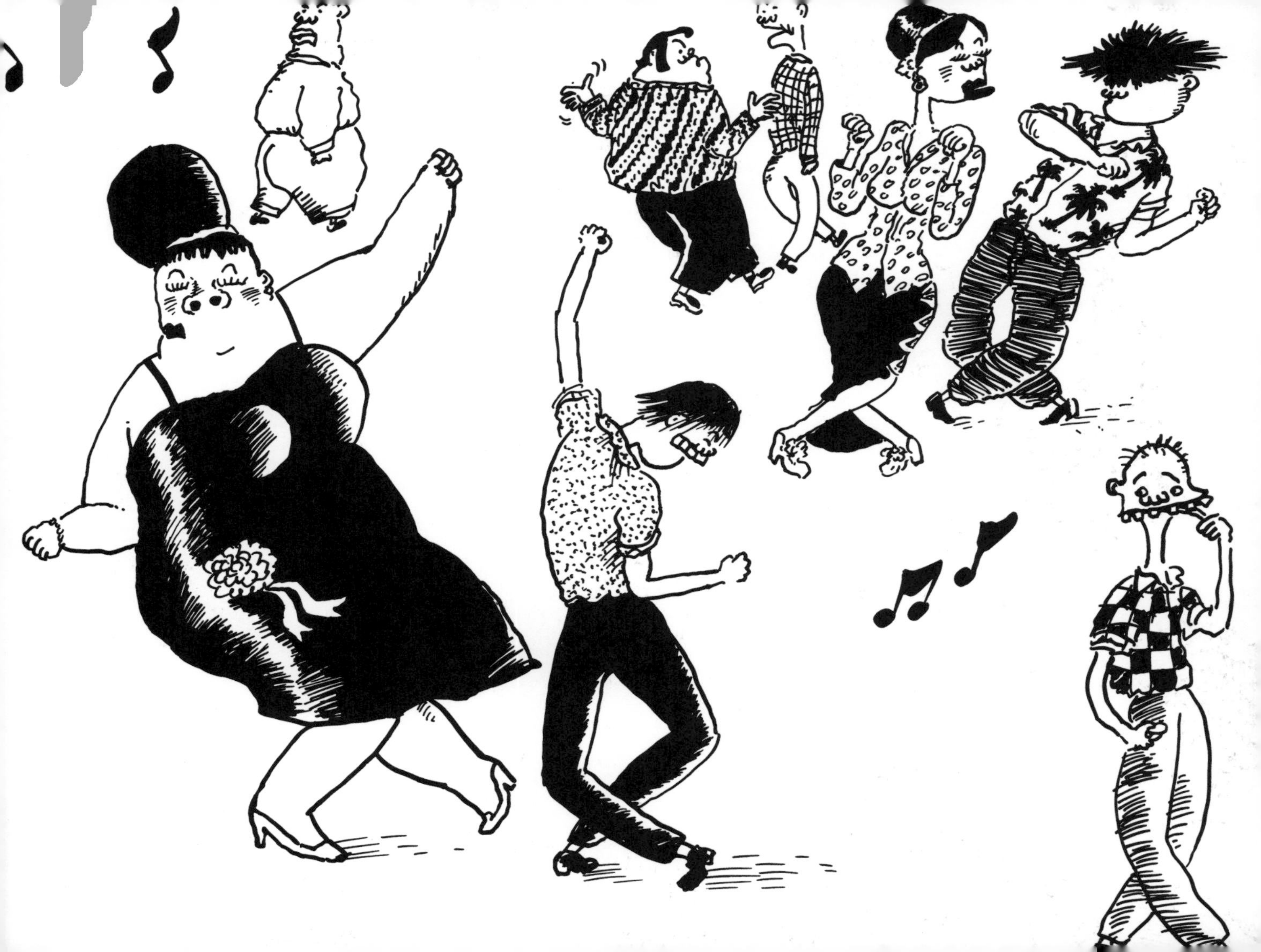

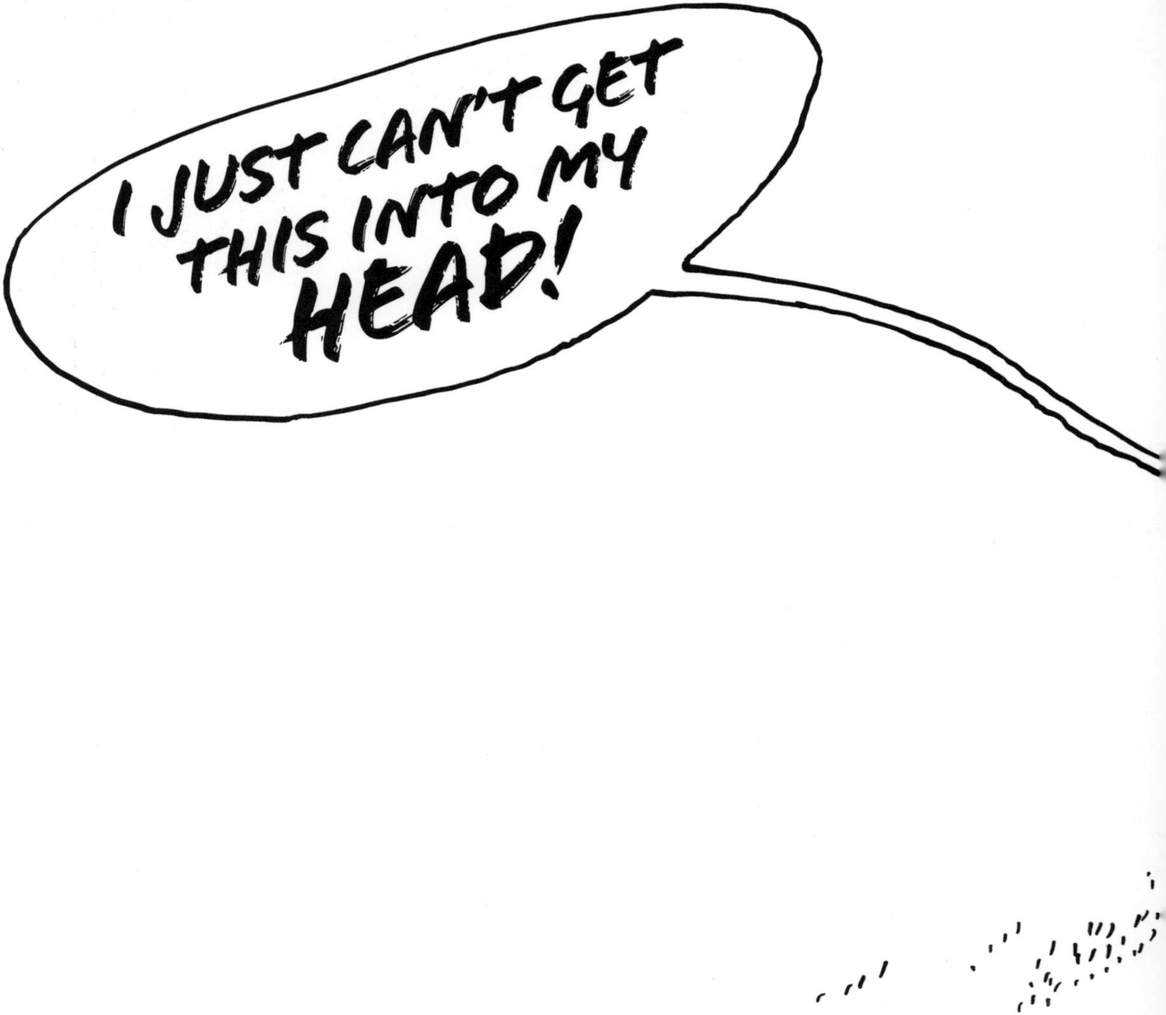
I JUST CAN'T GET THIS INTO MY HEAD!

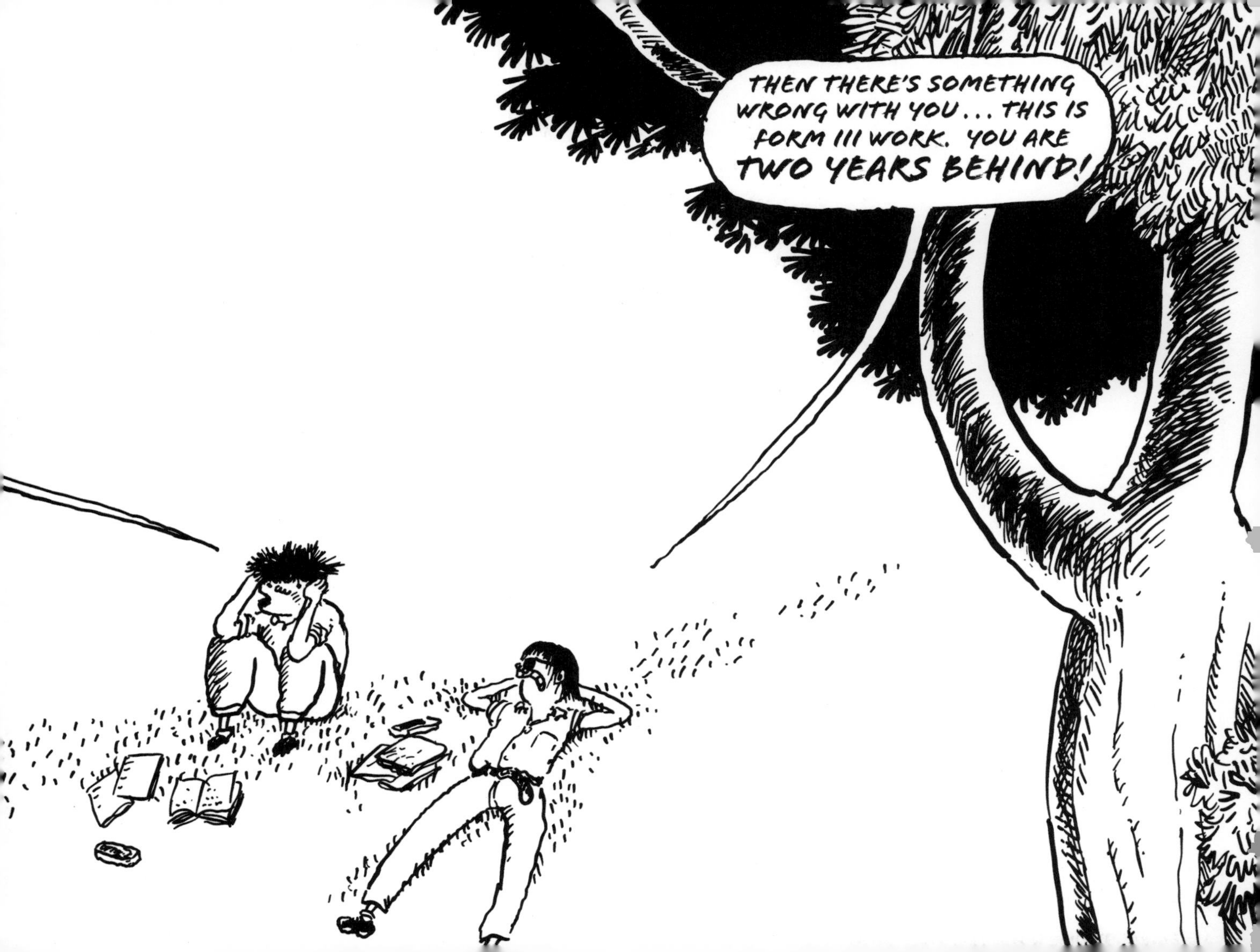
THEN THERE'S SOMETHING WRONG WITH YOU . . . THIS IS FORM III WORK. YOU ARE TWO YEARS BEHIND!

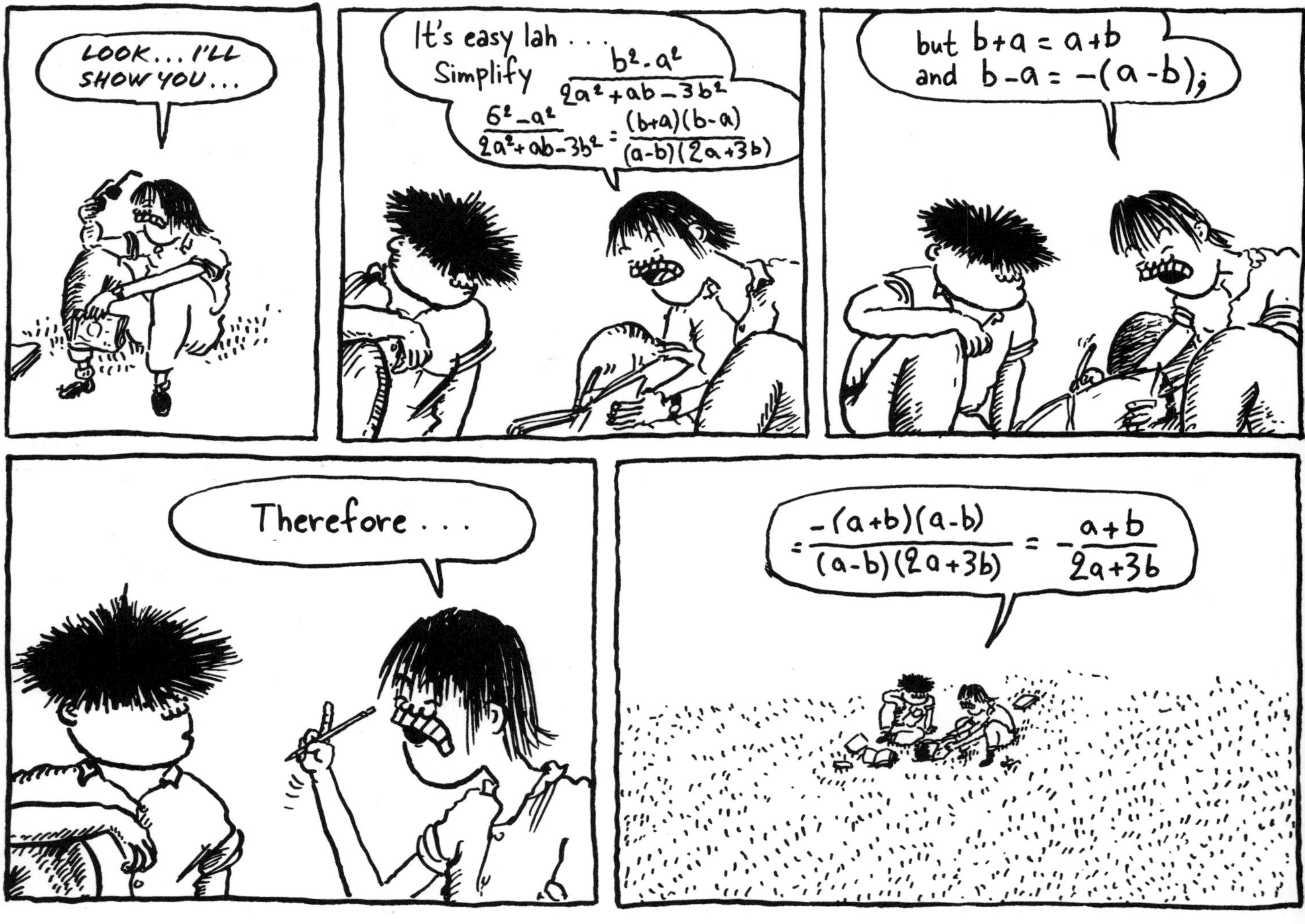
LOOK... I'LL SHOW YOU...
It's easy lah . . . Simplify $\frac{b^2 - a^2}{2a^2 + ab - 3b^2}$
$\frac{6^2 - a^2}{2a^2 + ab - 3b^2} = \frac{(b+a)(b-a)}{(a-b)(2a+3b)}$
but $b + a = a + b$
and $b - a = -(a - b)$;
Therefore . . .
$= \frac{-(a+b)(a-b)}{(a-b)(2a+3b)} = -\frac{a+b}{2a+3b}$

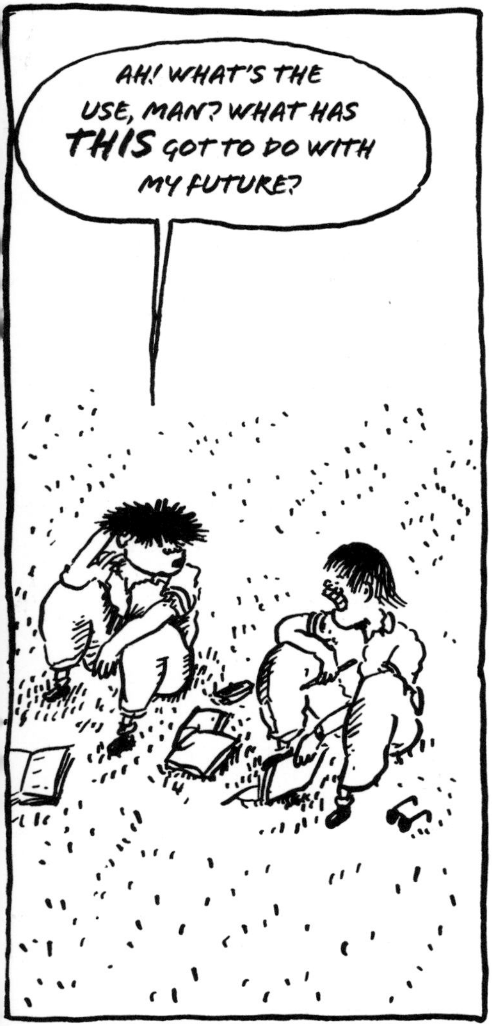
AH! WHAT'S THE USE, MAN? WHAT HAS **THIS** GOT TO DO WITH MY FUTURE?

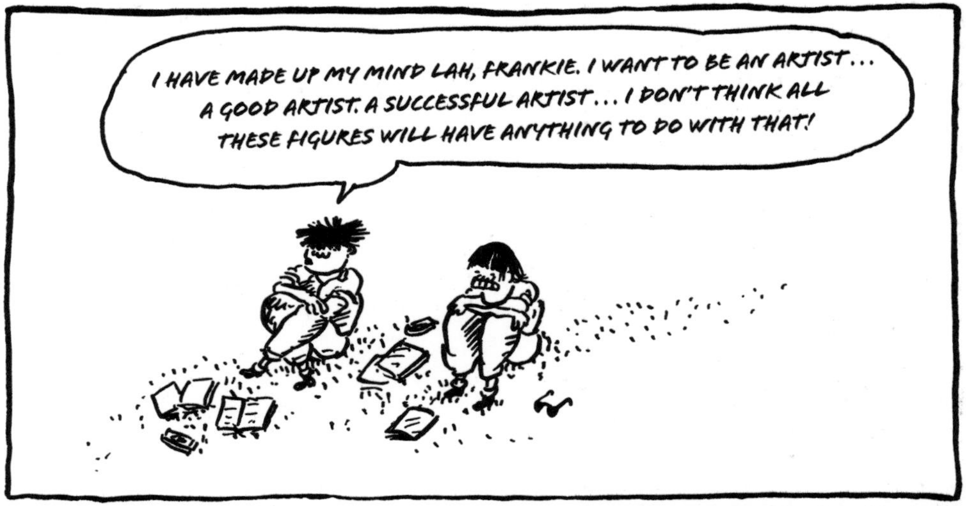
I HAVE MADE UP MY MIND LAH, FRANKIE. I WANT TO BE AN ARTIST... A GOOD ARTIST. A SUCCESSFUL ARTIST... I DON'T THINK ALL THESE FIGURES WILL HAVE ANYTHING TO DO WITH THAT!

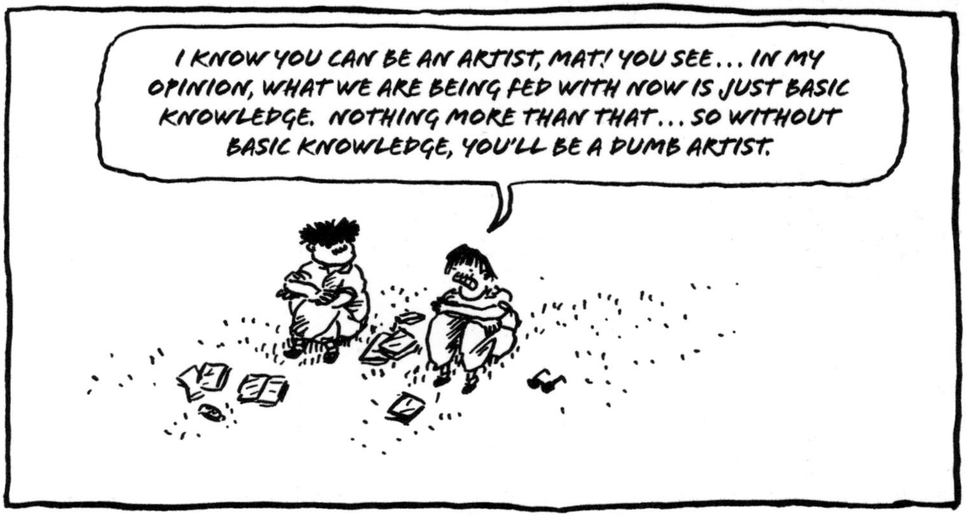
I KNOW YOU CAN BE AN ARTIST, MAT! YOU SEE... IN MY OPINION, WHAT WE ARE BEING FED WITH NOW IS JUST BASIC KNOWLEDGE. NOTHING MORE THAN THAT... SO WITHOUT BASIC KNOWLEDGE, YOU'LL BE A DUMB ARTIST.

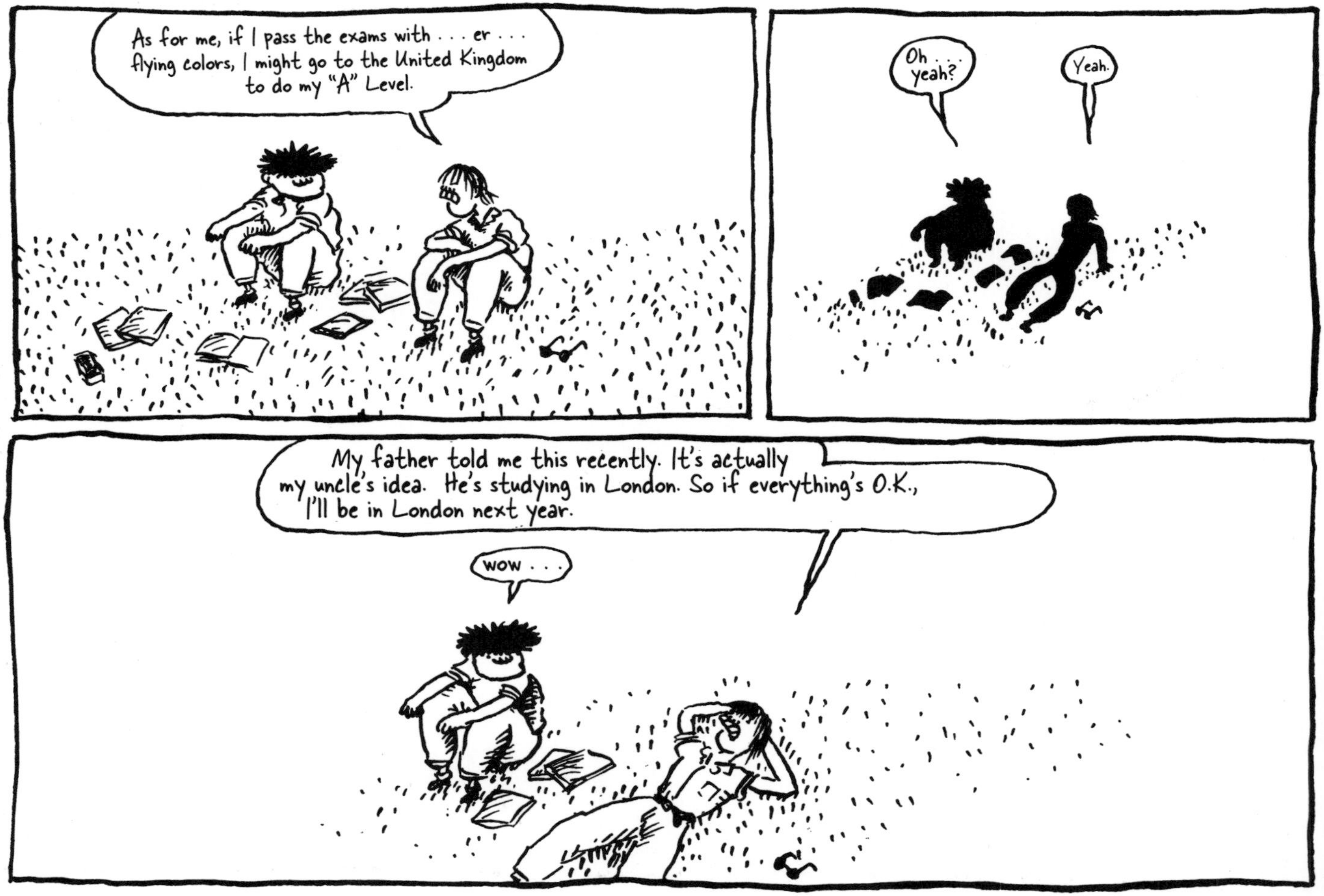
As for me, if I pass the exams with . . . er . . . flying colors, I might go to the United Kingdom to do my "A" Level.
Oh . . . yeah?
Yeah.
My father told me this recently. It's actually my uncle's idea. He's studying in London. So if everything's O.K., I'll be in London next year.
WOW . . .

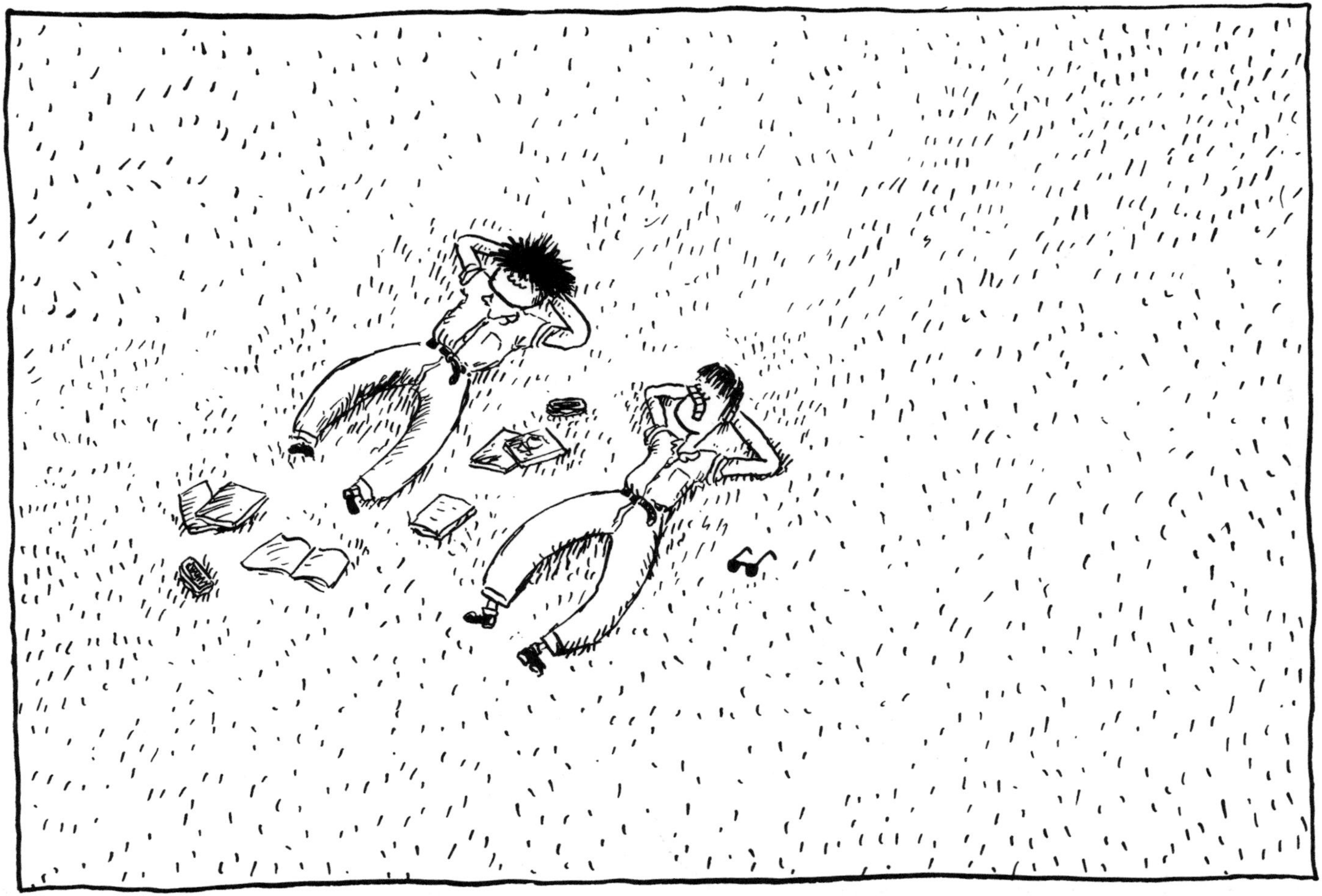

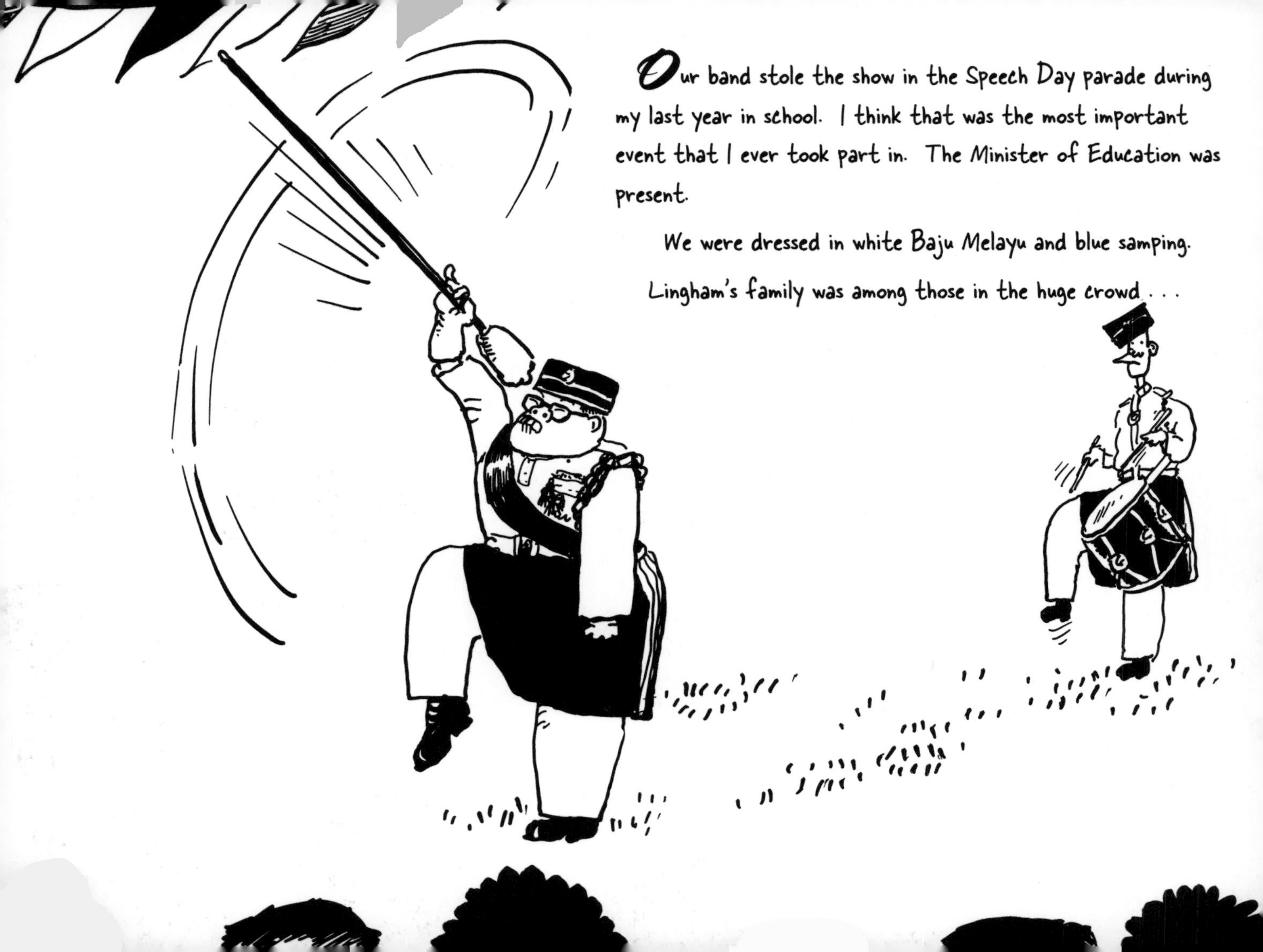
Our band stole the show in the Speech Day parade during my last year in school. I think that was the most important event that I ever took part in. The Minister of Education was present.
We were dressed in white Baju Melayu and blue samping.
Lingham's family was among those in the huge crowd . . .

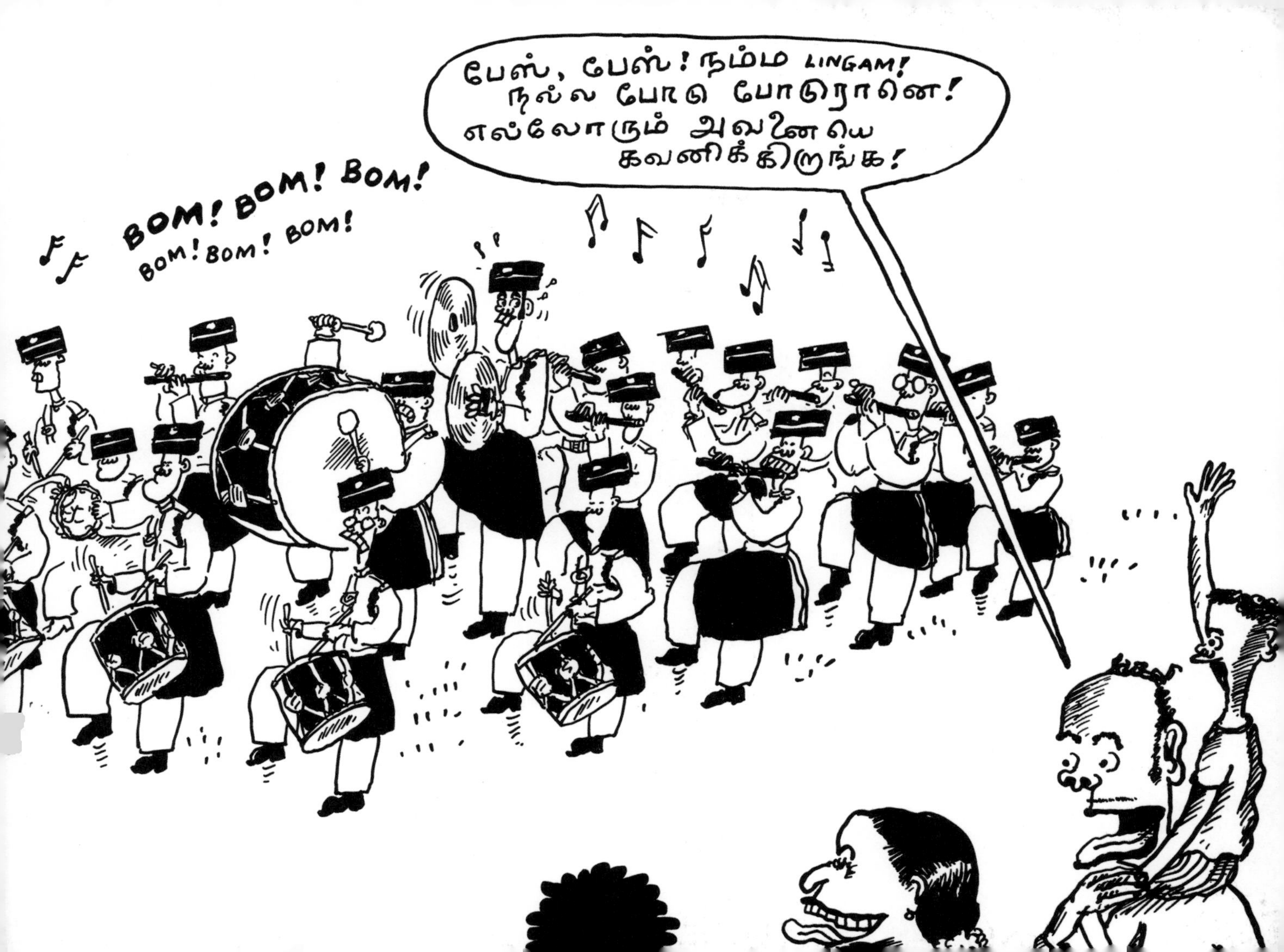
பேஷ், பேஷ்! நம்ம LINGAM!
நல்ல போடு போடுறானே!
எல்லோரும் அவனையே
கவணிக்கிறுங்க!
BOM! BOM! BOM!
BOM! BOM! BOM!

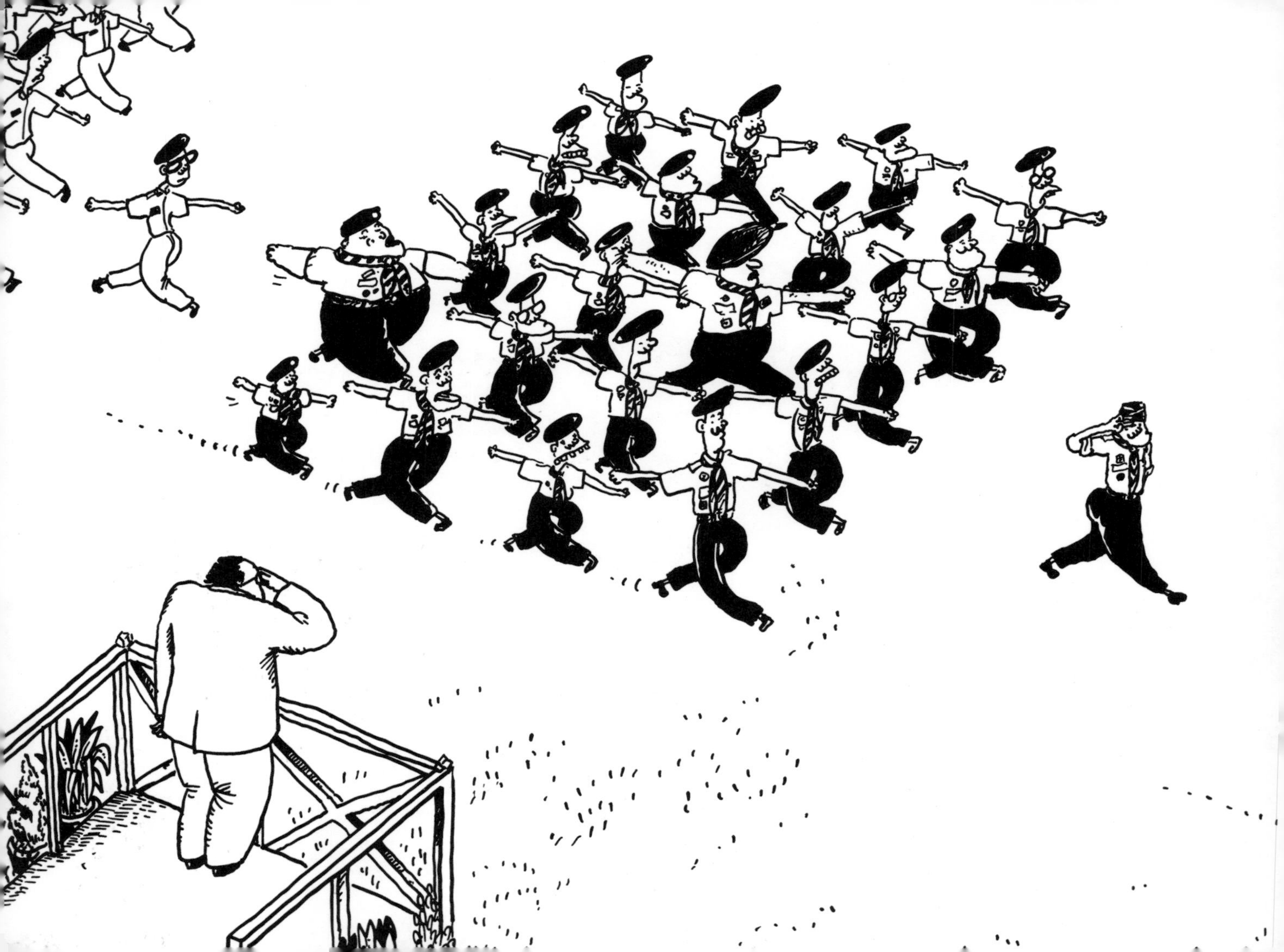

As the minister took the salute we played the school song, "Sedia Berkhidmat," and "Ob la di, Ob la da."

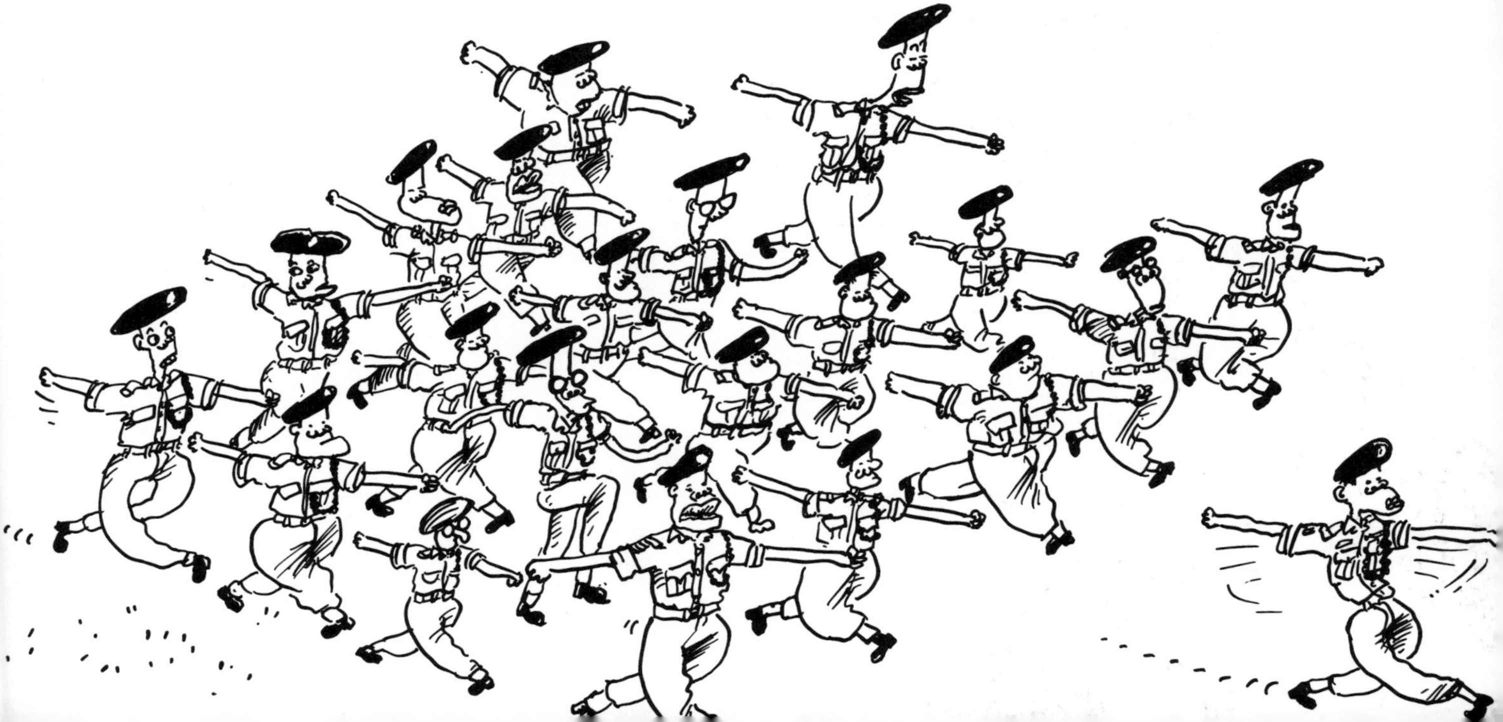

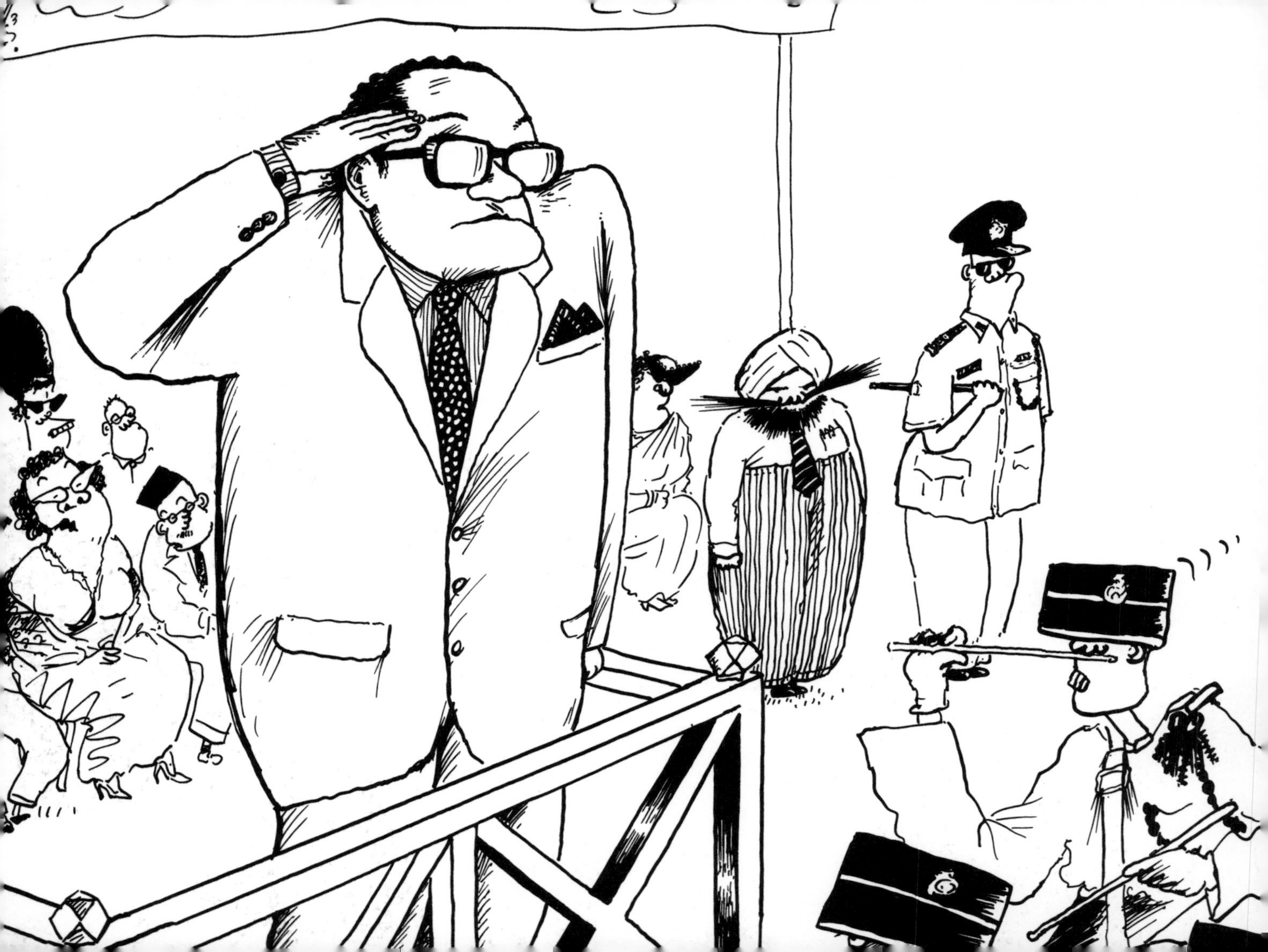

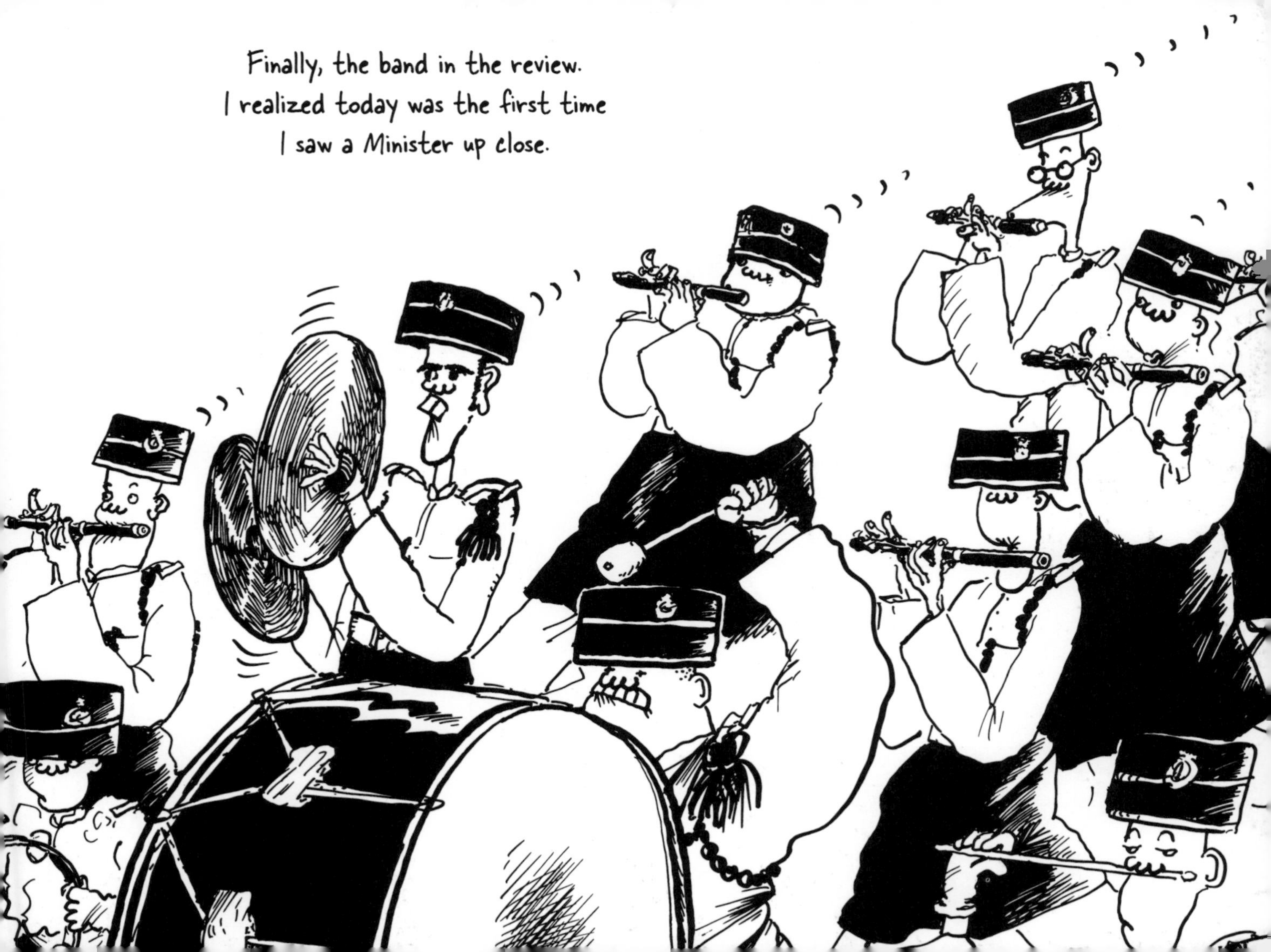
Finally, the band in the review.
I realized today was the first time
I saw a Minister up close.

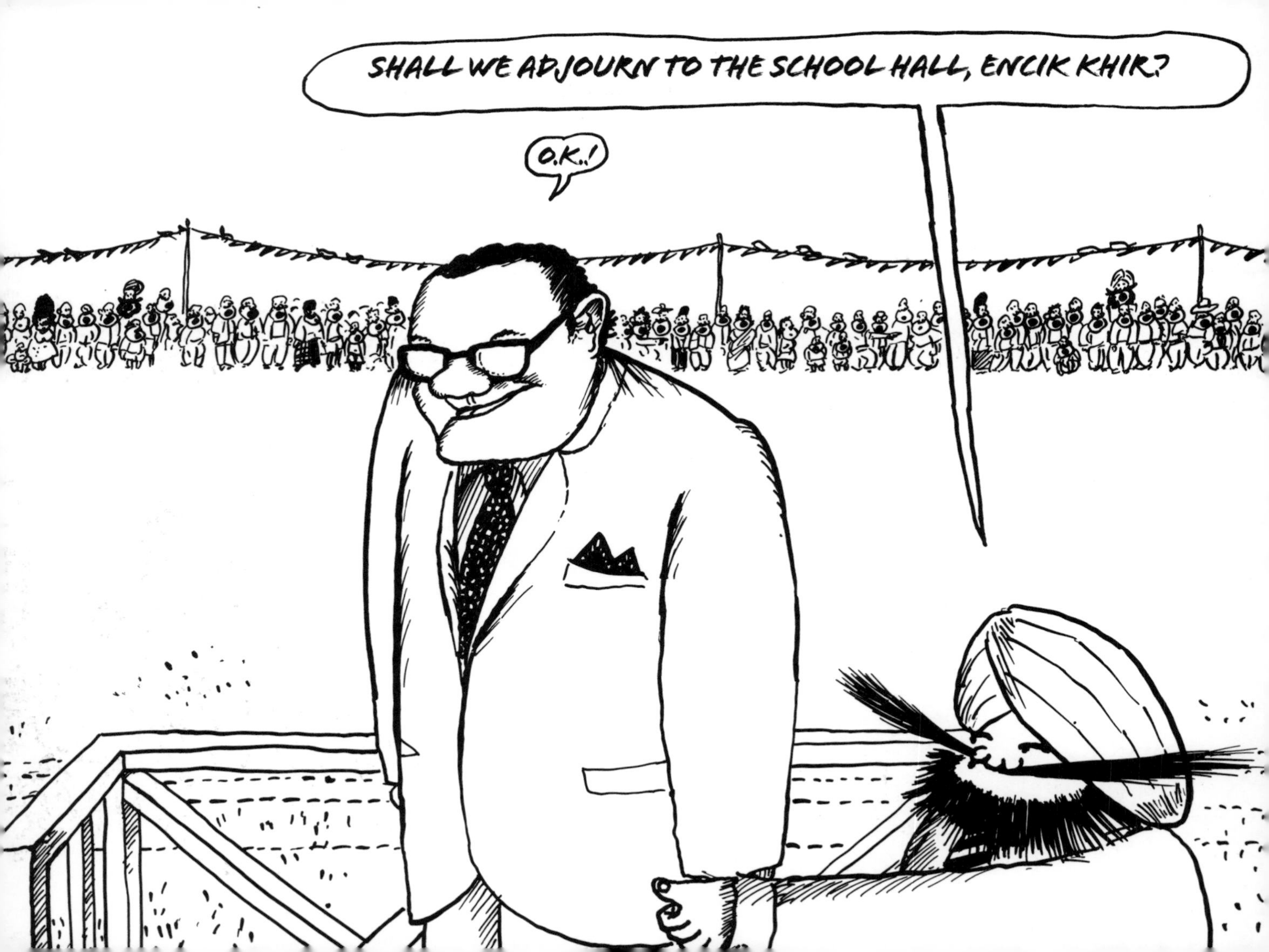
SHALL WE ADJOURN TO THE SCHOOL HALL, ENCIK KHIR?
O.K..!

However, it just wasn't Lingham's day!

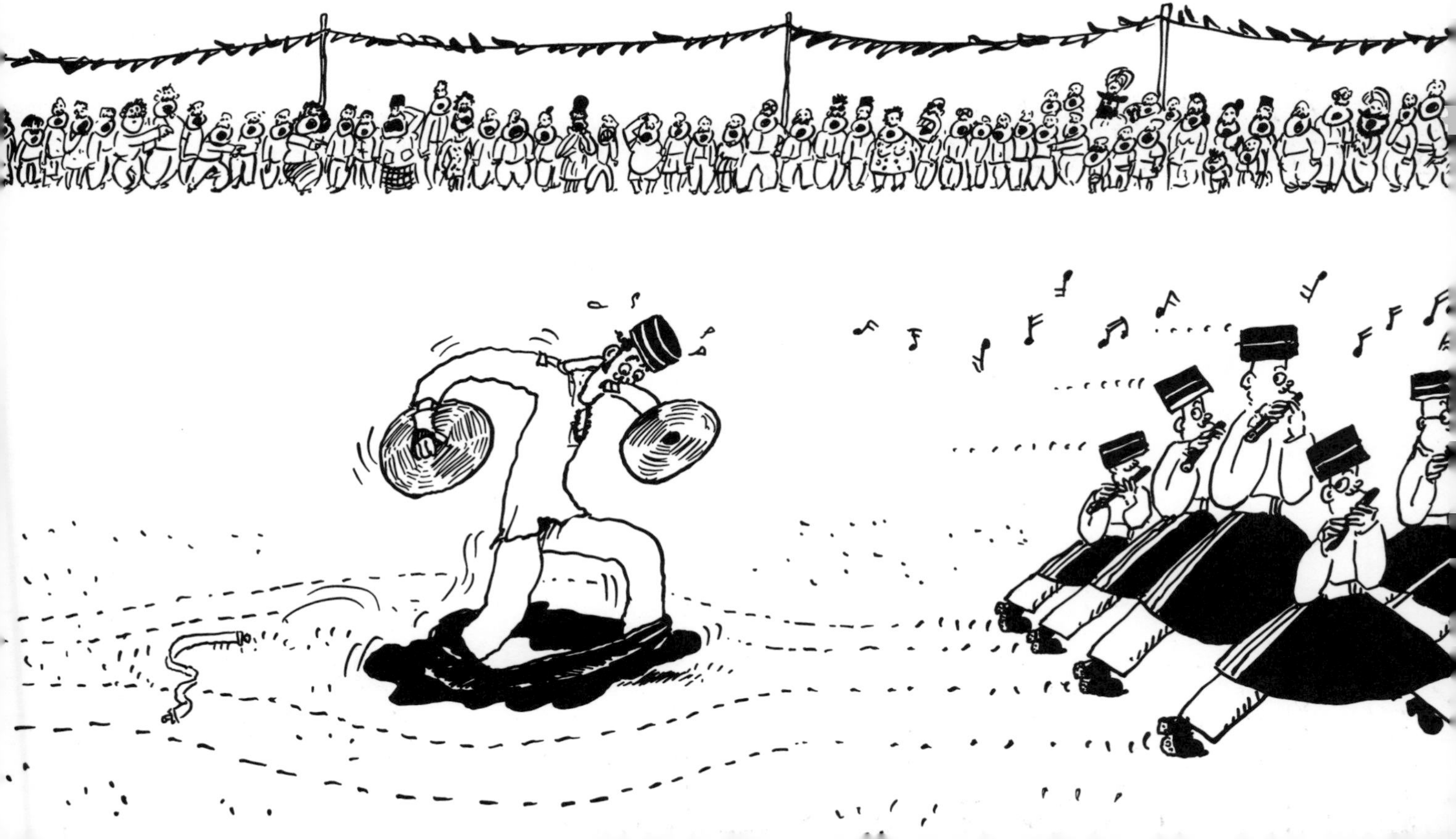

HELLO, MAT!

NORMAH...

HOW ARE YOU?

OH!... ER... O.K....

I NEED SOME HELP FROM YOU, ACTUALLY...

OH?

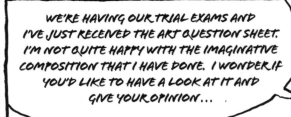

WE'RE HAVING OUR TRIAL EXAMS AND I'VE JUST RECEIVED THE ART QUESTION SHEET. I'M NOT QUITE HAPPY WITH THE IMAGINATIVE COMPOSITION THAT I HAVE DONE. I WONDER IF YOU'D LIKE TO HAVE A LOOK AT IT AND GIVE YOUR OPINION...

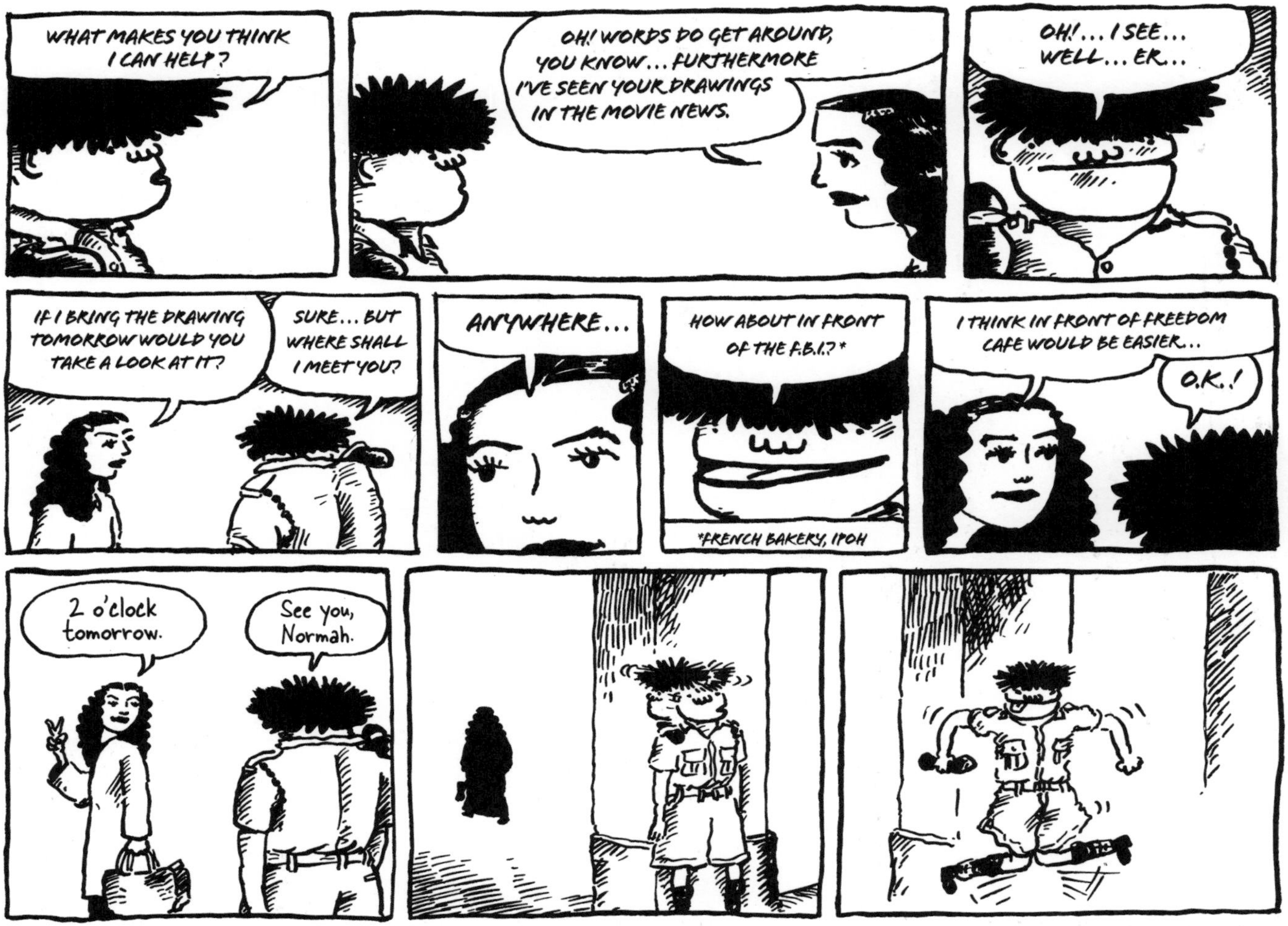
WHAT MAKES YOU THINK I CAN HELP?
OH! WORDS DO GET AROUND, YOU KNOW... FURTHERMORE I'VE SEEN YOUR DRAWINGS IN THE MOVIE NEWS.
OH!... I SEE... WELL... ER...
IF I BRING THE DRAWING TOMORROW WOULD YOU TAKE A LOOK AT IT?
SURE... BUT WHERE SHALL I MEET YOU?
ANYWHERE...
HOW ABOUT IN FRONT OF THE F.B.I.?*
*FRENCH BAKERY, IPOH
I THINK IN FRONT OF FREEDOM CAFE WOULD BE EASIER...
O.K.!
2 o'clock tomorrow.
See you, Normah.

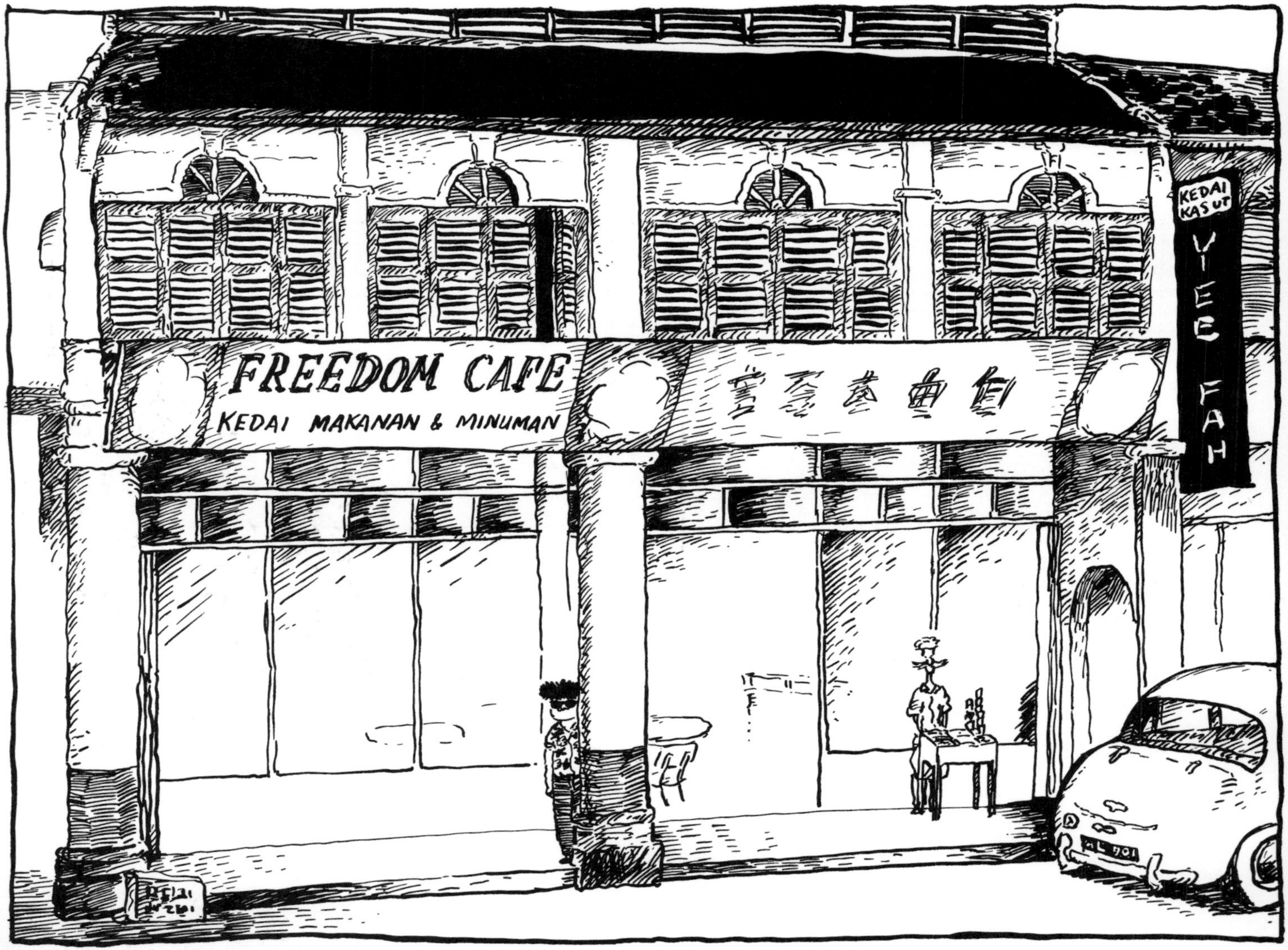
FREEDOM CAFE
KEDAI MAKANAN & MINUMAN
KEDAI KASUT
YEE FAH

HELLO!
HELLO!
I'll tell you what . . . why don't we have roti canai and a drink. I'm hungry.
O.K!

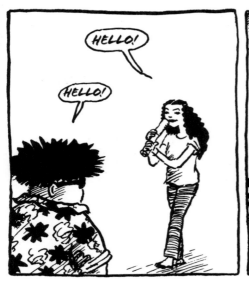

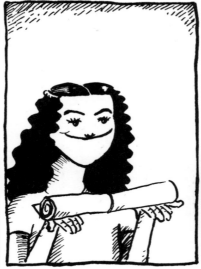

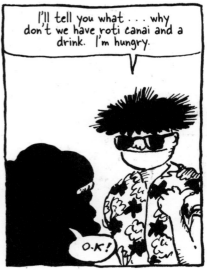

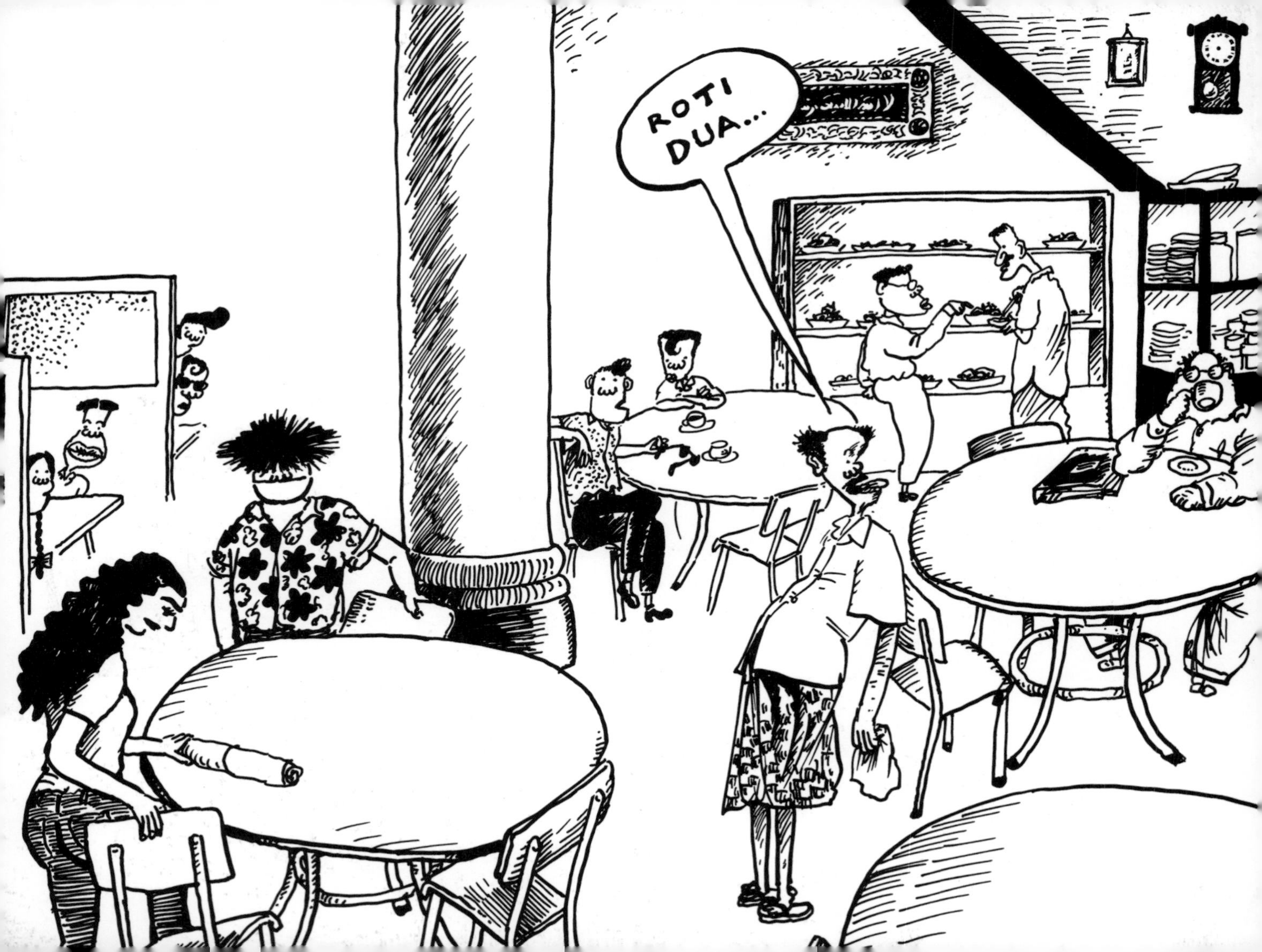
ROTI DUA...

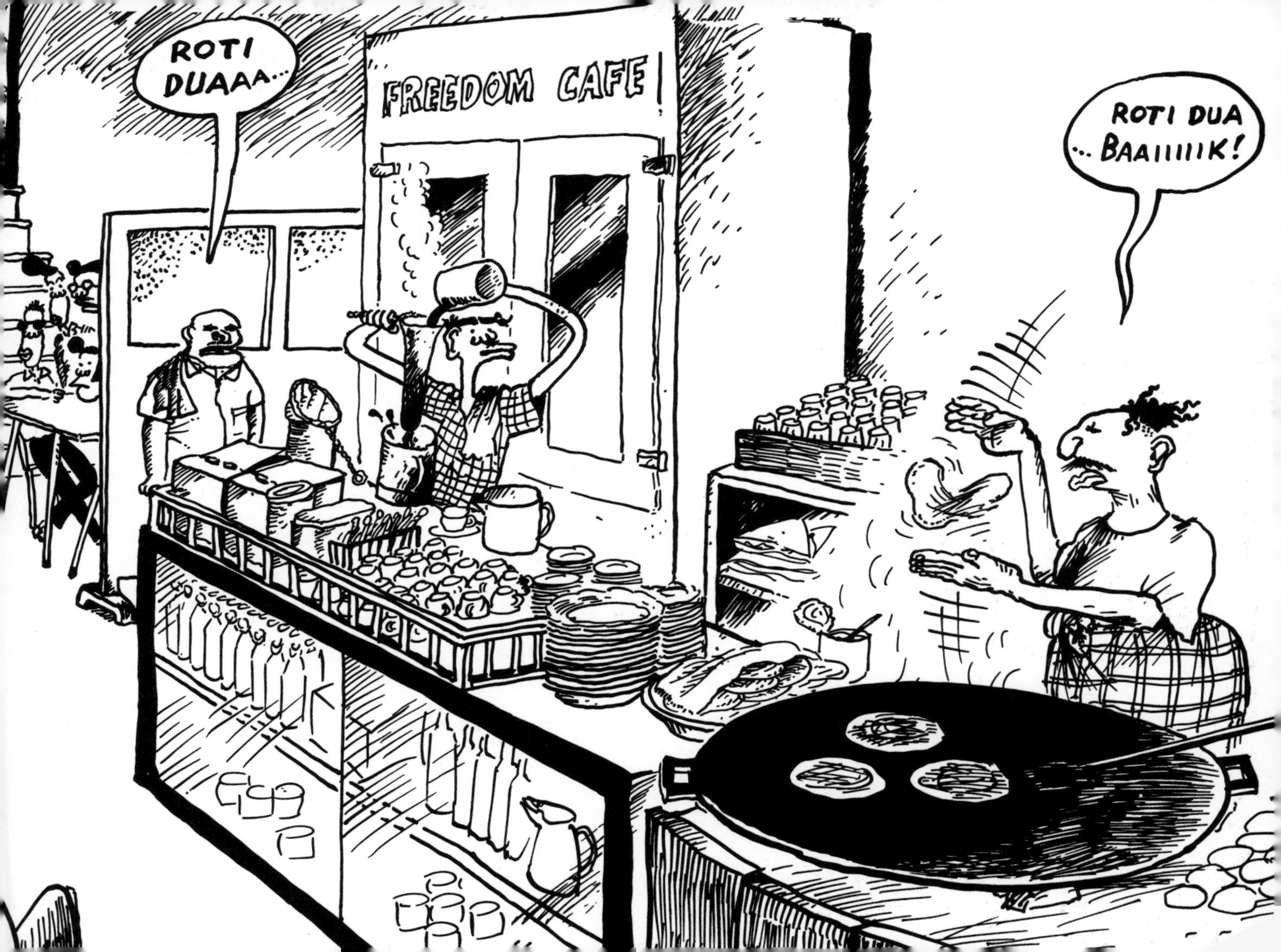
ROTI DUAAA...
FREEDOM CAFE
ROTI DUA ...BAAIIIIIK!

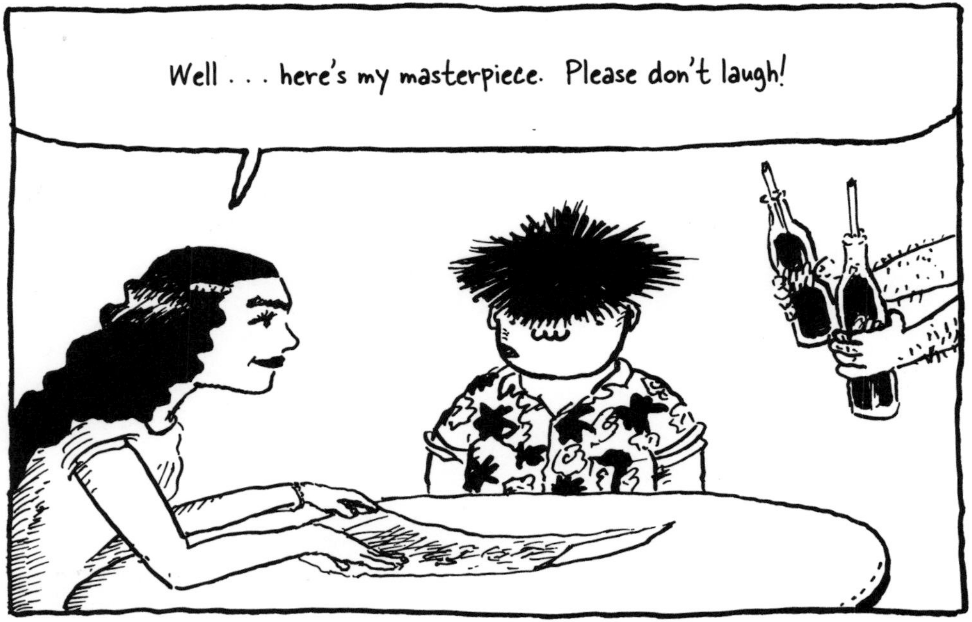
Well . . . here's my masterpiece. Please don't laugh!

I took a look at Normah's drawing. This is how our conversation went:

"For a start, all your figures are stiff."

"Is that so . . . ?"

"Yes. Look at this fellow here. Is he supposed to be sweeping?"

"Yes."

"Well, he looks like a policeman standing at attention."

"Oh! Ha! ha!"

"Make him bend a little bit . . . You know, try to make his hands 'move.'"

"Make him 'move.' I see."

"Another thing—all your characters here seem to be posing for you."

"What do you mean?"

"It's as if you are taking a photograph of a set-up situation."

"So . . . how?"

"I think you should make some of them show their backs to the artist. Make some squatting down . . . some bending down . . . and maybe some looking your way."

"Looking MY way?"

"Yes! As if they're wondering why you should be painting their picture . . ."

"Ha! ha! That's funny!"

"You see, art can be anything . . ."

(Obviously this was not my original line.)

"Anything?"

"It can be funny."

"I shall remember that . . . What about the colors . . .?"

"That's up to each individual's style. You have your own style. Your own taste. I have my style."

Tell me . . . what is your hobby?
I like to read poetry.
Masuri S.N. . . . Usman Awang . . . Latiff Mohiddin . . .
I see . . .

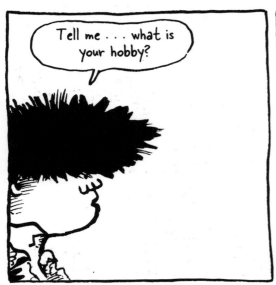

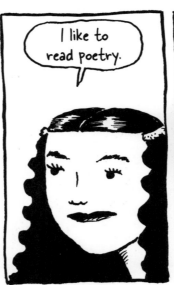

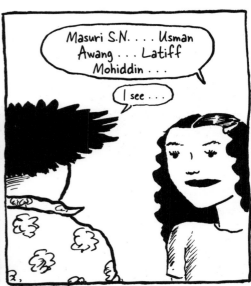

Say . . . er . . . would you like to go to a film with me after this?
What?
Would you like to go and see a film after this?

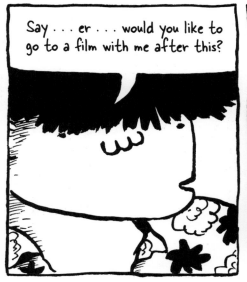

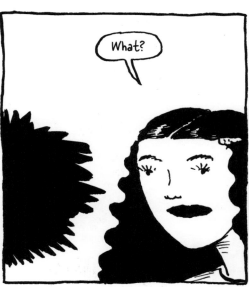

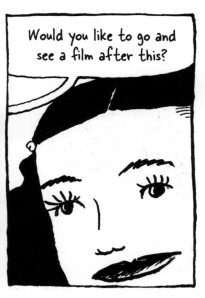

It's a Tarzan rerun . . . Let's go and see the 3 o'clock show . . . I always like Tarzan . . .!
Well . . . You want to go?

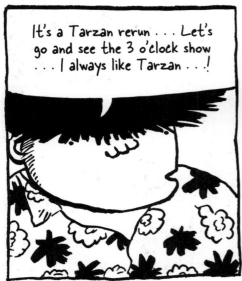

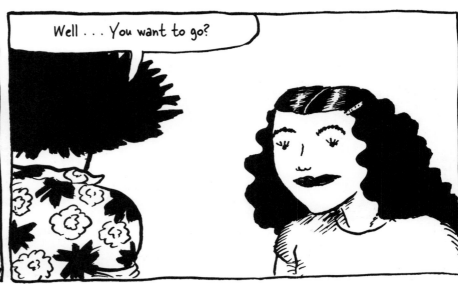

Come on . . . the afternoon is still young.

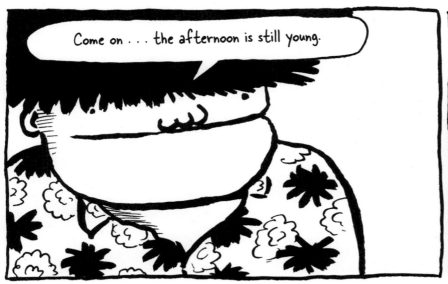

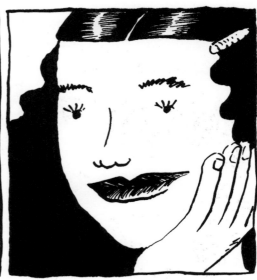

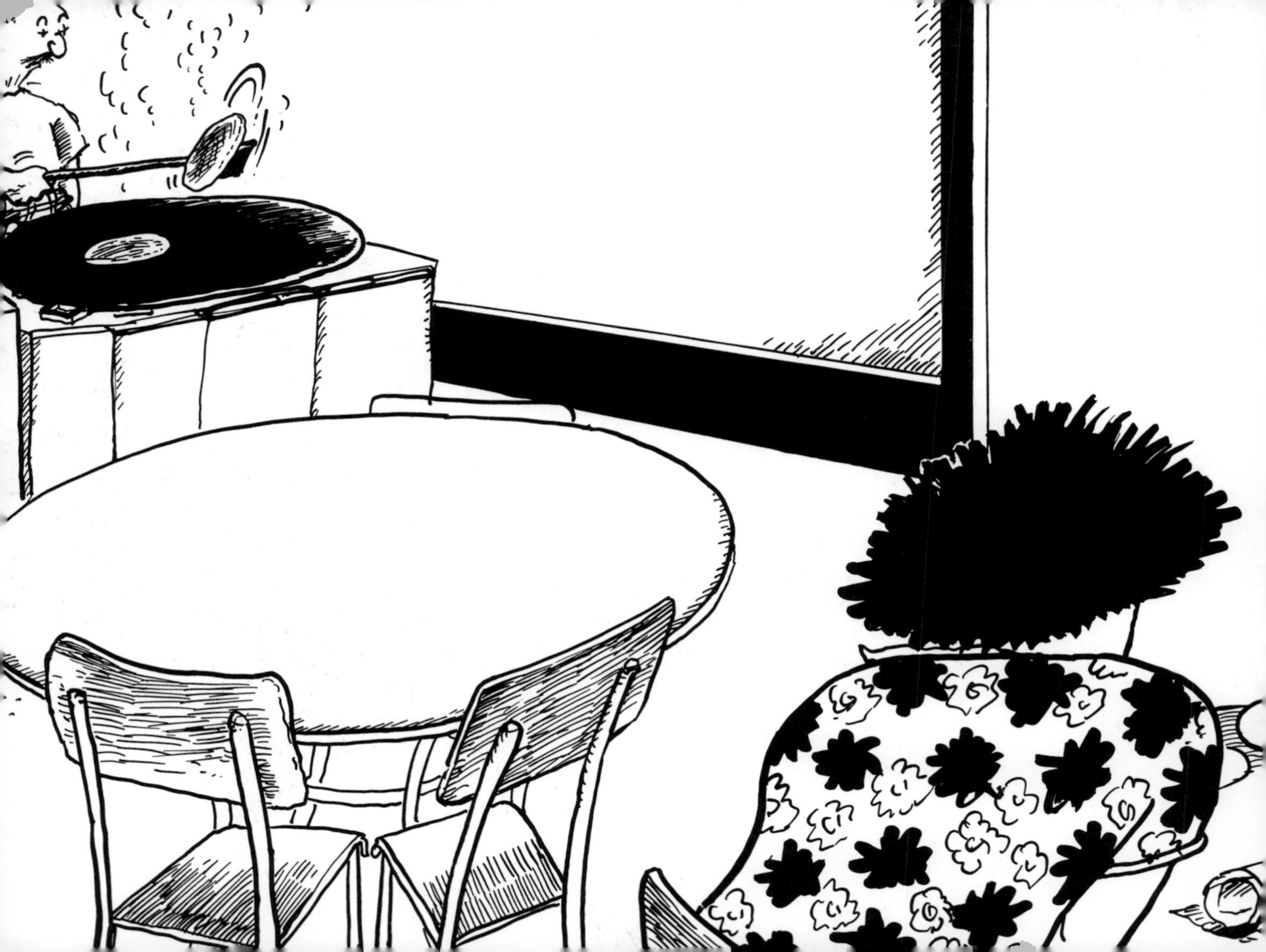

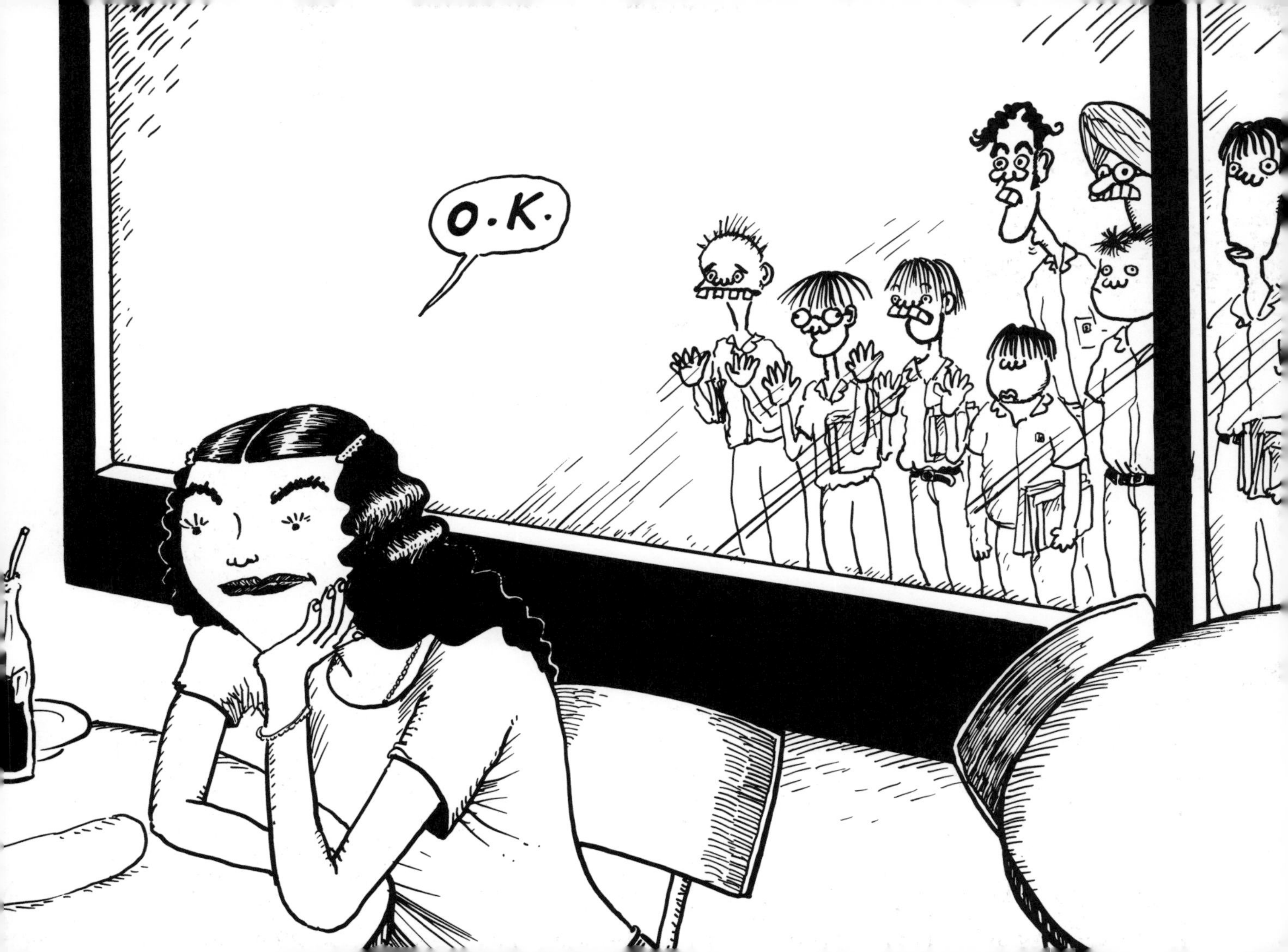
O.K.

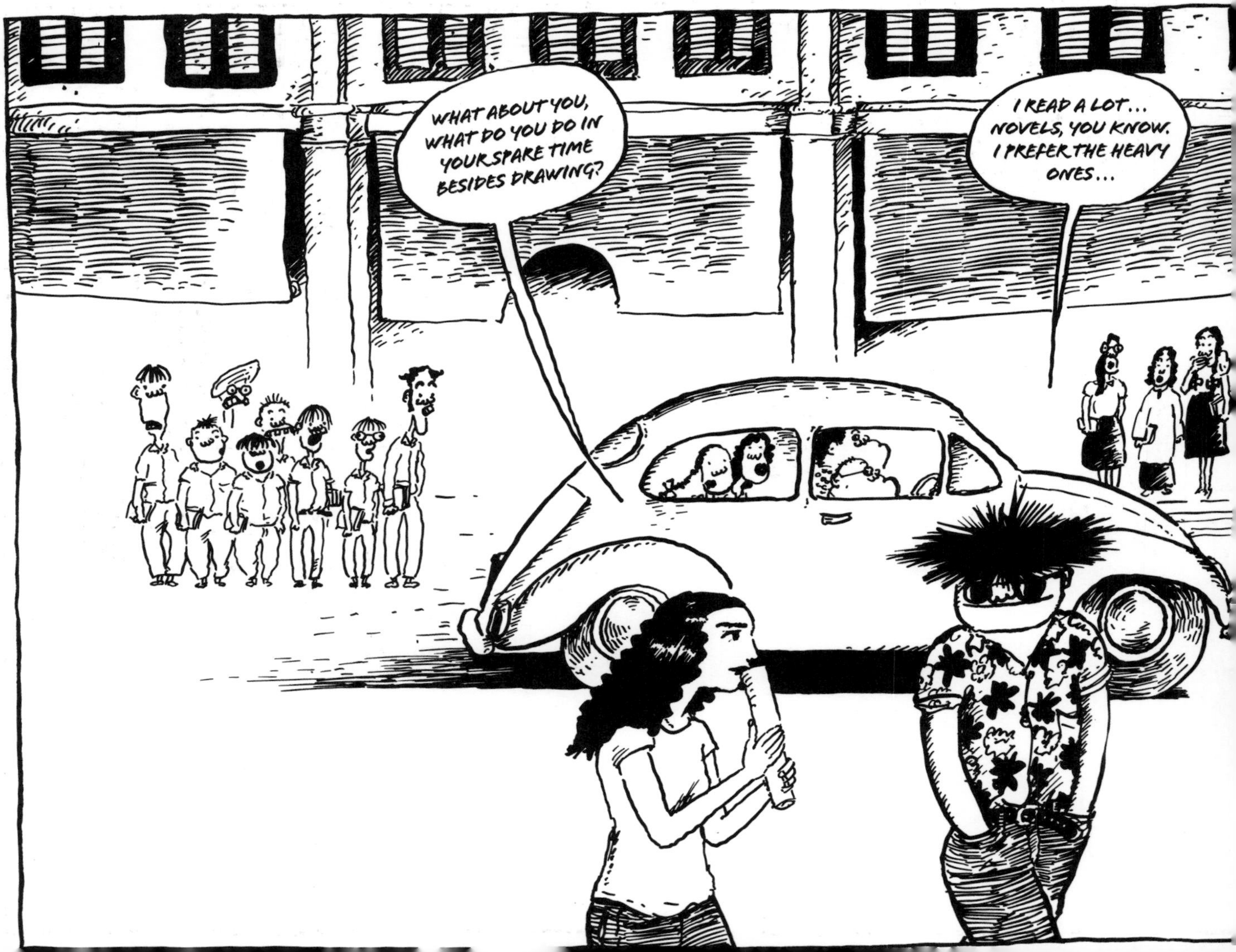
WHAT ABOUT YOU, WHAT DO YOU DO IN YOUR SPARE TIME BESIDES DRAWING?
I READ A LOT... NOVELS, YOU KNOW. I PREFER THE HEAVY ONES...

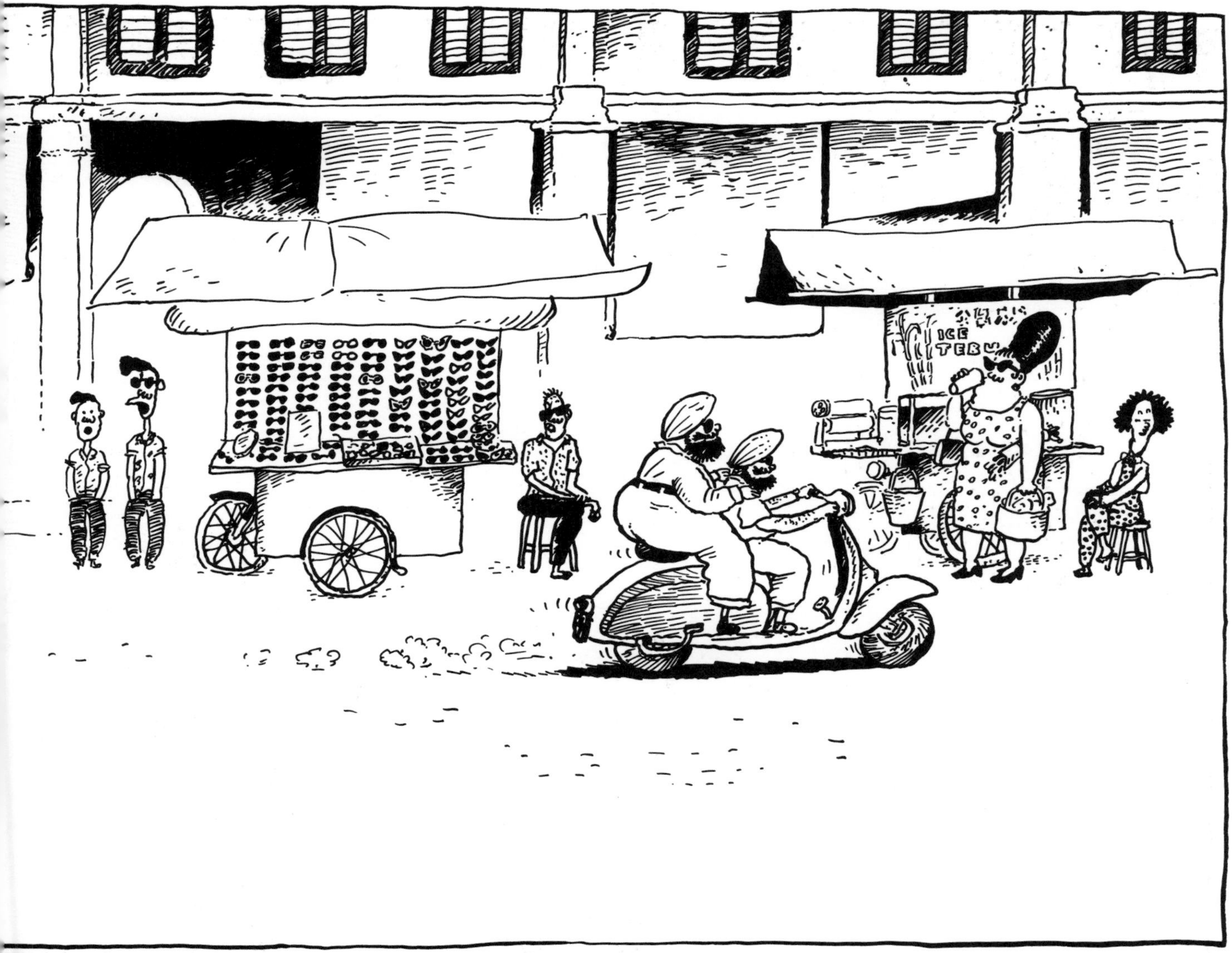
ICE
TEBU

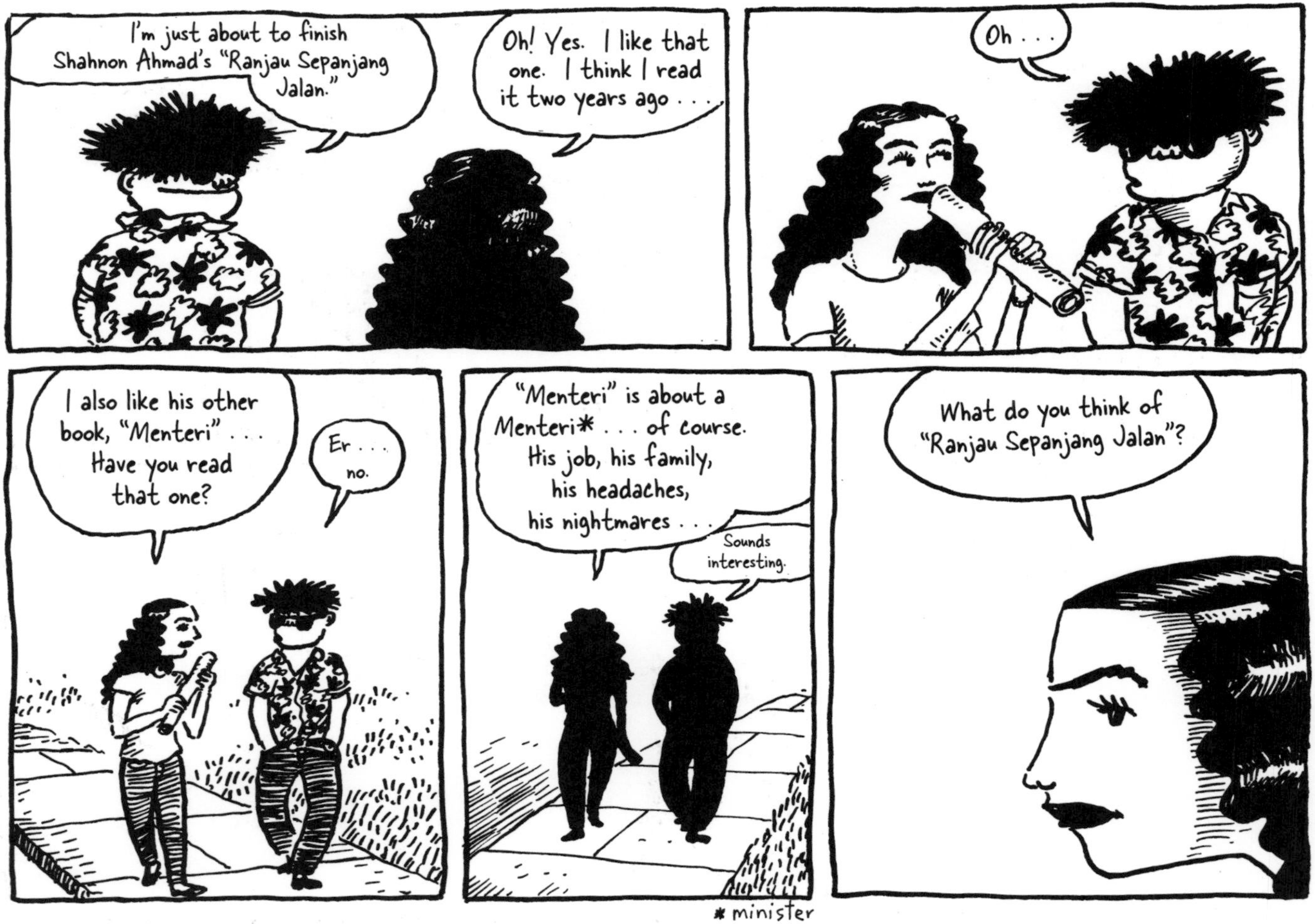
I'm just about to finish Shahnon Ahmad's "Ranjau Sepanjang Jalan."
Oh! Yes. I like that one. I think I read it two years ago . . .
Oh . . .
I also like his other book, "Menteri" . . . Have you read that one?
Er . . . no.
"Menteri" is about a Menteri* . . . of course. His job, his family, his headaches, his nightmares . . .
Sounds interesting.
* minister
What do you think of "Ranjau Sepanjang Jalan"?

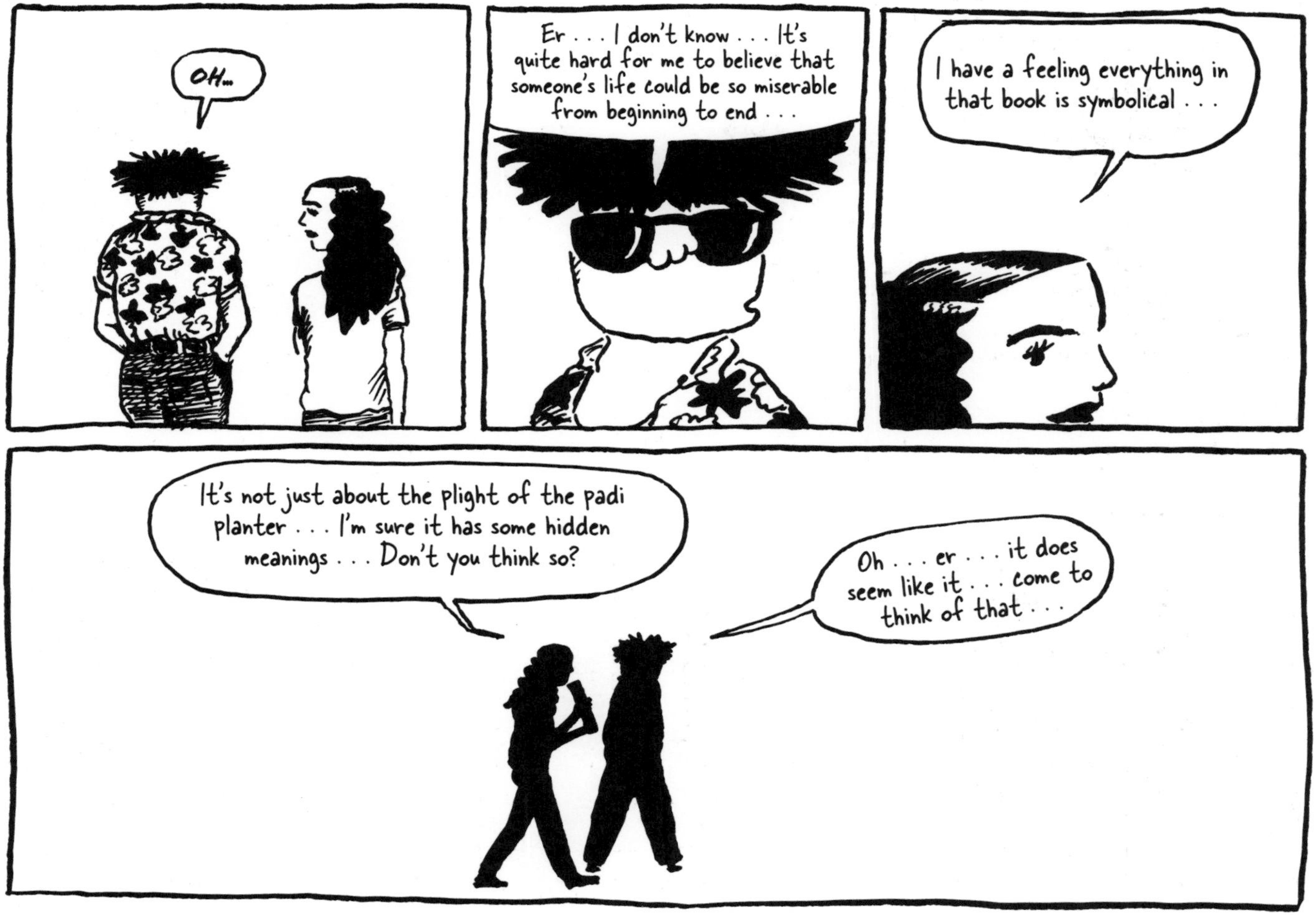
OH...
Er . . . I don't know . . . It's quite hard for me to believe that someone's life could be so miserable from beginning to end . . .
I have a feeling everything in that book is symbolical . . .
It's not just about the plight of the padi planter . . . I'm sure it has some hidden meanings . . . Don't you think so?
Oh . . . er . . . it does seem like it . . . come to think of that . . .

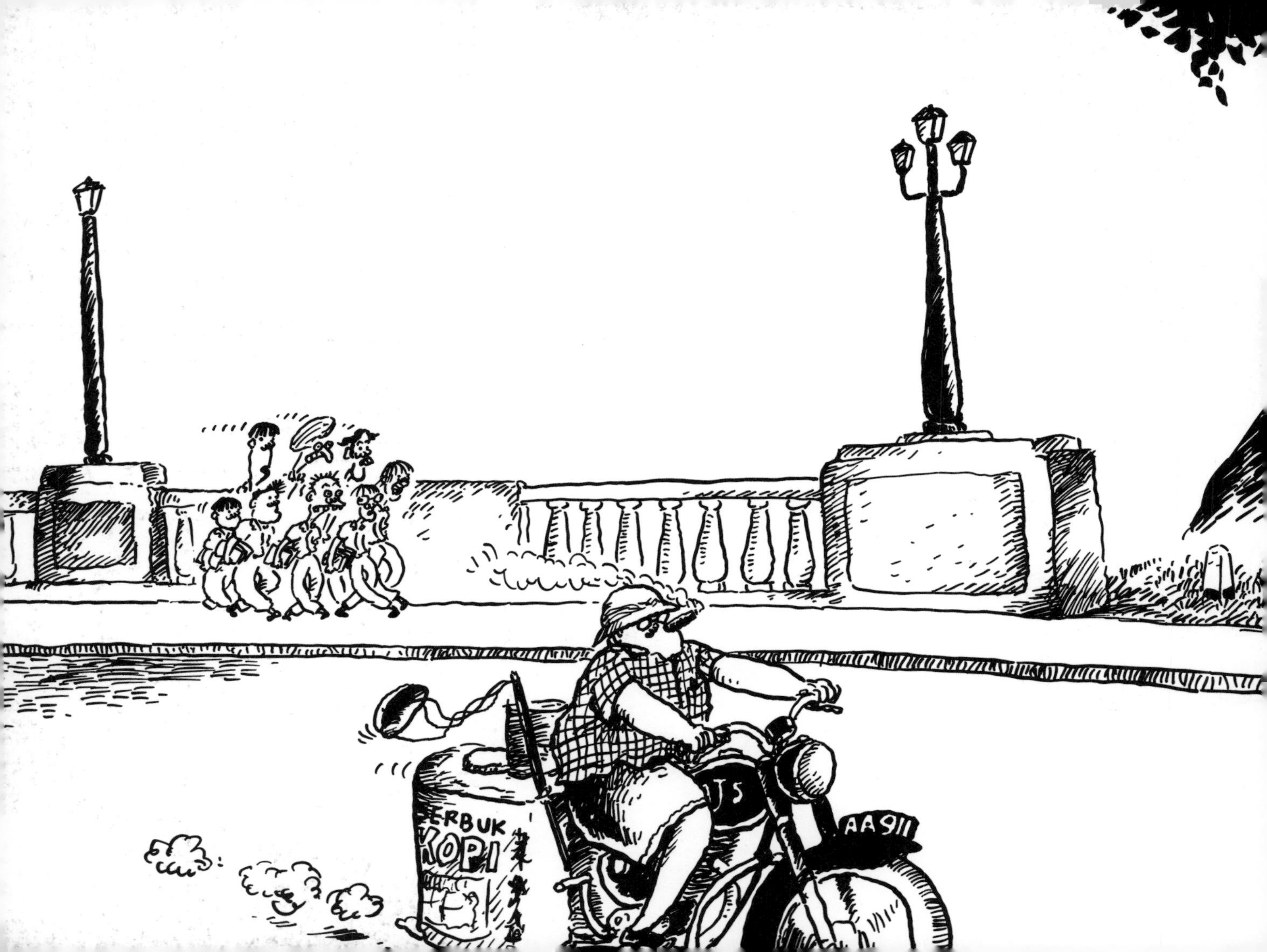
ERBUK
KOPI
AA911

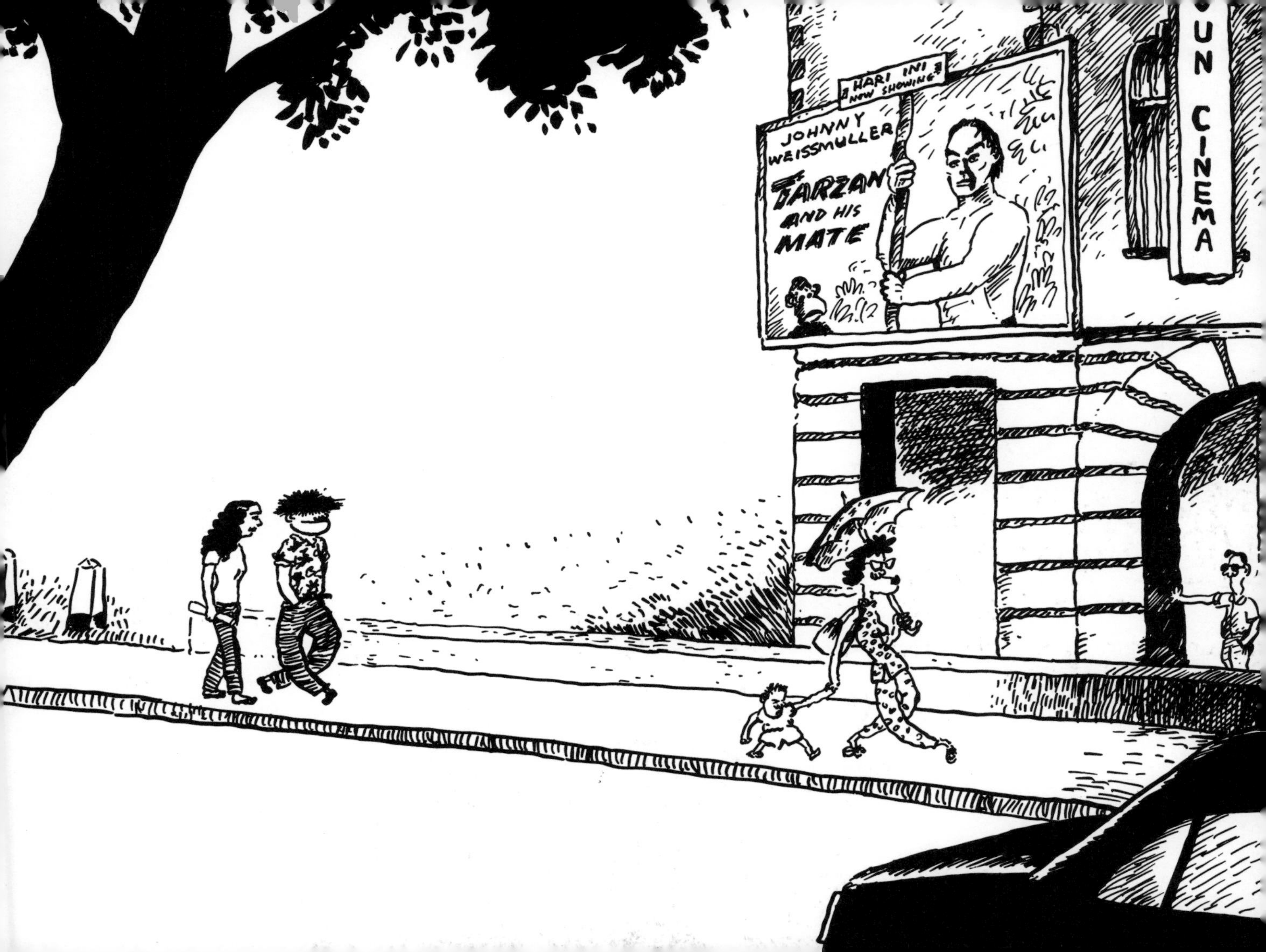
HARI INI
NOW SHOWING
JOHNNY WEISSMULLER
TARZAN AND HIS MATE
UN CINEMA

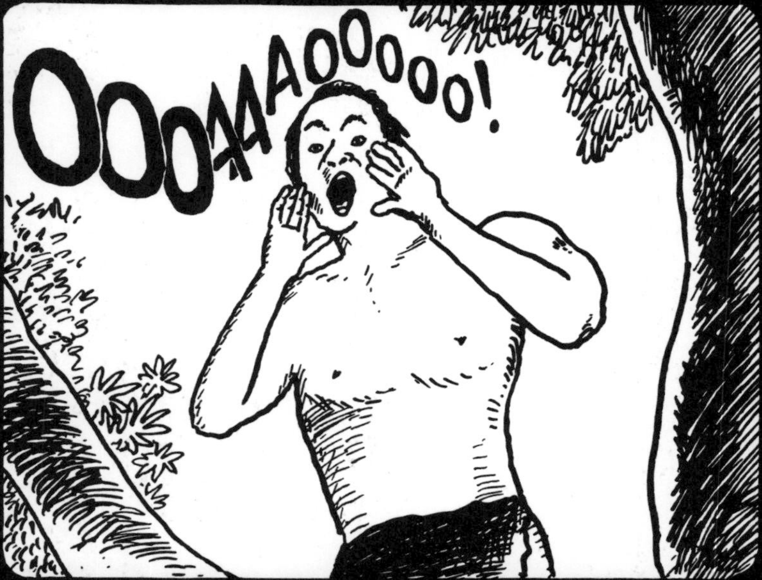
OOOWAOOOOO!

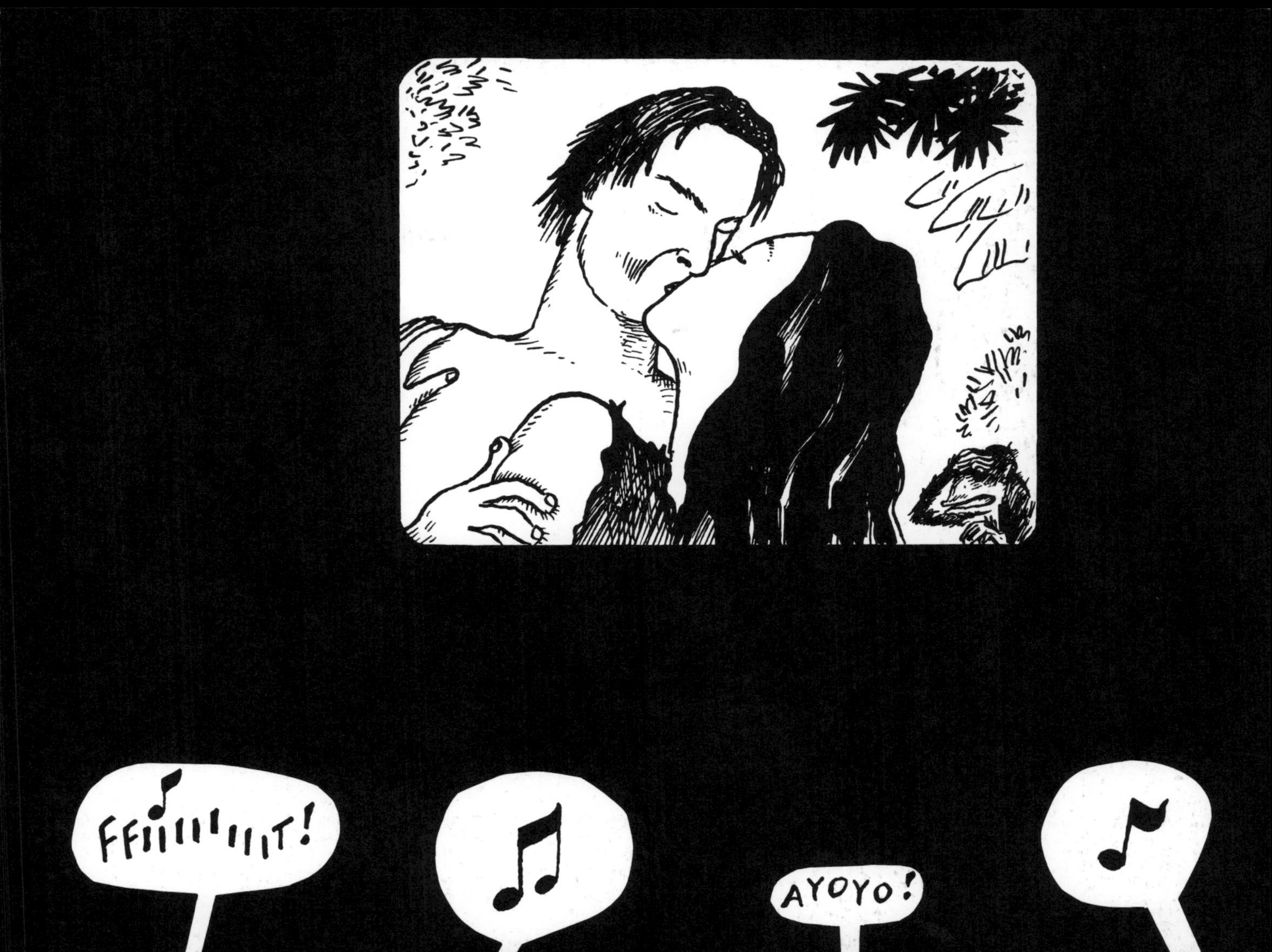
FFIIIIIIIIT!
AYOYO!

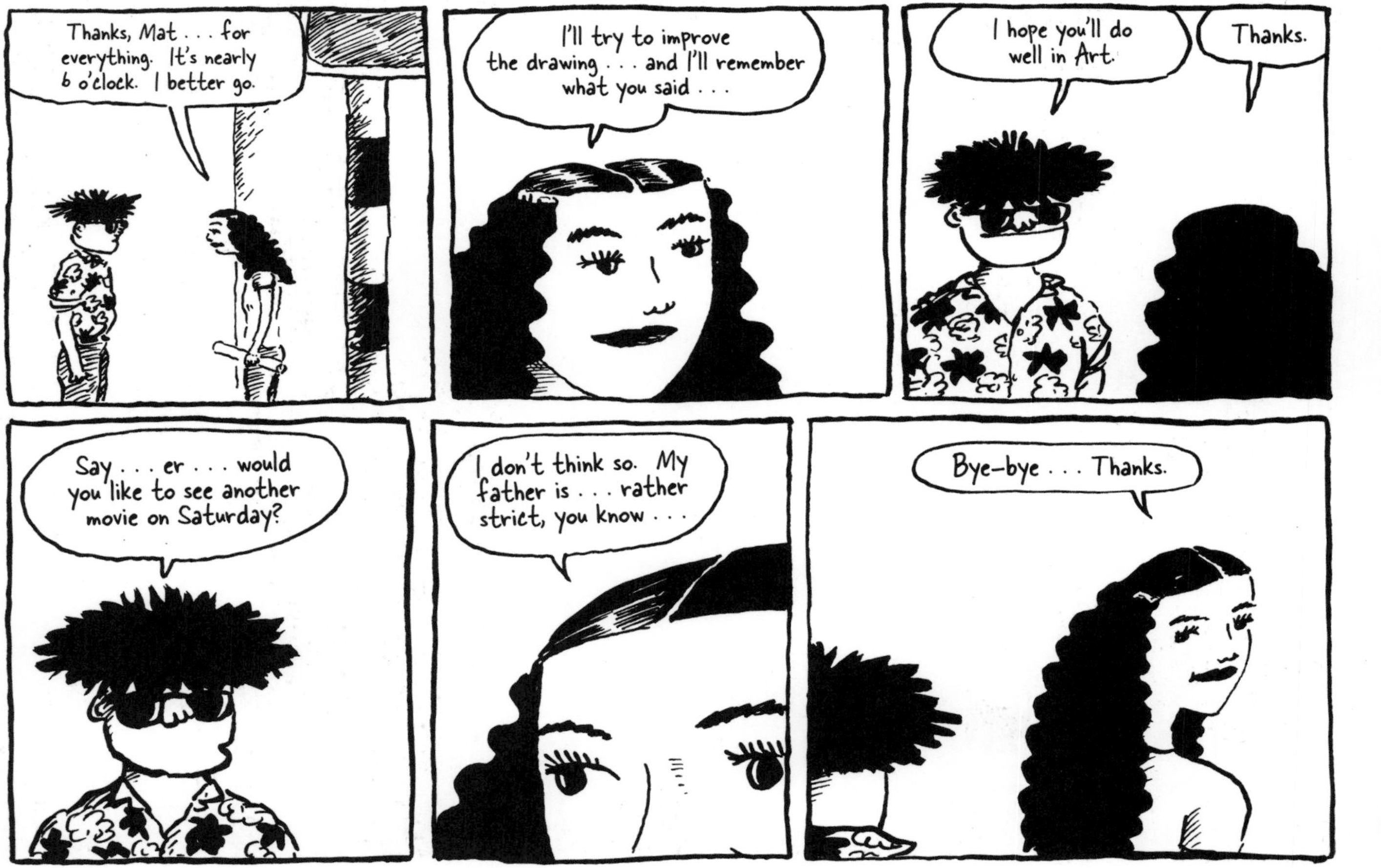
Thanks, Mat . . . for everything. It's nearly 6 o'clock. I better go.
I'll try to improve the drawing . . . and I'll remember what you said . . .
I hope you'll do well in Art.
Thanks.
Say . . . er . . . would you like to see another movie on Saturday?
I don't think so. My father is . . . rather strict, you know . . .
Bye-bye . . . Thanks.

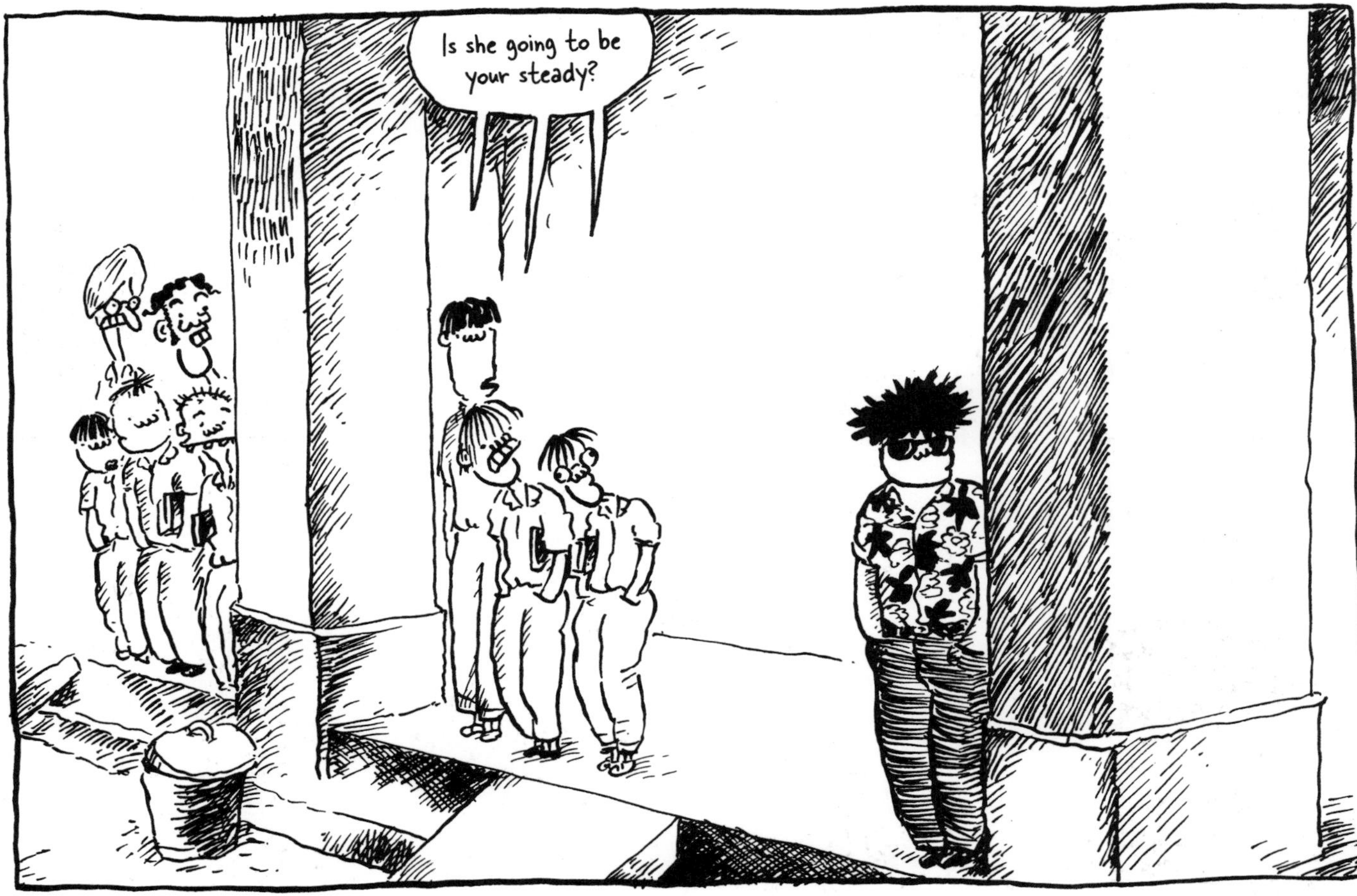
Is she going to be your steady?

In March the following year . . .

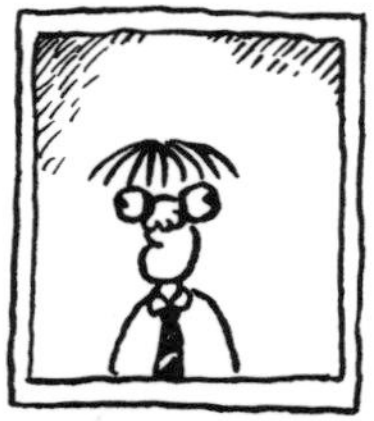

The first fellow to know his examination result was Jerry. He got 3rd Grade.

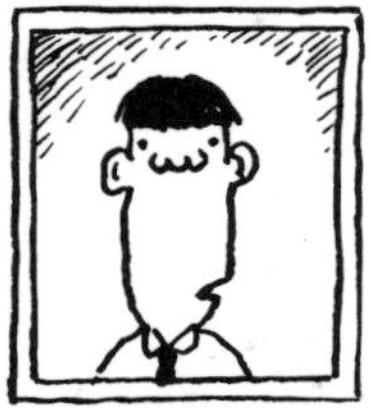

Din, of the T.R. Trio, also got 3rd Grade.

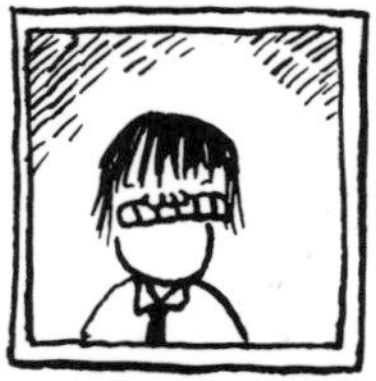

The First Graders were Frankie,

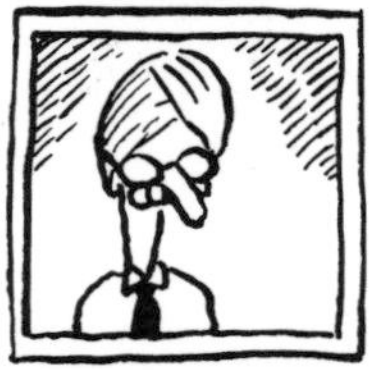

Tara Singh,

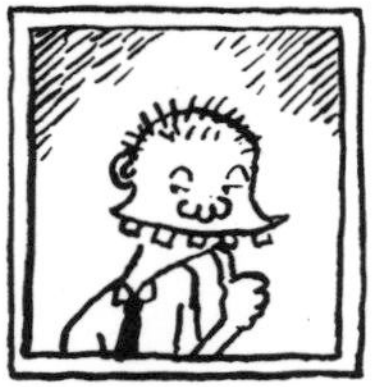

and Mat Sham.

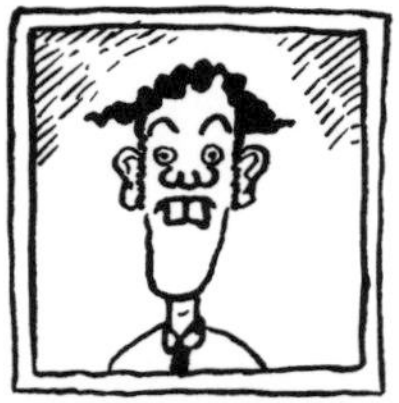

Lingham—3rd Grade.

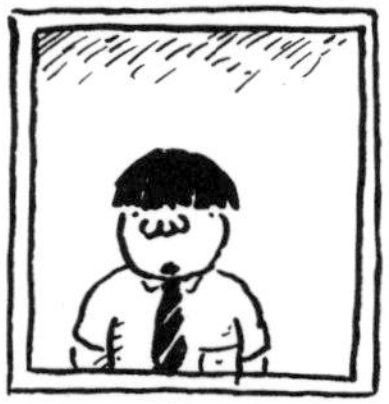

Hamdan—3rd Grade.

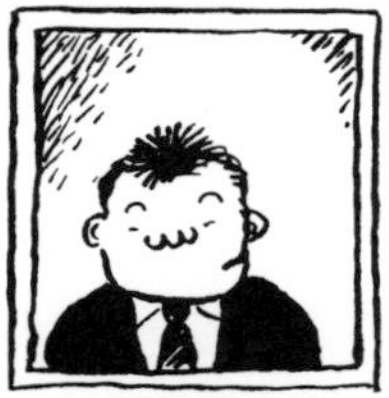

Neoh, the last member of the T.R. Trio—3rd Grade.

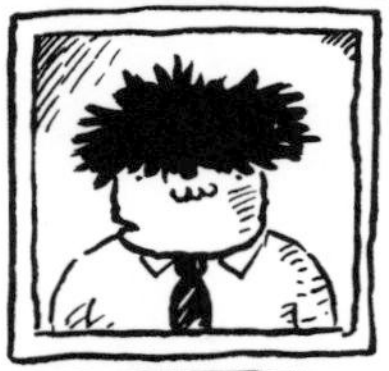

Myself—3rd Grade. I got 8 for Art.

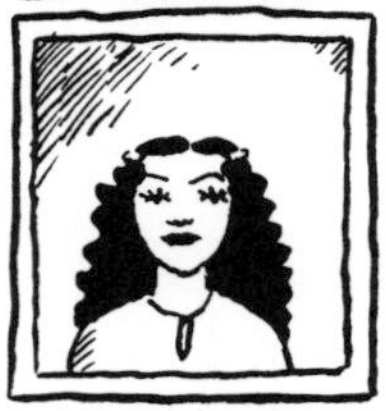

Normah—2nd Grade . . . And she obtained a distinction (2) in Art.

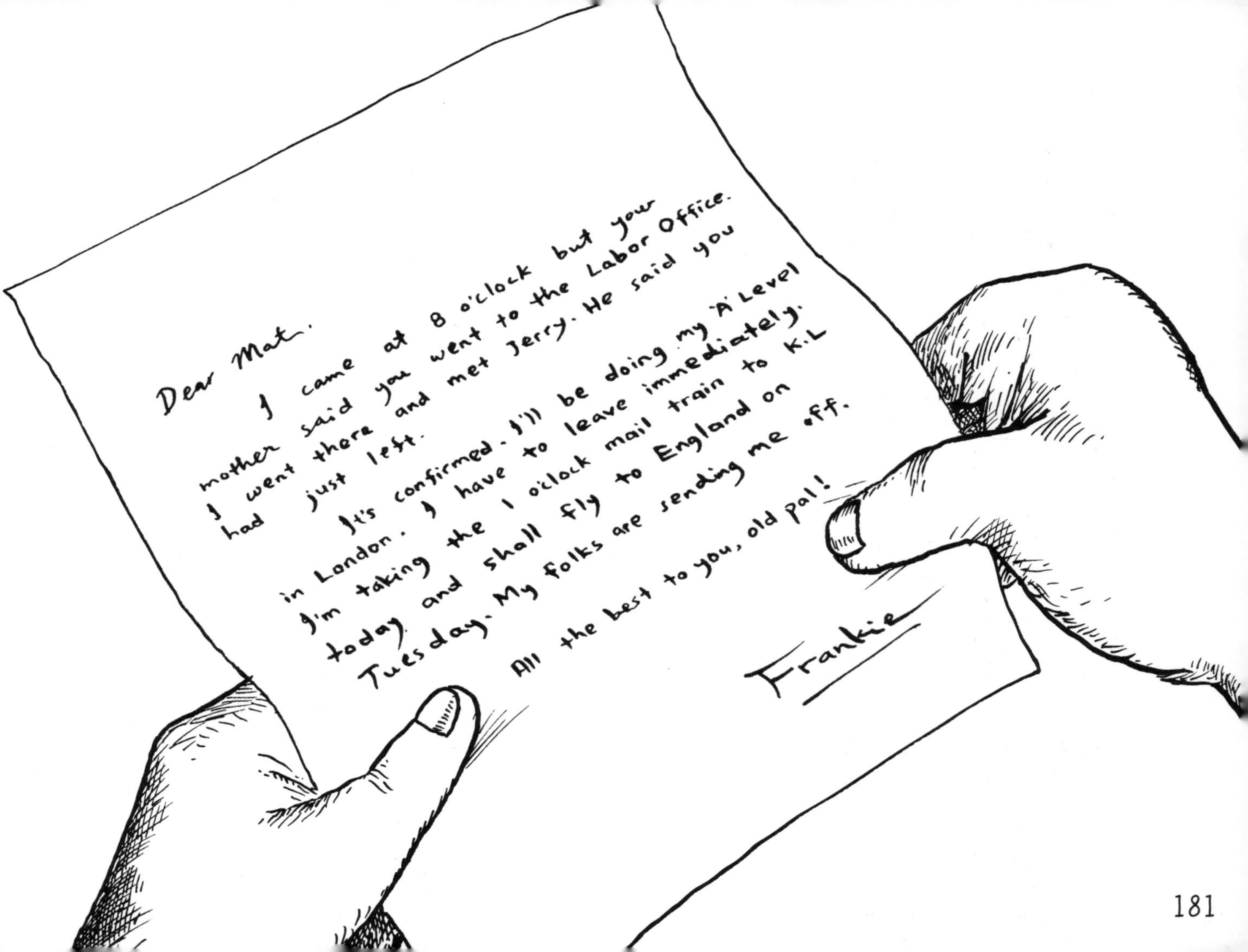
Dear Mat,
I came at 8 o'clock but your mother said you went to the Labor Office. I went there and met Jerry. He said you had just left.
It's confirmed. I'll be doing my 'A' Level in London. I have to leave immediately. I'm taking the 1 o'clock mail train to K.L today and shall fly to England on Tuesday. My folks are sending me off.
All the best to you, old pal!
Frankie

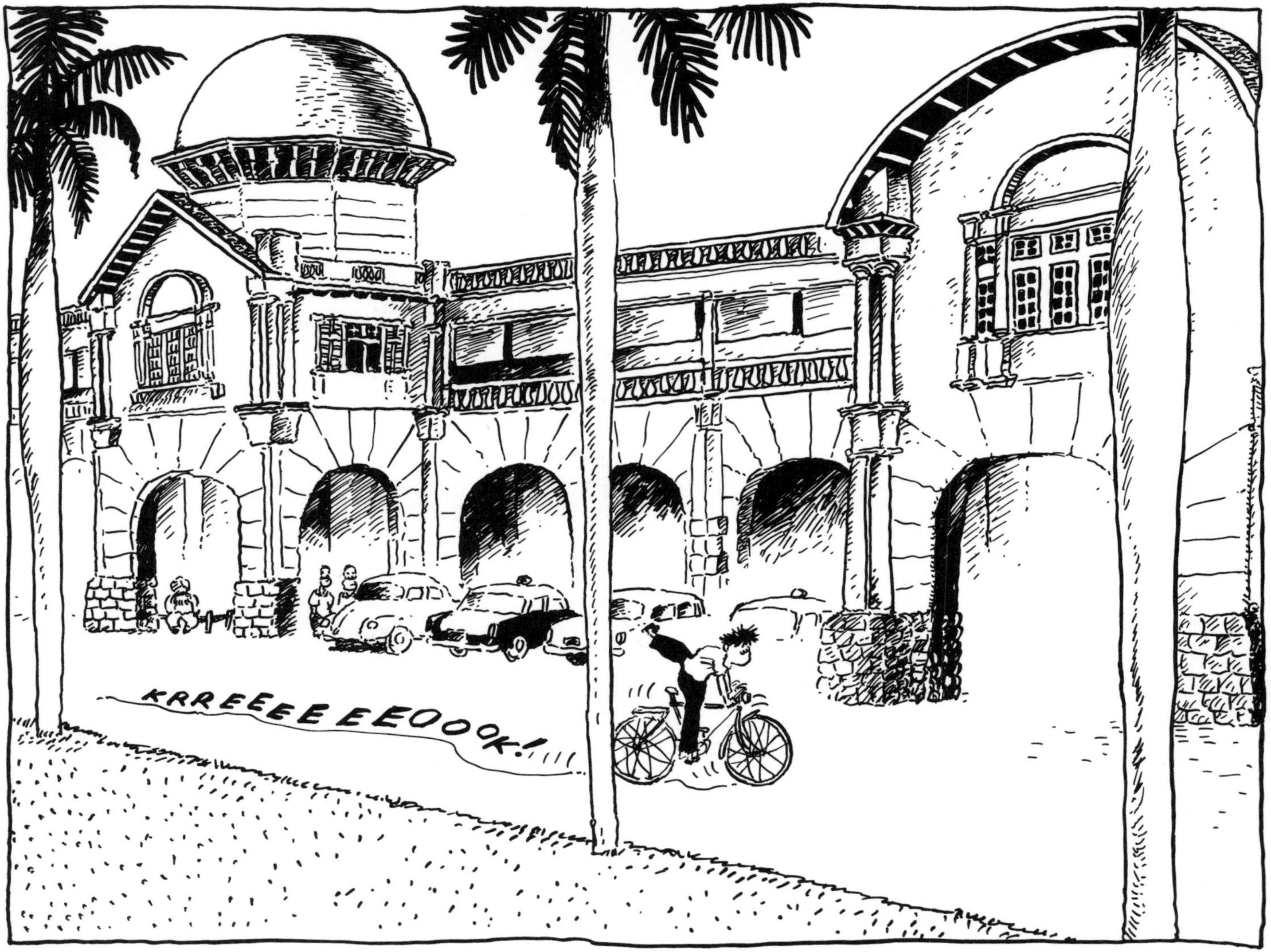
KRRREEEEEEEEOOOOK!

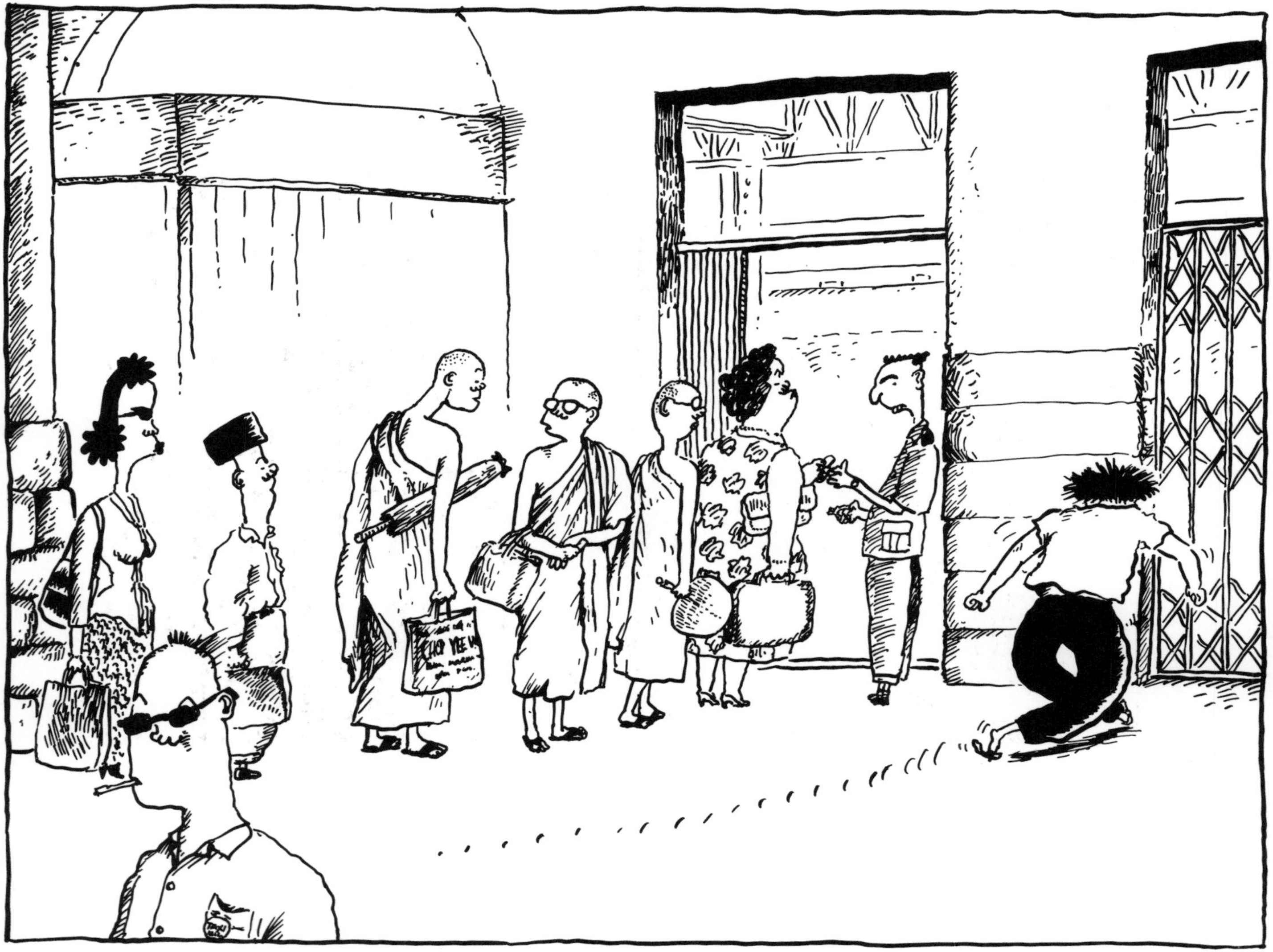

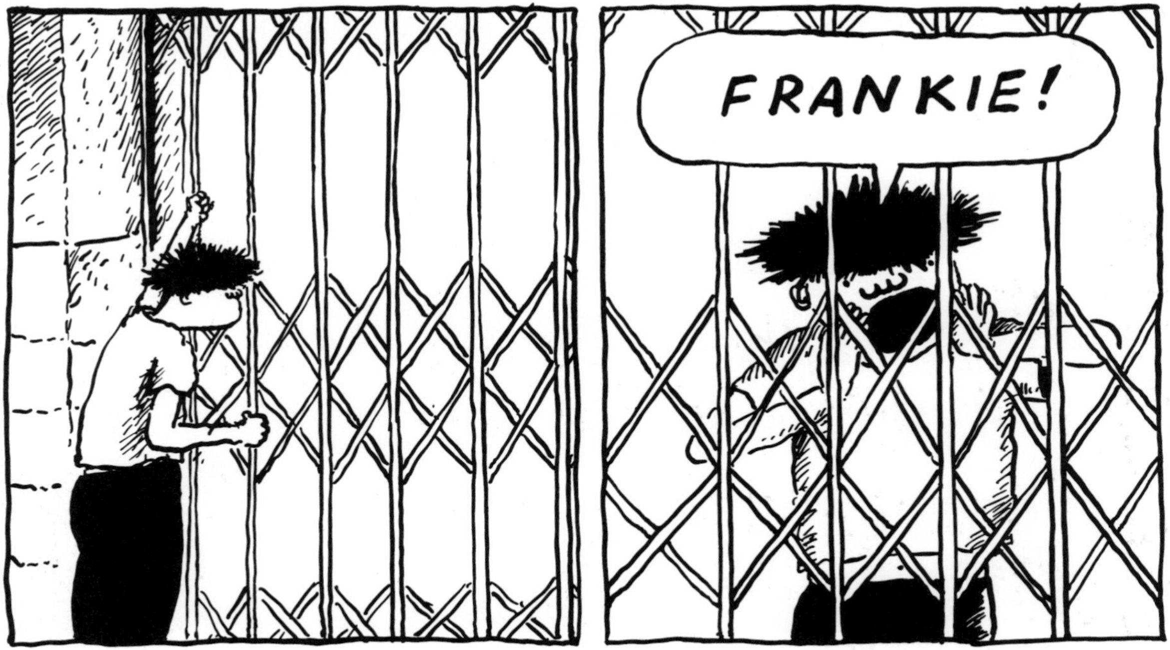
FRANKIE!

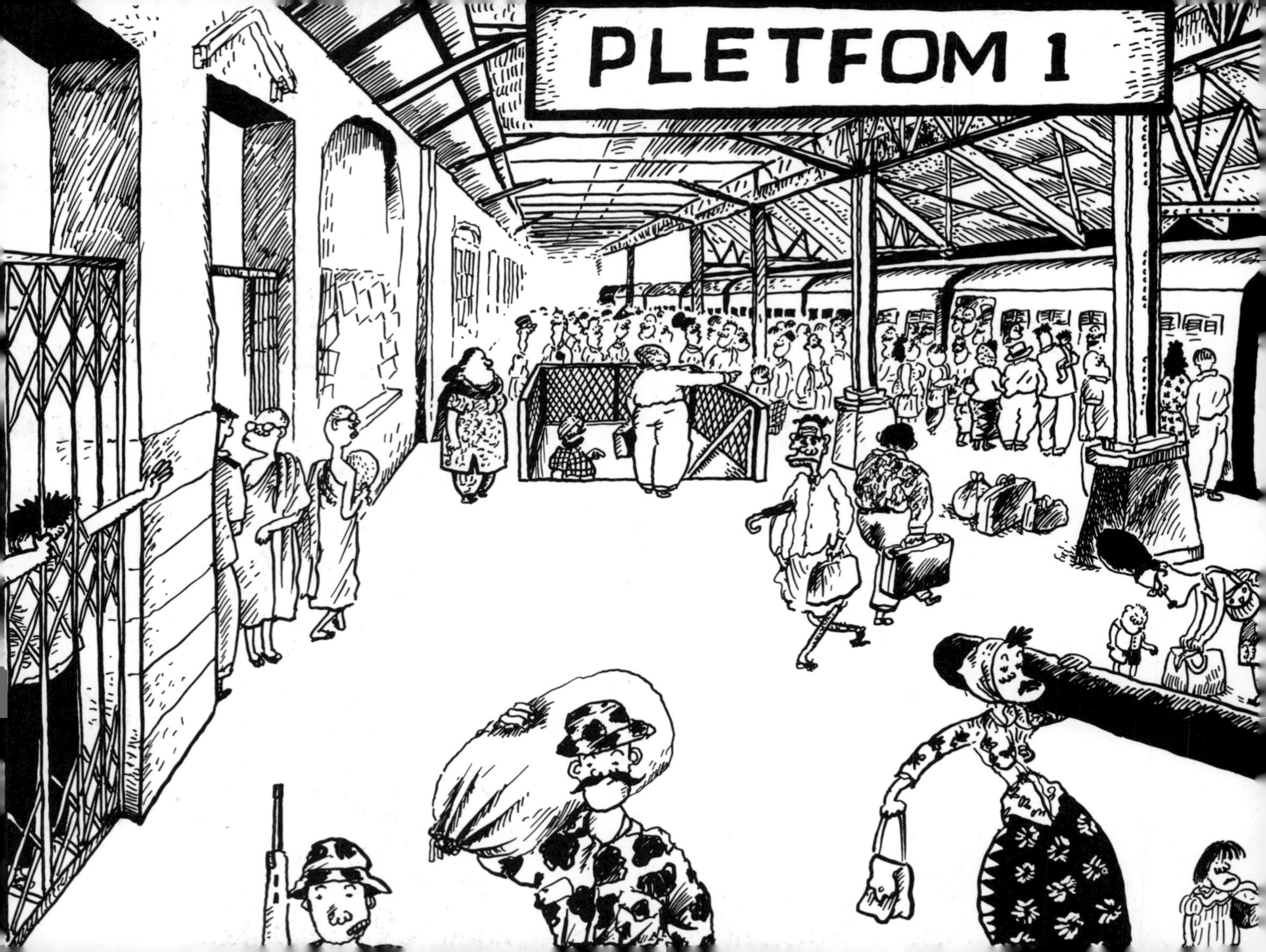
PLETFOM 1

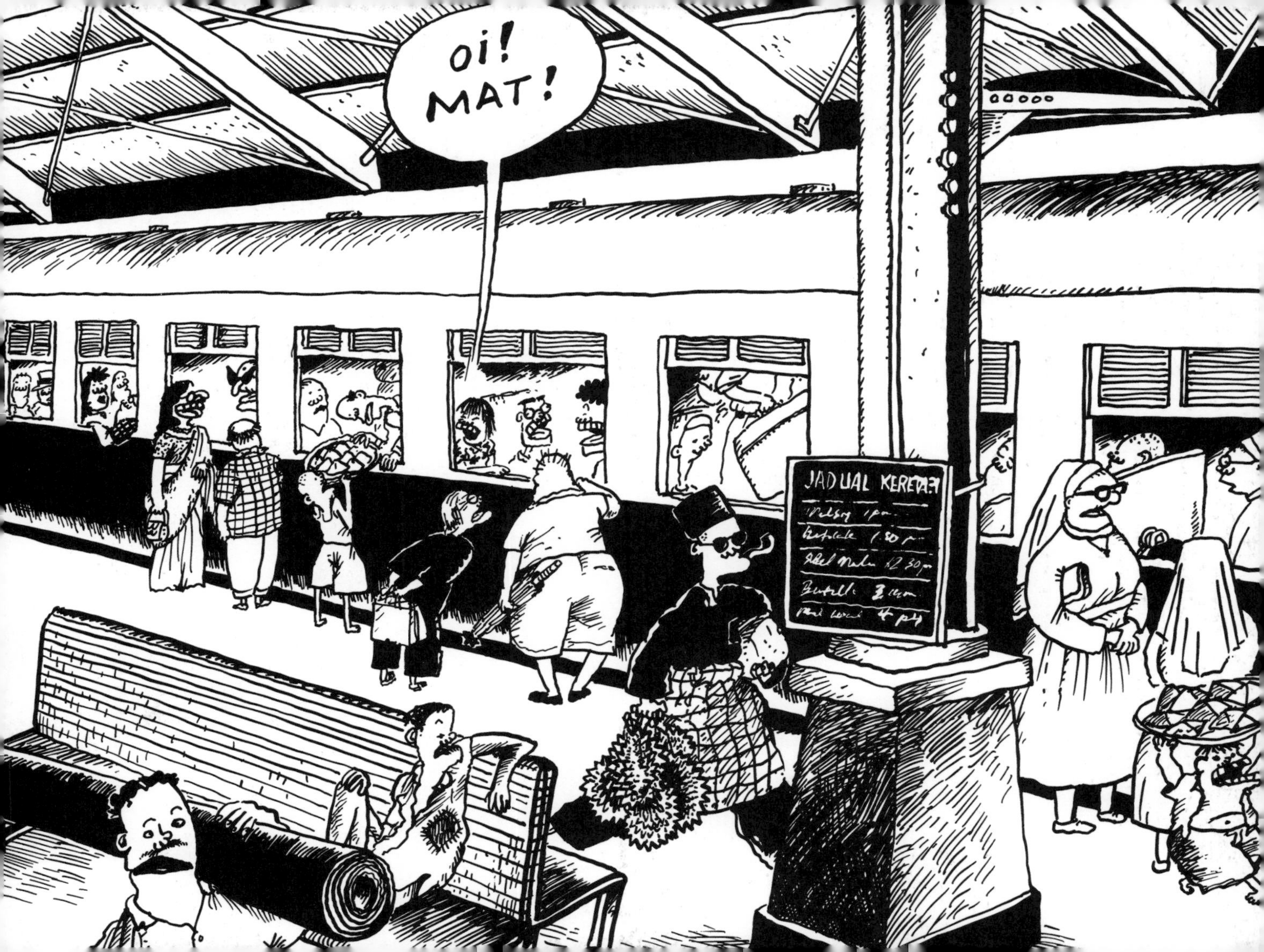
OI! MAT!
JADUAL KERETA

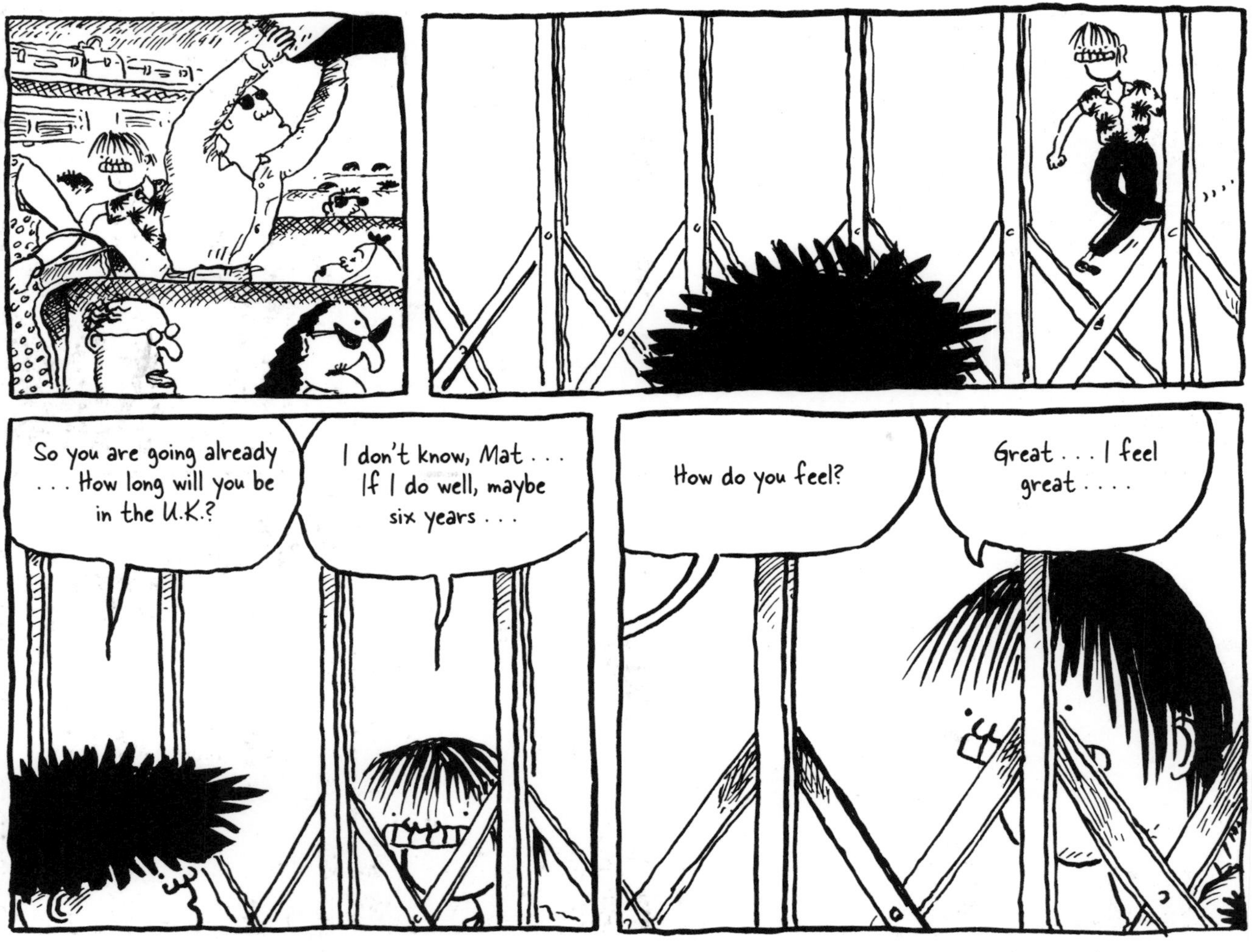
So you are going already . . . How long will you be in the U.K.?
I don't know, Mat . . . If I do well, maybe six years . . .
How do you feel?
Great . . . I feel great . . . .

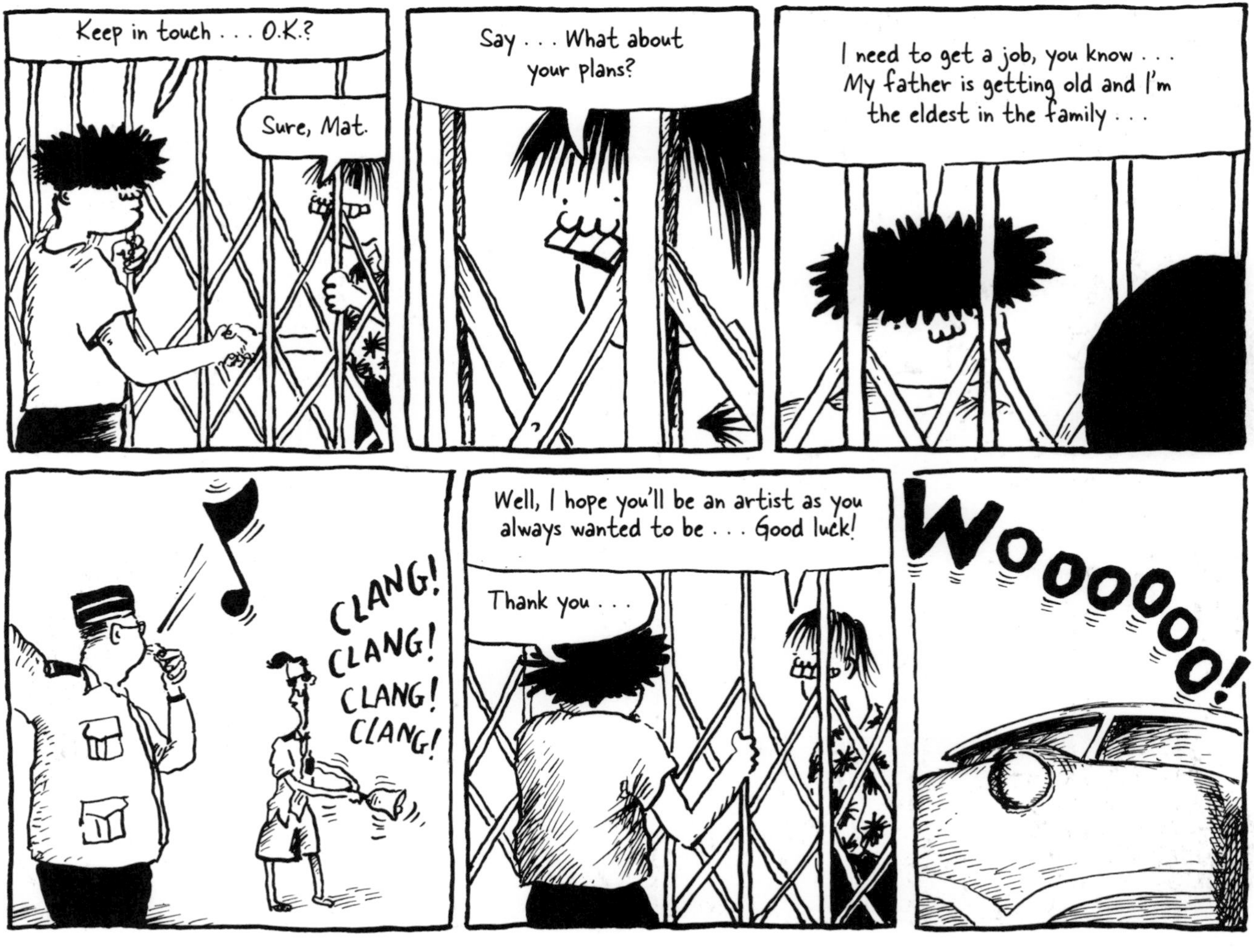
Keep in touch . . . O.K.?
Sure, Mat.
Say . . . What about your plans?
I need to get a job, you know . . . My father is getting old and I'm the eldest in the family . . .
CLANG! CLANG! CLANG! CLANG!
Well, I hope you'll be an artist as you always wanted to be . . . Good luck!
Thank you . . .
WOOOOOOO!

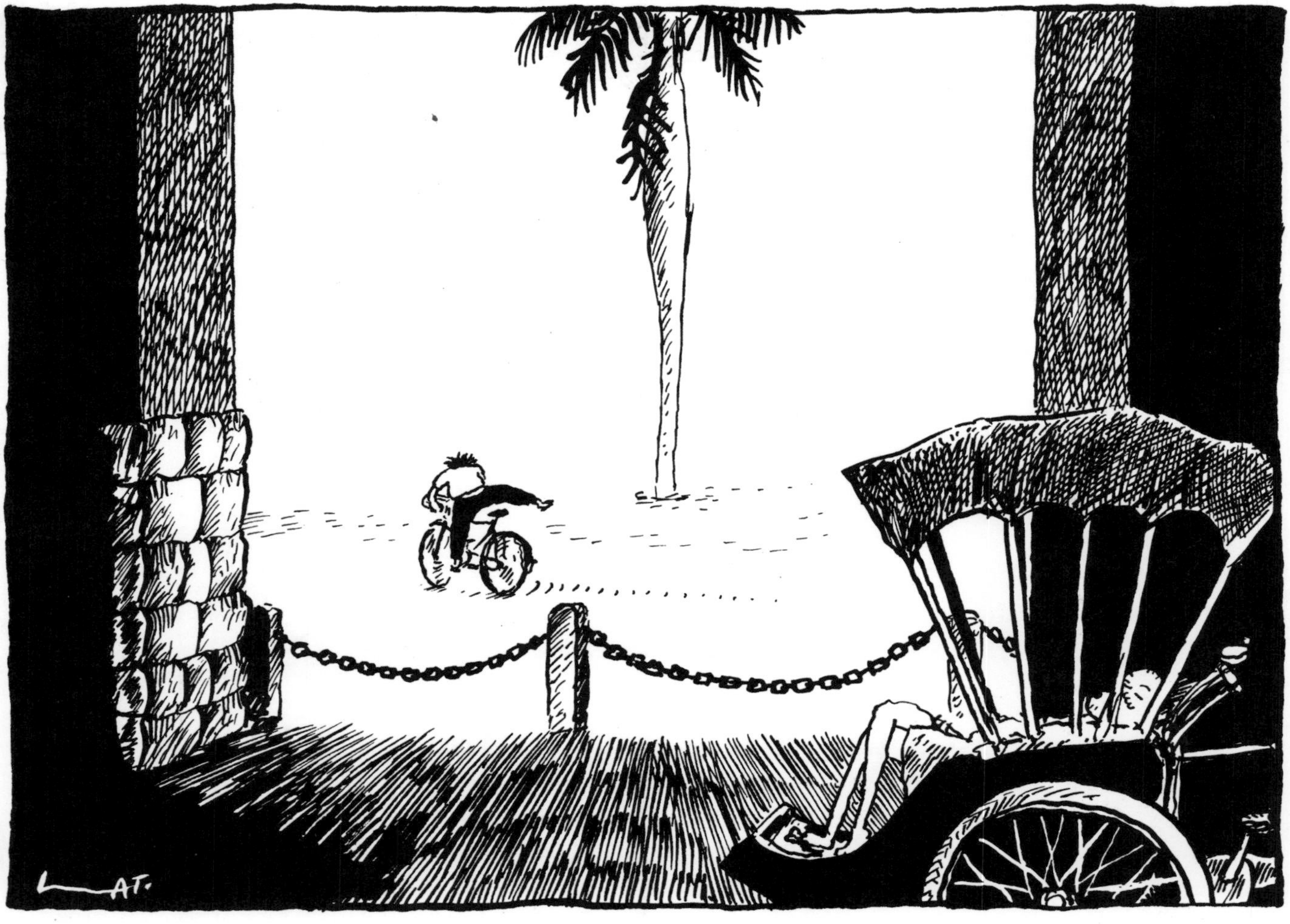
LAT.